Disney's TARZAN®

Adapted by
Kathleen W. Zoehfeld

Oil paintings by Glenn Harrington

Layout drawings by Judith Holmes Clarke
Cleanup drawings by Denise Shimabukuro, Lori Tyminski, Elizabeth Tate,
Samatha Clarke, and Caroline Egan

DISNEY
PRESS

New York

n a small island near the shore of her jungle home, Kala discovered a strange house, high up in a tree's branches. The faint crying coming from the house had drawn Kala away from her gorilla family. Cautiously, she crept through the door and looked around.

Amid a chaos of broken furniture, Kala found a baby. As she peered into his cradle, the baby giggled and reached for her.

Kala took the little one in her arms and held him close. The baby sighed and nuzzled her furry chest.

At that instant, the evil leopard Sabor leaped at Kala from a wooden beam above! Kala fought desperately, determined to keep the baby away from the cat's slashing claws.

As Kala fled, Sabor's paw became tangled in a rope. Kala clutched the baby closer to her chest and raced toward the safety of her family.

The apes gathered around Kala and gaped at the strange, furless baby.

"Um . . . where's his mama?" asked little Terk.

"I'm going to be his mother now," said Kala.

At that, Kerchak, leader of the ape family, loomed over them. "It's not our kind. I cannot let you put our family in danger," he declared.

"Does he look dangerous to you?" asked Kala, holding up the cooing infant.

Kerchak hesitated. "Was it alone?" he asked.

"Yes," said Kala. "Sabor killed his family."

Kerchak agreed to let Kala keep the baby.

"I know he'll be a good son," said Kala.

"I said he could stay," replied Kerchak. "That doesn't make him my son."

"Whatcha gonna call it?" asked Terk.

"I'm going to call *him* Tarzan," said Kala.

Kala and Tarzan and the other ape mothers and children cuddled in their nests for the night. As Kala sang Tarzan to sleep, she promised to always care for him.

Over the next few years, Tarzan grew up strong and curious, swinging from vines and mimicking the ways of the jungle animals.

One day Terk and her buddies were playing near the lagoon. Tarzan begged to join them. "I'd love to hang out with you," Terk whispered to Tarzan. "But the guys, they need a little convincing."

"What do I gotta do?" asked Tarzan gamely.

"You gotta . . . uh . . . go get an elephant hair," Terk said.

Tarzan stared down into the lagoon far below.

Then he took a deep breath and dove into the water! He'd show those guys he wasn't too little to play with them. Tarzan latched onto an elephant's tail and plucked a hair.

"Yeow!" cried the elephant.

"What is it?" asked the others.

"It's a piranha!" screamed a little elephant named Tantor.

"Piranha!" yelled the elephants. They began to stampede through the gorillas' feeding grounds!

When things finally settled down, Kerchak was angry. "What happened?" he demanded.

"It was my fault," said Tarzan. "We were playing and . . . well . . . I'm sorry."

"I should have known," said Kerchak. "Stampeding the elephants. He almost killed someone."

"He's only a child," argued Kala. "He'll learn."

"You can't learn to be one of us!" shouted Kerchak.

At those words, Tarzan ran off.

Tarzan was staring at his reflection in a jungle pool when Kala caught up with him. Sadly, Tarzan held his hand against hers. "Why am I so different?" he asked.

"Close your eyes," whispered Kala. "Now forget what you see." She put Tarzan's hand to his chest. "What do you feel?"

"My heart?" asked Tarzan.

"Come here," she said. She pressed his ear to her chest.

"Your heart," said Tarzan.

"See," said Kala. "They're exactly the same. Kerchak just can't see that."

"I'll make him see it," said Tarzan, beating his chest. "I'll be the best ape ever!"

"Oh, I bet you will," said Kala, with a smile.

As the years went by, Tarzan, Terk, and Tantor grew to be great friends. One day, while wrestling with Terk, Tarzan sensed something in the bushes. Just as he turned, Sabor leaped at him!

Kerchak grabbed the snarling leopard and threw her to the ground. Angry, Sabor raked Kerchak with her sharp claws.

Gripping his spear, Tarzan swung between Sabor and Kerchak. The gorillas gasped as they saw Tarzan wrestle Sabor into a deep pit. When they reappeared, Tarzan was victorious!

Respectfully, Tarzan laid the slain leopard at Kerchak's feet. But before either could speak, gunshots sounded.

Curious, Tarzan swung through the jungle toward the strange sound. From a treetop he looked down on the first humans he had ever seen.

"Clayton, wha-what is it?" asked Professor Porter.

"I thought I saw something," replied the hunter.

"Mr. Clayton," said Jane, "my father and I came on this expedition to study gorillas, and your shooting might be scaring them off."

"Ooo, Jane!" exclaimed Porter. "Look! A gorilla nest!"

"At last," said Clayton. "Our first sign in days." Clayton and Porter pressed on, looking for more nests. Jane was about to follow, when a papaya plopped on her head. A baby baboon jumped down to get it.

"Wait! Hold still!" Jane cried, as she whipped out her pencil and sketchbook. The baby snatched the book and ran.

When Jane caught up, the little baboon was admiring the portrait she had drawn. She pulled it from his hands, and he began to cry. The grown-up baboons moved in!

From his treetop, Tarzan watched as Jane ran off, with hundreds of snarling baboons in pursuit. He could see that she was headed for a deep chasm. As she tried to jump across, he swung down from his tree and scooped her up.

"Oh . . . I'm flying!" Jane cried.

Tarzan set her safely on a branch and began to study the curious new creature. Gently, he peeled off her glove and held his palm up to hers. They were alike!

Tarzan leaned against her and listened to her heartbeat. "Oh, oh, um," Jane stammered.

He smiled. Then he held her head against his chest. "Oh dear, oh dear," she sputtered. "Yes . . . it's a lovely heartbeat."

Tarzan pointed to himself. "Tarzan," he said.

"Tar-zan," repeated Jane. She pointed to herself. "Jane," she said.

"Jane," replied Tarzan.

"Exactly," said Jane.

Hearing a distant gunshot, Jane asked, "Can you take me to my camp?"

Tarzan took Jane by the waist, and off they swung. When they arrived, they found Terk and her friends having a clanging, banging good time with all of the camp equipment.

"Gorillas!" cried Jane, thrilled to catch a glimpse of the creatures she had come so far to study. To her amazement, she saw that Tarzan was part of their family!

As Clayton and her father approached, the gorillas disappeared into the jungle. Tarzan cast one more glance at Jane and then he fled, too.

Far away from the humans' camp, Kerchak told his family, "We will avoid the strangers."

"Why are you threatened by anyone different from you?" argued Tarzan.

"Protect this family and stay away from them!" demanded Kerchak.

Upset and confused, Tarzan climbed a high tree and spent the night alone.

The next day, as Jane was describing the strange ape-man to her father and Clayton, Tarzan himself dropped down from the trees.

Tarzan eyed Clayton and tried standing upright like him. He circled around, studying him.

"Fascinating!" exclaimed Porter. "He could be the missing link!"

"Or our link to the gorillas!" said Clayton, with a sinister smile.

For many days, Jane taught Tarzan about the human world. And Tarzan showed her the wonders of the jungle.

Clayton became impatient. "The ship could arrive any day. Now ask him straight out!"

"Tarzan," said Jane, "will you take us to the gorillas?"

"I can't," replied Tarzan. He knew that Kerchak did not want the gorillas and humans to meet.

The next morning, when Tarzan returned to camp, he saw men carrying Jane and Porter's belongings off to an awaiting ship.

"Tarzan!" cried Jane. "I was so afraid you wouldn't come in time. Daddy and I hope that you'll come with us."

"Go see England today, come home tomorrow?" asked Tarzan.

"Oh, no. It would be very difficult to come back . . . ever," whispered Jane.

"Jane must stay with Tarzan," said Tarzan.

"Here? No, I can't," Jane broke off and rushed away, crying.

Clayton approached and pretended to sympathize with Tarzan. "If only she could have spent more time with the gorillas."

"If Jane sees gorillas, she stays?" asked Tarzan. He decided to take Jane to his family.

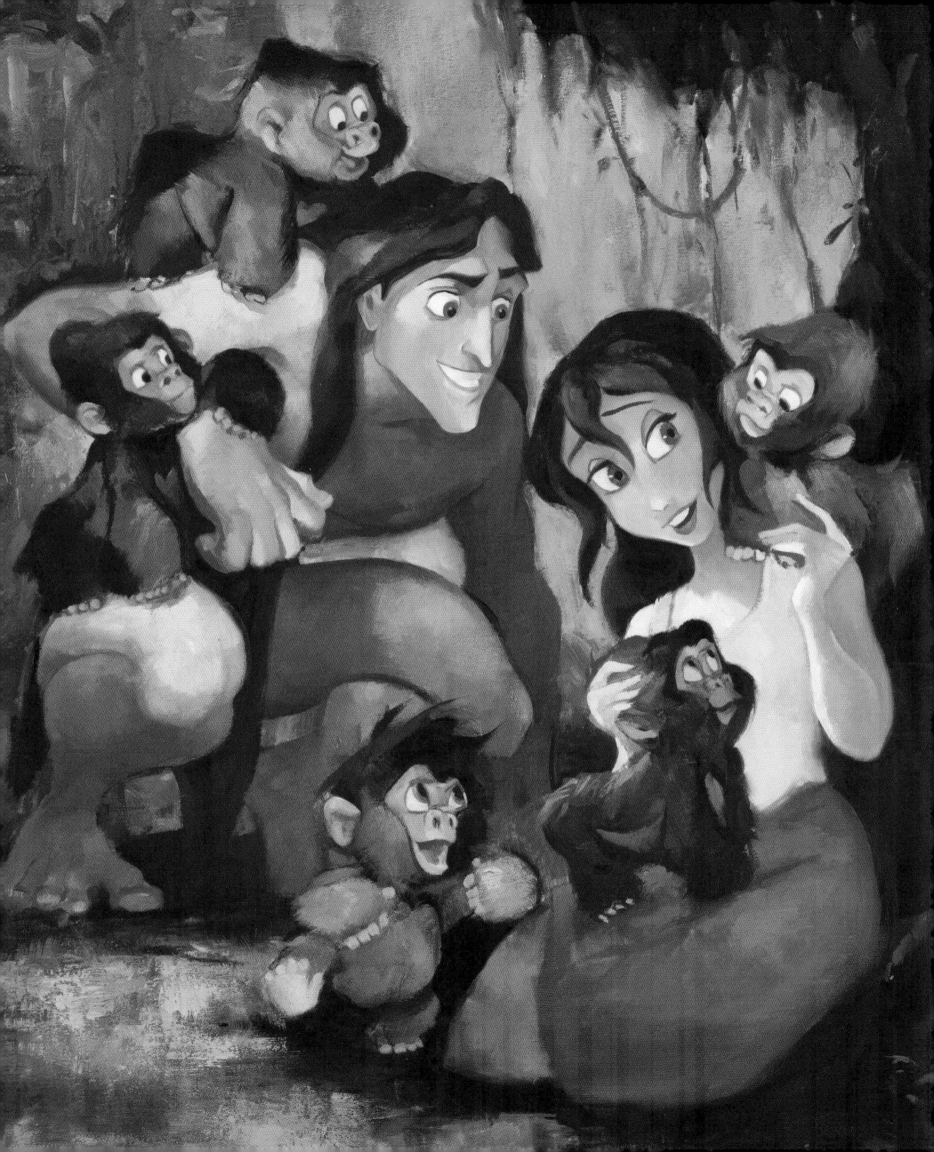

Tarzan asked Terk and Tantor to lure Kerchak away from the other gorillas. Then Tarzan led the humans to the nesting area.

"Isn't she beautiful?" whispered Jane, seeing Kala under a shelter of bushes.

"She's my mother," said Tarzan.

"Th-this is your mother?" asked Jane. Kala and the others shrank deeper into the bushes. Tarzan knelt down, saying soothing ape words. Jane and Porter imitated him. Soon the gorillas came out of their hiding places.

Jane and Porter were delighted, but Clayton only checked his map and drew an "X" to mark the gorillas' location.

"Oo oo ee eh ou," said Jane, mimicking Tarzan. The baby gorillas leaped around her joyfully. "What did I say?" she asked.

"Jane stays with Tarzan," said Tarzan.

"Oh, Tarzan, I can't," answered Jane sadly.

At that moment, Terk and Tantor crashed through the bushes with Kerchak right behind them.

When Kerchak saw the humans with his family, he was furious. As Clayton lifted his rifle to fire, Kerchak charged him and knocked his gun away.

Tarzan wrestled Kerchak off Clayton and struggled to hold the mighty ape. "Go!" he shouted at the humans.

Kerchak roared in anger as the humans fled.

"Kerchak, I'm sorry," said Tarzan.

"I asked you to protect our family," cried Kerchak. "And you betrayed us all."

Alone, Tarzan retreated into the jungle.

Kala found him.

"I'm so confused," Tarzan said sadly.

"Come," said Kala. "There's something I should have showed you long ago."

She led Tarzan to the tree house. Tarzan stared at the cradle. On the floor he found a portrait of two humans and a baby.

"Is this me?" he asked. "And this is my father . . . and my . . ."

"Now you know," said Kala, fighting back tears. "I just want you to be happy . . . whatever you decide."

Minutes later, Tarzan stepped out of the tree house, dressed in his father's clothes. Kala gasped. "No matter where I go, you will always be my mother," said Tarzan, embracing her.

Tarzan cast one last look at the beautiful jungle that had been his home. Then he climbed aboard the ship bound for England.

Suddenly, he heard Jane cry out from across the deck. She and her father were in the grips of two scruffy sailors.

It was too late: other sailors seized Tarzan.

"So sorry about the rude welcome," sneered Clayton, "but I couldn't have you making a scene when we put your furry friends in their cages."

"Why?" asked Tarzan.

"For three hundred pounds sterling a head!" exclaimed Clayton. "And I couldn't have done it without you."

Tarzan let out a cry of despair.

On shore, Terk and Tantor heard Tarzan's cry. Tantor trumpeted wildly, and they charged toward the ship.

Locked inside the hold, Tarzan pounded on the hull.

"Clayton betrayed us all," said Jane. "I am so sorry."

"No, I did this. I betrayed my family," cried Tarzan.

Suddenly the ship heeled over, throwing them all to one side.

"What was that?" asked Jane.

They heard the sound of trumpeting just as a huge elephant foot crashed through the deck above them.

"Tantor!" shouted Tarzan. He scrambled through the hole his friend had made. Jumping off the deck, Tarzan swam toward shore.

At the gorilla nesting grounds, Clayton and his men were rounding up the apes and throwing them into cages.

Tarzan raced through the jungle as Tantor, Terk, Jane, Porter, and their animal friends followed close behind.

Clayton was pointing his gun at Kerchak. "I think this one will be better off stuffed."

Tarzan burst into the clearing.

Clayton turned and aimed his rifle at Tarzan, but Kerchak leaped in to protect him, receiving the bullet himself. Clayton chased after Tarzan, following him up into the trees.

Struggling with Clayton on a thick tree limb, Tarzan grabbed his rifle and smashed it. Angrily, Clayton lunged at him, but the vines entangled him. As Clayton slashed at them he fell to his death.

Tarzan raced back to Kerchak. "Forgive me," Tarzan said.

"No, Tarzan, I misjudged you," said Kerchak. "Our family will look to you now. Take care of them, my son."

Everyone bowed, mourning the death of their leader. Then Tarzan rose and beat his chest, signaling his role as the apes' new leader.

Early the next morning, Tarzan made his way to the beach to say farewell to Jane and Porter. "I will miss you, Jane," Tarzan said softly.

As they were being rowed to the ship, Porter said, "Jane, dear, I can't help feeling that you should stay."

"I belong in England, with you," protested Jane.

"But you love him," said Porter. "Go on."

Jane jumped out of the boat and splashed through the water, falling into Tarzan's arms.

Porter smiled. "Captain," he said, "tell them you never found us. After all, people get lost in the jungle every day." He followed his daughter to shore.

Tarzan touched Jane's face and kissed her, while all the apes looked on.

"Oo oo ee eh ou," said Jane. The apes cheered.

Kala reached out her hand to welcome Jane, as Tarzan led his family back into the jungle.

Printed in the United States of America.

First Edition
1 3 5 7 9 10 8 6 4 2
ISBN: 0-7868-3220-7
Library of Congress Catalogue Card Number: 98-89391
This book is set in Janson Text and Khaki.

For more Disney Press fun, visit www.disneybooks.com

30°E 60° 90° 120° 150°

ARCTIC OCEAN
42–43

Europe-Asia
Boundary

A S I A
108–131

E U R O P E
90–107

A F R I C A
132–147

PACIFIC OCEAN
36–37

INDIAN OCEAN
40–41

A U S T R A L I A
NEW ZEALAND
OCEANIA
148–159

A N T A R C T I C A
160–163

YOU ARE HERE.

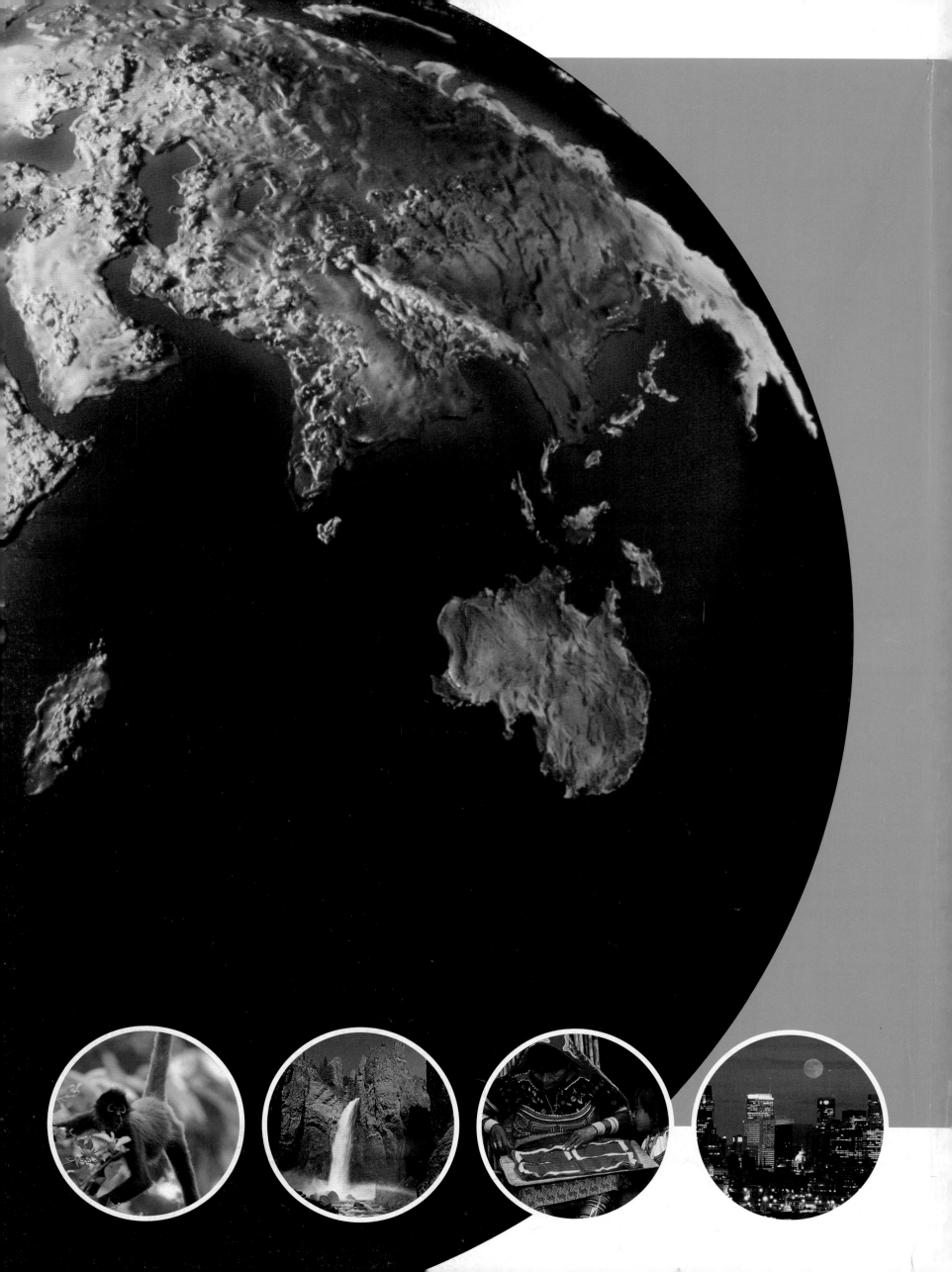

NATIONAL GEOGRAPHIC

WORLD ATLAS

FOR YOUNG EXPLORERS

THIRD EDITION

NATIONAL GEOGRAPHIC   WASHINGTON, DC

TABLE OF CONTENTS

North America: Grand Canyon, page 64

South America:
Llama, page 81

Europe: Colosseum, pages 96–97

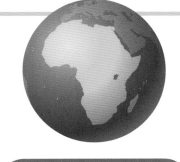

Antarctica: Penguins, pages 162–163

Australia, New Zealand, & Oceania: Maori man, page 152

Africa: Mother and child, page 137

HOW TO USE THIS ATLAS

This atlas is a window on your planet. Through it you can explore the world. To learn about maps, use the first section, Understanding Maps. Some basic facts about Earth as a planet are included in the section called Planet Earth. The Physical World includes world maps that focus on different aspects of nature, the environment, and the oceans. The Political World contains world maps about how humans live on the planet. After that, the maps, photographs, and essays are arranged by continent and region. You can look up specific places or just browse. Remember, it's your planet—learn it, love it, explore it!

WEB LINKS

Throughout the book you'll find black-and-yellow Web link icons for photos, videos, sounds, and games. You can get to all of these links through one URL: www.nationalgeographic.com/kids-world-atlas. This link takes you to the Web site specially designed to go with this atlas. Bookmark it and use it often. See pages 8-9 for how to use the Web site.

STATS & FACTS

At the left-hand edge of each continent opener and regional page is a bar that includes basic information about the subject. This feature is a great first stop if you're writing a report.

CHARTS & GRAPHS

Each region includes a chart or graph that shows information visually.

"YOU ARE HERE"

Locator globes help you see where one area is in relation to others. On regional pages (shown here), the area covered by the main map is yellow on the globe, and its continent is green. On pages with continent maps, the locator globe shows the whole continent in yellow. The surrounding land is brown.

SOUTHWEST ASIA

124 | SOUTHWEST ASIA

THE CONTINENT: ASIA

THE BASICS

STATS

This region, made up largely of deserts and mountains, includes the countries of the Arabian Peninsula and those that border the Persian Gulf. Islam is the dominant religion in each, and the two holiest places for Muslims—Mecca and Medina—are here. Arabic is the principal language everywhere but Iran, where most people speak Farsi. While water has been the most important natural resource here for millennia, global attention has focused in recent decades on the region's oil wealth. With the majority of the world's reserves found here, oil has brought outside influences and military conflict. Long a cradle of civilization, Southwest Asia continues to hold the world's gaze.

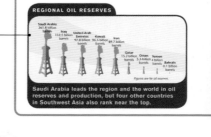

REGIONAL OIL RESERVES

Saudi Arabia leads the region and the world in oil reserves and production, but four other countries in Southwest Asia also rank near the top.

WHERE ARE THE PICTURES?

If you want to know where a picture in the regional sections of this atlas was taken, look for the map in the photo essay. Find the label that describes the picture you're curious about, and follow the line to its location.

ABOUT THE CONTINENT
ASIA
more about ASIA

WHERE THE PICTURES ARE

Maps use symbols to stand for many political and physical features. At right is the key to the symbols used in this atlas. If you are wondering what you're looking at on a map, check here.

INDEX AND GRID

Look through the index for the place-name you want. Next to it is a page number, a letter, and another number. Go to the page. Draw imaginary lines from the letter along the side of the map and the number along the top. Your place will be close to where the lines meet.

Río Muni (region), Equatorial Guinea **145** F2
Rivera, Uruguay **89** D4
Riverside, California **70** E2
Riviera (region), Europe **92** F3
Rivne, Ukraine **103** D6
Riyadh, Saudi Arabia **125** E4

COLOR BARS

Every section of this atlas has its own color. Look for the color on the Contents pages and across the top of every page in the atlas. Within that color bar, you'll see the name of the section and the title for each topic or map. These color bars are a handy way to find the section you want.

| North America |
| South America |
| Europe |
| Asia |
| Africa |
| Australia, New Zealand, & Oceania |
| Antarctica |

BAR SCALE

If you want to find out how far it is from one place on a map to another, use the scale. A bar scale appears on every map. It shows how distance on paper relates to distance in the real world.

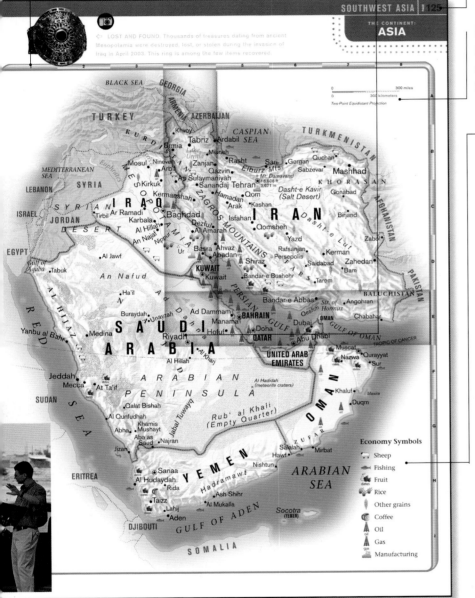

ECONOMY SYMBOLS

Each regional map has little pictures, or icons, that tell you the crops, farm animals, industries, and other economic activities that are common in each region. Each map has its own key, using the icons below.

Cattle	Sugarcane	Tobacco
Hogs	Sugar beets	Forest products
Sheep	Peanuts	Mining
Fishing	Potatoes	Coal
Bananas	Vegetable oil	Oil
Citrus	Cotton	Gas
Other fruit	Cacao	Manufacturing
Corn	Coffee	Tourism
Rice	Tea	Pollution
Other grains	Wine	

MAP KEY

• • • City / Town	791 ft / 241 m + Mountain peak with elevation above sea level	Waterfall	Dry / Salt Lake
⊛ Country capital		Dam	Glacier
⊙ State / Provincial capital	-282 ft. / -86 m • Low point with elevation below sea level	Canal	Swamp
• Small country		Ice Shelf	Sand
∴ Ruin	Defined boundary	Reef	Tundra
▪ Point of Interest	Undefined boundary	Lake	Lava
	Claimed boundary	Intermittent Lake	Below sea level
	River		

HOW TO USE THE ATLAS WEB SITE

As you can see by flipping through it, this atlas is chock full. There are photographs, statistics, quick facts and—most of all—lots of detailed maps and charts. And the companion Web site adds even more. You can watch videos of animals in their natural surroundings, listen to animal sounds and to music from many different cultures, find lots of country information, download pictures and maps for your school reports, play games that allow you to explore the world interactively, and even send e-postcards to your friends. The Web site extends specific subjects in the atlas and also helps you explore on your own, taking you deep into the resources of National Geographic and beyond. Throughout the book you will find these icons.

PHOTOS   VIDEO   AUDIO   GAMES

Some icons are placed near pictures. Others are with text. Each icon tells you that you can find more on that subject on the Web site. To follow any icon link, go to www.nationalgeographic.com/kids-world-atlas.

⇩ START HERE. There are three ways to find what you are looking for from the Home Page:
1. BY ATLAS PAGE NUMBER
2. BY TOPIC
3. BY ICON

NATIONAL GEOGRAPHIC

NATIONAL GEOGRAPHIC

WORLD ATLAS

FOR YOUNG EXPLORERS →

It's *your* planet. Learn it. Love it. Explore it!

THIRD EDITION

SEARCH BY

PAGE NUMBER 01 ⬍
COUNTRY
ANIMALS
MAPS
WORLD MUSIC
GAMES
OTHER FUN STUFF
ICONS

VIDEO   AUDIO   PHOTOS   GAMES

For more fun from
National Geographic Society
CLICK HERE!

NATIONAL GEOGRAPHIC
KIDS

Parents and Educators: E-Mail Newsletters | Shopping | Kids Privacy Policy | Education Guide | Subscriptions | Xpeditions Lesson Plans
To Purchase the National Geographic World Atlas for Young Explorers, Third Edition, Click Here
For more great content, including video, photos, news, and more, visit NationalGeographic.com

www.nationalgeographic.com/kids-world-atlas

1. SEARCH BY ATLAS PAGE NUMBER

⇐ **PAGE NUMBER PULL-DOWN MENU.** If you find an icon in the atlas and want to go directly to that link, use the page number pull-down menu. Just drag and click.

2. SEARCH BY TOPIC

⇨ **LIST OF TOPICS.** If you want to explore a specific topic, click on the entry in the topic list. This list is your portal to vast quantities of National Geographic information, photos, videos, games, and more, all arranged by subject. Say you're interested in Animals. One click takes you to the Animals choice page (below).

⇩ **CREATURE FEATURES.** Click to go to the National Geographic Kids' animal site. Click on an animal, and you will find a full feature about it, including photos, video, a range map, and other fun info.

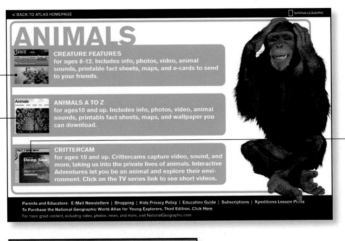

⇩ **CRITTERCAM.** Scientists put video cameras on animals to learn about the animal from its point of view. Click to see those videos, learn about the project, play games such as exploring the virtual world of a seal, and more.

⇐ **ANIMALS A TO Z.** This choice takes you to the animal site for adults and older kids. Use the list of animals in the upper right-hand corner of the page. Clicking on an animal there takes you to the profile of that animal.

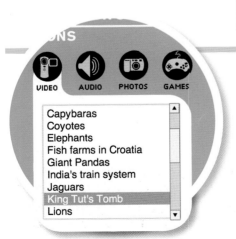

3. SEARCH BY ICON

⇐ **SELECT ONE OF FOUR ICONS.** If you want to find all the videos referenced in the atlas, or all of the audios, photos, or games, click on one of the icons. A list will drop down. Choose from the list, and you're there! Clicking on King Tut takes you to several King Tut videos.

EXPLORING YOUR WORLD

Earth is a big place. Even from space you can't see it all at one time. But with a map, you can see the whole world or just a part of it. Thanks to the Internet, you can download programs that allow you to experience Earth from space, pick a place you want to explore, and zoom closer and closer until you are "standing" among its buildings! These screenshots (right) take you from space to Chicago at the click of a mouse. You can even find a satellite view of your house (see below).

Compare the computer enhanced satellite images with the maps on the opposite page, and you will see how the same places can be shown in very different ways. You will want to explore all of them to really get to know your world.

FIND YOUR HOUSE

This image from SkylineGlobe shows National Geographic offices in Washington, D.C. To see your house, go to www.skylineglobe.com, one of several Web sites that allows you to view satellite imagery of the world.

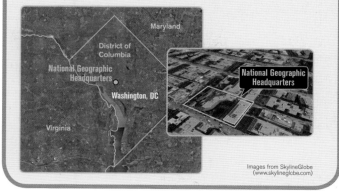

Images from SkylineGlobe (www.skylineglobe.com)

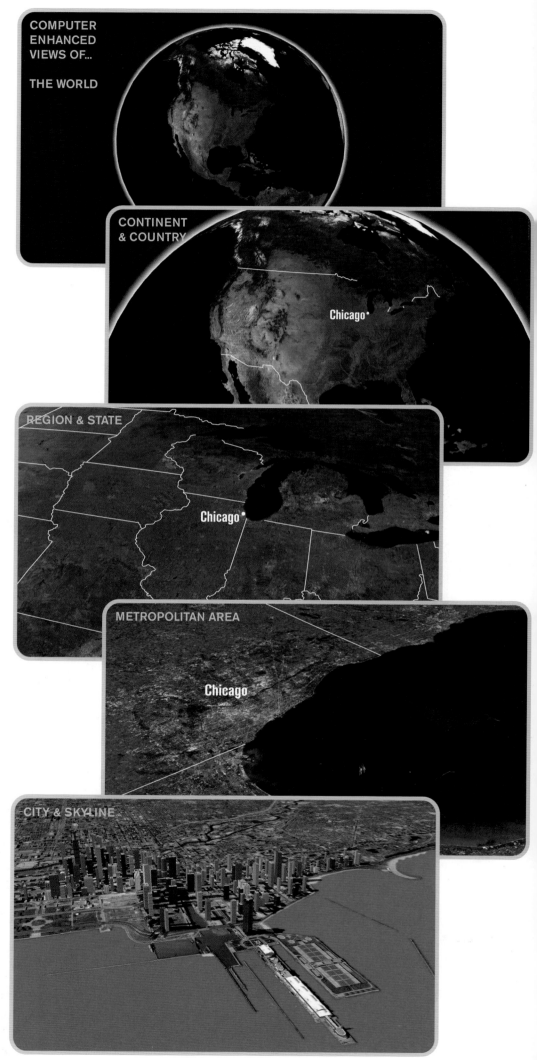

COMPUTER ENHANCED VIEWS OF...

THE WORLD

CONTINENT & COUNTRY

Chicago

REGION & STATE

Chicago

METROPOLITAN AREA

Chicago

CITY & SKYLINE

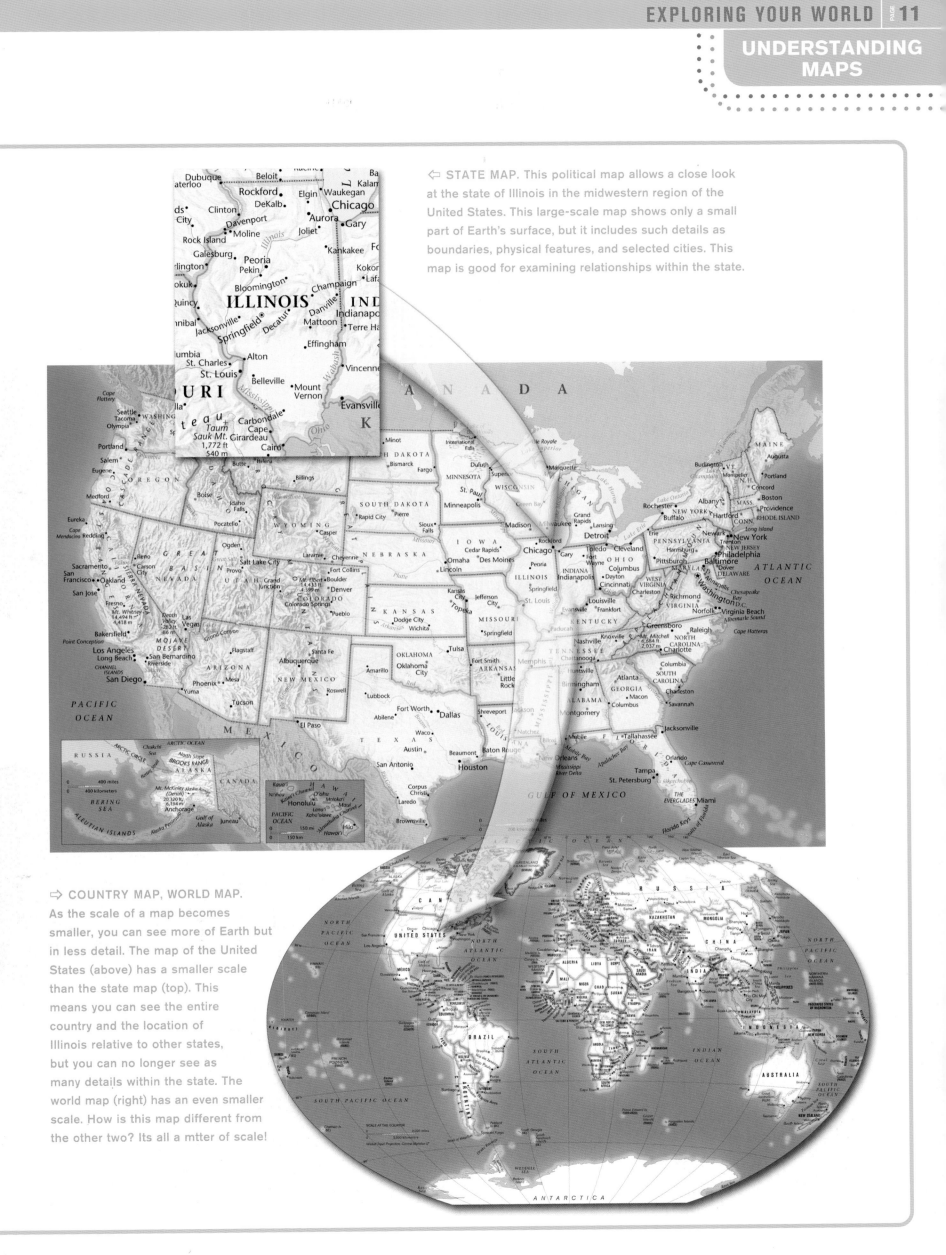

⇦ STATE MAP. This political map allows a close look at the state of Illinois in the midwestern region of the United States. This large-scale map shows only a small part of Earth's surface, but it includes such details as boundaries, physical features, and selected cities. This map is good for examining relationships within the state.

⇨ COUNTRY MAP, WORLD MAP. As the scale of a map becomes smaller, you can see more of Earth but in less detail. The map of the United States (above) has a smaller scale than the state map (top). This means you can see the entire country and the location of Illinois relative to other states, but you can no longer see as many details within the state. The world map (right) has an even smaller scale. How is this map different from the other two? Its all a mtter of scale!

KINDS OF MAPS

Maps are special tools that geographers use to tell a story about Earth. Some maps show physical features, such as mountains or vegetation. Maps also show climates or natural hazards and other things we cannot easily see. Other maps illustrate different human features on Earth—political boundaries, urban centers, and economic systems.

Maps are not perfect. A globe is a scale model of Earth with accurate relative sizes and locations. Because maps are flat, they involve distortions of size, shape, and direction. Also, cartographers—people who create maps—make choices about what information to include. Because of this, it is important to study many different types of maps to learn the complete story of Earth.

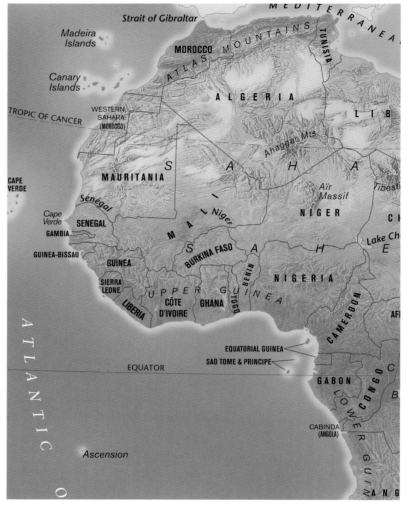

⇧ PHYSICAL MAPS. Earth's natural features—landforms, water bodies, and vegetation—are shown on physical maps. The map above uses color and shading to illustrate mountains, lakes, rivers, and deserts of western Africa. Country names and borders are added for reference, but they are not natural features.

⇐ MAP PROJECTIONS. To create a map, cartographers transfer an image of the round Earth to a flat surface, a process called projection. All projections involve distortion. For example, an interrupted projection (top map) shows accurate shapes and relative size of land areas, but oceans have gaps. Other types of projections are cylindrical, conic, or azimuthal—each with certain advantages, but all with some distortion.

MAKING MAPS

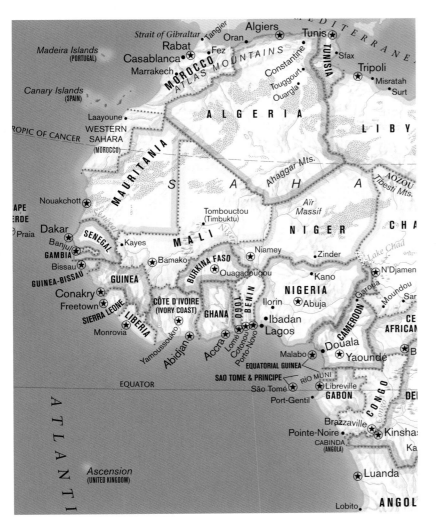

⇧ POLITICAL MAPS. These maps represent human characteristics of the landscape, such as boundaries, cities, and place-names. Natural features are added only for reference. On the map above, capital cities are represented with a star inside a circle, while other cities are located with black dots.

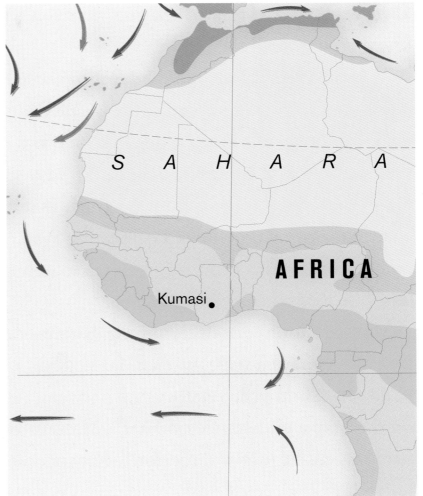

⇧ THEMATIC MAPS. Patterns related to a particular topic, or theme, such as population distribution, appear on these maps. The map above displays the region's climate zones, which range from tropical wet (bright green) to tropical wet and dry (light green) to semiarid (dark yellow) to arid or desert (light yellow).

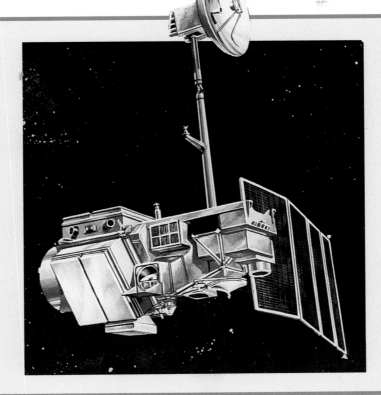

Long ago, cartographers worked with pen and ink, carefully hand-crafting maps based on explorers' observations and diaries. Today, map-making is a high-tech business. Cartographers use Earth data stored in "layers" in a Geographic Information System (GIS) and special computer programs to create maps that can be easily updated as new information becomes available. The cartographers at left are changing country labels on a map of the Balkans.

Satellites in orbit around Earth act as eyes in the sky, recording data about its land and ocean areas. The data is converted to numbers that are transmitted back to special computers, which are programmed to interpret the data. They record it in a form that cartographers can use to create maps.

HOW TO READ A MAP

Every map has a story to tell, but first you have to know how to read the map.

Maps are useful for finding places because every place on Earth has a special address called absolute location. Imaginary lines, called latitude and longitude, create a grid that makes finding places easy since these lines cross at the same spot every time. In addition, special tools, called Global Positioning Systems (GPS), communicate with orbiting satellites to determine absolute location.

Maps are useful for determining distance and direction. Maps have a scale, often a bar scale or a verbal scale, that shows the relationship between distance on the map and distance on Earth. Maps often have a compass rose to show direction. Many people think north is at the top of a map, but this is not always true. The compass rose indicates north for each map.

Maps represent other information by using a language of symbols. Knowing how to read these symbols provides access to a wide range of information. To find out what each symbol means, you must use the map key. Think of the map key as your secret decoder, identifying information represented by each symbol on the map.

⇨ LATITUDE AND LONGITUDE. Latitude and longitude lines help us determine locations on Earth. Lines of latitude run west to east, parallel to the Equator (below, left). These lines measure distance in degrees north or south, from the Equator (0° latitude) to the North Pole (90°N) or to the South Pole (90°S). One degree of latitude is approximately 70 statute miles (113 km).

Lines of longitude run north to south, meeting at the Poles (below, right). These lines measure distance in degrees east or west from 0° longitude (prime meridian) to 180° longitude. The prime meridian runs through Greenwich, England.

Latitude

Longitude

⇨ ABSOLUTE LOCATION. The imaginary grid composed of lines of latitude and longitude helps us locate places on a map. Suppose you are playing a game of global scavenger hunt. The clue says the prize is hidden at absolute location 30°S, 60°W. You know that the first number is south of the Equator, and the second is west of the prime meridian. On the map at left, find the line of latitude labeled 30°S. Now find the line of longitude labeled 60°W. Trace these lines with your fingers until they meet. Identify this spot. The prize must be located in central Argentina (see arrow, right).

SYMBOLS

There are three main types of map symbols: points, lines, and areas. Points, which can be either dots or small icons, represent the location or the number of things, such as schools, cities, or landmarks. Lines are used to show boundaries, roads, or rivers and can vary in color or thickness. Area symbols use patterns or color to show regions, such as a sandy area or a neighborhood.

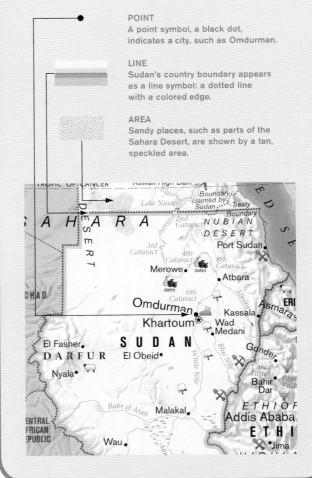

POINT
A point symbol, a black dot, indicates a city, such as Omdurman.

LINE
Sudan's country boundary appears as a line symbol: a dotted line with a colored edge.

AREA
Sandy places, such as parts of the Sahara Desert, are shown by a tan, speckled area.

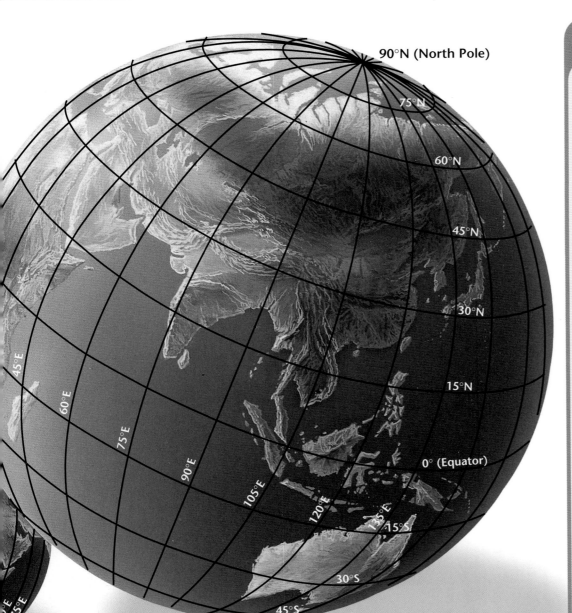

90°N (North Pole)

SCALE & DIRECTION

The scale on a map is shown as a fraction, as words, or as a line or bar. It relates distance on the map to distance in the real world. Sometimes the scale identifies the type of map projection. Maps may include an arrow or compass rose to indicate north on the map. Maps in this atlas are oriented north, so they do not use a north indicator.

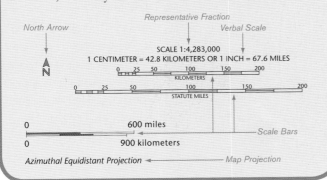

⇨ APPLYING WHAT YOU'VE LEARNED. Now that you know how to read a map, can you find places on the maps in this atlas? What about Sapporo in the eastern Asian country of Japan? The index at the back of this atlas tells you that Sapporo is on "page 121 B10." Along the edges of the map are letters and numbers. Place one finger on the B at the side and another finger on the 10 at the top. Now trace straight across from the B and down from the 10. Sapporo is where your fingers meet!

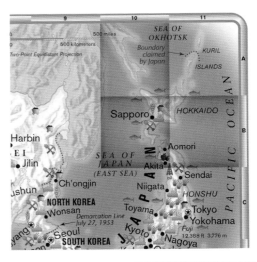

EARTH IN SPACE

Earth, the planet we call home, is part of a cosmic family called the solar system. It is one of the planets that revolve around a giant solar nuclear reactor that we call the Sun.

The extreme heat and pressure on the Sun cause atoms of hydrogen to combine in a process called fusion, producing new atoms of helium and releasing tremendous amounts of energy. The Sun is the essential source of energy that makes life on Earth possible. It also provides us with light and warmth.

Time on Earth is defined by our relationship to the Sun. It takes Earth, following a path called an orbit, approximately 365 days—one year—to make one full revolution around the Sun. As Earth makes its way around the Sun, it also turns on its axis, an imaginary line that passes between the Poles. This motion, called rotation, occurs once every 24 hours and results in day and night.

⇐ TIME ZONES. Long ago, when people lived in relative isolation, they measured time by the position of the Sun overhead. That meant that noon in one place was not the same as noon in a place 100 miles (160 km) to the west. Later, with the development of long-distance railroads, people needed to coordinate time. In 1884, a system of 24 standard time zones was adopted. Each time zone reflects the fact that Earth rotates west to east 15 degrees each hour. Time is counted from the prime meridian, which runs through Greenwich, England.

Note: Art shows relative sizes of the Sun and planets, but distances are not to scale.

⇧ SOLAR SYSTEM. The Sun and its family of planets are located near the outer edge of the Milky Way, a giant spiral galaxy. Earth is the third planet from the Sun and one of the four "terrestrial" planets. These planets—Mercury, Venus, Earth, and Mars—are made up of solid rocky material. Beyond these inner planets are the four gas giants—Jupiter, Saturn, Uranus, and Neptune. Recently, astronomers—scientists who study space—have named a new category called "dwarf" plnates, including Pluto, Ceres, and Eris. More of these dwarf planets may soon be identified. Many planets, including Earth, have one or more moons orbiting them. The art above names a few: Io, Callisto, Titan, Triton, and Charon.

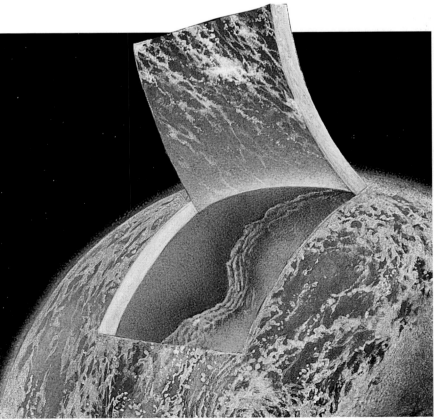

⇨ ENVELOPE OF AIR. Earth is enclosed within a thick layer of air called the atmosphere. Made up of a mix of nitrogen, oxygen, and other gases, the atmosphere provides us with the life-giving air that we breathe. It also protects us from dangerous radiation from the Sun. Weather systems move through the atmosphere, redistributing heat and moisture and creating Earth's climates.

EARTH IN MOTION

If we could step into a time machine and travel 500 million years into the past, we probably would not recognize Earth. Back then, most of the landmasses we call continents were joined together in a single giant landmass called Pangaea. So how did the continents break away from Pangaea and move to their current positions? Where will they be in another 500 million years?

Deep within Earth, pressure and heat cause rocks of the mantle to become partially molten, but near Earth's surface a thin shell of solid rock forms the crust. Currents of heat rise and fall within the mantle, causing the crust to break into large pieces, called plates, which very slowly move about on Earth's surface. These powerful forces are at work today, creating and destroying land features and reshaping Earth's surface.

⇨ CRUST IN MOTION. Earth's major plates are outlined in red on the map at right. Plate edges are the most active parts, with volcanoes and earthquakes (yellow dots on the map) resulting from plates moving together or grinding past each other.

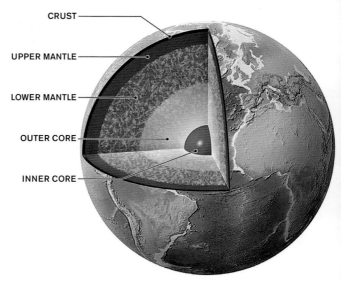

CRUST
UPPER MANTLE
LOWER MANTLE
OUTER CORE
INNER CORE

⇧ A LOOK WITHIN. The distance from Earth's surface to its center is 3,963 miles (6,370 km). There are four layers: a thin, rigid crust; the rocky mantle; the outer core, which is a layer of molten iron; and finally the inner core, which is solid iron.

CONTINENTS ON THE MOVE

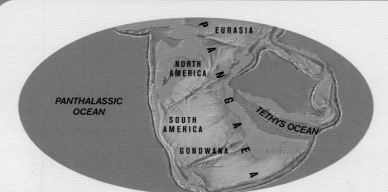

1 PANGAEA. About 240 million years ago, Earth's landmasses were joined together in one supercontinent that extended from Pole to Pole.

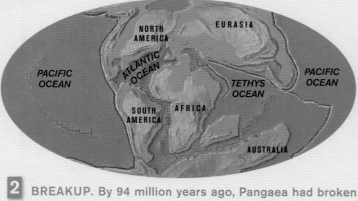

2 BREAKUP. By 94 million years ago, Pangaea had broken apart into landmasses that would become today's continents. Dinosaurs roamed Earth during a period of warmer climates.

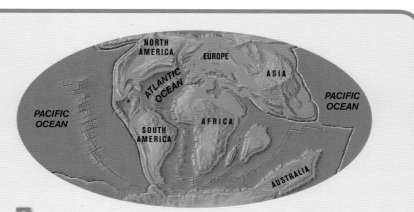

3 EXTINCTION. About 65 million years ago an asteroid smashed into Earth, creating the Gulf of Mexico (*). This impact may have resulted in the extinction of half the world's species, including the dinosaurs. This was one of several major extinctions.

4 ICE AGE. By 18,000 years ago, the continents had drifted close to their present positions, but most far northern and far southern lands were buried beneath huge glaciers.

Plate boundary
Earthquake

Earth Shapers

Earth's features are constantly undergoing change—being built up, destroyed, or just rearranged. Plates are in constant, very slow motion. Some plates collide, others pull apart, and still others slowly grind past each other. As the plates move, mountains are uplifted, volcanoes erupt, and new land is created.

⇧ VOLCANOES form when molten rock, called magma, rises to Earth's surface. Some volcanoes occur as one plate pushes beneath another plate. Other volcanoes result when a plate passes over a column of magma, called a hot spot, rising from the mantle.

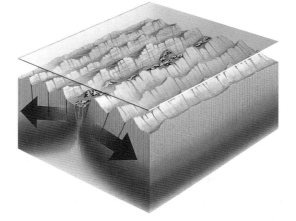

⇧ SPREADING results when oceanic plates move apart. The ocean floor cracks, magma rises, and new crust is created. The Mid-Atlantic Ridge spreads a few centimeters—about an inch—a year, pushing Europe and North America farther apart.

⇩ FAULTING happens when two plates grind past each other, creating large cracks along the edges of the plates. A famous fault is the San Andreas, in California, where the Pacific and North American plates meet, causing damaging earthquakes.

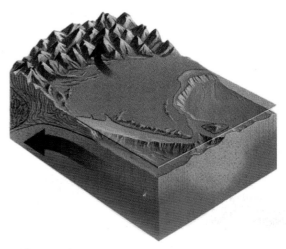

⇧ COLLISION of two continental plates causes plate edges to break and fold, creating mountains, Earth's highest landforms. The Himalaya are the result of the Indian plate colliding with the Eurasian plate, an ongoing process that began 50 million years ago.

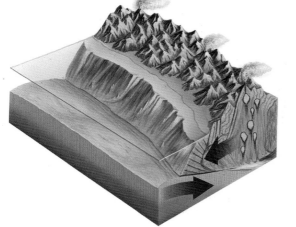

⇧ SUBDUCTION occurs when an oceanic plate dives under a continental plate. This often results in volcanoes and earthquakes, as well as mountain building.

THE PHYSICAL WORLD

Earth is dominated by large landmasses called continents—seven in all—and by an interconnected global ocean that is divided into four parts by the continents. More than 70 percent of Earth's surface is covered by oceans, and the remaining 30 percent is made up of land areas.

Different landforms give variety to the surface of the continents. The Rockies and Andes mark the western edge of North and South America, and the Himalaya tower above southern Asia. The Plateau of Tibet forms the rugged core of Asia, while the Northern European Plain extends from the North Sea to the Ural Mountains. Much of Africa is a plateau, and dry plains cover large areas of Australia. Beneath massive ice sheets, mountains rise more than 16,000 feet (4,877 m) in Antarctica.

Mountains and trenches make the ocean floors as varied as any continent (see pages 34–43). A mountain chain called the Mid-Atlantic Ridge runs the length of the Atlantic Ocean. In the western Pacific Ocean, trenches drop to depths greater than 35,000 feet (10,668 m).

⇨ LAND AND WATER. This world physical map shows Earth's seven continents—North America, South America, Europe, Africa, Asia, Australia, and Antarctica—as well as the four oceans: Pacific, Atlantic, Indian, and Arctic. Some people regard the area from Antarctica to 60°S, where the oceans merge, as a fifth ocean called the Southern Ocean.

SCALE AT THE EQUATOR
0   2,000 miles
0   2,000 kilometers
Winkel Tripel Projection, Central Meridian 0°

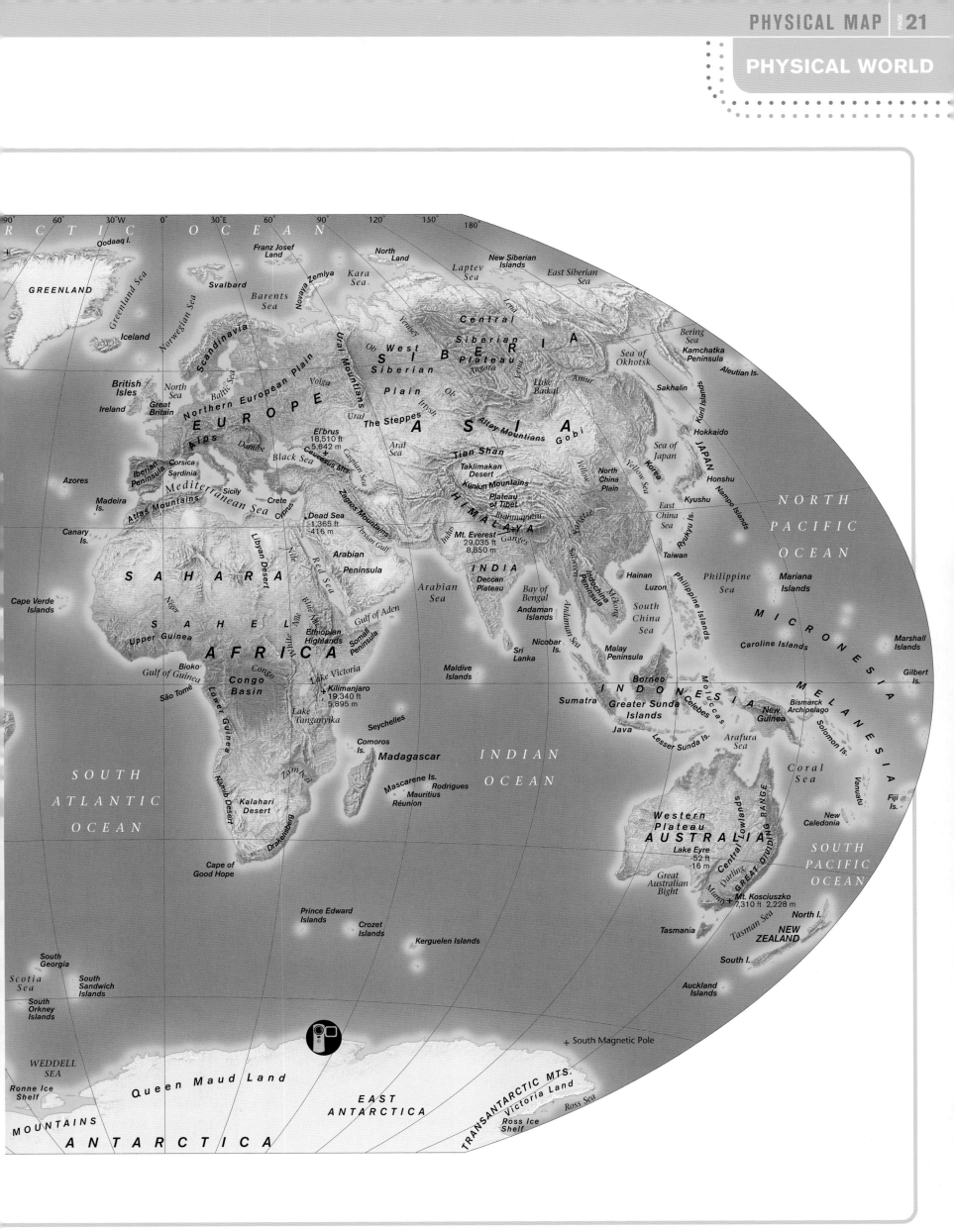

ARCTIC OCEAN

90° 60° 30°W 0° 30°E 60° 90° 120° 150° 180°

Oodaaq I.

GREENLAND

Greenland Sea

Svalbard

Franz Josef Land

North Land

New Siberian Islands

Laptev Sea

East Siberian Sea

Iceland

Norwegian Sea

Scandinavia

Barents Sea

Novaya Zemlya

Kara Sea

Central Siberian Plateau

Bering Sea

British Isles

North Sea

Baltic Sea

Northern European Plain

Ob

West Siberian Plain

SIBERIA

Angara

Lena

Kamchatka Peninsula

Aleutian Is.

Ireland

Great Britain

EUROPE

Volga

Yenisey

The Steppes

Ob

Irtysh

ASIA

Lake Baikal

Amur

Sakhalin

Kuril Islands

Sea of Okhotsk

Alps

Ural Mountains

Ural

El'brus 18,510 ft +5,642 m

Aral Sea

Altay Mountains

Gobi

Hokkaido

Sea of Japan

Iberian Peninsula

Corsica

Sardinia

Danube

Caucasus Mts.

Black Sea

Caspian Sea

Tian Shan

JAPAN

Honshu

Korea

North China Plain

Yellow

Sea of Japan

Azores

Sicily

Crete

Mediterranean Sea

Taklimakan Desert

Kunlun Mountains

Plateau of Tibet

Yellow Sea

Kyushu

Nampo Islands

Madeira Is.

Atlas Mountains

Cyprus

Dead Sea -1,365 ft -416 m

Zagros Mountains

Persian Gulf

Brahmaputra

HIMALAYA

Indus

Mt. Everest 29,035 ft 8,850 m

Ganges

East China Sea

Ryukyu Is.

Taiwan

NORTH PACIFIC OCEAN

Canary Is.

Libyan Desert

Nile

Red Sea

Arabian Peninsula

Arabian Sea

INDIA

Deccan Plateau

Bay of Bengal

Salween

Hainan

Indochina Peninsula

Mekong

Luzon

Philippine Islands

Philippine Sea

Mariana Islands

MICRONESIA

Cape Verde Islands

SAHARA

Blue Nile

Gulf of Aden

Andaman Islands

Andaman Sea

South China Sea

Marshall Islands

SAHEL

Niger

White Nile

Ethiopian Highlands

Somali Peninsula

Nicobar Is.

Malay Peninsula

Caroline Islands

Upper Guinea

AFRICA

Maldive Islands

Sri Lanka

Gilbert Is.

Bioko

Gulf of Guinea

Congo

Congo Basin

Lake Victoria

Kilimanjaro 19,340 ft 5,895 m

Borneo

Greater Sunda Islands

INDONESIA

Moluccas

Celebes

New Guinea

Bismarck Archipelago

MELANESIA

São Tomé

Lower Guinea

Lake Tanganyika

Sumatra

Java

Lesser Sunda Is.

Solomon Is.

Vanuatu

Seychelles

Comoros Is.

Madagascar

INDIAN OCEAN

Arafura Sea

Coral Sea

New Caledonia

Fiji Is.

SOUTH ATLANTIC OCEAN

Zambezi

Mascarene Is.

Rodrigues

Mauritius

Réunion

Darling

GREAT DIVIDING RANGE

Namib Desert

Kalahari Desert

Western Plateau

AUSTRALIA

Central Lowlands

Lake Eyre -52 ft -16 m

Drakensberg

Cape of Good Hope

Great Australian Bight

Murray

Mt. Kosciuszko 7,310 ft 2,228 m

SOUTH PACIFIC OCEAN

Prince Edward Islands

Crozet Islands

Tasmania

Tasman Sea

North I.

NEW ZEALAND

South Georgia

South Sandwich Islands

Kerguelen Islands

South I.

Scotia Sea

Auckland Islands

South Orkney Islands

+ South Magnetic Pole

WEDDELL SEA

Ronne Ice Shelf

Queen Maud Land

EAST ANTARCTICA

TRANSANTARCTIC MTS.

Victoria Land

Ross Sea

MOUNTAINS

ANTARCTICA

Ross Ice Shelf

THE LAND

A closer look at Earth's surface reveals many varied forms and features that make each place unique. The drawing (right) captures 42 natural and human-made features in an imaginary landscape that shows how these different land and water features relate to each other. For example, a large moving "river" of ice, called a glacier, descends from a high mountain range. A river passes through a valley and empties into a gulf. And a harbor, built by people, creates safe anchorage for ships.

Features such as these can be found all over the world because the same forces are at work wherever you might go. Internal forces such as volcanoes and the movement of the plates of Earth's crust are constantly creating and building up new landforms, while external forces such as wind, water, and ice continuously wear down surface features.

Earth is dynamic—constantly changing, never the same.

Dormant volcano
Ocean
Island
Archipelago
Point
Strait
Cape
Sound
Peninsula
Bay
Lagoon
Isthmus
Cliff
Gulf
Spit
Reef

RIVER

As a river moves through flatlands, it twists and turns. Above, the Rio Los Amigos winds through a rain forest in Peru.

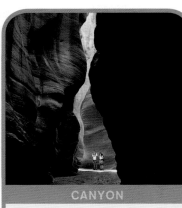

CANYON

Steep-sided valleys called canyons are created mainly by running water. Buckskin Gulch (above) is the deepest slot canyon in the American Southwest.

DESERT

Deserts are a land feature created by climate, specifically by a lack of water. Above, a camel caravan crosses the Sahara, in North Africa.

OASIS

Occasionally, water rises from deep below a desert, creating a refuge that supports trees and sometimes crops, as in this oasis in Africa.

Mountain peak

Mountain range

Glacier

Iceberg

Basin

Desert

Mesa

Oasis

Divide

Plateau

Waterfall

Escarpment

Valley

Lake

Canyon

Canal

Plain

Beach

River

Fork

Delta

Hills

Harbor

Tributary

Breakwater

A Name for Every Feature

Land has a vocabulary all its own, each name identifying a specific feature of the landscape. A cape, for example, is a broadish chunk of land extending out into the sea. It is not pointed, however, for then it would be a point. Nor does it have a narrow neck. A sizable cape or point with a narrow neck is a peninsula. The narrow neck, of course, is an isthmus.

Such specific identifiers have proven useful over the centuries. In the early days of exploration, even the simplest maps showed peninsulas, bays, and straits. Sailors used these landmarks to reach safe harbor or avoid disastrous encounters.

← EXPLORING THE LANDSCAPE. How many land and water features can you identify in the imaginary landscape at left? Definitions for these terms can be found in the glossary on pages 172–173.

MOUNTAIN

Mountains are Earth's tallest landforms, and Mount Everest (above) rises highest of all at 29,035 feet (8,850 m) above sea level.

GLACIER

Glaciers—"rivers" of ice—such as Alaska's Hubbard (above), move slowly from mountains to the sea. Global warming may be shrinking them.

VALLEY

Valleys, cut by running water or moving ice, may be broad and flat or narrow and steep, such as the Indus River Valley in Ladakh, India (above).

WATERFALL

Waterfalls form when a river reaches an abrupt change in elevation. Above, Kaitur Falls, in Guyana, descends 800 feet (244 m).

WORLD CLIMATE

Weather is the condition of the atmosphere—temperature, precipitation, humidity, wind—at a given place at a given time. Climate, however, is the average weather for a particular place over a long period of time. Different places on Earth have different climates, but climate is not a random occurrence. There is a pattern that is controlled by factors such as latitude, elevation, prevailing winds, temperature of ocean currents, and location on land relative to water. Climate is generally constant, but many are concerned that human activity may be causing a change in the patterns of climate.

THE BASICS

According to the National Oceanic and Atmospheric Administration (NOAA), 2005 ranks second only to 1998 as the hottest year on record. The global annual temperature for combined land and ocean surfaces was 1°F (.6°C) above the average established between 1880 and 2004.

Ice cores taken from Antarctica and Greenland have enabled scientists to gain detailed information about the history of Earth's climate and its atmosphere—especially the presence of greenhouse gases—dating back thousands of years.

Data collected by satellite imagery suggests that the Sahara, Earth's largest desert, had a wet climate that supported vast forests some 12,000 years ago. Extremely dry conditions did not begin until about 5,000 years ago.

According to climatologists, Earth had what is called the Little Ice Age, which lasted from the 17th century to the late 19th century. During that time, temperatures were cold enough to cause glaciers to advance.

⇩ CLIMATE GRAPHS.
Temperature and precipitation data provide a snapshot of the climate at a particular place. This information can be shown in a special type of graph called a climate graph (see below). Average monthly temperatures (scale on the left side of the graphs) are represented by the lines at the tops of the colored areas, while average monthly precipitation totals (scale on the right side of the graphs) are reflected in the bars. For example, the graph for Belém, Brazil, shows a constant warm temperature with abundant rainfall year-round. In contrast, the graph for Fairbanks, Alaska, shows a cool, variable temperature with only limited precipitation.

Resolute.
•Fairbanks

ROCKY MOUNTAINS

NORTH AMERICA
•Des Moines

Subarctic Current

North Pacific Drift

California Current

Gulf Stream

North Atlantic Drift

Labrador Current

Hawaiian Islands

TROPIC OF CANCER

Monterrey•

Gulf of Mexico

North Equatorial Current

PACIFIC OCEAN

Equatorial Countercurrent

EQUATOR

ATLANTIC OCEAN

South Equatorial Current

Peru Current

ANDES

AMAZONIA

•Belém

SOUTH AMERICA

Brazil Current

TROPIC OF CAPRICORN

Falkland Current

Antarctic Peninsula

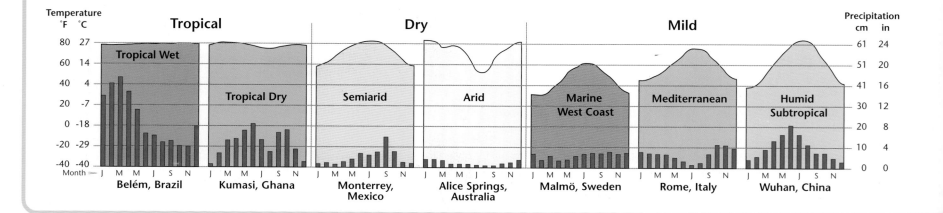

Temperature °F °C	**Tropical**		**Dry**		**Mild**			Precipitation cm in
80 27	Tropical Wet							61 24
60 14								51 20
40 4		Tropical Dry	Semiarid	Arid	Marine West Coast	Mediterranean	Humid Subtropical	41 16
20 -7								30 12
0 -18								20 8
-20 -29								10 4
-40 -40								0 0
Month —	J M M J S N	J M M J S N	J M M J S N	J M M J S N	J M M J S N	J M M J S N	J M M J S N	
	Belém, Brazil	Kumasi, Ghana	Monterrey, Mexico	Alice Springs, Australia	Malmö, Sweden	Rome, Italy	Wuhan, China	

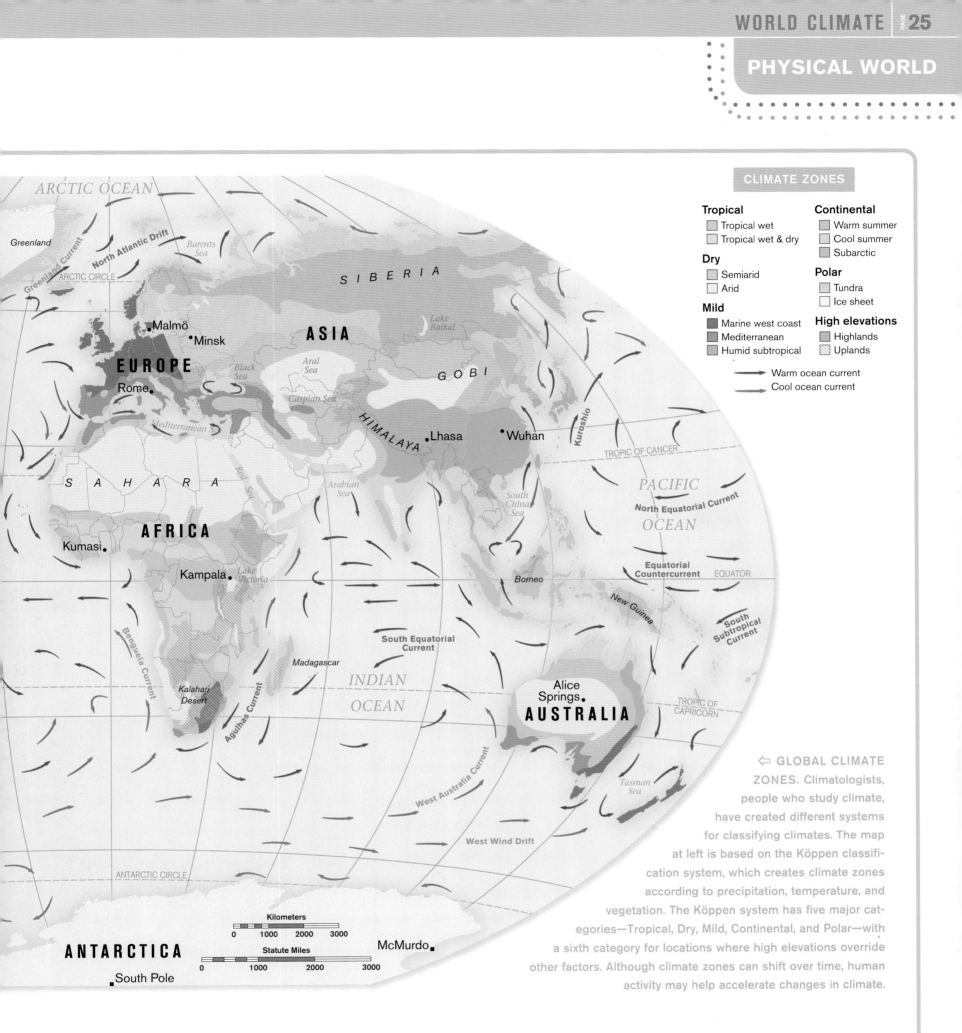

CLIMATE ZONES

Tropical
- ☐ Tropical wet
- ☐ Tropical wet & dry

Dry
- ☐ Semiarid
- ☐ Arid

Mild
- ☐ Marine west coast
- ☐ Mediterranean
- ☐ Humid subtropical

Continental
- ☐ Warm summer
- ☐ Cool summer
- ☐ Subarctic

Polar
- ☐ Tundra
- ☐ Ice sheet

High elevations
- ☐ Highlands
- ☐ Uplands

→ Warm ocean current
→ Cool ocean current

⇐ GLOBAL CLIMATE ZONES. Climatologists, people who study climate, have created different systems for classifying climates. The map at left is based on the Köppen classification system, which creates climate zones according to precipitation, temperature, and vegetation. The Köppen system has five major categories—Tropical, Dry, Mild, Continental, and Polar—with a sixth category for locations where high elevations override other factors. Although climate zones can shift over time, human activity may help accelerate changes in climate.

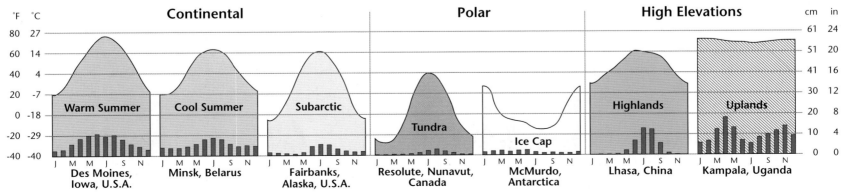

Continental	Polar	High Elevations
Warm Summer — Des Moines, Iowa, U.S.A. / Cool Summer — Minsk, Belarus / Subarctic — Fairbanks, Alaska, U.S.A.	Tundra — Resolute, Nunavut, Canada / Ice Cap — McMurdo, Antarctica	Highlands — Lhasa, China / Uplands — Kampala, Uganda

FACTORS INFLUENCING CLIMATE

Earth's climate is a bit like a big jigsaw puzzle. In order to understand it, you need to fit all the pieces together because climate is influenced by a number of different, but interrelated factors, including latitude, topography (shape of the land), elevation above sea level, wind systems, ocean currents, and distance from large water bodies. Climate has always affected the way we live, but scientists now believe that the way we live may also be affecting climate. Pollution from industries and motor vehicles may be contributing to global warming. And this could be causing Earth's climates to change.

⬇ TOPOGRAPHY. Mountain ranges are natural barriers to the movement of air. In North America, prevailing westerly winds carry air full of moisture from the Pacific Ocean to the coast. As air rises over the Coast Ranges, light precipitation falls. Farther inland, the much taller Sierra Nevada range triggers heavy precipitation as air rises higher. On the leeward side of the Sierra Nevada, sinking air warms, clouds evaporate, and dry "rain shadow" conditions prevail. As winds continue across the interior plateau, the air remains dry because there is not a significant source of moisture.

Windward (wet)   Leeward (dry)

Pacific Ocean   Wind

Coast Ranges   Sierra Nevada

Cool ▬▬ Warm ➤ Temperature changes as air moves over mountains

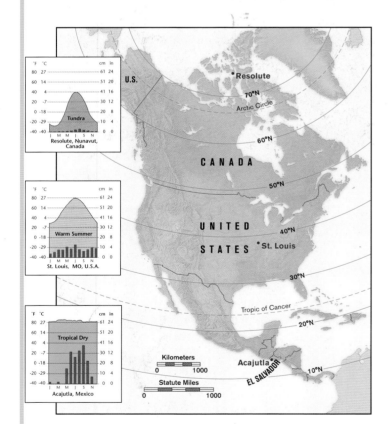

⬆ LATITUDE. Energy from the sun drives global climates. Latitude—distance north or south of the Equator—affects the amount of solar energy received. Places near the Equator (see Acajutla, El Salvador, above) have warm temperatures year-round. As distance from the Equator increases (see St. Louis, U.S.A., and Resolute, Canada, above), average temperatures decline, and cold winters become more pronounced.

⇨ ELEVATION. In general, climate conditions become cooler as elevation increases. Since cooler air holds less moisture, less precipitation falls. As temperature and moisture conditions change, vegetation also changes. In the mountain diagram (right), dense mixed forest grows near the base of the mountain on the windward side. As elevation increases and temperatures decline, the mixed forest changes to all evergreen, followed by alpine meadows, until finally the mountain's rocky peaks are covered by snow and ice. As air moves down the leeward slope of the mountain, it warms and evaporates moisture, causing the leeward side to be drier and have less vegetation.

WINDWARD

Cold winds over warm water
Cool onshore ocean winds
Desert winds
Warm onshore ocean winds

⇧ DIGGING OUT. Arctic winds roar across Canada, picking up moisture from the Great Lakes (see purple arrows on map, left). As the moisture-laden air crosses over the frozen land, temperatures fall and heavy precipitation—called lake effect snow—buries cars and roads, as shown here in Oswego, New York.

⇦ WARM CURRENT. The Gulf Stream, a warm ocean current averaging 50–93 miles (80–150 km) wide, sweeps up the East Coast of North America (see red arrow on map above). One branch continues across the North Atlantic Ocean and above the Arctic Circle. In this color-enhanced satellite image, the Gulf Stream looks like a dark red river moving up the coast. This "river" of warm water influences climate along its path, bringing moisture and mild temperatures to the East Coast of the United States and causing ice-free ports above the Arctic Circle in Europe.

LEEWARD

GLOBAL WARMING

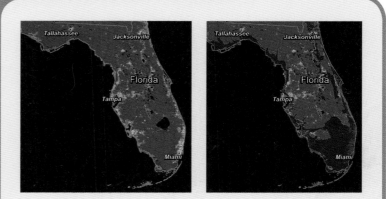

Earth's climate history has been a story of ups and downs, with warm periods followed by periods of bitter cold. The early part of the 20th century was marked by colder than average temperatures (see graph below), followed by a period of gradual and then steady increase. Scientists are concerned that the current warming trend may be more than a natural cycle. Evidence indicates that human activity is adding to the warming. One sign of change is melting glaciers in Greenland and Antarctica. If glaciers continue to melt, areas of Florida (shown above in red) and other coastal land will be under water.

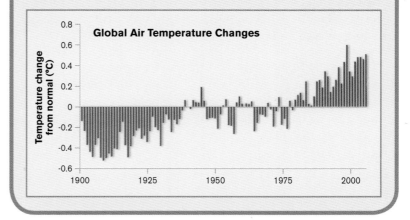

Global Air Temperature Changes

WORLD VEGETATION

Natural vegetation—plants that would grow under ideal circumstances at a particular place—depends on several factors. The climate is very important, as is the quality and type of soil that is available. Therefore, vegetation often reflects patterns of climate. (Compare the vegetation map at right with the world climate map on pages 24–25.) Forests thrive in places with ample precipitation; grasses are found in places with less precipitation or with only seasonal rainfall; and xerophytes—plants able to survive lengthy periods with little or no water—are found in arid areas that receive very little precipitation on a yearly basis. Grasses and shrubs cover almost half of Earth's land.

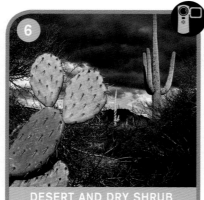

TEMPERATE BROADLEAF FOREST

Broadleaf trees that grow in mid-latitude areas with mild temperatures, such as this one in Shenandoah National Park, are deciduous, meaning they lose their leaves in winter. Many such forests have been cleared for cropland.

DESERT AND DRY SHRUB

Deserts, areas that receive less than 10 inches (25 cm) of rainfall a year, have vegetation that is specially adapted to survive under dry conditions, such as these dry shrubs and cacti growing in the Sonora Desert in Arizona.

TUNDRA

With only two to three months of temperatures above freezing, tundra plants are mostly dwarf shrubs, short grasses, mosses, and lichens. Much of Canada's Yukon has tundra vegetation, which turns red as winter approaches.

CONIFEROUS FOREST

Needleleaf trees with cones to protect their seeds from bitter winters grow in cold climates with short summers, such as British Columbia, Canada. These trees are important in lumber and paper-making industries.

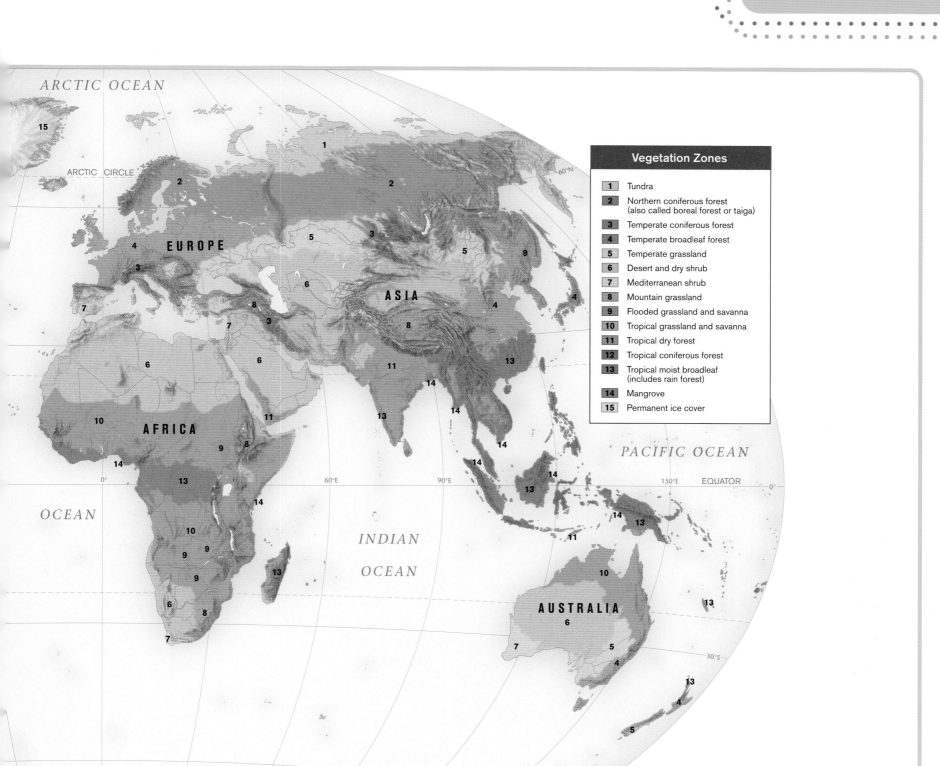

ARCTIC OCEAN

ARCTIC CIRCLE

EUROPE

ASIA

AFRICA

PACIFIC OCEAN

OCEAN

INDIAN OCEAN

AUSTRALIA

EQUATOR

Vegetation Zones

1	Tundra
2	Northern coniferous forest (also called boreal forest or taiga)
3	Temperate coniferous forest
4	Temperate broadleaf forest
5	Temperate grassland
6	Desert and dry shrub
7	Mediterranean shrub
8	Mountain grassland
9	Flooded grassland and savanna
10	Tropical grassland and savanna
11	Tropical dry forest
12	Tropical coniferous forest
13	Tropical moist broadleaf (includes rain forest)
14	Mangrove
15	Permanent ice cover

5 TEMPERATE GRASSLAND

Grasslands, such as this tall-grass prairie in southwestern Missouri, are found in areas where precipitation is too low to support forests. Many temperate grasslands have been converted to crop-land for grain production.

10 TROPICAL GRASSLAND

Tall grasses and scattered trees that can survive a hot, dry season dominate low latitude grasslands, also called savannas. Africa's grasslands are home to game animals, such as this male lion crossing the savanna in Botswana.

13 RAIN FOREST

A waterfall tumbles over a cliff in the Costa Rican rain forest. Rain forest trees can grow as much as 200 feet (61 m) above the forest floor. The overlapping branches of the tallest trees keep sunlight from reaching the forest floor.

CROPLAND

People remove natural vegetation in many places to create fields to grow crops to feed both people and animals. Here, a farmer in the Catskill Mountains of New York uses a mechanized harvester to cut corn to feed his dairy cows.

ENVIRONMENTAL HOT SPOTS

Around the world people are putting more and more pressure on the environment by dumping pollutants into the air and water and by removing natural vegetation to extract mineral resources or to turn the land into cropland for farming. In more developed countries, industries create waste and pollution; farmers use fertilizers and pesticides that run off into water supplies; and motor vehicles release exhaust fumes into the air. In less developed countries, forests are cut down for fuel or to clear land for farming; grasslands are turned into deserts as farmers and herders overuse the land; and expanding urban areas face problems of water quality and sanitation.

NORTH AMERICA

Toronto
Chicago
Boston
New York
San Francisco
Los Angeles
México

PACIFIC OCEAN

ATLANTIC OCEAN

Bogotá

SOUTH AMERICA

Lima

São Paulo
Rio de Janeiro

Santiago

Buenos Aires

Cities
- Megacity, over 10 million
- 5 to 10 million

Pollution
- Areas most sensitive to acid rain
- Frequent pollution from shipping

Desertification
- Areas at highest risk of desertification

Deforestation
- Current tropical forest
- Cleared tropical forest
- Current temperate forest
- Cleared temperate forest

ENDANGERED

Human activity poses the greatest threat to Earth's biodiversity—its rich variety of species. Loss of habitat puts many species, including those at right, at great risk. Experts estimate that species are becoming extinct at a rate 100 to 1,000 times higher than natural loss would cause.

Monarch Butterfly

Giant Tree Frog

California Condor

Asian Elephant

Rafflesia Flower

Napoleon Wrasse Fish

POLLUTION

Poor air quality is a serious environmental problem. Industrial plants are a major source of pollution. Smoke containing particles that contribute to acid rain is released from a factory in Poland (above).

⇩ HUMAN FOOTPRINT. This map uses population density, land use, transportation, and energy production and use to identify areas of Earth where human impact is greatest.

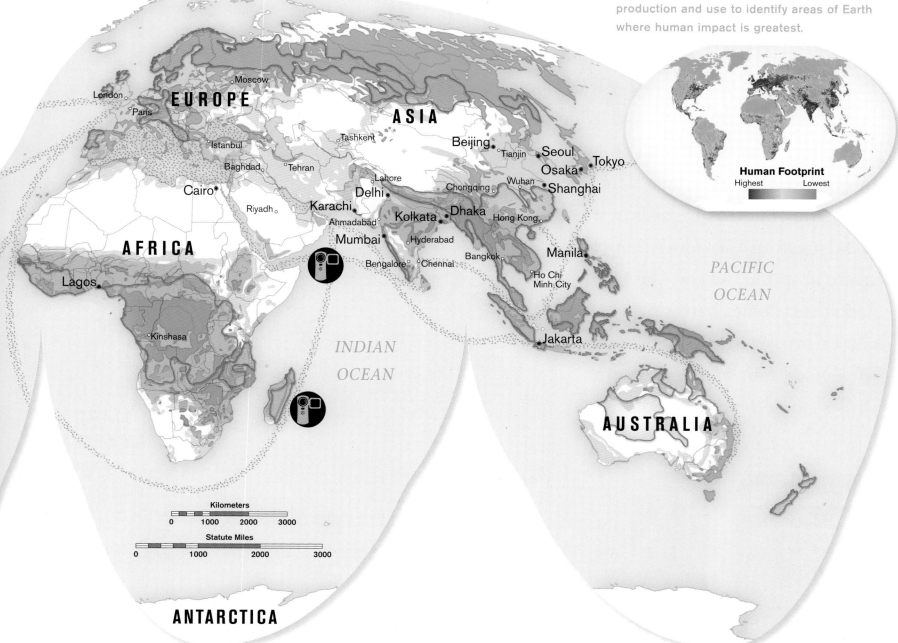

Human Footprint
Highest — Lowest

EUROPE
ASIA
AFRICA
PACIFIC OCEAN
INDIAN OCEAN
AUSTRALIA
ANTARCTICA

London
Paris
Moscow
Istanbul
Tashkent
Baghdad
Tehran
Cairo
Riyadh
Lahore
Delhi
Beijing
Tianjin
Seoul
Osaka
Tokyo
Chongqing
Wuhan
Shanghai
Karachi
Ahmadabad
Kolkata
Dhaka
Hong Kong
Mumbai
Hyderabad
Bangkok
Manila
Bengalore
Chennai
Ho Chi Minh City
Lagos
Kinshasa
Jakarta

Kilometers
0   1000   2000   3000

Statute Miles
0   1000   2000   3000

DEFORESTATION

Loss of forest cover, such as on this hillside in Malaysia, contributes to a buildup of carbon dioxide in the atmosphere, as well as to a loss of biodiversity. This is a frequent problem in the tropics.

DESERTIFICATION

Villagers in Mauritania, Africa, shovel sand away from their schoolhouse. In semiarid areas, which receive limited and often unreliable rainfall, land that is overgrazed or overcultivated can become desertlike.

DAMAGED REEFS

Coral reefs, such as this one in the Indian Ocean near the Maldives, can be damaged by increases in ocean temperatures. If a reef dies, a habitat for the many marine creatures that live there is lost.

NATURAL DISASTERS

Every world region has its share of natural disasters—the menacing mix just varies from place to place. The Ring of Fire—grinding tectonic plate boundaries that follow the coasts of the Pacific Ocean—shakes with volcanic eruptions and earthquakes. Coastal lives and livelihoods here and along other oceans can be swept away by quake-caused tsunamis. The U.S. heartland endures blizzards in winter and dangerous tornadoes that can strike in spring, summer, or fall. Tropical cyclones batter many coastal areas with ripping winds, torrents of rain, and huge storm surges along their deadly paths.

KINDS OF DISASTERS

EARTHQUAKE
A shaking of Earth's crust caused by a volcanic eruption or by the release of energy along a fault in the crust

TORNADO
A violently rotating column of air that touches Earth's surface during intense thunderstorm activity

TROPICAL CYCLONE
A huge weather system, fueled by warm water, that can become a rotating storm packing winds of at least 74 miles per hour (119 kmph); called hurricanes in the Atlantic Ocean and eastern Pacific, cyclones in the Bay of Bengal and Indian Ocean, and typhoons in the western Pacific

TSUNAMI
Ocean waves caused by an undersea earthquake or by a volcanic eruption

VOLCANIC ERUPTION
The upward movement and usually forceful release of molten material and gases from Earth's interior onto the surface

⬆ TORNADO. This funnel cloud churns past Union City, Oklahoma. There are more of these storms in "Tornado Alley" (see map) than anywhere else on Earth.

➡ TSUNAMI. People and pets alike fight to survive the deadly Indian Ocean tsunami of December 2004. The storm, triggered by an undersea earthquake, killed more than 225,000 people.

NORTH AMERICA

ROCKY MOUNTAINS

Tri-State Tornado (1925)

Galveston Hurricane (1900)

Hurricane Katrina (2005)

Hurricane Mitch (1998)

Hawaiian Islands

PACIFIC OCEAN

ATLANTIC OCEAN

SOUTH AMERICA

ANDES

Kilometers
0 1000 2000 3000

Statute Miles
0 1000 2000 3000

Winkel Tripel Projection

ARCTIC OCEAN

ASIA

EUROPE

ALPS

Ivanova-Yaroslav
(1984)

AFRICA

HIMALAYA

Great Rift Valley

Bangladesh Cyclone
(1970)

Daultipur-
Salturia
(1989)

Andaman Sea
(1941)

Coast of Sumatra
(2004)

Moro Gulf
(1976)

PACIFIC
OCEAN

INDIAN
OCEAN

AUSTRALIA

→ Typical hurricane, typhoon, or cyclone track	○ 20–21st century earthquake greater than 6.5 magnitude	· Known recorded tsunami (quake epicenter)
▬ Plate boundary or fault line	● Notable tornado of the 20–21st century	▲ Notable volcanic eruption of the 20–21st century
▬ "Tornado Alley" (highest concentration of tornadoes worldwide)	● Notable hurricane, typhoon, or cyclone of the 20–21st century	▴ Known volcanic eruption during the past 10,000 years

ANTARCTICA

⇧ VOLCANIC ERUPTION.
Dormant for 500 years,
Mount Pinatubo, in the
Philippines, erupted in June
1991, causing the deaths
of at least 300 people
and the evacuation of
tens of thousands of
others. Ash and
other material
ejected into the
atmosphere slightly
lowered global
temperatures for
a year.

⇦ NATURAL HAZARDS.
When they take human
lives and destroy property,
natural hazards become natural
disasters. This map shows areas
that have been hardest hit by natural
disasters between 1900 and 2006.

⇩ TROPICAL CYCLONE. Hurricane Katrina made
landfall along the U.S. Gulf Coast on August 29, 2005.
Four days later, U.S. Army National Guard soldiers assisted
stranded victims in New Orleans, Louisiana.

TRACKING QUAKES

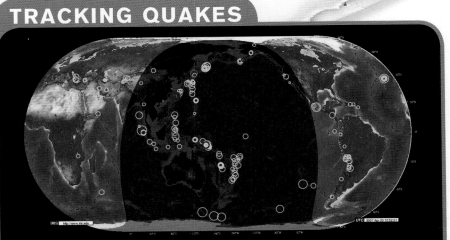

Track seismic events and learn more about them, using the link on page 175.

INVESTIGATING THE OCEANS

The map at right shows that more than 70 percent of Earth's surface is under water, mainly covered by four great oceans. There is growing support for a fifth ocean, called the Southern Ocean, in the area from Antarctica to 60°S latitude. The oceans are really interconnected bodies of water that together form one global ocean.

The ocean floor is as varied as the surface of the continents, but mapping the oceans is challenging. Past explorers cut their way through jungles of the Amazon and conquered icy heights of the Himalaya, but explorers could not march across the floor of the Pacific Ocean, which in places descends to more than 35,000 feet (10,668 m) below the surface of the water.

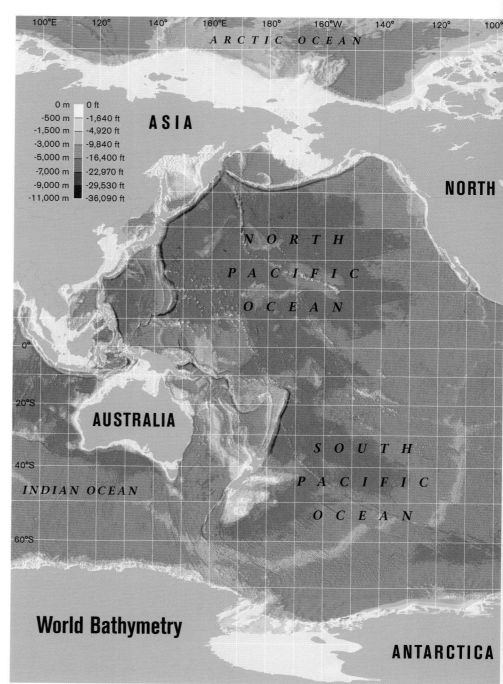

World Bathymetry

⇩ UNDERWATER LANDSCAPES. The landscape of the ocean floor is varied and constantly changing. A continental edge that slopes gently beneath the water is called a continental shelf. Mountain ranges, called mid-ocean ridges, rise where ocean plates are spreading and magma flows out to create new land. Other plates plunge into trenches more than 6 miles (10 km) deep. And magma, rising through vents called hot spots, pushes through ocean plates, creating seamounts and volcanoes.

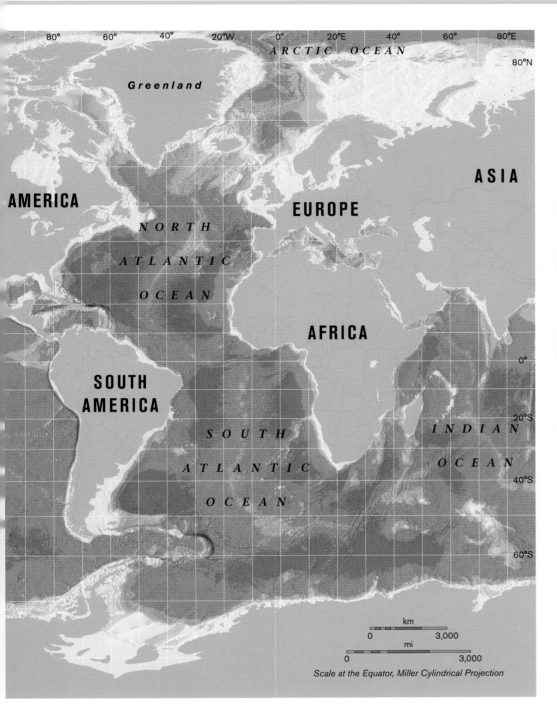

Scale at the Equator, Miller Cylindrical Projection

⇧ FROM OCEAN TO SATELLITE. In the 1990s, scientists developed the Argo Float to collect data from below the ocean surface. Argo Floats sink to a preset depth, often thousands of feet, where they gather data, such as temperature and salt content. At regular intervals, the floats rise to the surface (above) and transmit the data collected to a satellite. Then the cycle starts over again.

⇩ EYE ON THE OCEAN. The Sea-Viewing Wide Field-of-View Sensor (SeaWiFS) satellite records digital images of ocean colors that are used to identify and follow plant and animal activity in the oceans.

⇦ SEEING WITH YOUR EARS. Special instruments, such as this acoustic buoy, use sound waves bounced off the ocean floor to record variations in water temperature. This technique, called Acoustic Thermometry of Ocean Climate (ATOC), may someday help monitor long-term climate changes.

PACIFIC OCEAN

THE BASICS

STATS

Surface area
65,436,200 sq mi
(169,479,000 sq km)

Percent of Earth's water area
47%

Greatest depth
Challenger Deep
(in the Mariana Trench)
-35,827 ft (-10,920 m)

Surface temperatures
Summer high: 82°F (28°C)
Winter low: 30°F (−1°C)

Tides
Highest: 30 ft (9 m)
near Korean peninsula
Lowest: 1 ft (0.3 m)
near Midway Islands

GEO WHIZ

The Pacific Ocean has more islands—tens of thousands of them—than any other ocean.

The ocean's name comes from the Latin *Mare Pacificum*, meaning "peaceful sea," but earthquake and volcanic activity along the Ring of Fire generate powerful waves called tsunamis, which cause death and destruction when they slam ashore.

With the greatest area of tropical waters, the Pacific is also home to the largest number of coral reefs, including Earth's longest: Australia's 1,429-mile- (2,300-km-) long Great Barrier Reef.

The Hawaiian monk seal, the most endangered marine mammal in U.S. waters, lives only on a few islands in the remote northwestern end of the Hawaiian archipelago.

The Pacific Ocean, largest of Earth's oceans, is about 15 times larger than the United States and covers more than 30 percent of Earth's surface. The edges of the Pacific are often called the Ring of Fire because many active volcanoes and earthquakes occur where the ocean plate is moving under the edges of continental plates.

⇧ IN THE MIDST OF DANGER. A false-clown anemonefish swims among the tentacles of a sea anemone off the coast of the Philippines, in the western Pacific. This colorful fish is immune to the anemone's paralyzing sting.

The southwestern Pacific is dotted with many islands. Also in the western Pacific, the Challenger Deep in the Mariana Trench plunges to 35,827 feet (10,920 m) below sea level. Most of the world's fish catch (see page 56) comes from the Pacific, and oil and gas reserves there are an important energy source.

⇦ CIRCLE OF LIFE. Atolls, such as this one near Okinawa, Japan, are ocean landforms created by tiny marine animals called corals. These creatures live in warm tropical waters. The circular shape of atolls often marks the coastline of sunken volcanic islands.

SCALE AT THE EQUATOR
0   1,000 miles
0   1,000 kilometers
Mercator Projection

ASIA

Sea of Okhotsk

Sakhalin

Amur

Kuril Basin

Hokkaido

Kuril

Sea of Japan (East Sea)

Honshu

Japan Trench

Korea

Yellow

Yellow Sea

Kyushu

Izu Trench

Yangtze

East China Sea

Ryukyu Is.

Taiwan

Ryukyu Trench

Bonin Trench

Palau Ridge

Philippine Sea

Philippine Trench

Luzon

West Mariana Basin

Mariana Trough

Mariana Islands

Mariana Trench

East Mariana Basin

PHILIPPINE ISLANDS

Sulu Basin

Mindanao

Palau

Kyushu

Palau Trench

Yap Trench

Challenger Deep World's greatest ocean depth -35,827 ft -10,920 m

Borneo

Celebes Basin

West Caroline Basin

East Caroline Basin

Caroline Islands

INDONESIA

Celebes

Greater Sunda Islands

Banda Sea

Weber Basin

New Guinea

Bismarck Archipelago

Lesser Sunda Islands

Continental Shelf

North Australian Basin

Coral Sea Basin

Great Barrier Reef

Cos

TROPIC OF CAPRICORN

AUSTRALIA

South Australian Basin

Tasman Plain

Tasmania

INDIAN OCEAN

South Tasman Rise

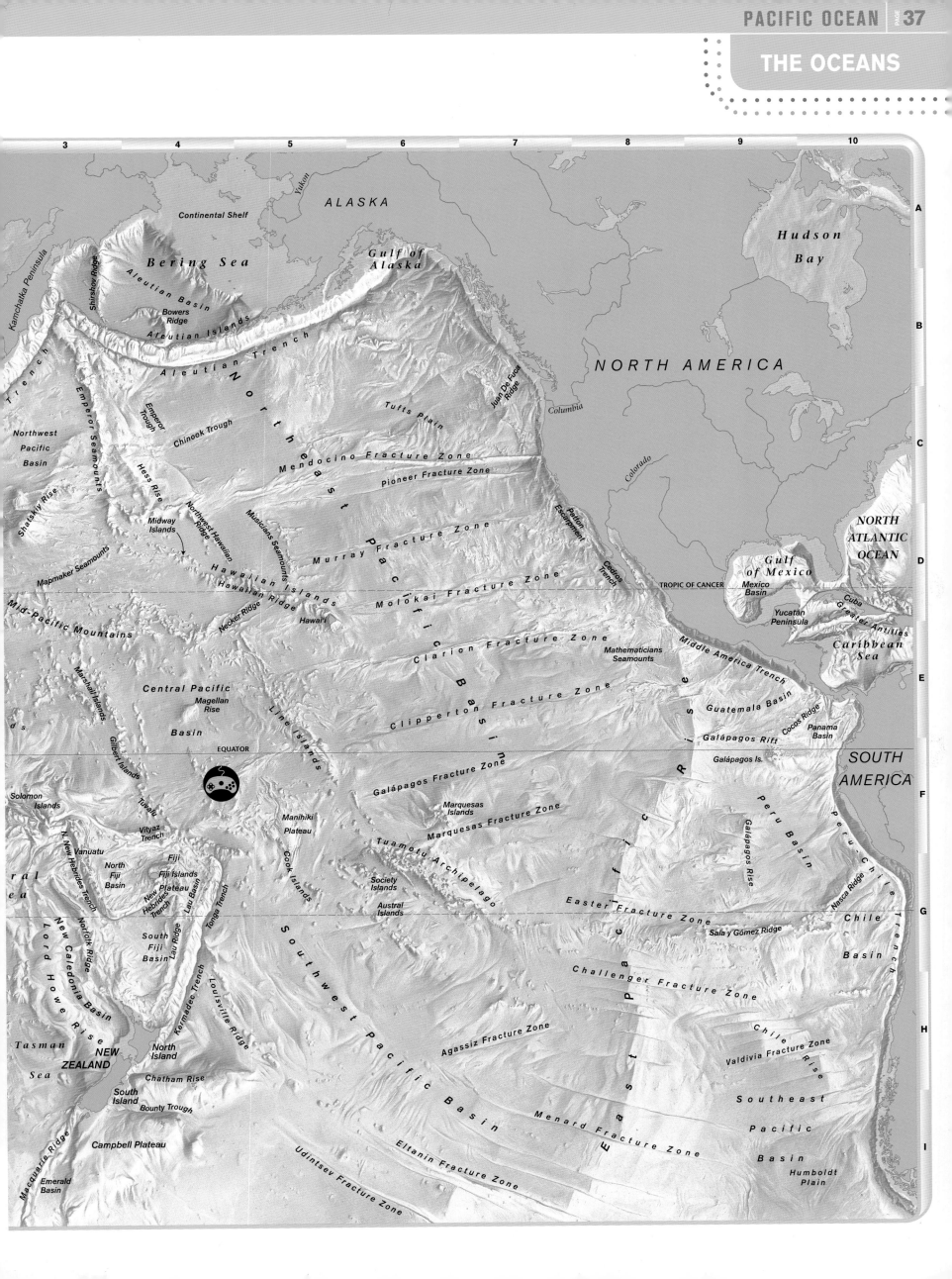

ATLANTIC OCEAN

Among Earth's great oceans, the Atlantic is second only to the Pacific in size. The floor of the Atlantic is split by the Mid-Atlantic Ridge, which is part of the Mid-Ocean Ridge—the longest mountain chain on Earth. The Atlantic poses many hazards to human activity. Tropical storms called hurricanes form in the warm tropical waters off the west coast of Africa and move across the ocean to bombard the islands of the Caribbean and coastal areas of North America with damaging winds, waves, and rain in the late summer and fall. In the cold waters of the North Atlantic, sea ice and icebergs pose a danger to shipping, especially during winter and spring.

The Atlantic has rich deposits of oil and natural gas, but drilling has resulted in pollution problems. In addition, the Atlantic has important marine fisheries, but overfishing has put some species at risk. Sea lanes between Europe and the Americas are among the most heavily trafficked in the world.

THE BASICS

STATS

Surface area
35,338,500 sq mi
(91,526,400 sq km)

Percent of Earth's water area
25%

Greatest depth
Puerto Rico Trench
-28,232 ft (-8,605 m)

Surface temperatures
Summer high: 86°F (30°C)
Winter low: 28°F (-2°C)

Tides
Highest: 52 ft (16 m)
Bay of Fundy, Canada
Lowest: 1.5 ft (0.5 m)
Gulf of Mexico and Mediterranean Sea

GEO WHIZ

In 2005, the Atlantic Ocean produced a record-setting 15 hurricanes. For the first time in a single season, 4 hurricanes—Emily, Katrina, Rita, and Wilma—reached category 5 level, with sustained winds of at least 155 miles per hour (249 kmph).

The Atlantic Ocean is about half the size of the Pacific, but it's growing. Spreading along the Mid-Atlantic Ridge allows molten rock from Earth's interior to escape and form new ocean floor.

Fishermen in the North Atlantic were eyewitnesses to the volcanic eruption that created the island of Surtsey, off the southeastern coast of Iceland, in November 1963.

Each year, the amount of water that flows into the Atlantic Ocean from the Amazon River is equal to 20 percent of Earth's available fresh water.

⇧ CAMOUFLAGE ON ICE. A young harp seal, called a pup, rests on the ice in Canada's Gulf of St. Lawrence. Pups are cared for by their mothers for only 12 days. Then, they must survive on their own.

⇧ HIDDEN DANGER. Icebergs (above, right) are huge blocks of ice that break away, or calve, from the edges of glaciers. They pose a danger to ships because only about 10 percent of their bulk is visible above the waterline. A tragic disaster associated with an iceberg was the 1912 sinking of the RMS *Titanic*, whose ghostly ruins are shown above, left.

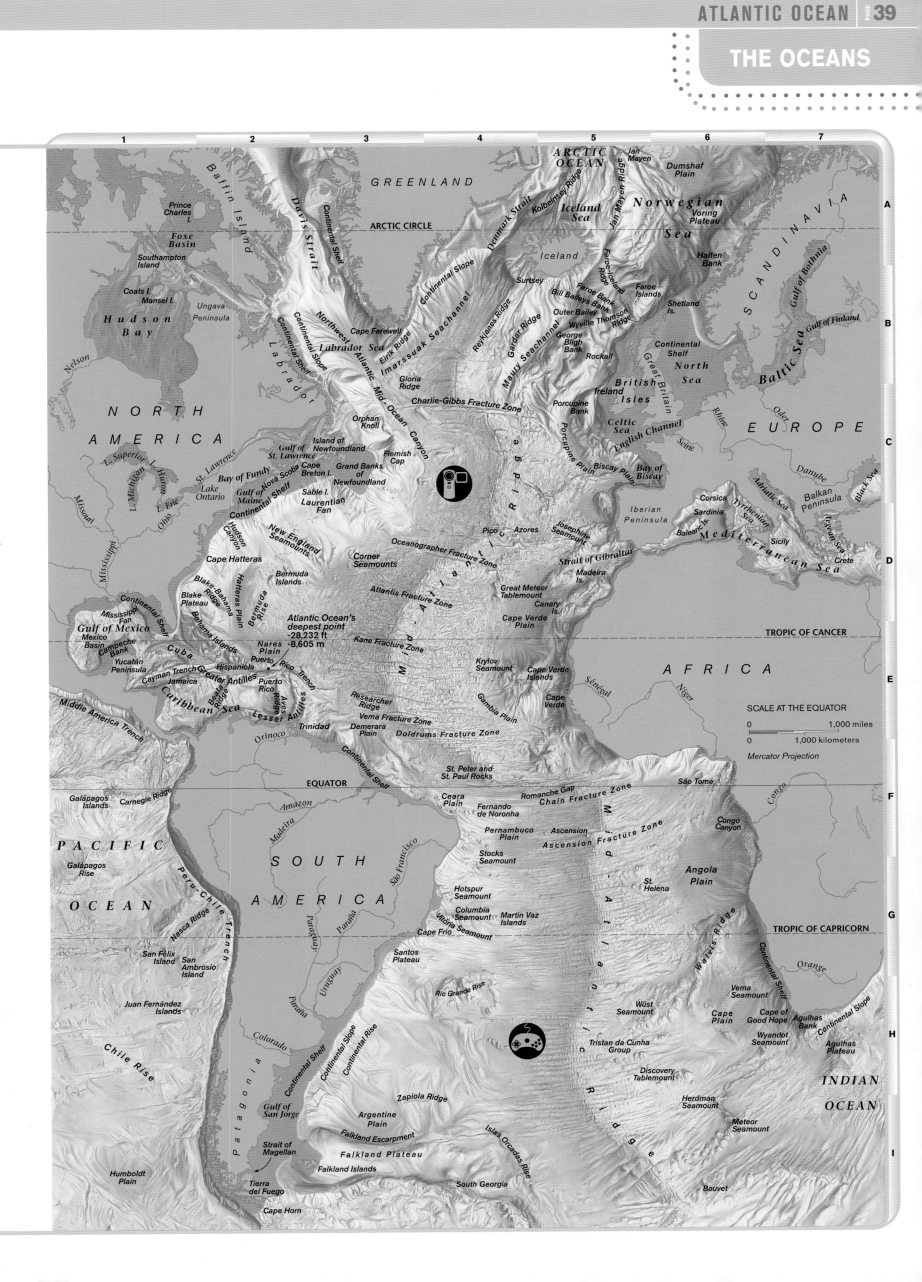

ARCTIC OCEAN

GREENLAND

Jan Mayen

Dumshaf Plain

Kolbeinsey Ridge

Iceland Sea

Jan Mayen Ridge

Norwegian Sea

Voring Plateau

SCANDINAVIA

Gulf of Bothnia

ARCTIC CIRCLE

Denmark Strait

Iceland

Surtsey

Faroe-Iceland Ridge

Faroe Bank

Bill Bailey's Bank

Outer Bailey

Faroe Islands

Halten Bank

Shetland Is.

Gulf of Finland

Baltic Sea

Prince Charles I.

Foxe Basin

Southampton Island

Coats I.

Mansel I.

Ungava Peninsula

HUDSON BAY

Baffin Island

Davis Strait

Continental Shelf

Cape Farewell

Northwest Atlantic Mid-Ocean Canyon

Continental Slope

Labrador Sea

Eirik Ridge

Imarssuak Seachannel

Reykjanes Ridge

Gardar Ridge

Maury Seachannel

Wyville Thomson Ridge

George Bligh Bank

Rockall

Great Britain

Continental Shelf

North Sea

British Isles

Celtic Sea

Rhine

Odra

EUROPE

Nelson

Continental Shelf

Continental Slope

Labrador

Gloria Ridge

Charlie-Gibbs Fracture Zone

Porcupine Bank

Ireland

English Channel

Porcupine Plain

Biscay Plain

Bay of Biscay

Seine

Danube

NORTH AMERICA

L. Superior

L. Huron

Missouri

L. Michigan

L. Erie

Ohio

St. Lawrence

Lake Ontario

Bay of Fundy

Cape Breton I.

Gulf of Nova Scotia

Gulf of St. Lawrence

Island of Newfoundland

Orphan Knoll

Grand Banks of Newfoundland

Flemish Cap

Iberian Peninsula

Corsica

Sardinia

Balearics

Adriatic Sea

Tyrrhenian Sea

Balkan Peninsula

Black Sea

Sicily

Aegean Sea

Crete

Mediterranean Sea

Continental Shelf

Sable I.

Laurentian Fan

New England Seamounts

Hudson Canyon

Cape Hatteras

Corner Seamounts

Oceanographer Fracture Zone

Pico

Azores

Josephine Seamount

Strait of Gibraltar

Madeira Is.

Mississippi

Bermuda Islands

Blake-Bahama Ridge

Hatteras Plain

Bermuda Rise

Atlantis Fracture Zone

Great Meteor Tablemount

Canary Is.

Cape Verde Plain

Blake Plateau

Continental Shelf

Mississippi Fan

Gulf of Mexico

Mexico Basin

Campeche Bank

Bahama Islands

Atlantic Ocean's deepest point -28,232 ft -8,605 m

Nares Plain

Kane Fracture Zone

Krylov Seamount

Cape Verde Islands

TROPIC OF CANCER

AFRICA

Yucatán Peninsula

Cuba

Greater Antilles

Cayman Trench

Jamaica

Hispaniola

Puerto Rico Trench

Beata Ridge

Aves Ridge

Puerto Rico

Researcher Ridge

Gambia Plain

Cape Verde

Sénégal

Niger

SCALE AT THE EQUATOR

0 ———— 1,000 miles

0 ———— 1,000 kilometers

Mercator Projection

Middle America Trench

Caribbean Sea

Lesser Antilles

Trinidad

Orinoco

Vema Fracture Zone

Demerara Plain

Doldrums Fracture Zone

Continental Shelf

St. Peter and St. Paul Rocks

Romanche Gap

Chain Fracture Zone

São Tomé

Congo

EQUATOR

Galápagos Islands

Carnegie Ridge

Amazon

Madeira

Ceara Plain

Fernando de Noronha

Ascension

Ascension Fracture Zone

Congo Canyon

PACIFIC OCEAN

Galápagos Rise

São Francisco

Pernambuco Plain

Stocks Seamount

St. Helena

Angola Plain

SOUTH AMERICA

Peru-Chile Trench

Nasca Ridge

Paraguay

Paraná

Hotspur Seamount

Columbia Seamount

Vitória Seamount

Cape Frio

Martin Vaz Islands

TROPIC OF CAPRICORN

Walvis Ridge

Continental Shelf

Orange

San Félix Island

San Ambrosio Island

Juan Fernández Islands

Uruguay

Paraná

Santos Plateau

Rio Grande Rise

Vema Seamount

Cape Plain

Cape of Good Hope

Agulhas Bank

Continental Slope

Wüst Seamount

Wyandot Seamount

Agulhas Plateau

Chile Rise

Colorado

Continental Shelf

Continental Slope

Continental Rise

Zapiola Ridge

Tristan da Cunha Group

Discovery Tablemount

Herdman Seamount

INDIAN OCEAN

Patagonia

Gulf of San Jorge

Argentine Plain

Rio Grande Rise

Mid-Atlantic Ridge

Meteor Seamount

Humboldt Plain

Strait of Magellan

Falkland Escarpment

Falkland Plateau

Islas Orcadas Rise

Bouvet

Tierra del Fuego

Falkland Islands

South Georgia

Cape Horn

INDIAN OCEAN

THE BASICS

STATS

Surface area
28,839,800 sq mi
(74,694,800 sq km)

Percent of Earth's water area
21%

Greatest depth
Java Trench
-23,376 ft (-7,125 m)

Surface temperatures
Summer high: 90°F (32°C)
Winter low: 30°F (-1°C)

Tides
Highest: 36 ft (11 m)
Lowest: 2 ft (0.6 m)
Both along Australia's west coast

GEO WHIZ

Each day tankers carrying 17 million barrels of crude oil from the Persian Gulf enter the waters of the Indian Ocean, transporting their cargo for distribution around the world.

Some of the world's largest breeding grounds for humpback whales are in the Indian Ocean, the Arabian Sea, and off the east coast of Africa.

The Bay of Bengal is sometimes called Cyclone Alley because of the large number of tropical storms that occur each year between May and November.

Sailors from what is now Indonesia used seasonal winds called monsoons to reach Africa's east coast. They arrived on the continent long before Europeans did.

The earthquake that caused the tsunami that killed more than 225,000 people in countries bordering the Indian Ocean in December 2004 created waves as high as 49 feet (15 m).

The Indian Ocean has several strategic chokepoints—narrow straits through which shipping must pass. They include Bab el Mandeb, between the Gulf of Aden and the Red Sea; the Strait of Hormuz, between the Persian Gulf and the Arabian Sea; the Gulf of Suez, between the Red Sea and the Suez Canal; and the Strait of Malacca, between Sumatra and the Malay Peninsula.

The Indian Ocean stretches from Africa's east coast to the southern coast of Asia and the western coast of Australia. It is the third largest of Earth's great oceans. Changing air pressure systems over the warm waters of the Indian Ocean trigger South Asia's famous monsoon climate— a weather pattern in which winds reverse directions seasonally. The Bay of Bengal, an arm of the Indian Ocean, experiences devastating tropical storms, similar to hurricanes, but called cyclones in this region. Islands along the eastern edge of the Indian Ocean plate experience earthquakes that sometimes cause destructive ocean waves, called tsunamis.

The Arabian Sea, Persian Gulf, and Red Sea, also extensions of the Indian Ocean, are important sources of oil and natural gas reserves and account for an estimated 40 percent of the world's offshore oil production. The sea routes of the Indian Ocean connect the Middle East to the rest of world, carrying much needed energy resources on huge tanker ships.

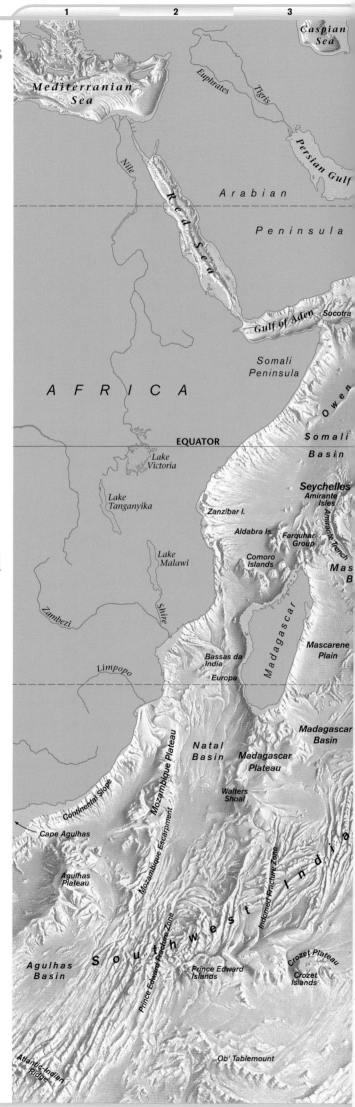

⟸ LIVING FOSSIL. A coelacanth swims in the warm waters of the western Indian Ocean off the Comoro Islands. Once thought to have become extinct 65 million years ago along with the dinosaurs, a living coelacanth was discovered in 1938.

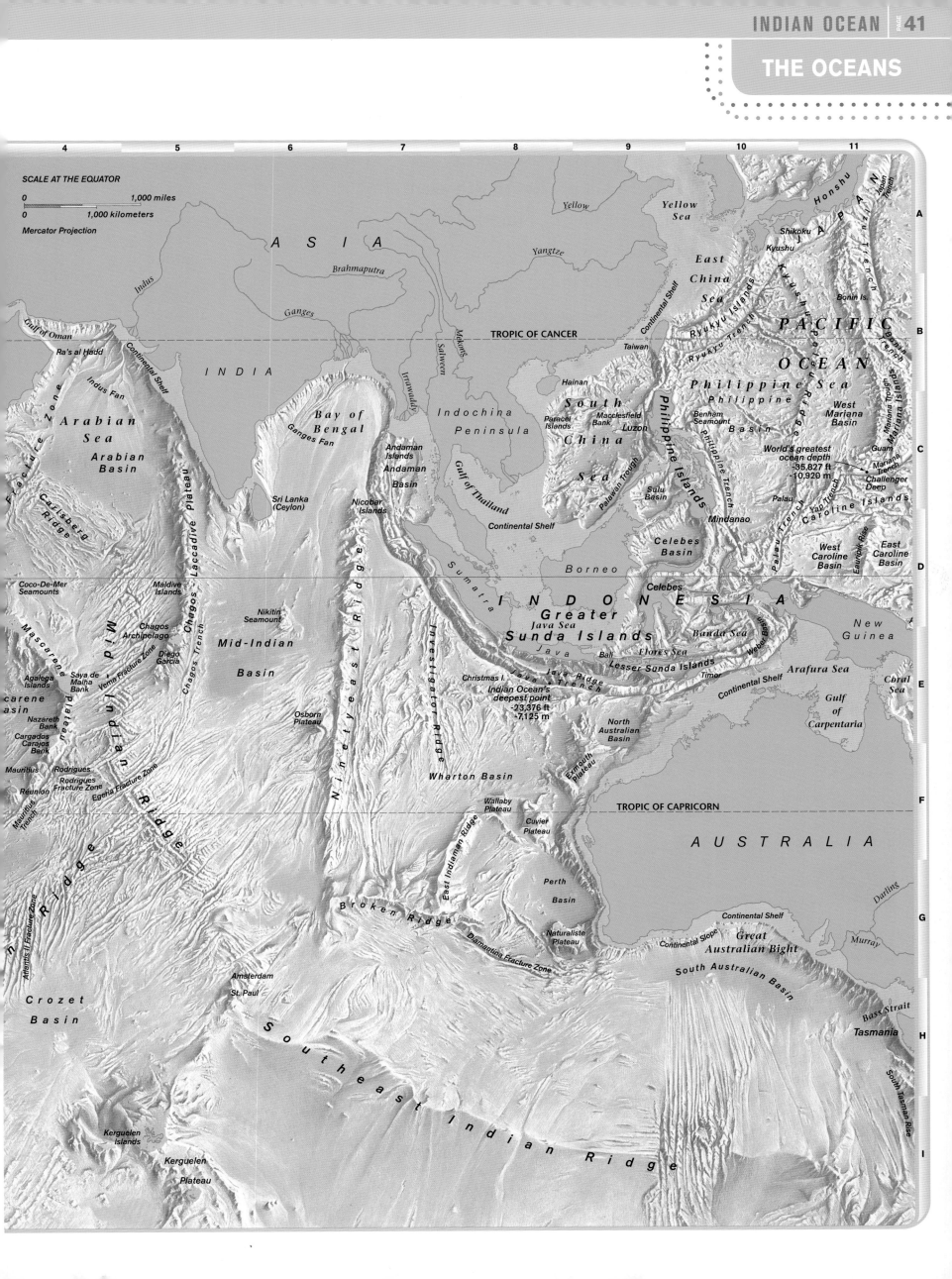

4   5   6   7   8   9   10   11

SCALE AT THE EQUATOR

0   1,000 miles
0   1,000 kilometers

Mercator Projection

A S I A

Yellow

Yellow
Sea

Brahmaputra

Yangtze

Ganges

Honshu

Izu Trench

Japan Trench

Shikoku

Kyushu

J A P A N

Bonin Is.

Indus

Gulf of Oman

Ra's al Hadd

Continental Shelf

TROPIC OF CANCER

Continental Shelf

East
China
Sea

Ryukyu Islands

Ryukyu Trench

Kyushu-Palau Ridge

PACIFIC
OCEAN

Bonin Trench

I N D I A

Taiwan

Philippine
Sea

West
Mariana
Basin

Mariana Trough

Mariana Islands

Salween

Irrawaddy

Mekong

Hainan

Philippine
Islands

Benham
Seamount

Philippine
Basin

Guam

Mariana
Trench

Challenger
Deep

Arabian
Sea

Arabian
Basin

Carlsberg
Ridge

Fracture Zone

Continental Shelf

Indus Fan

Chagos-Laccadive Plateau

Bay of
Bengal

Ganges Fan

Indochina
Peninsula

Gulf of Thailand

Andaman
Islands

Andaman
Basin

South
China
Sea

Paracel
Islands

Macclesfield
Bank

Luzon

Palawan Trough

Mindanao

World's greatest
ocean depth
-35,827 ft
-10,920 m

Palau

Palau Trench

Yap Trench

Caroline Islands

East
Caroline
Basin

Eauripik Rise

West
Caroline
Basin

Sri Lanka
(Ceylon)

Nicobar
Islands

Ninetyeast Ridge

Continental Shelf

Sulu
Basin

Celebes
Basin

Celebes

I N D O N E S I A

New
Guinea

Coco-De-Mer
Seamounts

Maldive
Islands

Chagos
Archipelago

Diego
Garcia

Chagos Trench

Vema Fracture Zone

Mascarene Plateau

Mid-Indian Ridge

Nikitin
Seamount

Mid-Indian

Basin

Borneo

Sumatra

Java Sea

Java

Greater
Sunda Islands

Bali

Flores Sea

Banda Sea

Weber Basin

Lesser Sunda Islands

Timor

Continental Shelf

Arafura Sea

Gulf
of
Carpentaria

Coral
Sea

Agalega
Islands

Saya de
Malha
Bank

Mascarene
Basin

Nazareth
Bank

Cargados
Carajos
Bank

Mauritius

Rodrigues

Réunion

Rodrigues
Fracture Zone

Egeria Fracture Zone

Mauritius Trench

Investigator Ridge

Osborn
Plateau

Christmas I.

Java Ridge

Java Trench

Indian Ocean's
deepest point
-23,376 ft
-7,125 m

North
Australian
Basin

Exmouth
Plateau

Wharton Basin

Atlantis II Fracture Zone

Ridge

Wallaby
Plateau

East Indiaman Ridge

Cuvier
Plateau

TROPIC OF CAPRICORN

A U S T R A L I A

Broken Ridge

Diamantina Fracture Zone

Perth
Basin

Naturaliste
Plateau

Continental Shelf

Continental Slope

Great
Australian Bight

South Australian Basin

Darling

Murray

Crozet
Basin

Amsterdam

St. Paul

Bass Strait

Tasmania

Southeast Indian Ridge

South Tasman Rise

Kerguelen
Islands

Kerguelen
Plateau

THE BASICS

STATS

Surface area
5,390,000 sq mi (13,960,100 sq km)

Percent of Earth's water area
4%

Greatest depth
Molloy Hole: -18,599 ft (-5,669 m)

Surface temperatures
Summer high: 29°F (-1.7°C)
Winter low: 28°F (-2°C)

Tides
Less than a 1-ft (0.3-m) variation
throughout the ocean

GEO WHIZ

Satellite monitoring of Arctic sea
ice, which began in the late 1970s,
shows that the extent of the sea ice is
shrinking by approximately 8 percent
every 10 years. Scientists think this may
be caused by global warming.

The geographic North Pole lies roughly
in the middle of the Arctic Ocean under
13,000 feet (3,962 m) of water.

Many of the features on the Arctic
Ocean floor are named for early Arctic
explorers and bordering landmasses.

Mapping of the Arctic Ocean floor did
not begin until 2001. The initial research
was by a joint U.S.-German operation
called AMORE (Arctic Mid-Ocean Ridge
Expedition). Surprise findings included
12 volcanoes, hydrothermal vents, and a
vast continental shelf off Siberia.

ARCTIC OCEAN

The Arctic Ocean lies mostly north of the Arctic Circle, bounded by North America, Europe, and Asia. Unlike the other oceans, the Arctic is subject to persistent cold throughout the year. Also, because of its very high latitude, the Arctic experiences winters of perpetual night and summers of continual daylight. Except for coastal margins, the Arctic Ocean is covered by permanent drifting pack ice that averages almost 10 feet (3 m) in thickness. Some scientists are concerned that the polar ice may be melting due to global warming, putting at risk the habitat of polar bears and other arctic animals.

⇐ ARCTIC RESEARCH. Scientists wearing cold weather survival suits prepare to measure salt content, nutrients, and plant and animal life in ice and meltwater. They also monitor changes related to global warming, such as the shrinking of the polar ice cap.

⇒ FREE RIDE. A baby polar bear catches a ride as its mother crosses Canada's Arctic. Polar bear populations are showing signs of stress as sea ice shrinks.

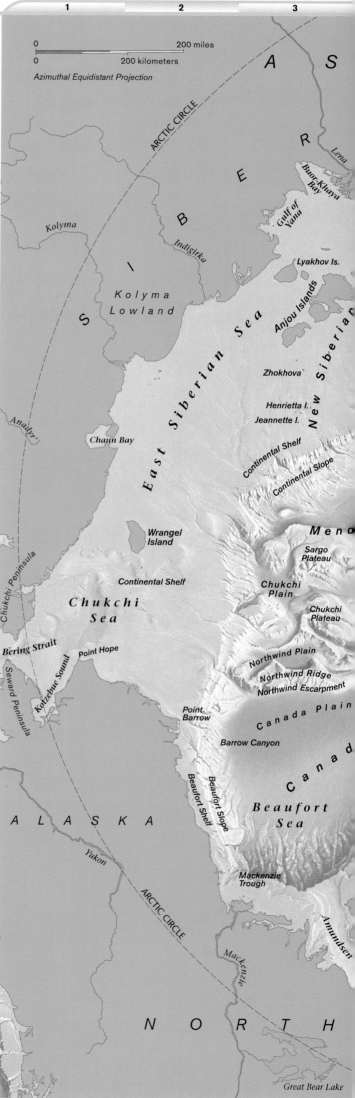

Azimuthal Equidistant Projection

200 miles
200 kilometers

ARCTIC CIRCLE

S I B E R I A

Lena
Kolyma
Buor-Khaya Bay
Gulf of Yana
Indigirka
Lyakhov Is.
Kolyma Lowland
Anjou Islands
New Siberian
East Siberian Sea
Zhokhova
Henrietta I.
Jeannette I.
Continental Shelf
Continental Slope
Anadyr
Chaun Bay
Wrangel Island
Meno
Sargo Plateau
Chukchi Plain
Continental Shelf
Chukchi Plateau
Chukchi Sea
Chukchi Peninsula
Bering Strait
Point Hope
Northwind Plain
Northwind Ridge
Northwind Escarpment
Seward Peninsula
Kotzebue Sound
Point Barrow
Canada Plain
Barrow Canyon
Canad
Beaufort Shelf
Beaufort Slope
Beaufort Sea
ALASKA
Yukon
Mackenzie Trough
ARCTIC CIRCLE
Amundsen
Mackenzie
N O R T H
Great Bear Lake

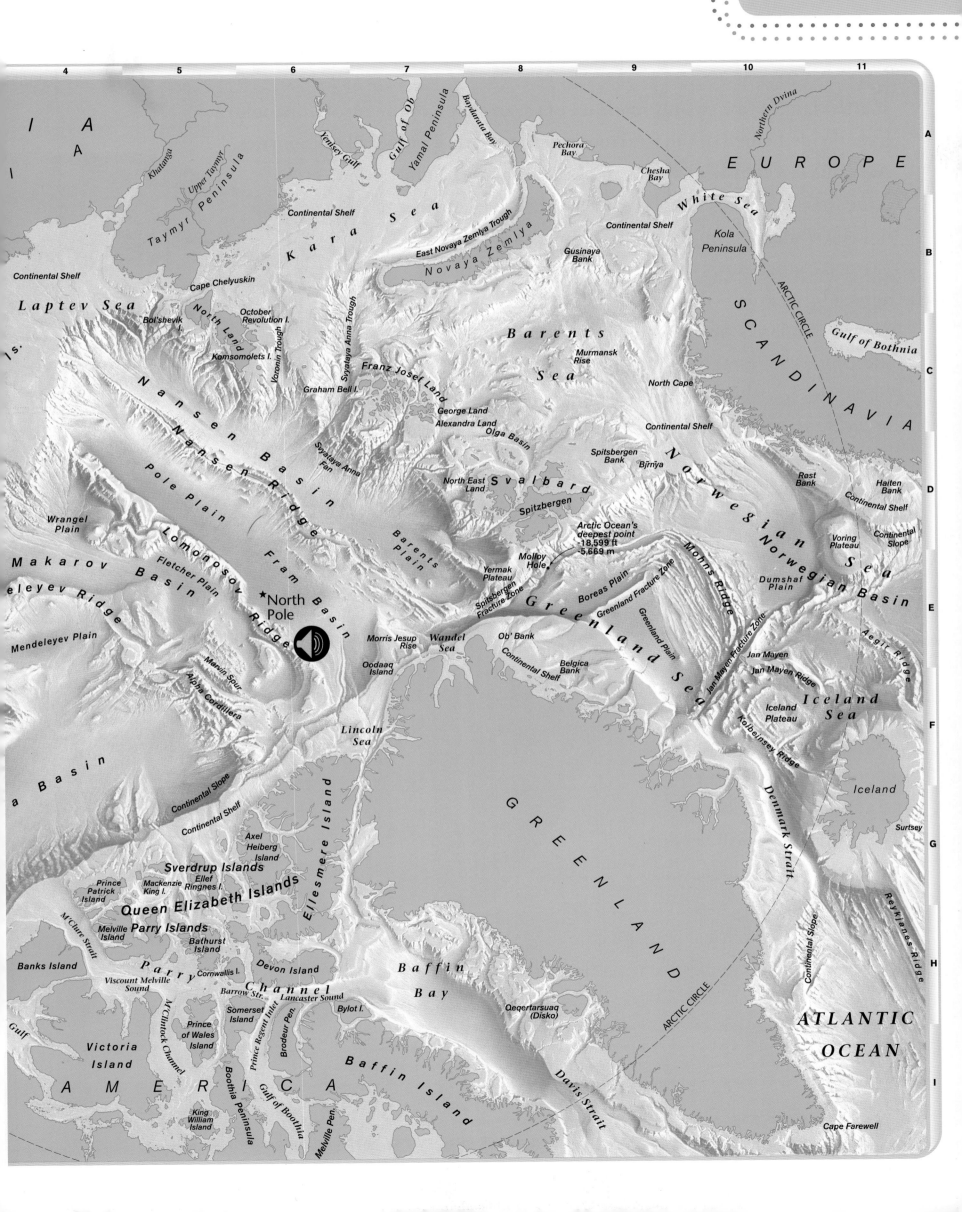

4   5   6   7   8   9   10   11

A
B
C
D
E
F
G
H
I

EUROPE

Northern Dvina

Pechora Bay
Chesha Bay
White Sea
SCANDINAVIA
ARCTIC CIRCLE
Gulf of Bothnia

Kola Peninsula

Continental Shelf

Murmansk Rise

North Cape

Barents Sea

Continental Shelf

Gusinaya Bank

Spitsbergen Bank
Bjrnya
Norwegian Sea
Røst Bank
Haiten Bank
Continental Shelf
Continental Slope

Khatanga
Upper Taymyr
Taymyr Peninsula
Yenisey Gulf
Gulf of Ob
Yamal Peninsula
Baydarata Bay

Kara Sea

Continental Shelf

East Novaya Zemlya Trough
Novaya Zemlya

Continental Shelf

Cape Chelyuskin

Bol'shevik
October Revolution I.
North Land
Komsomolets I.
Voronin Trough
Graham Bell I.

Svyataya Anna Trough
Svyataya Anna Fan

Franz Josef Land

George Land
Alexandra Land
Olga Basin

North East Land
Svalbard
Spitzbergen

Voring Plateau

Laptev Sea

Continental Shelf

Is.

Nansen Basin
Nansen Ridge
Pole Plain

Wrangel Plain

Makarov
eleyev Ridge
Mendeleyev Plain

Lomonosov Ridge
Fletcher Plain
Basin

Fram Basin

Barents Plain

Arctic Ocean's deepest point -18,599 ft -5,669 m

Molloy Hole
Yermak Plateau
Spitsbergen Fracture Zone

Boreas Plain
Greenland Fracture Zone
Greenland Plain
Greenland Sea
Mohns Ridge
Dumshaf Plain

Jan Mayen Fracture Zone
Jan Mayen
Jan Mayen Ridge

Norwegian Basin

Aegir Ridge

★ North Pole

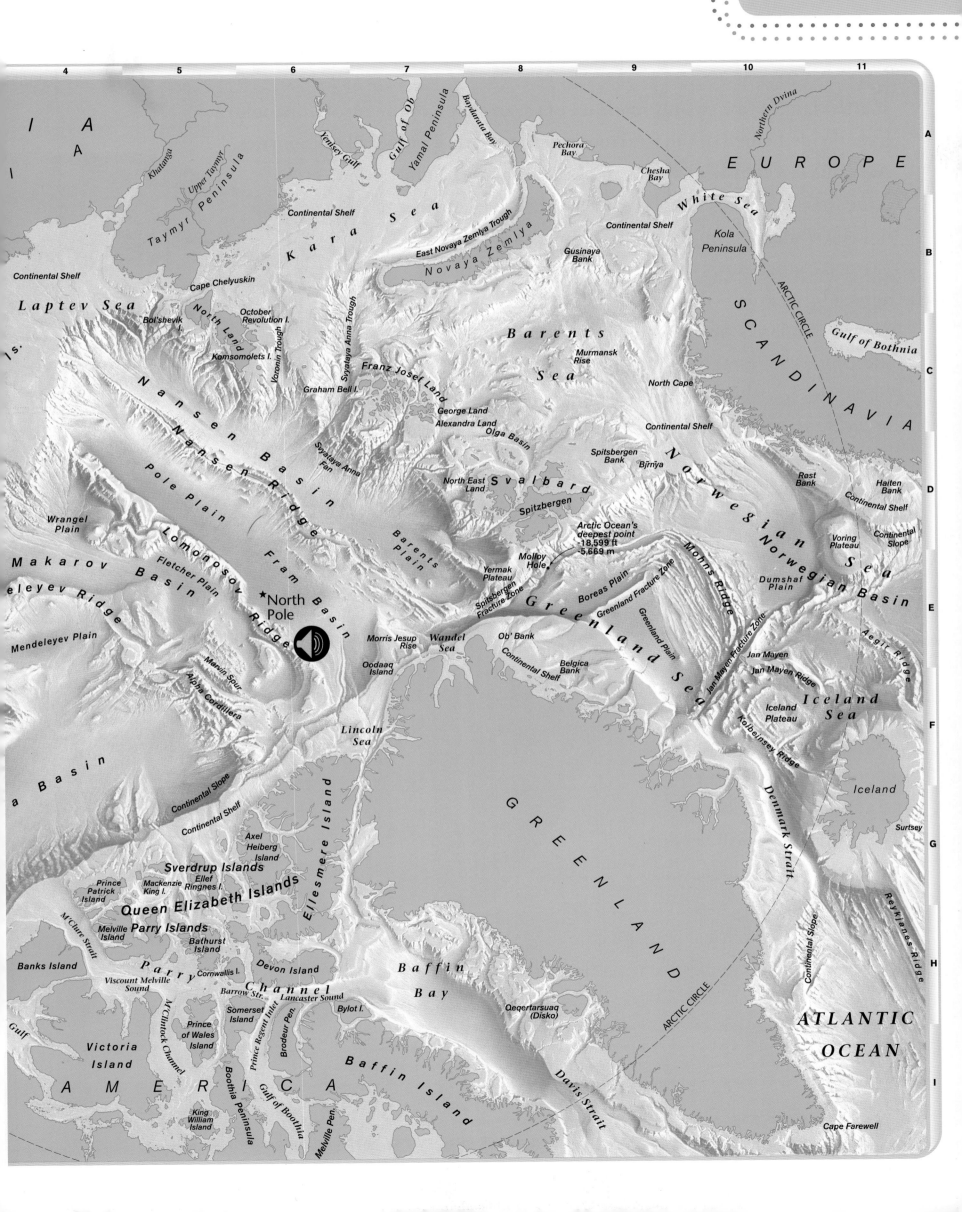

Marvin Spur
Alpha Cordillera

Morris Jesup Rise
Oodaaq Island

Wandel Sea

Ob' Bank
Continental Shelf
Belgica Bank

Kolbeinsey Ridge
Iceland Plateau
Iceland Sea

Lincoln Sea

a Basin

Continental Slope
Continental Shelf

Ellesmere Island

GREENLAND

Iceland

Surtsey

Denmark Strait

Reykjanes Ridge

Axel Heiberg Island

Sverdrup Islands
Prince Patrick Island
Mackenzie King I.
Ellef Ringnes I.
Queen Elizabeth Islands
Melville Island
Parry Islands
Bathurst Island
Cornwallis I.
Devon Island

M'Clure Strait
Banks Island
Viscount Melville Sound
Parry Channel
Barrow Str.
Lancaster Sound
Somerset Island
Bylot I.
Baffin Bay

Qeqertarsuaq (Disko)

ARCTIC CIRCLE

Continental Slope

ATLANTIC OCEAN

Gulf

Victoria Island
M'Clintock Channel
Prince of Wales Island
Prince Regent Inlet
Brodeur Pen.
Boothia Peninsula
Gulf of Boothia

AMERICA
King William Island
Melville Pen.

Baffin Island

Davis Strait

Cape Farewell

THE POLITICAL WORLD

Earth's land area is mainly made up of seven giant continents, but people have divided much of the land into smaller political units called countries. Australia is a continent with a single country, and Antarctica is set aside for scientific research. But the other five continents include almost 200 independent countries. The political map (right) shows boundaries—imaginary lines agreed by treaties—that separate countries. Some boundaries, such as the one between the United States and Canada, are very stable and have been recognized for many years. Other boundaries, such as the one between Ethiopia and Eritrea in northeast Africa, are relatively new and still disputed.

Countries come in all shapes and sizes. Russia and Canada are giants. Other countries, such as Luxembourg in western Europe, are small. Some countries are long and skinny—look at Chile in South America! Still other countries—like Indonesia and Japan in Asia—are made up of groups of islands. The political map is a clue to the diversity that makes Earth so fascinating.

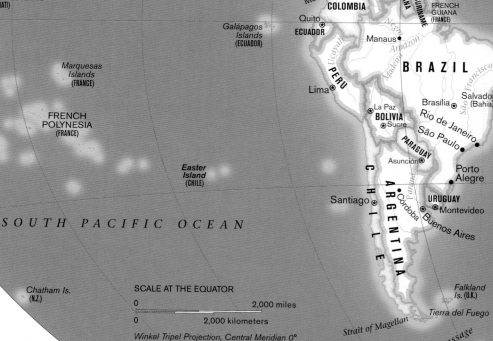

⇨ COUNTRIES AND CAPITALS. The world political map looks a bit like a patchwork quilt. Each country's boundary is outlined in one color. Some countries also include territory beyond the main land area. For example, the United States is outlined in bright green, but so are Alaska and Hawai'i, which are also U.S. states. Most countries have one city—called the capital—that is the center of political decision-making. For example, Beijing is the capital of China. But a few countries have more than one capital, such as La Paz and Sucre in Bolivia. The capital of each country is marked with a star inside a circle.

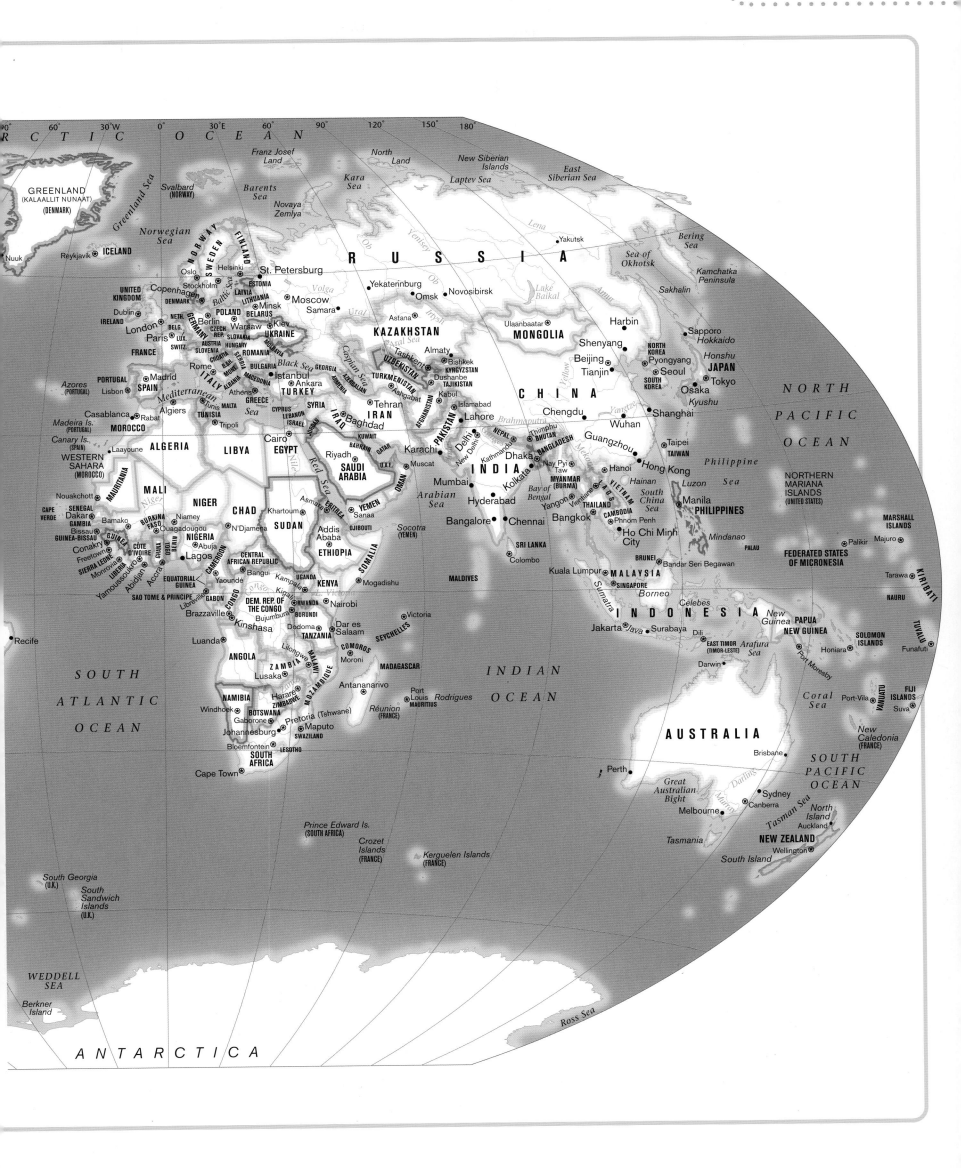

ARCTIC OCEAN

60° 30°W 0° 30°E 60° 90° 120° 150° 180°

GREENLAND
(KALAALLIT NUNAAT)
(DENMARK)

Franz Josef
Land

North
Land

New Siberian
Islands

East
Siberian Sea

Nuuk

Svalbard
(NORWAY)

Barents
Sea

Novaya
Zemlya

Kara
Sea

Laptev Sea

Reykjavík ⊛ ICELAND

Greenland Sea

Norwegian
Sea

Yakutsk

Bering
Sea

Kamchatka
Peninsula

R U S S I A

Sea of
Okhotsk

Oslo
Stockholm

Helsinki
St. Petersburg

Yekaterinburg
Omsk
Novosibirsk

Lake
Baikal

Sakhalin

Amur

Harbin

Sapporo
Hokkaido

UNITED
KINGDOM
Copenhagen
Dublin
IRELAND
London
Paris

Moscow
Samara

Ob

Astana

Ulaanbaatar

MONGOLIA

Shenyang

NORTH
KOREA
Pyongyang
Seoul

Honshu

JAPAN

Tokyo

FINLAND
ESTONIA
LATVIA
LITHUANIA
Minsk
BELARUS
Berlin
POLAND
Warsaw
Kiev
UKRAINE

Volga

KAZAKHSTAN
Aral Sea
Almaty
Bishkek
Tashkent
KYRGYZSTAN
UZBEKISTAN
Dushanbe
TAJIKISTAN
Ashgabat
TURKMENISTAN

Beijing
Tianjin

SOUTH
KOREA

Osaka

Kyushu

Madrid
SPAIN

Rome
ITALY

Istanbul

Ankara
TURKEY

GEORGIA
ARMENIA
AZERBAIJAN

Tehran

Kabul
AFGHANISTAN
Islamabad

CHINA

C H I N A

Chengdu

Yellow
Yangtze

Wuhan

Shanghai

NORTH
PACIFIC
OCEAN

Azores
(PORTUGAL)
Lisbon
PORTUGAL

Madeira Is.
(PORTUGAL)

Casablanca
Rabat

Algiers
TUNISIA
MALTA

Athens
GREECE
CYPRUS
LEBANON
ISRAEL
SYRIA
IRAQ
Baghdad

Mediterranean
Sea

Tripoli

Cairo

Lahore
PAKISTAN
Delhi
New Delhi
NEPAL
Kathmandu
Guangzhou
Hong Kong

Taipei
TAIWAN

Philippine
Sea

Luzon

NORTHERN
MARIANA
ISLANDS
(UNITED STATES)

Canary Is.
(SPAIN)
MOROCCO
WESTERN
SAHARA
(MOROCCO)

ALGERIA

LIBYA

EGYPT

Nile

Red Sea

BAHRAIN
QATAR
U.A.E.
Riyadh
SAUDI
ARABIA

KUWAIT

Muscat
OMAN

Karachi

Thimphu
BHUTAN
BANGLADESH
Dhaka

Mumbai

INDIA

Kolkata

Nay Pyi
Taw
MYANMAR
(BURMA)

Bay of
Bengal

Brahmaputra

Hanoi
Hainan

VIETNAM

South
China
Sea

Manila
PHILIPPINES

Mindanao

PALAU

Nouakchott
MAURITANIA

MALI

NIGER

CHAD

N'Djamena
SUDAN

Khartoum

Asmara
ERITREA
DJIBOUTI

Sanaa
YEMEN

Addis
Ababa
ETHIOPIA

Socotra
(YEMEN)

Arabian
Sea

Hyderabad

Bangalore
Chennai

Yangon

Bangkok
THAILAND
CAMBODIA
Phnom Penh

LAOS
Vientiane

Mekong

Ho Chi Minh
City

MALDIVES

SRI LANKA
Colombo

FEDERATED STATES
OF MICRONESIA

MARSHALL
ISLANDS

Palikir

Majuro

Tarawa
KIRIBATI

NAURU

CAPE
VERDE
SENEGAL
Dakar
GAMBIA
GUINEA-BISSAU
Bissau
Conakry
GUINEA
Freetown
SIERRA LEONE
Monrovia
LIBERIA

BURKINA
FASO
Niamey
Ouagadougou

NIGERIA
Abuja
Lagos
BENIN
TOGO
GHANA
Accra
CÔTE
D'IVOIRE
Yamoussoukro
Abidjan

CAMEROON
Yaoundé
CENTRAL
AFRICAN REPUBLIC
Bangui

Kampala
UGANDA

KENYA

SOMALIA

Mogadishu

BRUNEI
Bandar Seri Begawan

Kuala Lumpur
MALAYSIA
SINGAPORE

Borneo

Celebes

New
Guinea

PAPUA
NEW GUINEA

SOLOMON
ISLANDS

Honiara

TUVALU

Funafuti

SÃO TOMÉ & PRÍNCIPE
EQUATORIAL
GUINEA
Libreville
GABON
Brazzaville
CONGO
Kinshasa
DEM. REP. OF
THE CONGO

RWANDA
Kigali
BURUNDI
Bujumbura

Congo

Nairobi

Dodoma
TANZANIA
Dar es
Salaam

Victoria
SEYCHELLES

Lake Victoria

INDONESIA

Jakarta
Java
Surabaya

Dili
EAST TIMOR
(TIMOR-LESTE)

Arafura
Sea

Darwin

Port Moresby

New
Caledonia
(FRANCE)

VANUATU

FIJI
ISLANDS

Port-Vila

Suva

Recife

SOUTH
ATLANTIC
OCEAN

Luanda

ANGOLA

ZAMBIA
Lusaka

MALAWI
Lilongwe

COMOROS
Moroni

MADAGASCAR

Antananarivo

INDIAN
OCEAN

Coral
Sea

AUSTRALIA

SOUTH
PACIFIC
OCEAN

NAMIBIA
Windhoek

BOTSWANA
Gaborone
Pretoria (Tshwane)
Johannesburg
Bloemfontein
SOUTH
AFRICA
Cape Town

Harare
ZIMBABWE
MOZAMBIQUE
Maputo
SWAZILAND
LESOTHO

Réunion
(FRANCE)

Port
Louis
MAURITIUS

Rodrigues

Great
Australian
Bight

Perth

Darling

Murray

Brisbane

Sydney
Canberra
Melbourne

Tasman Sea

North
Island

Auckland

Prince Edward Is.
(SOUTH AFRICA)

Crozet
Islands
(FRANCE)

Kerguelen Islands
(FRANCE)

Tasmania

NEW ZEALAND
Wellington

South Island

South Georgia
(U.K.)

South
Sandwich
Islands
(U.K.)

WEDDELL
SEA

Berkner
Island

Ross Sea

A N T A R C T I C A

WORLD POPULATION

How big is a billion? It's hard to imagine. But Earth's population is 6.7 billion and rising, with more than a billion living in both China and India. And more than 80 million people are added to the world each year. Most growth occurs in the less-developed countries of Asia, Africa, and Latin America, while some countries in Europe are hardly increasing at all. Population changes can create challenges for countries. Fast-growing countries with young populations need food, housing, and schools. Countries with low growth rates and older populations need workers to sustain their economies.

MOST POPULOUS COUNTRIES

(mid-2006 data)

1. China 1,311,000,000
2. India 1,122,000,000
3. United States 300,000,000
4. Indonesia 225,000,000
5. Brazil 187,000,000
6. Pakistan 166,000,000
7. Bangladesh 147,000,000
8. Russia 142,000,000

MOST CROWDED COUNTRIES

Population Density
(People per sq mi/sq km; mid-2006 data)

1. Monaco 44,000/16,988
2. Singapore 18,652/7,202
3. Malta 3,278/1,266
4. Bahrain 2,793/1,078
5. Bangladesh 2,637/1,018
6. Maldives 2,573/993
7. Mauritus 1,572/615
8. Nauru 1,529/590

⇨ DENSITY. Demographers, people who study population, use density to measure how concentrated population is. For example, the population density of Egypt is almost 200 people per square mile (77 per sq km). This assumes that the population is evenly spread throughout the country, but this is not the case in Egypt. Almost all of the people live along the banks of the Nile River. Likewise, Earth's population is not evenly spread across the land. Some places, like central Australia, are almost empty, but others, such as Europe or India, are very crowded.

⇨ CITY DWELLERS. Almost half the world's people have shifted from rural areas to urban centers, with some countries adding more than 100 million to their urban populations between 1950 and 2000 (see map, right). In more-developed countries, about 74 percent of the population is urban, compared with just 43 percent in less-developed countries. But the fastest growing urban areas are in less-developed countries, where thousands flock to cities, such as Dhaka, Bangladesh (photo, far right), in search of a better life. By 2015 there could be as many as 22 cities with populations of 10 million or more.

Los Angeles

México

PACIFIC OCEAN

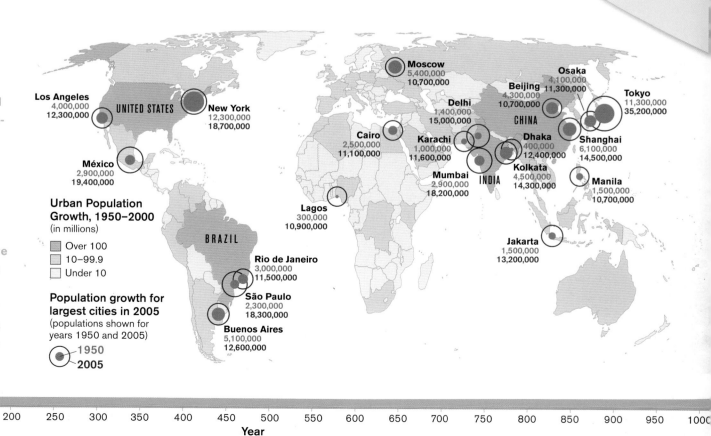

Los Angeles
4,000,000
12,300,000

UNITED STATES

New York
12,300,000
18,700,000

Moscow
5,400,000
10,700,000

Osaka
4,100,000
11,300,000

Beijing
4,300,000
10,700,000

Tokyo
11,300,000
35,200,000

Delhi
1,400,000
15,000,000

CHINA

México
2,900,000
19,400,000

Cairo
2,500,000
11,100,000

Karachi
1,000,000
11,600,000

Dhaka
400,000
12,400,000

Shanghai
6,100,000
14,500,000

Mumbai
2,900,000
18,200,000

INDIA

Kolkata
4,500,000
14,300,000

Manila
1,500,000
10,700,000

Lagos
300,000
10,900,000

BRAZIL

Urban Population Growth, 1950–2000
(in millions)

■ Over 100
■ 10–99.9
□ Under 10

Population growth for largest cities in 2005
(populations shown for years 1950 and 2005)

◉ 1950
○ 2005

Rio de Janeiro
3,000,000
11,500,000

São Paulo
2,300,000
18,300,000

Buenos Aires
5,100,000
12,600,000

Jakarta
1,500,000
13,200,000

50   100   150   200   250   300   350   400   450   500   550   600   650   700   750   800   850   900   950   1000
Year

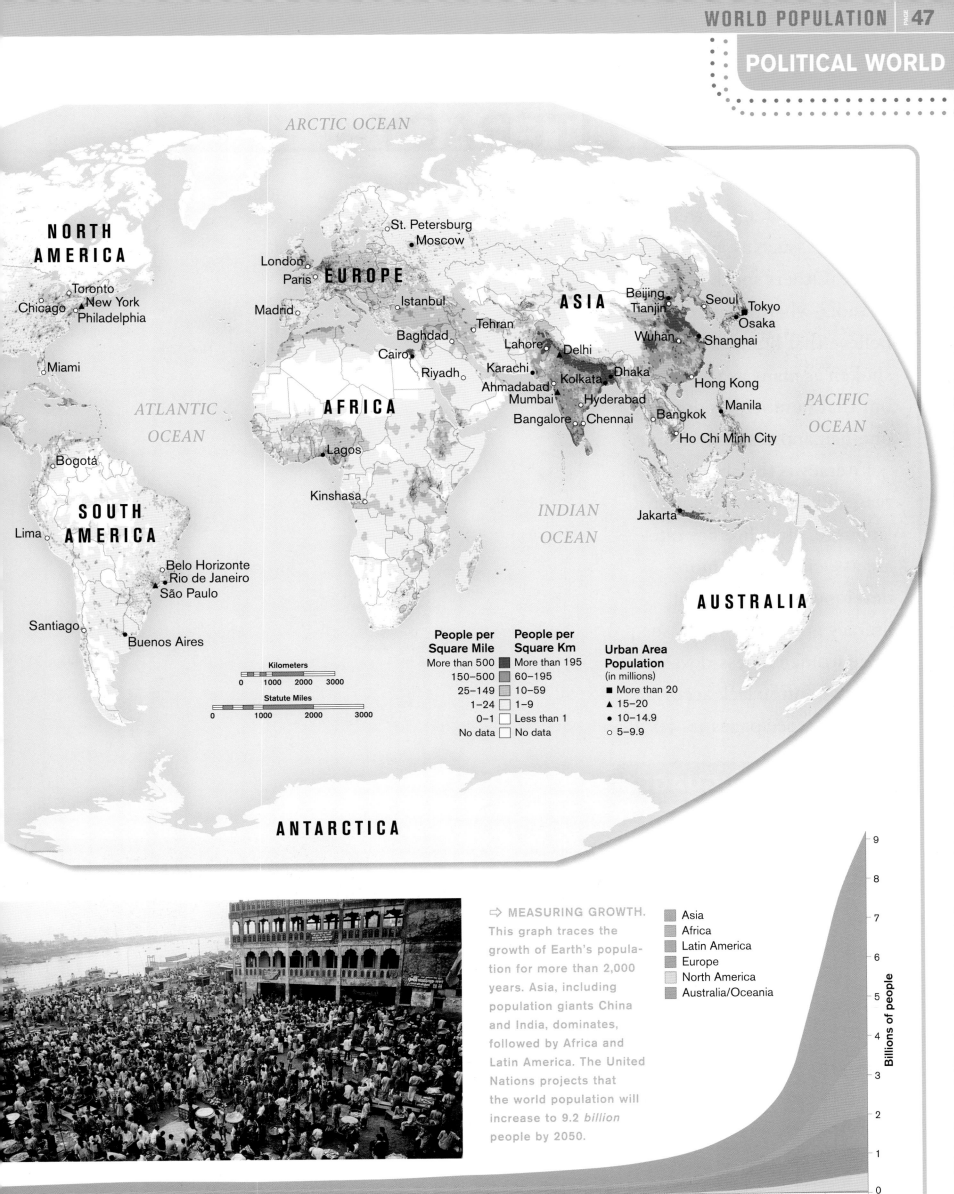

ARCTIC OCEAN

NORTH
AMERICA

St. Petersburg
Moscow

London
Paris
EUROPE

Madrid

Chicago
Toronto
New York
Philadelphia

Miami

ATLANTIC
OCEAN

Bogotá

SOUTH
AMERICA

Lima

Santiago

Belo Horizonte
Rio de Janeiro
São Paulo

Buenos Aires

Istanbul

AFRICA

Lagos

Kinshasa

Tehran

Baghdad
Cairo

Riyadh

ASIA

Lahore
Karachi

Ahmadabad
Mumbai
Bangalore

Beijing
Tianjin

Wuhan

Delhi

Kolkata
Dhaka
Hyderabad
Chennai

Seoul Tokyo
Osaka

Shanghai

Hong Kong

Bangkok Manila

Ho Chi Minh City

PACIFIC
OCEAN

INDIAN
OCEAN

Jakarta

AUSTRALIA

People per Square Mile
More than 500
150–500
25–149
1–24
0–1
No data

People per Square Km
More than 195
60–195
10–59
1–9
Less than 1
No data

Urban Area Population
(in millions)
■ More than 20
▲ 15–20
● 10–14.9
○ 5–9.9

Kilometers
0 1000 2000 3000

Statute Miles
0 1000 2000 3000

ANTARCTICA

⇨ **MEASURING GROWTH.**
This graph traces the
growth of Earth's popula-
tion for more than 2,000
years. Asia, including
population giants China
and India, dominates,
followed by Africa and
Latin America. The United
Nations projects that
the world population will
increase to 9.2 *billion*
people by 2050.

Asia
Africa
Latin America
Europe
North America
Australia/Oceania

Billions of people

9
8
7
6
5
4
3
2
1
0

1050 1100 1150 1200 1250 1300 1350 1400 1450 1500 1550 1600 1650 1700 1750 1800 1850 1900 1950 2000 2050
Year

WORLD LANGUAGES & LITERACY

Earth's 6.7 billion people live in 193 independent countries, but they speak more than 5,000 languages. Some countries, such as Japan, have one official language. Others speak many languages, such as India, where 23 are official. Experts believe that humans may once have spoken as many as 10,000 languages, but that number has dropped by one-half and is still declining.

Literacy is the ability to read and write in one's native language. High literacy rates are associated with more-developed countries. But literacy is also a gender issue, since women in less-developed countries often lack access to education (see pages 52–53).

Major Language Families Today

- Afro-Asiatic
- Altaic
- Austro-Asiatic
- Austronesian
- Dravidian
- Indo-European
- Japanese/Korean
- Kam-Tai
- Niger-Congo
- Nilo-Saharan
- Sino-Tibetan
- Uralic
- Other

NORTH AMERICA

Toronto

New York

Los Angeles

México

PACIFIC OCEAN

ATLANTIC OCEAN

SOUTH AMERICA

São Paulo

Buenos Aires

LEADING LANGUAGES

Some languages have only a few hundred speakers, but 23 languages stand out with more than 50 million speakers each. Earth's population giant, China, has 873 million speakers of Mandarin, more than double the next largest group of language speakers. Colonial expansion, trade, and migration account for the spread of the other most widely spoken languages. With growing use of the Internet, English is becoming the language of the technology age.

Population (in millions)

Language	Population
Chinese (Mandarin)	873
Spanish	322
English	309
Arabic	220
Hindi	180
Portuguese	177
Bengali	171
Russian	145
Japanese	122
German	95

Languages

Language colors are keyed to the map.

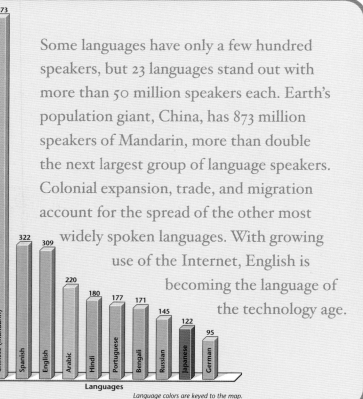

⇧ EDUCATION AND LITERACY. These Nenet boys in Siberia spend hours learning the national language—Russian—but this may result in the loss of their native language. Literacy means good jobs in the future for these boys and economic success for their country.

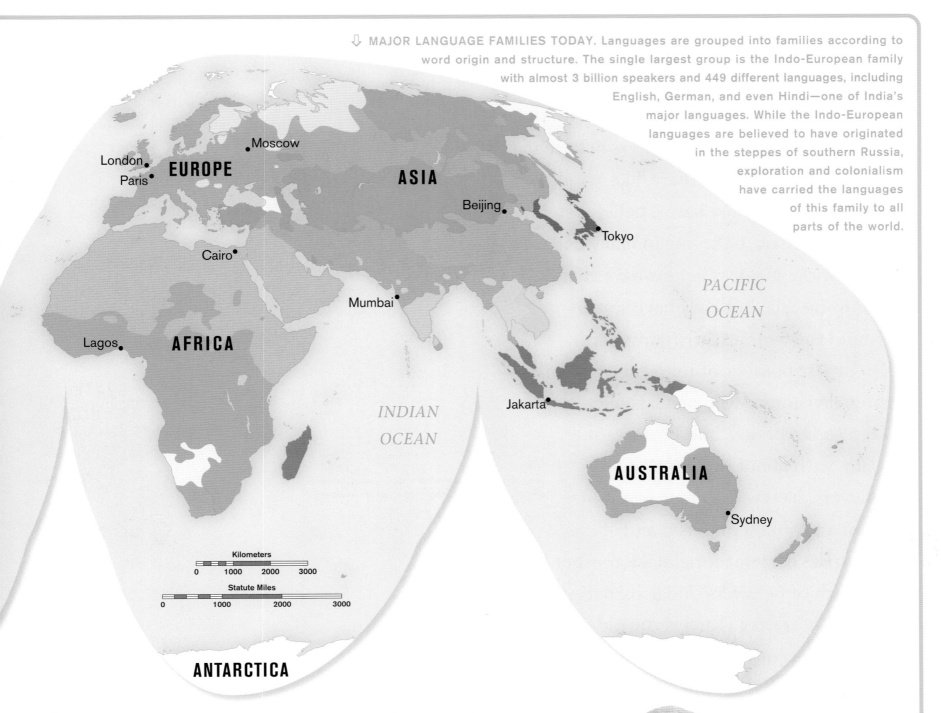

⇩ MAJOR LANGUAGE FAMILIES TODAY. Languages are grouped into families according to word origin and structure. The single largest group is the Indo-European family with almost 3 billion speakers and 449 different languages, including English, German, and even Hindi—one of India's major languages. While the Indo-European languages are believed to have originated in the steppes of southern Russia, exploration and colonialism have carried the languages of this family to all parts of the world.

Moscow

London
Paris   EUROPE

ASIA

Beijing

Tokyo

Cairo

PACIFIC
OCEAN

Mumbai

AFRICA

Lagos

Jakarta

INDIAN
OCEAN

AUSTRALIA

Sydney

Kilometers
0   1000   2000   3000

Statute Miles
0   1000   2000   3000

ANTARCTICA

⇩ ONE LANGUAGE, TWO FORMS. Some languages, including Chinese, use characters instead of letters. The Golden Arches provide a clue to the meaning of the characters on the restaurant sign. Many signs, such as the one in the foreground, also show words in pinyin, a spelling system that uses the Western alphabet.

⇧ UNIVERSAL LANGUAGE. The widespread use of technology—for example, the electronic games that hold the attention of these children in France—has crossed over the language barrier. Computers, the Internet, and electronic communications devices use a universal language that knows no national borders.

WORLD RELIGIONS

Rooted in people's attempts to explain the unknown, religion takes many forms. Some belief systems, such as Christianity, Islam, and Judaism, are monotheistic, meaning that followers believe in just one supreme being. Others, like Hinduism, Shintoism, and most native belief systems, are polytheistic, believing in many gods.

All of the major religions have their origins in Asia, but they have spread around the world. Christianity, with the largest number of followers, has three divisions—Roman Catholic, Eastern Orthodox, and Protestant. Islam, with about one-fifth of all believers, has two main divisions— Sunni and Shia. Hinduism and Buddhism account for almost another one-fifth of believers. Judaism, dating back some 4,000 years, is the oldest of all the major monotheistic religions.

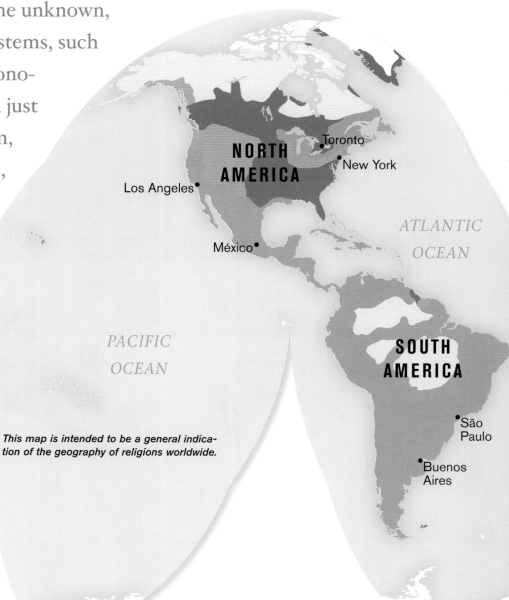

This map is intended to be a general indication of the geography of religions worldwide.

BUDDHISM

Founded about 2,500 years ago in northern India by a Hindu prince, Gautama Buddha, Buddhism spread throughout East and Southeast Asia. Buddhist temples have statues, such as the Mihintale Buddha (above) in Sri Lanka.

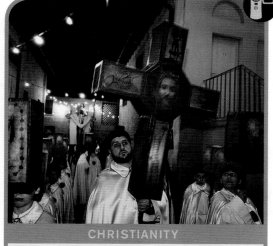

CHRISTIANITY

Based on the teachings of Jesus Christ, a Jew born some 2,000 years ago in the area of modern-day Israel, Christianity has spread worldwide and actively seeks converts. Followers in Switzerland (above) participate in a procession with lanterns and crosses.

HINDUISM

Dating back more than 4,000 years, Hinduism is practiced mainly in India. Hindus follow sacred texts known as the Vedas and believe in reincarnation. During the festival of Diwali, Hindus light candles (above) to symbolize the victory of good over evil.

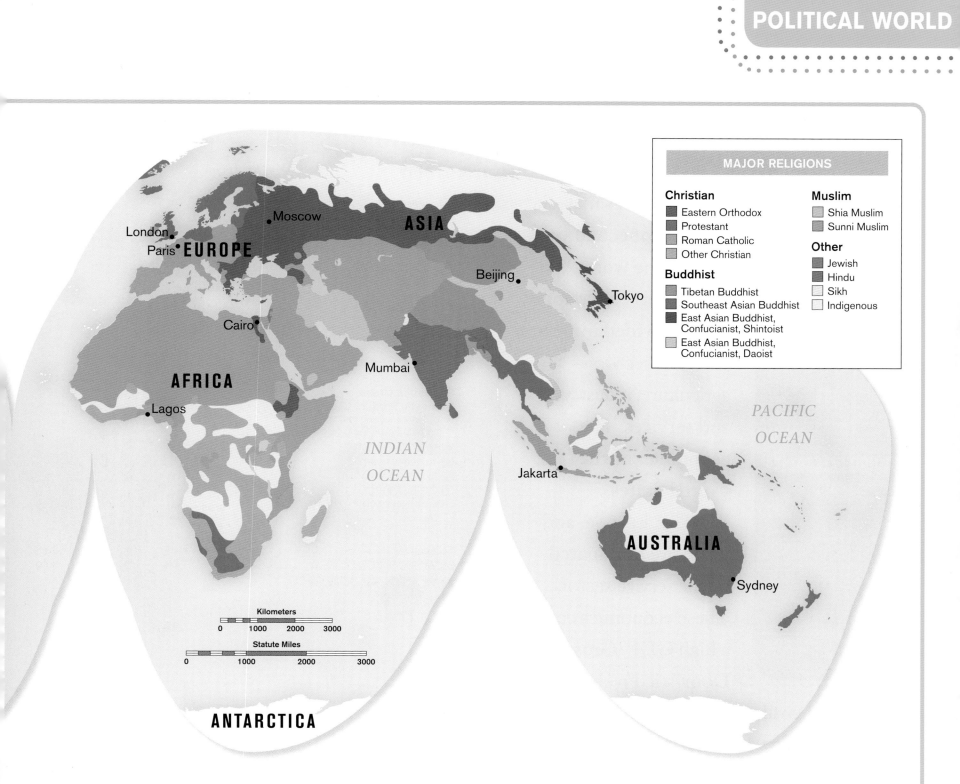

Moscow

ASIA

London
Paris • EUROPE

Beijing •

Tokyo

Cairo •

AFRICA

Mumbai •

PACIFIC
OCEAN

Lagos •

INDIAN
OCEAN

Jakarta •

AUSTRALIA

Sydney •

Kilometers
0   1000   2000   3000

Statute Miles
0   1000   2000   3000

ANTARCTICA

MAJOR RELIGIONS

Christian
- Eastern Orthodox
- Protestant
- Roman Catholic
- Other Christian

Buddhist
- Tibetan Buddhist
- Southeast Asian Buddhist
- East Asian Buddhist, Confucianist, Shintoist
- East Asian Buddhist, Confucianist, Daoist

Muslim
- Shia Muslim
- Sunni Muslim

Other
- Jewish
- Hindu
- Sikh
- Indigenous

ISLAM

Muslims believe that the Koran, Islam's sacred book, records the words of Allah (God) as revealed to the Prophet Muhammad around A.D. 610. Believers (above) circle the Kabah in the Haram Mosque in Mecca, the spiritual center of the faith.

JUDAISM

The traditions, laws, and beliefs of Judaism date back to Abraham, the founder, and the Torah, the first five books of the Old Testament. Followers (above) pray before the Western Wall, which stands below Islam's Dome of the Rock in Jerusalem.

RELIGIOUS FOLLOWERS

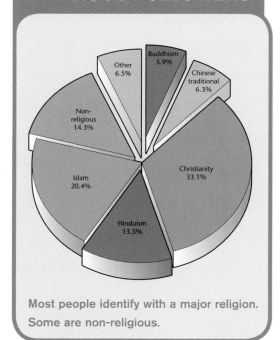

- Buddhism 5.9%
- Chinese traditional 6.3%
- Other 6.5%
- Non-religious 14.3%
- Christianity 33.1%
- Islam 20.4%
- Hinduism 13.5%

Most people identify with a major religion. Some are non-religious.

WORLD ECONOMIES

People use resources together with human energy and ingenuity to produce goods and services that meet their needs and generate income. This map shows patterns of economic activity around the world.

A country's economy can be divided into three parts, or sectors—agriculture, industry, and services. The economies of the United States, Western Europe, and Japan are dominated by the service sector. These economies enjoy a high GDP (Gross Domestic Product) per capita—the value of goods and services produced each year, averaged per person in each country. In contrast, some economies in Africa and Asia still depend mostly on agriculture. Many farmers produce only enough crops to support their own families—a practice called subsistence farming—and therefore have a low standard of living. Other economies, such as those of oil-producing countries of the Middle East, have a very high GDP per capita, but wealth is unevenly divided among the population, and many people remain poor.

No country produces everything its people need or want. Therefore, trade is a critical part of the world economy.

HIGHEST GDP PER CAPITA*

1.	Liechtenstein	$101,654
2.	Luxembourg	$87,955
3.	Norway	$71,674
4.	Qatar	$56,512
5.	Iceland	$54,858
6.	Ireland	$52,440
7.	Switzerland	$51,771
8.	Denmark	$50,965
9.	United States	$44,315
10.	Sweden	$42,383

LOWEST GDP PER CAPITA*

1.	Democratic Republic of the Congo	$115
2.	Burundi	$125
3.	Malawi	$164
4.	Ethiopia	$177
5.	Liberia	$185
6.	Guinea-Bissau	$192
7.	Myanmar	$230
8.	Eritrea	$244
9.	Sierra Leone	$254
10.	Rwanda	$261

*All data as of 2006.

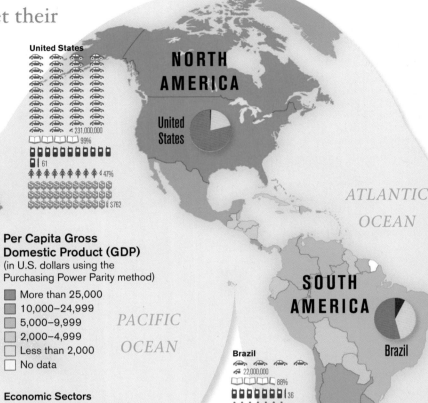

United States

🚗🚗🚗🚗🚗🚗🚗🚗🚗🚗🚗🚗🚗🚗🚗🚗🚗🚗
🚗🚗🚗🚗🚗🚗🚗🚗🚗🚗🚗 🚗 231,000,000
99%
▯▯▯▯▯▯▯▯▯▯▯
▮ 61
🌲🌲🌲🌲🌲🌲🌲🌲🌲 🌲 47%
$$$$$$$$$$$$$
$$$$$$$$$$$$ $762

NORTH AMERICA

United States

ATLANTIC OCEAN

Per Capita Gross Domestic Product (GDP)
(in U.S. dollars using the Purchasing Power Parity method)

■ More than 25,000
■ 10,000–24,999
■ 5,000–9,999
□ 2,000–4,999
□ Less than 2,000
□ No data

Economic Sectors
(composition of GDP by sector)

Service   Agriculture

Industry

PACIFIC OCEAN

SOUTH AMERICA

Brazil

🚗🚗🚗🚗
🚗 22,000,000
88%
▯▯▯▯▯▯▯▯ 36
🌲🌲🌲🌲🌲🌲🌲 35%
$$$ $60

Brazil

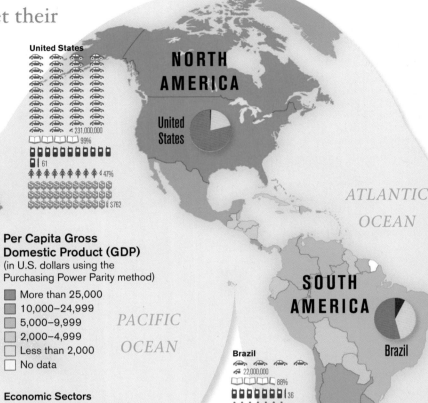

⬆ INDUSTRY. A man assembles a hybrid Prius car on an automated assembly line in a Toyota factory in Japan. Manufacture of cars is an important industrial activity and a key part of the global economy.

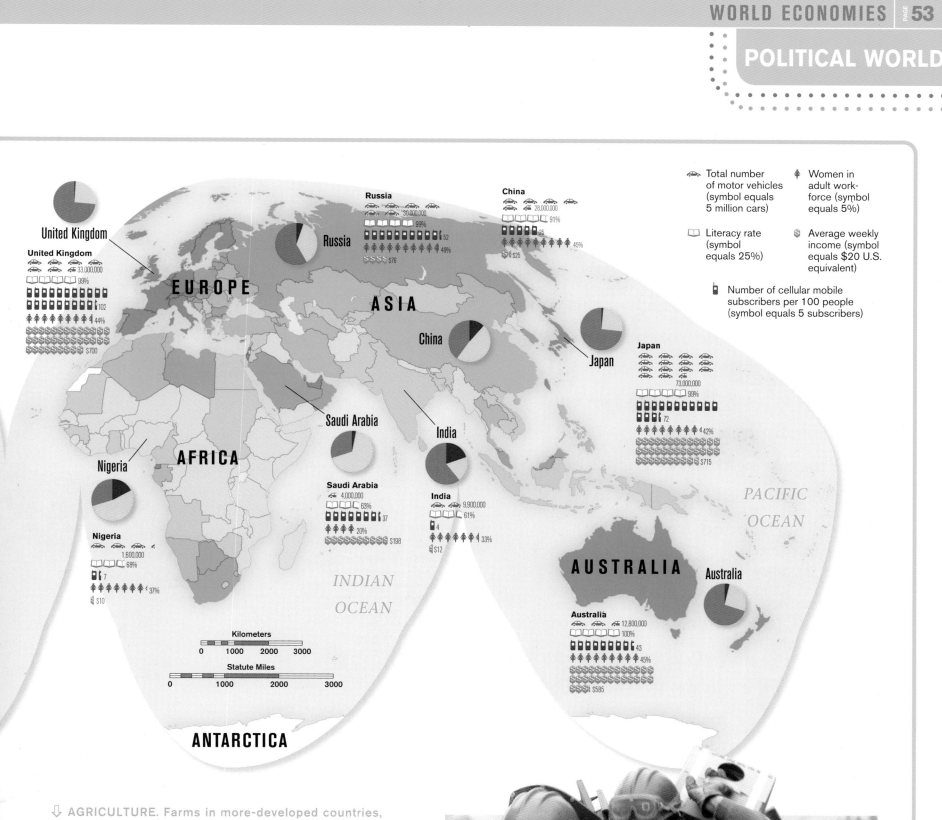

Russia

China

EUROPE

ASIA

China

Japan

Russia

Japan

United Kingdom

Saudi Arabia

India

Nigeria

AFRICA

Saudi Arabia

India

PACIFIC OCEAN

INDIAN OCEAN

AUSTRALIA

Australia

ANTARCTICA

Legend:

🚗 Total number of motor vehicles (symbol equals 5 million cars)

📖 Literacy rate (symbol equals 25%)

📱 Number of cellular mobile subscribers per 100 people (symbol equals 5 subscribers)

🌲 Women in adult work-force (symbol equals 5%)

$ Average weekly income (symbol equals $20 U.S. equivalent)

United Kingdom
🚗🚗🚗🚗🚗🚗🚗 33,000,000
📖📖📖📖 99%
📱📱📱📱📱📱📱📱📱📱📱 102
🌲🌲🌲🌲🌲🌲🌲🌲🌲 44%
$$$$$$$$$ $700

Russia
🚗🚗🚗🚗🚗🚗 30,000,000
📖📖📖📖 99%
📱📱📱📱📱📱📱📱📱📱 52
🌲🌲🌲🌲🌲🌲🌲🌲🌲 49%
$$$$ $76

China
🚗🚗🚗🚗🚗🚗 28,000,000
📖📖📖 91%
📱📱📱📱📱 25
🌲🌲🌲🌲🌲🌲🌲🌲 45%
$ $25

Japan
🚗🚗🚗🚗🚗🚗🚗🚗🚗 73,000,000
📖📖📖📖 99%
📱📱📱📱 72
🌲🌲🌲🌲🌲🌲🌲🌲 42%
$$$$$$$$$ $715

Nigeria
🚗🚗🚗 1,600,000
📖📖📖 68%
📱 7
🌲🌲🌲🌲🌲🌲🌲 37%
$ $10

Saudi Arabia
🚗 4,000,000
📖📖📖📖📖📖 63%
📱📱📱📱📱📱📱 37
🌲🌲🌲🌲 20%
$$$$$$$$$ $198

India
🚗🚗 9,900,000
📖📖 61%
📱 4
🌲🌲🌲🌲🌲🌲 33%
$ $12

Australia
🚗🚗 12,800,000
📖📖📖📖 100%
📱📱📱📱📱📱📱📱 43
🌲🌲🌲🌲🌲🌲🌲🌲🌲 45%
$$$$$$$$$ $585

Kilometers
0 1000 2000 3000

Statute Miles
0 1000 2000 3000

⇩ AGRICULTURE. Farms in more-developed countries, such as this one in Saskatchewan, Canada, use machinery to make agriculture more efficient and productive. Farmers in less-developed countries often use less-efficient traditional farming tools and methods.

⇧ SERVICES. People employed in the service sector, such as these national forest firefighters in Washington State, use their skills and training to provide services rather than products. Teachers, lawyers, and store clerks, among others, are also part of the service sector.

WORLD WATER

Water is Earth's most precious resource. Although more than two-thirds of Earth is covered by water, fresh water, which is needed by plants and animals—including humans—is only about 2.5 percent of all the water on Earth. Much of this is trapped deep underground or frozen in ice sheets and glaciers. Of the small amount of water that is fresh, less than 1 percent is available for human use.

The map at right shows Earth's major watersheds—large areas in which all surface and groundwater drains into a large river. Unfortunately, human activity often puts great stress on vital watersheds. For example, in Brazil, plans are being made to build large dams on the Amazon. This will alter the natural flow of water in this giant watershed. And heavy use of chemical fertilizers and pesticides has created toxic runoff that threatens the health of the Mississippi watershed in the United States.

Access to clean fresh water is critical for human health. But in many places, safe water is scarce due to population pressure and pollution.

WATER FACTS

Rivers that have been dammed to generate electricity are the source of almost 90 percent of Earth's renewable energy resources.

North America's Great Lakes hold about 20 percent of Earth's available fresh water.

If all the glaciers and ice sheets on Earth's surface melted, they would raise the level of Earth's oceans by about 230 feet (70 m). It is estimated that during the last ice age when glaciers covered about one-third of the land, sea level was 400 feet (122 m) lower than it is today.

Desalination is the process of removing salt from ocean water so that it can be used for irrigation, water for livestock, and for drinking. Most of the world's desalination plants are in the arid countries of the Arabian Peninsula.

Because of the water cycle, Earth has roughly the same amount of water now as it has had for two billion years.

If all the world's water were placed in a gallon jug, the fresh water available for humans to use would equal only about one tablespoon.

Primary Watersheds
Annual renewable water
(cubic meters per person, 1995)

- More than 10,000
- 4,000–10,000
- 1,700–3,999
- 1,000–1,699
- Fewer than 1,000
- No data available

Amazon Watershed name

NORTH AMERICA

Yukon
Mackenzie
Thelon
Fraser
Nelson
Columbia
St. Lawrence
Sacramento
Hudson
Susquehanna
Colorado
Mississippi
Alabama & Tombigbee
Yaqui
Rio Grande
Brazos
Rio Grande de Santiago
Balsas
Usumacinta

ATLANTIC OCEAN

PACIFIC OCEAN

Magdalena
Orinoco

SOUTH AMERICA

Amazon
Parnaíba
Tocantins
São Francisco
Lake Titicaca
Paraná
Uruguay
Colorado
Negro
Chubut

⇨ BIG SPLASH! Water sports are a favorite recreational activity, especially in hot places such as Albuquerque, New Mexico, where these young people cool down in a giant wave pool.

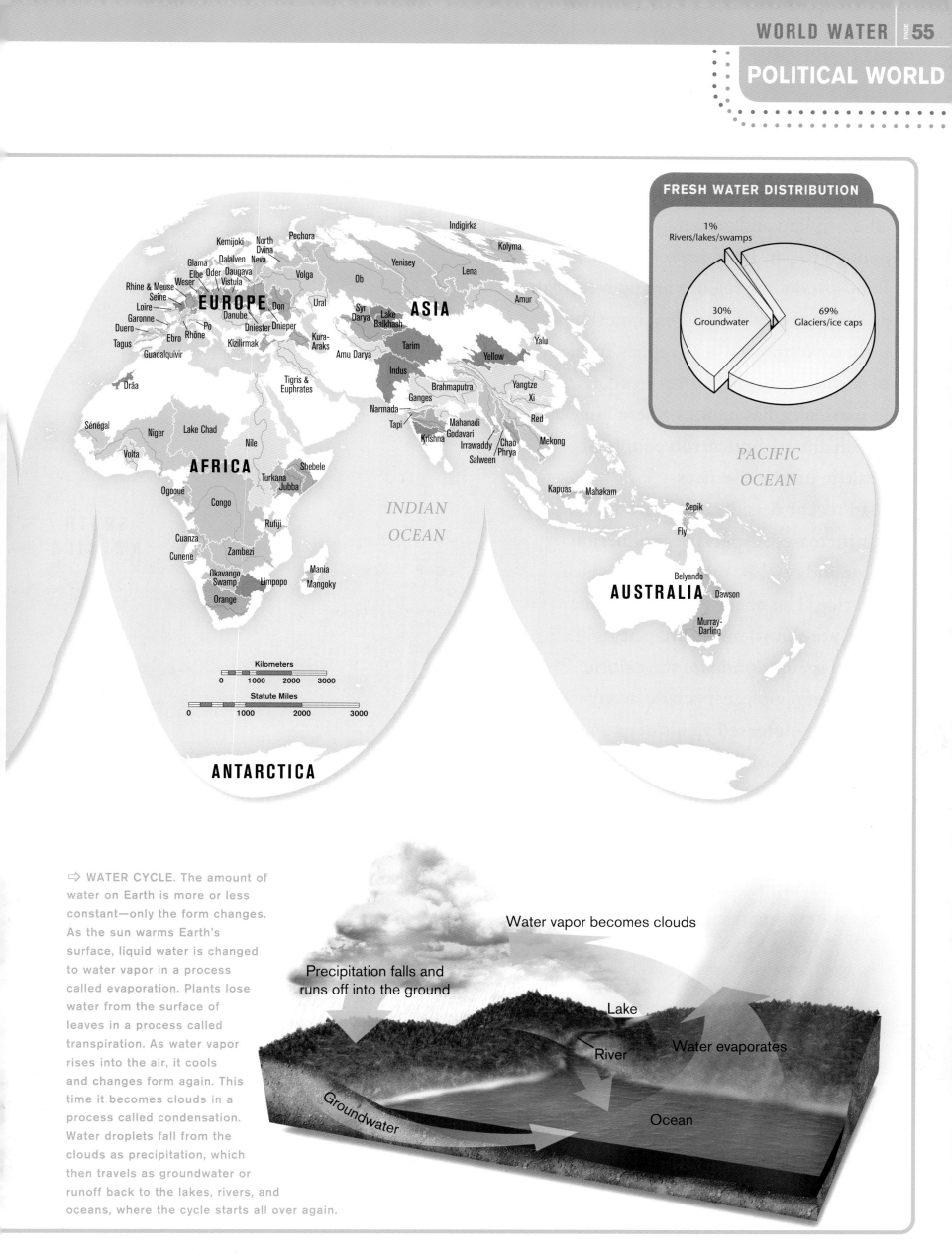

FRESH WATER DISTRIBUTION

1%
Rivers/lakes/swamps

30%
Groundwater

69%
Glaciers/ice caps

EUROPE

ASIA

AFRICA

AUSTRALIA

ANTARCTICA

PACIFIC OCEAN

INDIAN OCEAN

Kemijoki
North Dvina
Pechora
Indigirka
Kolyma
Glama
Dalalven
Neva
Yenisey
Lena
Elbe
Oder
Daugava
Volga
Ob
Amur
Rhine & Meuse
Weser
Vistula
Seine
Ural
Loire
Don
Syr Darya
Lake Balkhash
Yalu
Garonne
Danube
Duero
Po
Dniester Dnieper
Tarim
Yellow
Ebro
Rhône
Kizilirmak
Kura-Araks
Tagus
Amu Darya
Indus
Yangtze
Xi
Guadalquivir
Kura-Araks
Brahmaputra
Red
Drãa
Tigris & Euphrates
Ganges
Narmada
Mekong
Sénégal
Niger
Lake Chad
Tapi
Krishna
Mahanadi
Godavari
Irrawaddy
Chao Phrya
Salween
Volta
Nile
AFRICA
Turkana
Jubba
Shebele
Ogooué
Congo
Rufiji
Cuanza
Cunene
Zambezi
Okavango Swamp
Limpopo
Mania
Mangoky
Orange
Kapuas
Mahakam
Sepik
Fly
Belyando
Dawson
Murray-Darling

Kilometers
0   1000   2000   3000

Statute Miles
0   1000   2000   3000

⇨ WATER CYCLE. The amount of water on Earth is more or less constant—only the form changes. As the sun warms Earth's surface, liquid water is changed to water vapor in a process called evaporation. Plants lose water from the surface of leaves in a process called transpiration. As water vapor rises into the air, it cools and changes form again. This time it becomes clouds in a process called condensation. Water droplets fall from the clouds as precipitation, which then travels as groundwater or runoff back to the lakes, rivers, and oceans, where the cycle starts all over again.

Water vapor becomes clouds

Precipitation falls and runs off into the ground

Lake

River

Water evaporates

Groundwater

Ocean

WORLD FOOD

Earth produces enough food for all its inhabitants—all 6.7 billion and growing—but not everyone gets enough to eat. It's a matter of distribution. Food-producing regions are unevenly spread around the world, and it is sometimes difficult to move food supplies from areas of surplus to areas of great need. Africa, in particular, has regions where hunger and malnourishment rob people of healthy, productive lives.

In recent decades, food production has increased, especially production of meat and cereals, such as corn, wheat, and rice. The major grain-producing areas are shown on the map at right. Cereal grains dominate the calorie supply of people, especially in Africa and Asia. But increased yields of grain require intensive use of fertilizers and irrigation, which are not only expensive but also possibly a threat to the environment. Most advances in food production have occurred in Asia and Latin America, but new research now focuses on Africa.

⇨ FISHING AND AQUACULTURE. The world's yearly catch of ocean fish is more than four times what it was in 1950. The most heavily harvested areas are in the North Atlantic and western Pacific Oceans. Overfishing is becoming a serious problem. At least seven of the most-fished species are considered to be at their limit.

Aquaculture—raising fish and seaweed in controlled ponds—accounts for 40 percent of the fish people eat. This practice began some 4,000 years ago in China, where it continues today, accounting for about two-thirds of total output. Fish are among the most widely traded food products, with 75 percent of the total catch sold on the international market each year.

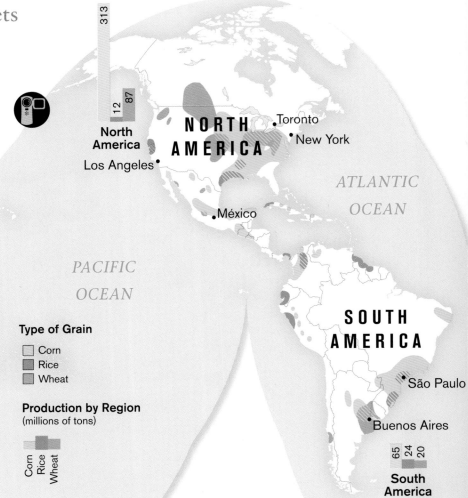

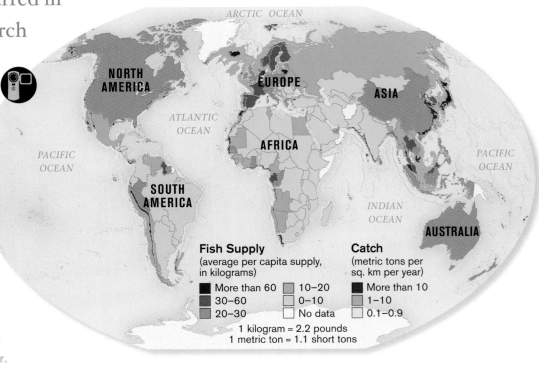

GRAIN TRADE

Major Importers   Major Exporters

Japan 22.4
South Korea 12.1
Mexico 9.5
Egypt 9.2
Brazil 7.7

United States 76.3
France 22.7
Argentina 21.7
Canada 17.7
Australia 16.2

Millions of metric tons annually

Moscow

ASIA

London
Paris
EUROPE

161
83
3
Europe

Beijing

Tokyo

570
308
199
Asia

PACIFIC
OCEAN

Cairo

AFRICA

Mumbai

Lagos

49
19
21
Africa

Jakarta

INDIAN
OCEAN

0.6
0.4
25
Australia/
Oceania

AUSTRALIA

Sydney

Kilometers
0 1000 2000 3000

Statute Miles
0 1000 2000 3000

ANTARCTICA

⇧ CASTING NETS. Fishermen in Orissa, India, cast their nets on the Birupa River. Fish is an important source of protein in their diets. Any surplus catch can be sold in the local market.

STAPLE GRAINS

CORN. A staple in prehistoric México and Peru, corn (or maize) is native to the New World. By the time Columbus's crew first tasted it, corn was already a hardy crop in much of North and South America.

WHEAT. Among the two oldest grains (barley is the other), wheat was important in ancient Mediterranean civilizations. Today, it is the most widely cultivated grain. Wheat grows best in temperate climates.

RICE. Originating in Asia many millennia ago, rice is the staple grain for about half the world's people. It is a labor-intensive plant that grows primarily in paddies (flooded fields) and thrives in the hot, humid tropics.

WORLD ENERGY & MINERALS

Almost everything people do—from cooking to powering a space shuttle—requires energy. But energy comes in different forms. Traditional energy sources, still used by many people in the developing world, include burning dried animal dung and wood. Industrialized countries and urban centers around the world rely on coal, oil, and natural gas—called fossil fuels because they formed from decayed plant and animal material accumulated from long ago. Fossil fuel deposits, either in the ground or under the ocean floor, are unevenly distributed on Earth (see map, right), and only some countries can afford to buy them.

Carbon dioxide from the burning of fossil fuels as well as other emissions may be contributing to global warming. Concerned scientists are looking at new ways to harness renewable sources of energy, such as water, wind, and sun.

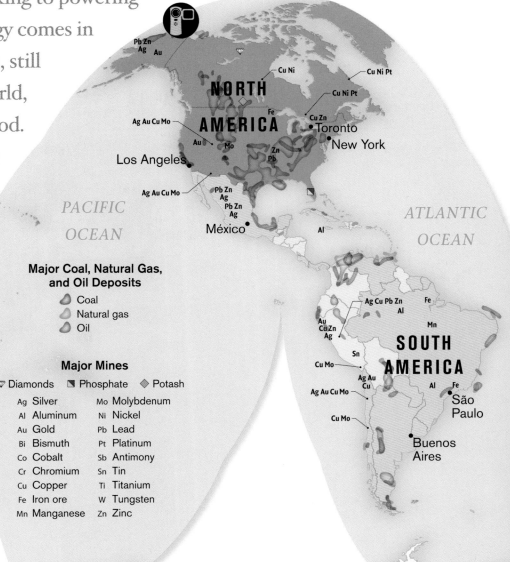

Major Coal, Natural Gas, and Oil Deposits
- Coal
- Natural gas
- Oil

Major Mines

▽ Diamonds   ◼ Phosphate   ◇ Potash

Ag	Silver	Mo	Molybdenum
Al	Aluminum	Ni	Nickel
Au	Gold	Pb	Lead
Bi	Bismuth	Pt	Platinum
Co	Cobalt	Sb	Antimony
Cr	Chromium	Sn	Tin
Cu	Copper	Ti	Titanium
Fe	Iron ore	W	Tungsten
Mn	Manganese	Zn	Zinc

OIL, GAS, AND COAL

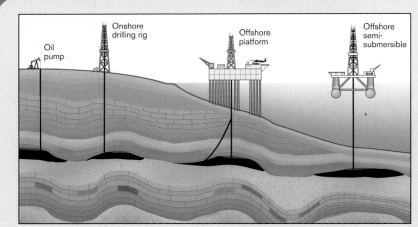

⇧ DRILLING FOR OIL AND GAS. The type of equipment depends on whether oil or natural gas is in the ground or under the ocean. This illustration shows some of the different kinds of onshore and offshore drilling equipment.

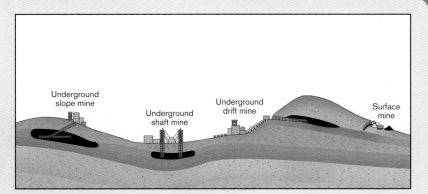

⇧ COAL MINING. The mining of coal made the industrial revolution possible, and coal still provides a major energy source. Work that was once done by people using picks and shovels now relies heavily on mechanized equipment. This diagram shows some of the various kinds currently in use.

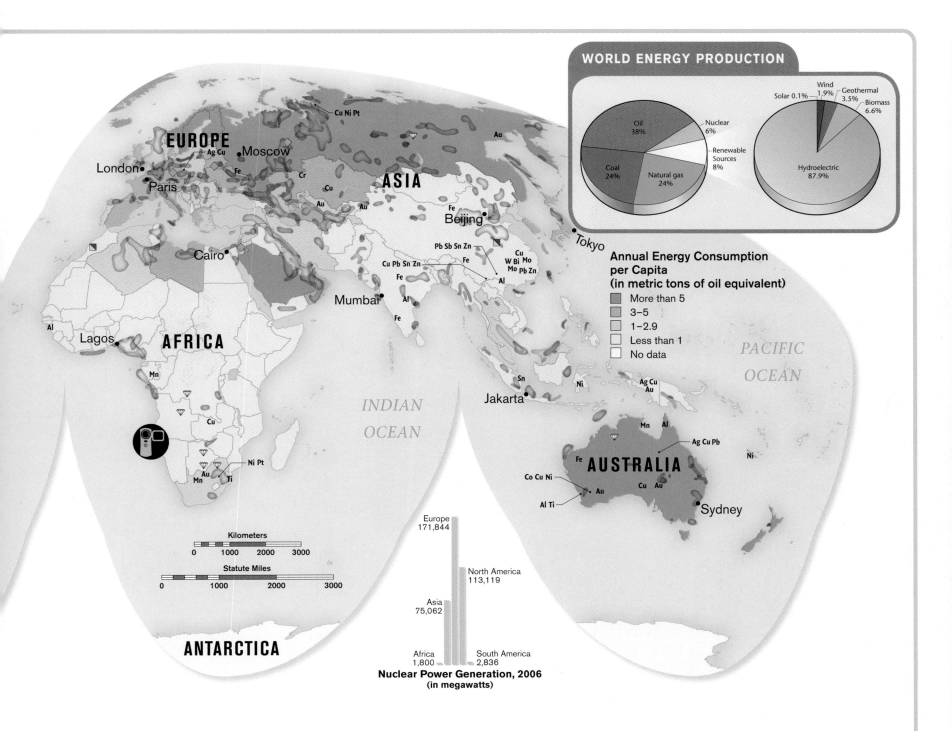

EUROPE
London
Paris
Moscow
Cu Ni Pt
Ag Cu
Fe
Cr
Cu
Au
Au
ASIA
Au
Cairo
AFRICA
Al
Lagos
Mn
Cu
Fe
Pb Sb Sn Zn
Cu Pb Sn Zn
Fe
Al
Fe
Mumbai
Al
Fe
Beijing
Tokyo
Cu W Bi Mo Mo Pb Zn
Al
Sn
Jakarta
Ni
Ag Cu Au
Ni
Ni Pt
Cu
Au
Ti
Mn
Au
Mn
Al
Fe
AUSTRALIA
Ag Cu Pb
Ni
Co Cu Ni
Au
Cu Au
Al Ti
Sydney

INDIAN OCEAN
PACIFIC OCEAN

ANTARCTICA

WORLD ENERGY PRODUCTION

Oil 38%
Nuclear 6%
Renewable Sources 8%
Natural gas 24%
Coal 24%

Solar 0.1%
Wind 1.9%
Geothermal 3.5%
Biomass 6.6%
Hydroelectric 87.9%

Annual Energy Consumption per Capita (in metric tons of oil equivalent)
- More than 5
- 3–5
- 1–2.9
- Less than 1
- No data

Kilometers
0 1000 2000 3000

Statute Miles
0 1000 2000 3000

Europe 171,844
North America 113,119
Asia 75,062
Africa 1,800
South America 2,836

Nuclear Power Generation, 2006 (in megawatts)

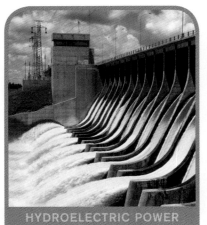

HYDROELECTRIC POWER

Hydroelectric plants, such as Santiago del Estero in Argentina (above), use dams to harness running water to generate clean, renewable energy.

GEOTHERMAL POWER

Geothermal power, originating from groundwater heated by magma, provides energy for this power plant in Iceland. Swimmers enjoy the warm, mineral-rich waters of a lake created by the power plant.

SOLAR POWER

Solar panels on Samso Island in Denmark capture and store energy from the sun, an environmentally friendly alternative to the use of fossil fuels.

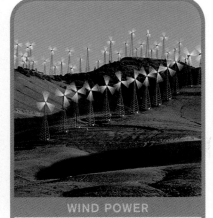

WIND POWER

Strong winds blowing through California's mountain passes spin the blades of windmills on an energy farm, powering giant turbines that generate electricity for the state.

THE CONTINENT:
NORTH AMERICA

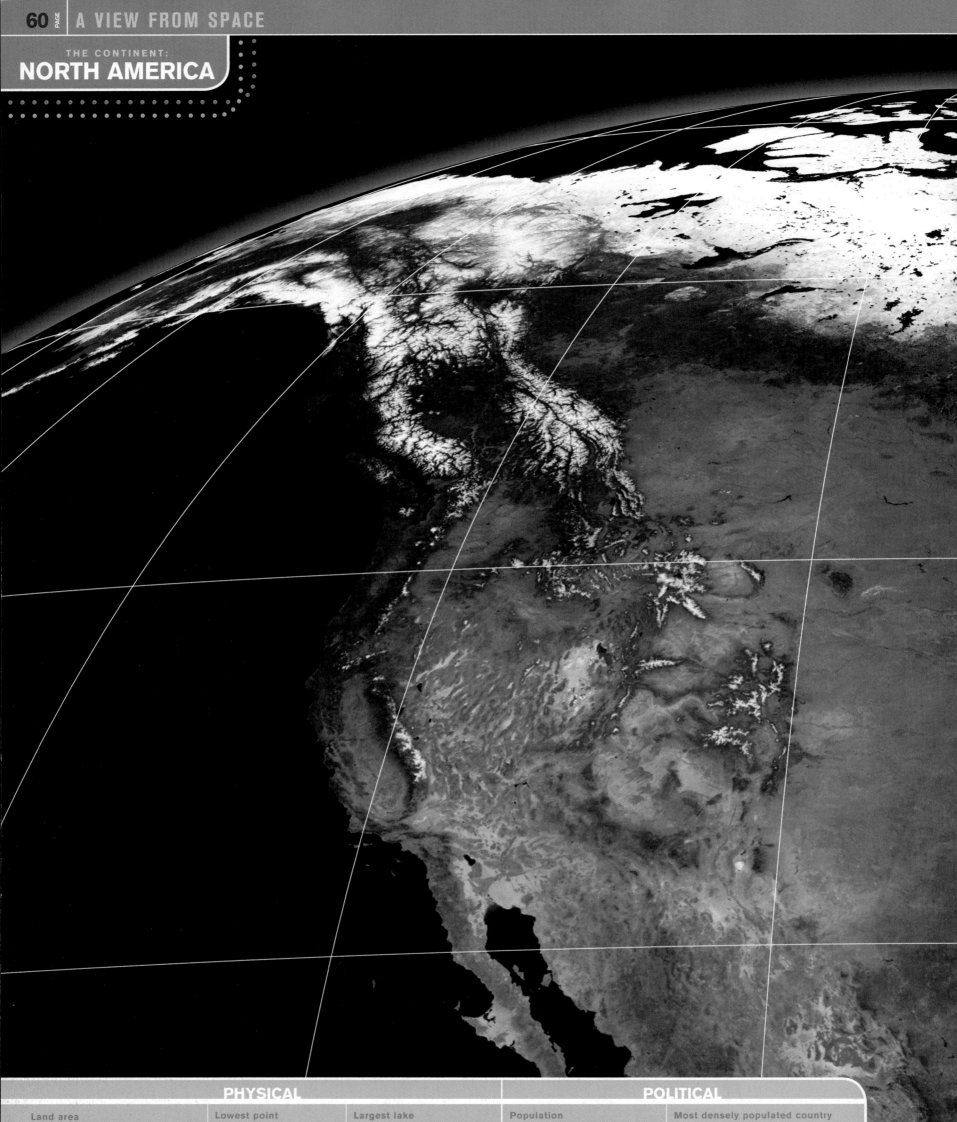

PHYSICAL

Land area
9,449,000 sq mi (24,474,000 sq km)

Highest point
Mount McKinley (Denali), Alaska
20,320 ft (6,194 m)

Lowest point
Death Valley, California
-282 ft (-86 m)

Longest river
Mississippi-Missouri,
United States
3,710 mi (5,971 km)

Largest lake
Lake Superior, U.S.-Canada
31,700 sq mi (82,100 sq km)

POLITICAL

Population
520,000,000

Largest metropolitan area
México City, México
Pop. 19,411,000

Largest country
Canada
3,855,101 sq mi (9,984,670 sq km)

Most densely populated country
Barbados
1,626 people per sq mi (628 per sq km)

Economy
Farming: cattle, grains, cotton, sugar
Industry: machinery, metals, mining
Services

North America

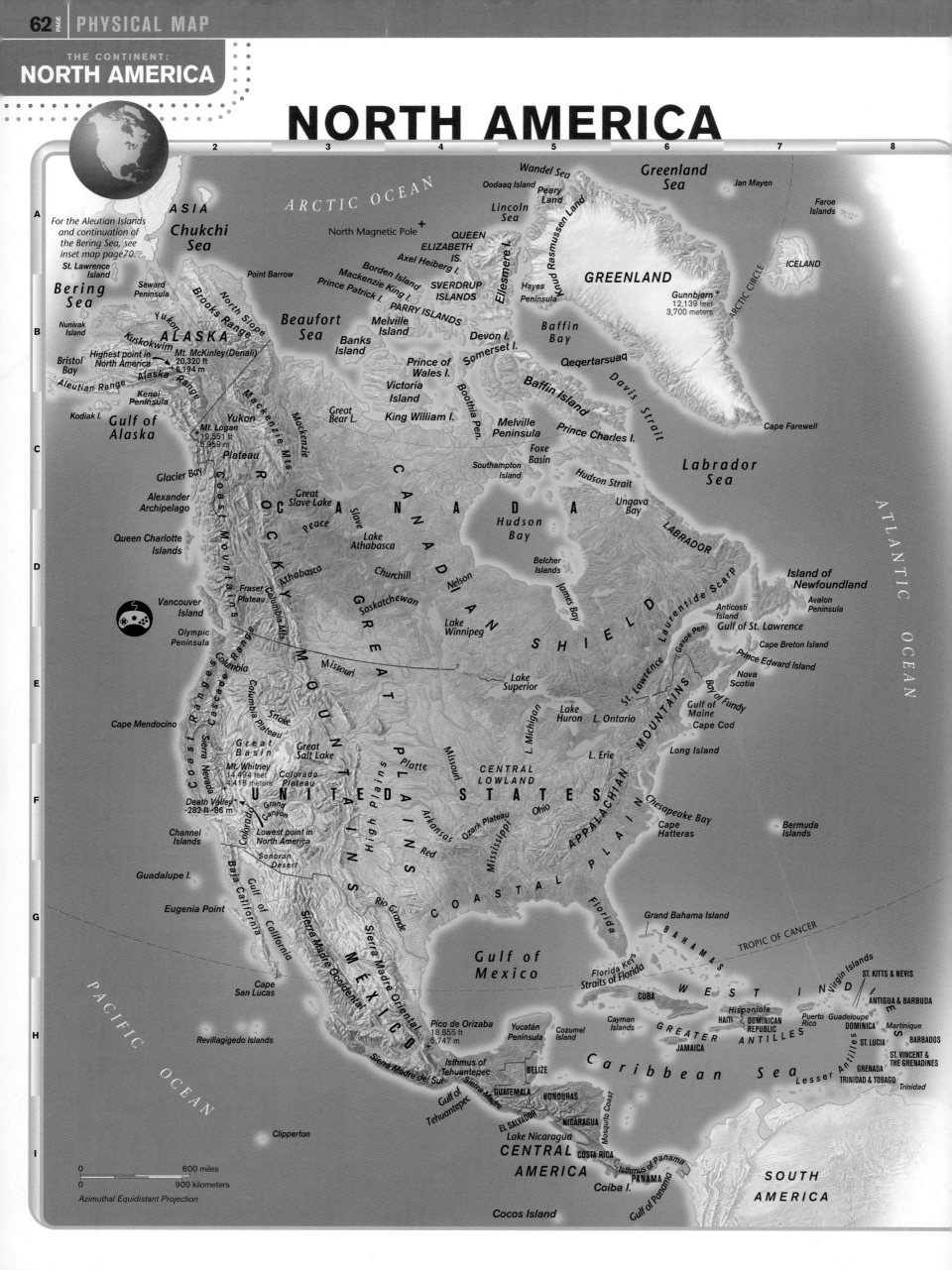

NORTH AMERICA

For the Aleutian Islands and continuation of the Bering Sea, see inset map page 70.

ARCTIC OCEAN

ASIA
Chukchi Sea

Wandel Sea
Oodaaq Island
Peary Land
North Magnetic Pole +
Lincoln Sea
QUEEN ELIZABETH IS.
Axel Heiberg I.
Borden Island
Mackenzie King I.
Prince Patrick I.
PARRY ISLANDS
Melville Island
Banks Island
Devon I.
Somerset I.
Prince of Wales I.
Victoria Island
King William I.
Boothia Pen.
Melville Peninsula
Prince Charles I.
Foxe Basin

Greenland Sea
Jan Mayen
Faroe Islands
ICELAND
ARCTIC CIRCLE

GREENLAND
Gunnbjørn +
12,139 feet
3,700 meters

St. Lawrence Island
Bering Sea
Nunivak Island
Bristol Bay
Kodiak I.
Seward Peninsula
Point Barrow
North Slope
Brooks Range
Yukon
Kuskokwim
ALASKA
Highest point in North America →
Mt. McKinley (Denali)
20,320 ft
6,194 m
Aleutian Range
Kenai Peninsula
Alaska Range
+ Mt. Logan
19,551 ft
5,959 m
Gulf of Alaska
Yukon
Plateau
Mackenzie Mts.
Beaufort Sea
Great Bear L.
Mackenzie
Southampton Island

Hayes Peninsula
Baffin Bay
Qeqertarsuaq
Davis Strait
Cape Farewell
Labrador Sea

Knud Rasmussen Land
SVERDRUP ISLANDS
Ellesmere I.

Glacier Bay
Alexander Archipelago
Queen Charlotte Islands
Vancouver Island
Olympic Peninsula
Coast Mountains
Columbia Mts.
Fraser Plateau
Athabasca
Peace
Slave
Lake Athabasca
Great Slave Lake
Churchill
Saskatchewan
Nelson
Lake Winnipeg
Hudson Bay
James Bay
Belcher Islands
Ungava Bay
LABRADOR
Laurentide Scarp
Island of Newfoundland
Avalon Peninsula
Anticosti Island
Gulf of St. Lawrence
Cape Breton Island
Prince Edward Island

CANADIAN SHIELD

ATLANTIC OCEAN

Cape Mendocino
Coast Ranges
Cascades
Columbia
Snake
Sierra Nevada
Great Basin
Great Salt Lake
Mt. Whitney
14,494 feet
4,418 meters
Colorado Plateau
Columbia Plateau
Snake
Missouri
Lake Superior
L. Michigan
Lake Huron
L. Ontario
L. Erie
St. Lawrence
APPALACHIAN MOUNTAINS
Gaspé Pen.
Nova Scotia
Bay of Fundy
Gulf of Maine
Cape Cod
Long Island
Bermuda Islands

ROCKY MOUNTAINS

GREAT PLAINS

CENTRAL LOWLAND

UNITED STATES

Death Valley
-282 ft -86 m
Grand Canyon
Colorado
Lowest point in North America
Channel Islands
Guadalupe I.
Eugenia Point
Baja California
Gulf of California
Platte
High Plains
Arkansas
Red
Ozark Plateau
Mississippi
Ohio
Missouri
Chesapeake Bay
Cape Hatteras
COASTAL PLAIN
Florida

Cape San Lucas
Revillagigedo Islands
Sierra Madre del Sur
Sierra Madre Oriental
Sierra Madre Occidental
MÉXICO
Rio Grande
Pico de Orizaba
18,855 ft
5,747 m
Yucatán Peninsula
Cozumel Island
Cayman Islands
Gulf of Mexico
Florida Keys
Straits of Florida
CUBA
BAHAMAS
Grand Bahama Island
TROPIC OF CANCER
JAMAICA
HAITI
Hispaniola
DOMINICAN REPUBLIC
Puerto Rico
Virgin Islands
ST. KITTS & NEVIS
ANTIGUA & BARBUDA
Guadeloupe
DOMINICA
Martinique
ST. LUCIA
BARBADOS
ST. VINCENT & THE GRENADINES
GRENADA
TRINIDAD & TOBAGO
Trinidad
GREATER ANTILLES
Lesser Antilles
WEST INDIES
Caribbean Sea

PACIFIC OCEAN

Clipperton
Isthmus of Tehuantepec
Gulf of Tehuantepec
Sierra Madre
BELIZE
GUATEMALA
HONDURAS
EL SALVADOR
NICARAGUA
Lake Nicaragua
COSTA RICA
Mosquito Coast
Isthmus of Panama
PANAMA
Coiba I.
Gulf of Panama
Cocos Island
CENTRAL AMERICA
SOUTH AMERICA

0 ——— 600 miles
0 ——— 900 kilometers
Azimuthal Equidistant Projection

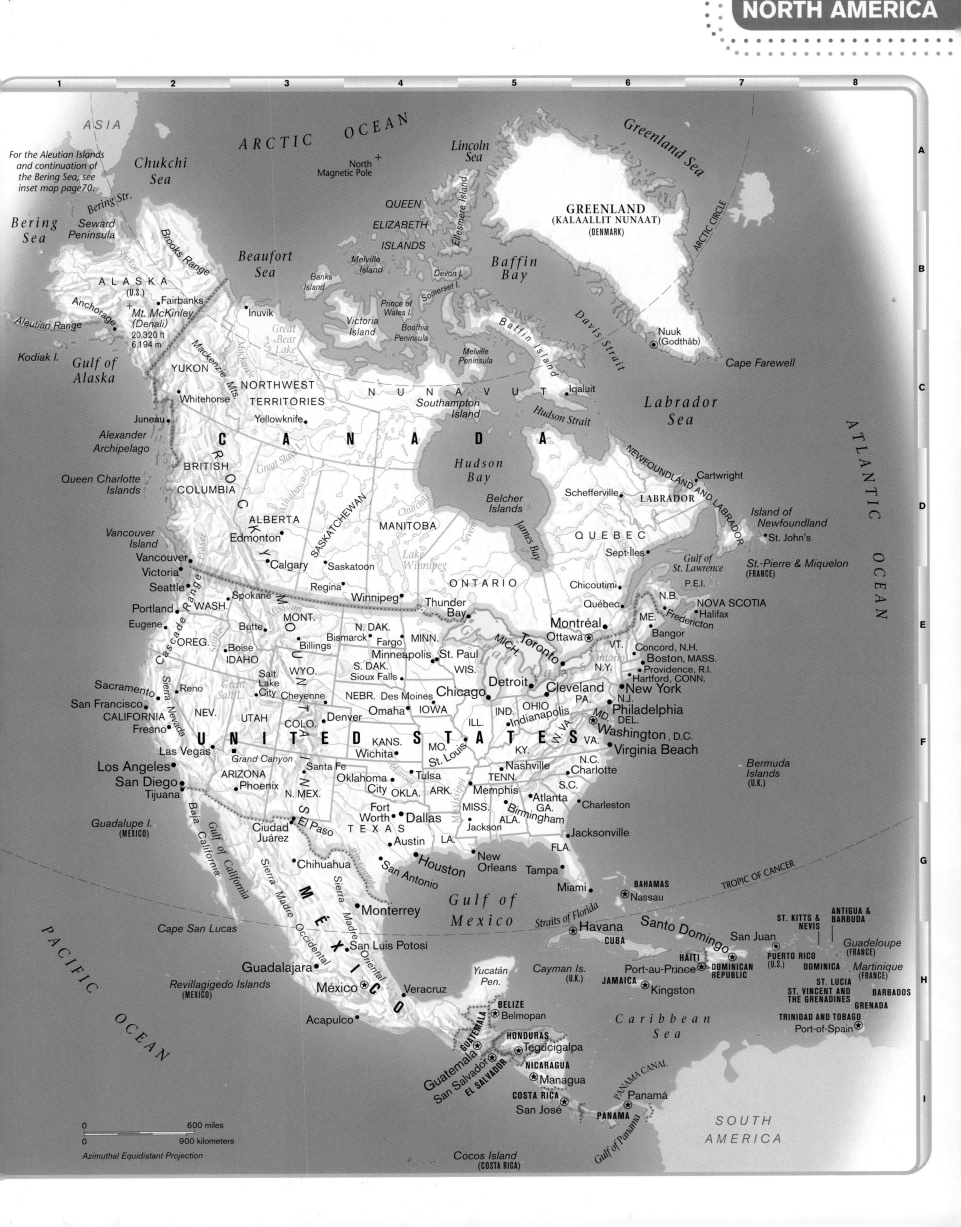

ASIA

ARCTIC OCEAN

Chukchi Sea

For the Aleutian Islands
and continuation of
the Bering Sea, see
inset map page70.

Bering Sea

Seward Peninsula

Bering Str.

North Magnetic Pole +

QUEEN ELIZABETH ISLANDS

Lincoln Sea

Greenland Sea

Beaufort Sea

Melville Island

Banks Island

Devon I.

Prince of Wales I.

Somerset I.

Ellesmere Island

Baffin Bay

GREENLAND
(KALAALLIT NUNAAT)
(DENMARK)

ARCTIC CIRCLE

ALASKA (U.S.)

Anchorage •

+ Fairbanks

Mt. McKinley (Denali)
20,320 ft
6,194 m

Brooks Range

Inuvik •

Victoria Island

Boothia Peninsula

Great Bear Lake

Melville Peninsula

Southampton Island

• Iqaluit

Baffin Island

Davis Strait

Nuuk (Godthåb) •

• Cape Farewell

Aleutian Range

Kodiak I.

Gulf of Alaska

YUKON

Mackenzie Mts.

Whitehorse •

NORTHWEST TERRITORIES

• Yellowknife

N U N A V U T

Hudson Strait

Labrador Sea

C A N A D A

Juneau •

Alexander Archipelago

BRITISH COLUMBIA

Great Slave Lake

Athabasca

Great Slave Lk.

Hudson Bay

Belcher Islands

Schefferville •

• Cartwright

NEWFOUNDLAND AND LABRADOR

LABRADOR

Queen Charlotte Islands

Fraser

ALBERTA

SASKATCHEWAN

MANITOBA

Churchill

Lake Winnipeg

ONTARIO

James Bay

Severn

Q U E B E C

Island of Newfoundland

• St. John's

Vancouver Island

Edmonton •

Calgary •

Saskatoon •

Sept-Îles •

Chicoutimi •

Gulf of St. Lawrence

St.-Pierre & Miquelon (FRANCE)

Vancouver •

Victoria •

Regina •

Winnipeg •

Thunder Bay •

Québec •

P.E.I.

N.B.

NOVA SCOTIA

ATLANTIC OCEAN

Seattle •

Spokane •

WASH.

Cascade Range

ROCKY

Portland •

Eugene •

OREG.

Butte •

MONT.

N. DAK.

Bismarck •

Fargo •

MINN.

Minneapolis •

St. Paul •

WIS.

MICH.

Toronto •

Ottawa ✪

Montréal •

VT.

Concord, N.H.

Fredericton •

Halifax •

ME.

Bangor •

N.H.

Boston, MASS.

Providence, R.I.

Hartford, CONN.

Boise •

IDAHO

Billings •

WYO.

S. DAK.

Sioux Falls •

Detroit •

Cleveland •

New York •

N.Y.

Sacramento •

Reno •

NEV.

Sierra Nevada

Great Salt Lk.

Salt Lake City •

Cheyenne •

NEBR.

Des Moines •

IOWA

Chicago •

IND.

OHIO

PA.

Philadelphia •

N.J.

San Francisco •

CALIFORNIA

Fresno •

UTAH

COLO.

Denver •

Omaha •

ILL.

Indianapolis •

MD.

DEL.

Washington, D.C.

Las Vegas •

UNITED STATES

KANS.

MO.

St. Louis •

KY.

W. VA.

VA.

Virginia Beach •

Los Angeles •

Grand Canyon

ARIZONA

Santa Fe •

Wichita •

Oklahoma City •

Nashville •

TENN.

N.C.

Charlotte •

San Diego •

Tijuana •

Phoenix •

N. MEX.

OKLA.

Tulsa •

ARK.

Memphis •

MISS.

Atlanta •

GA.

S.C.

Charleston •

Guadalupe I. (MEXICO)

Baja California

Gulf of California

Ciudad Juárez •

El Paso •

Fort Worth •

Dallas •

TEXAS

Austin •

LA.

Jackson •

Birmingham •

ALA.

Jacksonville •

FLA.

Sierra Madre Occidental

Chihuahua •

San Antonio •

Houston •

New Orleans •

Tampa •

Mississippi

Arkansas

Cape San Lucas

Sierra Madre Oriental

M É X I C O

Monterrey •

San Luis Potosí •

Gulf of Mexico

Miami •

BAHAMAS

Nassau ✪

Straits of Florida

TROPIC OF CANCER

PACIFIC OCEAN

Guadalajara •

Veracruz •

Yucatán Pen.

Cayman Is. (U.K.)

Havana ✪

CUBA

Santo Domingo

San Juan •

ST. KITTS & NEVIS

ANTIGUA & BARBUDA

Revillagigedo Islands (MEXICO)

México ✪

Acapulco •

BELIZE

Belmopan ✪

Caribbean Sea

HAITI

Port-au-Prince •

JAMAICA

Kingston ✪

DOMINICAN REPUBLIC

PUERTO RICO (U.S.)

Guadeloupe (FRANCE)

DOMINICA

Martinique (FRANCE)

ST. LUCIA

ST. VINCENT AND THE GRENADINES

BARBADOS

GRENADA

GUATEMALA

Guatemala ✪

HONDURAS

Tegucigalpa ✪

EL SALVADOR

San Salvador ✪

NICARAGUA

Managua ✪

COSTA RICA

San José •

PANAMA

Panamá ✪

PANAMA CANAL

TRINIDAD AND TOBAGO

Port-of-Spain ✪

Gulf of Panama

Cocos Island (COSTA RICA)

SOUTH AMERICA

Bermuda Islands (U.K.)

0   600 miles
0   900 kilometers

Azimuthal Equidistant Projection

North America
LAND OF CONTRASTS

From the windswept tundra of Alaska to the rain forest of Panama, the third-largest continent stretches 5,500 miles (8,850 km), spanning natural environments that support wildlife from polar bears to jaguars. Over thousands of years, Native American groups spread across these varied landscapes. But this rich mosaic of cultures largely disappeared before the onslaught of European fortune hunters and land seekers. While abundant resources and fast-changing technology have brought prosperity to Canada and the United States, other countries wrestle with the most basic needs. Promise and problems abound across this contrasting realm of 23 countries and 520 million people.

⇧ STORY IN THE ROCKS. Slanting sun rays reveal layers in the rocks of the Grand Canyon. Each rock layer—oldest on the canyon floor, youngest at the canyon's rim—tells us about Earth's changing history.

⇦ DRESSED TO CELEBRATE. This boy in México's southern state of Chiapas wears traditional clothing, including a brightly colored string tie and a broad-brimmed sombrero with elaborate stitching around the edge.

⇩ HOLD TIGHT. These daring rafters are running the roaring rapids of the Kicking Horse River in British Columbia, Canada's westernmost province. Rivers tumbling down the steep slopes of the Rocky Mountains provide many recreational opportunities.

⇦ STREET MUSIC. People from around the world visit New Orleans, Louisiana, to hear jazz musicians fill the air with their music.

⇨ NIGHT SONG. This coyote sends his mournful howl into the dark Montana night. Members of the dog family, coyotes originated in the southwestern United States but are now found throughout North America—even in urban areas.

THE CONTINENT:
NORTH AMERICA

more about
NORTH AMERICA

⇧ DWELLINGS FROM THE PAST. Between A.D. 1000 and A.D. 1300 native people known as Ancestral Puebloans built cliff dwellings called pueblos, such as this one in Mesa Verde, Colorado.

⇧ MAYA TREASURE. Pyramid of the Magician marks the ruins of Uxmal on the Yucatán Peninsula. Nearly four million people of Maya descent still live in southern México and Central America.

⇐ FROZEN SUMMER. Because it lies so far north, even summers are cold in Greenland. Here local people navigate their boat among icebergs in waters off the village of Augpilagtoq.

⇓ HIGH FLYER. A young Kutchin boy sails off a snow bank on snowshoes in Canada's Yukon. The Kutchin, an Athabascan tribe, live in the forested lands of eastern Alaska and western Canada. The name Kutchin means "people."

⇑ FISH BAIT. Palometa fish investigate the toes of a vacationer wading in the warm waters of the Caribbean near St. John in the U.S. Virgin Islands. Tropical waters are habitat for many species of fish.

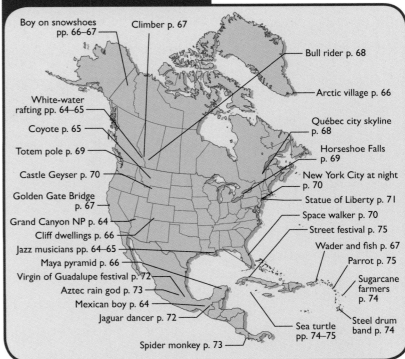

WHERE THE PICTURES ARE

Boy on snowshoes pp. 66–67
Climber p. 67
Bull rider p. 68
Arctic village p. 66
White-water rafting pp. 64–65
Québec city skyline p. 68
Coyote p. 65
Horseshoe Falls p. 69
Totem pole p. 69
New York City at night p. 70
Castle Geyser p. 70
Statue of Liberty p. 71
Golden Gate Bridge p. 67
Space walker p. 70
Grand Canyon NP p. 64
Street festival p. 75
Cliff dwellings p. 66
Wader and fish p. 67
Jazz musicians pp. 64–65
Parrot p. 75
Maya pyramid p. 66
Sugarcane farmers p. 74
Virgin of Guadalupe festival p. 72
Aztec rain god p. 73
Mexican boy p. 64
Steel drum band p. 74
Jaguar dancer p. 72
Sea turtle pp. 74–75
Spider monkey p. 73

⇓ DON'T LOOK DOWN. Clinging to a sheer rock face, this young woman demonstrates great skill as she climbs a cliff in Banff National Park in Canada. Covering more than 2,500 square miles (6,475 sq km) in the Canadian Rockies, Banff is a major tourist attraction.

⇑ WESTERN GATEWAY. The Golden Gate Bridge marks the entrance to San Francisco Bay. Beyond the bridge, captured above in the warm glow of twilight, is the California port city named after the bay.

THE CONTINENT:
NORTH AMERICA

CANADA

Topped only by Russia in area, Canada has just 33 million people—fewer than live in the U.S. state of California. Ancient rocks yield abundant minerals. Lakes and rivers in Québec are tapped for hydro-power, and wheat farming and cattle ranching thrive across the western Prairie Provinces. Vast forests attract loggers, and mountain slopes provide a playground for nature lovers. Enormous deposits of oil sands lie waiting for technology to find a cheap way to convert them to hundreds of billions of barrels of oil. Most Canadians live within a hundred miles (160 km) of the U.S. border. Here, too, are its leading cities: Asia-focused Vancouver, ethnically diverse Toronto, capital Ottawa, and French-speaking Montréal.

THE BASICS

STATS

Area
3,855,101 sq mi (9,984,670 sq km)

Population
32,600,000

Predominant languages
English, French (both official)

Predominant religion
Christianity (Roman Catholic, Protestant)

GDP per capita
$39,135

Life expectancy
80 years

Literacy rate
97%

GEO WHIZ

Canada ranks second behind Saudi Arabia in largest oil reserves thanks to oil contained in the Athabasca tar sands in northern Alberta.

The Inuit territory of Nunavut has issued license plates for cars, motorcycles, and snowmobiles in the shape of a polar bear.

Canada is a constitutional monarchy with Britain's Queen Elizabeth II as its head of state.

Montréal is the second most populous French-speaking city in the world after Paris, France.

Canada's many bays, inlets, and islands give it the longest coastline of any country: 151,023 miles (243,042 km).

Geologists believe Manicouagan Reservoir in Québec may have been created by the impact of a meteorite more than 200 million years ago.

⇨ COWBOY TRADITION. Across the continent's western regions, rodeos showcase cowboy skills of riding, roping, and racing. This bull rider at the Calgary Stampede in Alberta, Canada, fights for balance atop 1,300 pounds (590 kg) of bucking bull.

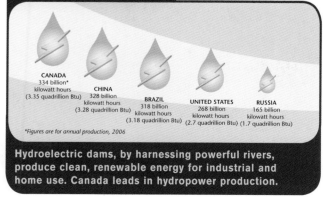

ENERGY FROM WATER

CANADA
334 billion*
kilowatt hours
(3.35 quadrillion Btu)

CHINA
328 billion
kilowatt hours
(3.28 quadrillion Btu)

BRAZIL
318 billion
kilowatt hours
(3.18 quadrillion Btu)

UNITED STATES
268 billion
kilowatt hours
(2.7 quadrillion Btu)

RUSSIA
165 billion
kilowatt hours
(1.7 quadrillion Btu)

*Figures are for annual production, 2006

Hydroelectric dams, by harnessing powerful rivers, produce clean, renewable energy for industrial and home use. Canada leads in hydropower production.

⇨ FRENCH ENCLAVE. Chateau Frontenac sparkles in Québec City's nighttime skyline. Settled by the French in the early 1600s, the province of Québec has maintained close ties to Europe and to its French heritage.

ARCTIC CIRCLE

Tuktoyaktuk
oil

ALASKA
(U.S.)

Inuvik

gas

MACKENZIE MOUNTAINS

YUKON

SELWYN MTS.

oil

Mt. Logan
19,551 ft
5,959 m

St. Elias Mts.

Haines
Junction

ROCKY MOUNTAINS

Whitehorse

PACIFIC OCEAN

gas C

QUEEN
CHARLOTTE
IS.

Prince Rupert

Dawson Creek
oil

Prince George

BRITISH
COLUMBIA

gas

Vancouver
Island

BANFF
N.P.

Vancouver

Victoria

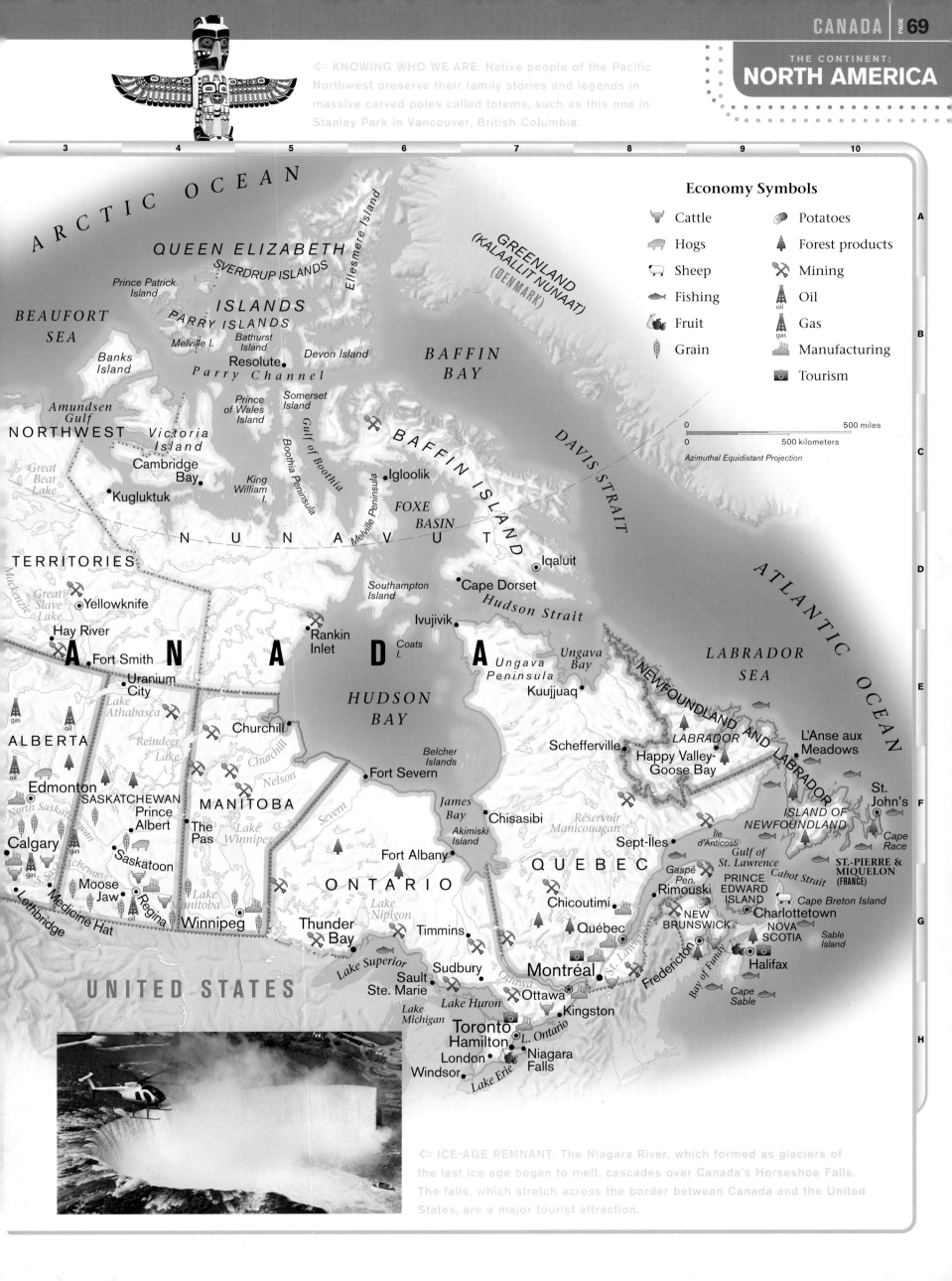

⟸ KNOWING WHO WE ARE. Native people of the Pacific Northwest preserve their family stories and legends in massive carved poles called totems, such as this one in Stanley Park in Vancouver, British Columbia.

Economy Symbols

Cattle
Hogs
Sheep
Fishing
Fruit
Grain

Potatoes
Forest products
Mining
Oil
Gas
Manufacturing
Tourism

500 miles
500 kilometers
Azimuthal Equidistant Projection

ARCTIC OCEAN

QUEEN ELIZABETH
SVERDRUP ISLANDS
Prince Patrick Island
ISLANDS
PARRY ISLANDS
Melville I.
Bathurst Island
Devon Island
Ellesmere Island

BEAUFORT SEA

Banks Island

Resolute
Parry Channel

GREENLAND
(KALAALLIT NUNAAT)
(DENMARK)

BAFFIN BAY

Amundsen Gulf

NORTHWEST

Great Bear Lake

Victoria Island

Cambridge Bay

Kugluktuk

Prince of Wales Island

King William I.

Somerset Island

Gulf of Boothia

Boothia Peninsula

Melville Peninsula

Igloolik

BAFFIN ISLAND

FOXE BASIN

DAVIS STRAIT

TERRITORIES

N U N A V U T

Iqaluit

ATLANTIC OCEAN

C A N A D A

Great Slave Lake

Yellowknife

Hay River

Fort Smith

Uranium City

Mackenzie

ALBERTA

gas
oil

Lake Athabasca

Reindeer Lake

Edmonton

Calgary
gas
oil

North Saskatchewan

Medicine Hat

Lethbridge

Moose Jaw

SASKATCHEWAN
Prince Albert

Saskatoon

Regina
oil

Lake Manitoba

MANITOBA

Churchill
Churchill

Nelson

The Pas

Lake Winnipeg

Winnipeg

Rankin Inlet

Coats I.

HUDSON BAY

Fort Severn

Belcher Islands

Southampton Island

Cape Dorset

Hudson Strait

Ivujivik

Ungava Peninsula

Ungava Bay

Kuujjuaq

LABRADOR SEA

Schefferville

Happy Valley-Goose Bay

LABRADOR

NEWFOUNDLAND AND LABRADOR

L'Anse aux Meadows

St. John's

ISLAND OF NEWFOUNDLAND

Cape Race

James Bay

Akimiski Island

Fort Albany

Chisasibi

Réservoir Manicouagan

Sept-Îles

QUEBEC

Chicoutimi

Québec

Rimouski

Gaspé Pen.

Île d'Anticosti

Gulf of St. Lawrence

Cabot Strait

ST.-PIERRE & MIQUELON (FRANCE)

PRINCE EDWARD ISLAND

Cape Breton Island

Charlottetown

NOVA SCOTIA

Sable Island

ONTARIO

Lake Nipigon

Thunder Bay

Timmins

Lake Superior

Sault Ste. Marie

Sudbury

Severn

St. Lawrence

NEW BRUNSWICK

Fredericton

Bay of Fundy

Cape Sable

Halifax

Montréal

Ottawa

Kingston

Lake Huron

Lake Michigan

Toronto

Hamilton

London

Windsor

L. Ontario

Niagara Falls

Lake Erie

Ottawa

UNITED STATES

⟸ ICE-AGE REMNANT. The Niagara River, which formed as glaciers of the last ice age began to melt, cascades over Canada's Horseshoe Falls. The falls, which stretch across the border between Canada and the United States, are a major tourist attraction.

3 4 5 6 7 8 9 10
A B C D E F G H

THE CONTINENT:
NORTH AMERICA

THE BASICS

STATS

Area
3,794,083 sq mi (9,826,630 sq km)

Population
300,000,000

Predominant languages
English, Spanish

Predominant religion
Christianity (Protestant,
Roman Catholic)

GDP per capita
$44,315

Life expectancy
78 years

Literacy rate
97%

GEO WHIZ

Florida is known as the lightning capital of the United States. Sea breezes from the Gulf of Mexico and the Atlantic Ocean collide over the warm Florida peninsula, producing thunderstorms and the lightning associated with them.

Hawai'i is politically part of the United States but geographically part of the Polynesian cultural region of Oceania.

At 379.1 feet (115.3 m), Hyperion, a coast redwood in California's Redwood National Forest, is the world's tallest living tree. It is more than 70 feet (21 m) higher than the Statue of Liberty.

Lake Michigan is the only one of the Great Lakes located entirely within the United States. Each of the other four lakes spans the U.S.-Canada border.

In 2006, 18 whooping crane chicks made a historic migration from Wisconsin to Florida following an ultralight aircraft as part of Operation Migration.

UNITED STATES

From "sea to shining sea" the United States is blessed with a rich bounty of natural resources. Mineral treasures abound—oil, coal, iron, and gold— and croplands are among the most productive in the world. Americans have used—and too often overused— this storehouse of raw materials to build an economic base unmatched by any other country. An array of high-tech businesses populate the "Sunbelt" of the South and West. By combining its natural riches and the creative ideas of its ethnically diverse population, this land of opportunity has become the leading global power.

⇧ CALLING HOME.
A U.S. astronaut takes an extravehicular space walk high above planet Earth, during a mission of the space shuttle *Atlantis*.

⇦ WORLD CITY. The lights of Manhattan glitter around New York City's Chrysler Building. The city's influence as a financial and cultural center extends across the United States and around the world.

⇨ LETTING OFF STEAM.
Castle Geyser is just one of many active geological features in Yellowstone National Park in Wyoming. The park is part of a region that sits on top of a major tectonic hot spot.

⇦ LADY LIBERTY. The Statue of Liberty, a gift from France, stands in New York City's harbor. The statue has become a symbol of hope for millions of immigrants coming to the United States in search of a better life.

CANADA

4 5 6 7 8 9 10 11

A
B
C
D
E
F
G

Lake of the Woods
Isle Royale
Lake Superior
St. Lawrence

MAINE
Great Falls
Minot
International Falls
Duluth
Marquette
Burlington
Montpelier
Augusta
MONTANA
NORTH DAKOTA
Bismarck
Fargo
MINNESOTA
Superior
VT.
N.H.
Portland
Billings
St. Paul
WISCONSIN
Lake Michigan
Lake Huron
Niagara Falls
Lake Ontario
Concord
Boston
YELLOWSTONE N.P.
SOUTH DAKOTA
Pierre
Minneapolis
Green Bay
Milwaukee
Madison
Grand Rapids
Lansing
NEW YORK
Albany
Rochester
Buffalo
Providence
RHODE ISLAND
CONN.
Hartford
WYOMING
Casper
Rapid City
Sioux Falls
Missouri
Mississippi
Lake Erie
Erie
Detroit
MICHIGAN
Harrisburg
PA.
Philadelphia
Long Island
New York
Newark
NEW JERSEY
Cheyenne
Laramie
NEBRASKA
Cedar Rapids
IOWA
Rockford
Chicago
Gary
Fort Wayne
Toledo
Cleveland
OHIO
Pittsburgh
Trenton
Fort Collins
Grand Junction
Boulder
Denver
Mt. Elbert 14,433 ft 4,399 m
Omaha
Des Moines
Peoria
ILLINOIS
Springfield
INDIANA
Indianapolis
Dayton
Columbus
WEST VIRGINIA
MD.
Dover
DELAWARE
Baltimore
Annapolis
Washington, D.C.
Colorado Springs
COLORADO
Lincoln
Kansas City
MISSOURI
St. Louis
Evansville
Cincinnati
Louisville
Charleston
Richmond
VIRGINIA
Chesapeake Bay
Pueblo
Topeka
KANSAS
Jefferson City
Frankfort
KENTUCKY
Norfolk
Virginia Beach
MESA VERDE N.P.
Dodge City
Wichita
Springfield
Paducah
Knoxville
Nashville
Mt. Mitchell +6,684 ft 2,037 m
NORTH CAROLINA
Greensboro
Raleigh
Cape Hatteras
Santa Fe
Albuquerque
OKLAHOMA
Tulsa
Fort Smith
Memphis
TENNESSEE
Chattanooga
Charlotte
SOUTH CAROLINA
Columbia
NEW MEXICO
Roswell
Amarillo
Oklahoma City
ARKANSAS
Little Rock
Huntsville
Birmingham
Atlanta
GEORGIA
Columbia
Charleston
El Paso
Lubbock
Fort Worth
Abilene
Dallas
Shreveport
Jackson
MISSISSIPPI
ALABAMA
Montgomery
Columbus
Macon
Savannah
TEXAS
Waco
Natchez
Mobile
Jacksonville
Austin
Beaumont
Baton Rouge
LOUISIANA
Biloxi
Mobile Bay
Tallahassee
FLORIDA
Orlando
Cape Canaveral
San Antonio
Houston
New Orleans
Mississippi River Delta
Tampa
St. Petersburg
Lake Okeechobee
Corpus Christi
Laredo
GULF OF MEXICO
THE EVERGLADES
Miami
BAHAMAS
Brownsville
Florida Keys
Straits of Florida

MEXICO

ATLANTIC OCEAN

Kaua'i
Ni'ihau
HAWAI'I
O'ahu
Moloka'i
Maui
Honolulu
Lana'i
Kaho'olawe
Principal Hawaiian Islands
0 150 mi
0 150 km
Hilo
Hawai'i

200 miles
0
200 kilometers
0
Albers Conic Equal-Area Projection

Economy Symbols

⚊ Cattle	⚊ Sugarcane	⚊ Forest products
⚊ Hogs	⚊ Sugar beets	⚊ Mining
⚊ Fishing	⚊ Peanuts	⚊ Coal
⚊ Citrus	⚊ Potatoes	⚊ Oil
⚊ Other fruit	⚊ Cotton	⚊ Gas
⚊ Corn	⚊ Coffee	⚊ Manufacturing
⚊ Rice	⚊ Wine	⚊ Tourism
⚊ Other grains	⚊ Tobacco	

NATION OF IMMIGRANTS

Mexico 161,445*

*Figures represent the total number of legal permanent residents between 2003 and 2005

India 84,681
China 69,967
Philippines 60,748
Cuba 36,261

From its founding, the United States has attracted people from other lands. Today, most immigrants come from Latin America and Asia.

THE CONTINENT:
NORTH AMERICA

MÉXICO & CENTRAL AMERICA

⇧ PAST MEETS PRESENT.
A boy prepares to become a jaguar dancer in Tabasco State, México. This dance to bring rain dates back to the Olmec culture.

México and most Central American countries share a backbone of mountains, a legacy of powerful Native American empires, and a largely Spanish colonial history. Once-abundant rain forests now are largely gone. México dwarfs its seven Central American neighbors in area, population, and natural resources. Its economy boasts a rich diversity of agricultural crops, highly productive oil fields, a growing manufacturing base, and strong trade with the U.S. and Canada. Overall, Central American countries rely on agricultural products such as bananas and coffee, though tourism is increasing. Modern-day México and Central America struggle to fulfill the hopes of growing populations, some of whom search for better lives by migrating—both legally and illegally—north to the United States.

THE BASICS

STATS

Largest country
México
758,449 sq mi (1,964,375 sq km)

Smallest country
El Salvador
8,124 sq mi (21,041 sq km)

Most populous country
México
108,300,000

Least populous country
Belize
300,000

Predominant languages
English, Spanish, Mayan, various Amerindian languages

Predominant religion
Christianity (Roman Catholic, Protestant)

Highest GDP per capita
México
$7,594

Lowest GDP per capita
Nicaragua
$908

Highest life expectancy
Costa Rica
79 years

Highest literacy rate
Costa Rica
96%

GEO WHIZ

México takes its name from the word "Mexica," another name for the Aztec, the last of the indigenous cultures to rule México before it fell to Spanish conquerors in 1521.

Scientists believe that the crater of the comet that struck Earth 65 million years ago, causing the dramatic climate changes that led to the extinction of the dinosaurs, is at Chicxulub, on the Yucatán Peninsula.

Coral colonies growing along much of the coast of Belize form the longest barrier reef in the Western Hemisphere and the second longest in the world, after Australia's Great Barrier Reef.

Vampire bats, which are only about the size of an adult person's thumb, drink the blood of other animals to survive. They are found throughout Central America.

A new set of locks on the Panama Canal will allow ships with 2.5 times the cargo capacity of ships now traveling the canal to take this shortcut between the Atlantic and Pacific Oceans.

⇨ CELEBRATION.
Traditional costumes and musical instruments combine with Christian beliefs during the annual Virgin of Guadalupe festival, observed throughout México. The festival marks the appearance of the Virgin Mary to a peasant in 1531.

Tijuana
Mexicali
Nogáles
Hermos
BAJA CALIFORNIA
Gulf of California
Ciu
Ob
La Paz
Culia
Cape
San Lucas
M
Puer

1

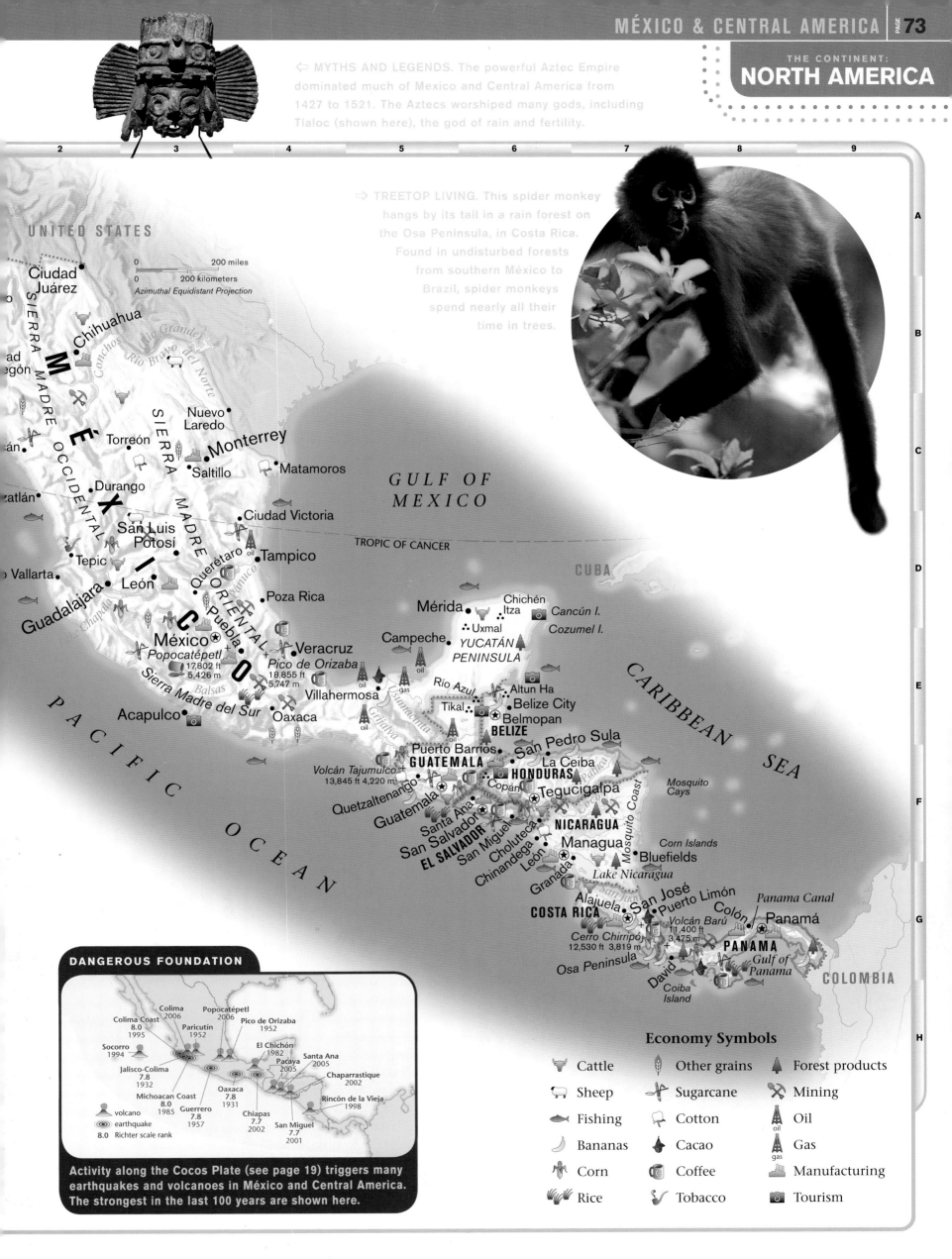

THE CONTINENT:
NORTH AMERICA

⇐ MYTHS AND LEGENDS. The powerful Aztec Empire dominated much of Mexico and Central America from 1427 to 1521. The Aztecs worshiped many gods, including Tlaloc (shown here), the god of rain and fertility.

2   3   4   5   6   7   8   9

⇨ TREETOP LIVING. This spider monkey hangs by its tail in a rain forest on the Osa Peninsula, in Costa Rica. Found in undisturbed forests from southern México to Brazil, spider monkeys spend nearly all their time in trees.

A

UNITED STATES

0   200 miles
0   200 kilometers
Azimuthal Equidistant Projection

B

Ciudad Juárez

SIERRA MADRE OCCIDENTAL

Chihuahua

Rio Grande
Río Bravo del Norte
Conchos

Nuevo Laredo

Torreón
Monterrey

Saltillo
Matamoros

C

Durango

Mazatlán

Ciudad Victoria

GULF OF MEXICO

CUBA

Puerto Vallarta

San Luis Potosí

SIERRA MADRE ORIENTAL

Tepic

Tampico

TROPIC OF CANCER

D

Guadalajara

León
Querétaro

Poza Rica

Mérida
Chichén Itza
Cancún I.
Cozumel I.

Lake Chapala

México
Popocatépetl
17,802 ft
5,426 m

Puebla

Campeche

YUCATÁN PENINSULA

Balsas

Veracruz
Pico de Orizaba
18,855 ft
5,747 m

Río Azul

E

Acapulco

Sierra Madre del Sur

Oaxaca

Villahermosa

oil
gas

Tikal
Altun Ha
Belize City
Belmopan
BELIZE

CARIBBEAN SEA

PACIFIC OCEAN

Puerto Barrios
San Pedro Sula
La Ceiba

GUATEMALA
HONDURAS

Volcán Tajumulco
13,845 ft 4,220 m

Copán
Tegucigalpa

Mosquito Cays

F

Quetzaltenango

Guatemala

Santa Ana
San Salvador
EL SALVADOR

San Miguel

Choluteca

NICARAGUA

Chinandega
León

Managua

Bluefields

Mosquito Coast

Corn Islands

Granada
Lake Nicaragua

G

Alajuela
San José
Puerto Limón
Colón
Panamá
Panama Canal

COSTA RICA

Cerro Chirripó
12,530 ft 3,819 m

Volcán Barú
11,400 ft
3,475 m

PANAMA

Osa Peninsula

David

Coiba Island

Gulf of Panama

COLOMBIA

H

DANGEROUS FOUNDATION

Colima 2006
Colima Coast
8.0
1995

Popocatépetl 2006
Paricutín
1952

Pico de Orizaba
1952

Socorro 1994

El Chichón 1982
Santa Ana 2005
Pacaya 2005

Jalisco-Colima
7.8
1932

Michoacan Coast
8.0
1985

Oaxaca
7.8
1931

Chaparrastique 2002

Guerrero
7.8
1957

Rincón de la Vieja
1998

Chiapas
7.7
2002

▲ volcano
◉ earthquake
8.0 Richter scale rank

San Miguel
7.7
2001

Activity along the Cocos Plate (see page 19) triggers many earthquakes and volcanoes in México and Central America. The strongest in the last 100 years are shown here.

Economy Symbols

Cattle	Other grains	Forest products
Sheep	Sugarcane	Mining
Fishing	Cotton	Oil
Bananas	Cacao	Gas
Corn	Coffee	Manufacturing
Rice	Tobacco	Tourism

WEST INDIES & THE BAHAMAS

THE BASICS

STATS

Largest country
Cuba
42,803 sq mi (110,860 sq km)

Smallest country
St. Kitts and Nevis
104 sq mi (269 sq km)

Most populous country
Cuba
11,300,000

Least populous country
St. Kitts and Nevis
50,000

Predominant languages
Spanish, English, French, French patois

Predominant religion
Christian (Roman Catholic, Protestant, and others)

Highest GDP per capita
Bahamas
$18,869

Lowest GDP per capita
Haiti
$505

Highest life expectancy
Cuba
77 years

Highest literacy rate
Barbados
100%

GEO WHIZ

Voodoo, a religion that combines elements of West African spiritualism and Roman Catholic saints, is common in Haiti, the Dominican Republic, Cuba, Jamaica, and the Bahamas.

On the seafloor just off San Salvador, in the Bahamas, there is a bronze monument marking the site where Christopher Columbus is believed to have anchored his ship in 1492.

Pico Duarte (10,417 ft/3,175 m), on the island of Hispaniola, is the highest peak in the Caribbean.

Boiling Lake, in Morne Trois Pitons National Park on Dominica, is one of the world's largest thermal lakes.

Grenada, which is nicknamed the Spice Island, is one of the world's chief sources of nutmeg, mace, and other spices.

⇧ RHYTHM OF THE TROPICS. When traditional drums were banned in Trinidad in 1884, plantation workers looked for new instruments, including 55-gallon (208-L) oil drums, which were the origin of today's steel drums or "pans."

This region of tropical islands stretches from the Bahamas, off the eastern coast of Florida, to Trinidad and Tobago, off the northern coast of South America. The Greater Antilles—Cuba, Jamaica, Hispaniola, and U.S. territory Puerto Rico—account for nearly 90 percent of the region's land area and most of its 40 million people. A necklace of smaller islands called the Lesser Antilles plus the Bahamas make up most of the rest of this region. Lush vegetation, warm waters, and scenic beaches attract vacationers from across the globe. While these visitors bring much needed income, most people in this region remain poor.

⇦ WHITE GOLD. Sugarcane is an important economic resource throughout the Caribbean. This woman carries freshly cut cane on her head in a field in Barbados.

FUN IN THE SUN

Figures represent tourist arrivals, 2004

Dominican Republic	3,450,000*
Cuba	2,017,000
Bahamas	1,561,000
Jamaica	1,415,000
Barbados	552,000
Trinidad and Tobago	443,000
St. Lucia	296,000
Antigua and Barbuda	245,384
St. Kitts and Nevis	118,000
Grenada	98,244

These island countries are the region's most popular destinations for tourists seeking sandy beaches, blue waters, and warm breezes.

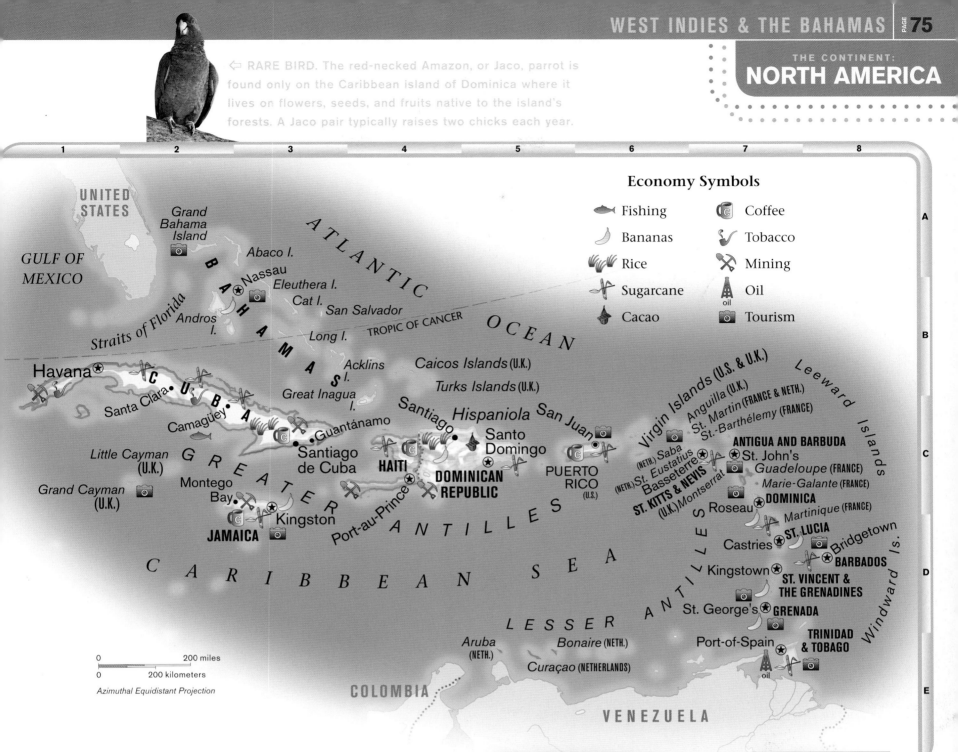

⇐ RARE BIRD. The red-necked Amazon, or Jaco, parrot is found only on the Caribbean island of Dominica where it lives on flowers, seeds, and fruits native to the island's forests. A Jaco pair typically raises two chicks each year.

Economy Symbols

- Fishing
- Coffee
- Bananas
- Tobacco
- Rice
- Mining
- Sugarcane
- Oil
- Cacao
- Tourism

UNITED STATES

GULF OF MEXICO

Grand Bahama Island

Abaco I.

Nassau

Eleuthera I.

Cat I.

San Salvador

Straits of Florida

Andros I.

Long I.

TROPIC OF CANCER

ATLANTIC OCEAN

BAHAMAS

Acklins I.

Caicos Islands (U.K.)

Turks Islands (U.K.)

Havana

CUBA

Santa Clara

Camagüey

Great Inagua I.

Guantánamo

Santiago

Hispaniola

San Juan

Virgin Islands (U.S. & U.K.)

Anguilla (U.K.)

St. Martin (FRANCE & NETH.)

St.-Barthélemy (FRANCE)

Leeward Islands

Little Cayman (U.K.)

GREATER

Santiago de Cuba

Santo Domingo

HAITI

DOMINICAN REPUBLIC

PUERTO RICO (U.S.)

(NETH.) Saba

(NETH.) St. Eustatius

Basseterre

ST. KITTS & NEVIS

(U.K.) Montserrat

ANTIGUA AND BARBUDA

St. John's

Guadeloupe (FRANCE)

Marie-Galante (FRANCE)

DOMINICA

Martinique (FRANCE)

Grand Cayman (U.K.)

Montego Bay

Kingston

JAMAICA

Port-au-Prince

ANTILLES

Roseau

ST. LUCIA

Castries

Bridgetown

BARBADOS

CARIBBEAN SEA

Kingstown

ST. VINCENT & THE GRENADINES

St. George's

GRENADA

Windward Is.

LESSER ANTILLES

Aruba (NETH.)

Bonaire (NETH.)

Curaçao (NETHERLANDS)

Port-of-Spain

TRINIDAD & TOBAGO

oil

0   200 miles
0   200 kilometers
Azimuthal Equidistant Projection

COLOMBIA

VENEZUELA

⇓ WATER WORLD. The clear waters of the Caribbean allow face-to-face interaction with sea life, such as this green sea turtle. Adult sea turtles can remain under water for two hours without breathing.

⇑ CELEBRATION. Stilt walkers in brightly colored costumes tower above this street in Old Havana, Cuba, during the annual celebration of Carnival. Introduced by Catholic colonizers from Spain, this festival occurs prior to the beginning of the religious season of Lent.

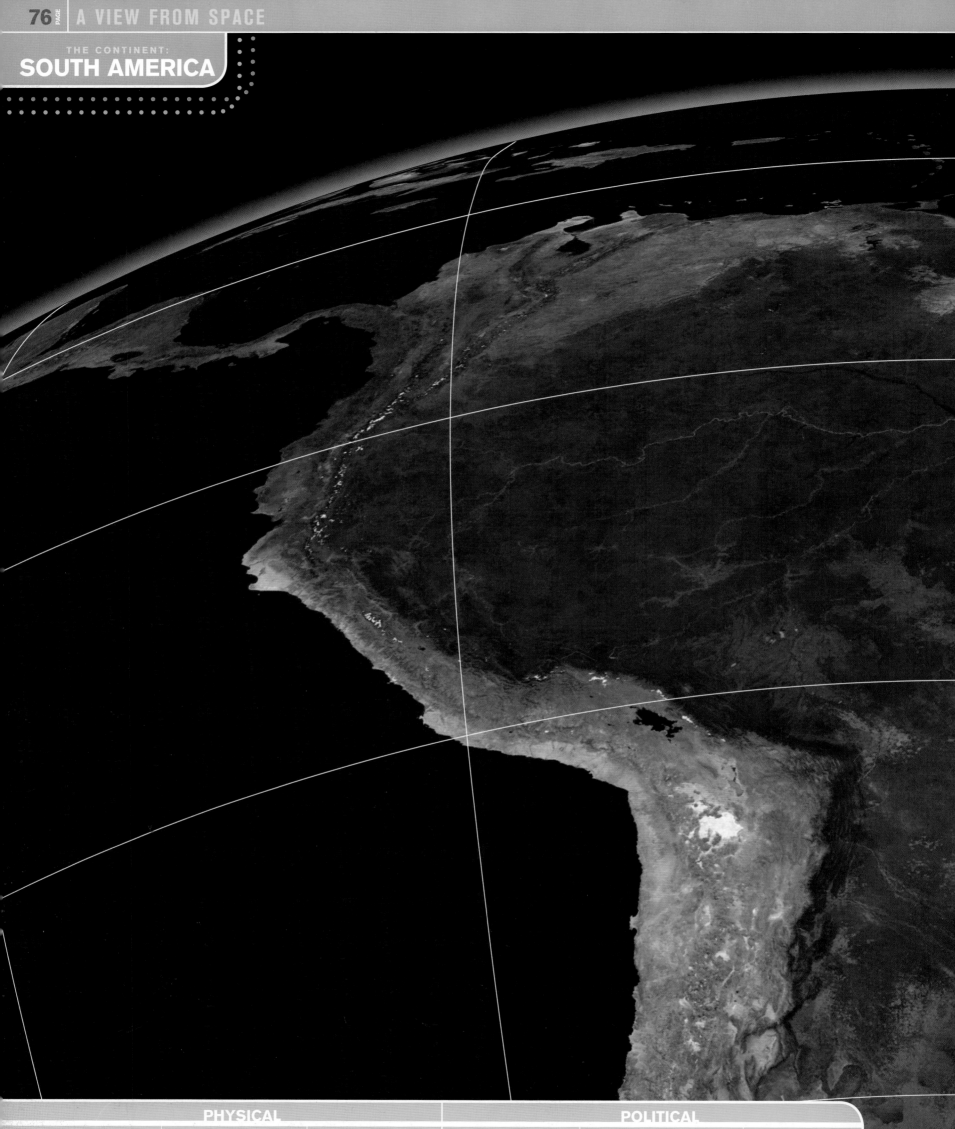

THE CONTINENT:
SOUTH AMERICA

PHYSICAL

Land area
6,880,000 sq mi (17,819,000 sq km)

Lowest point
Laguna del Carbón, Argentina
-344 ft (-105 m)

Largest lake
Lake Titicaca, Bolivia-Peru
3,200 sq mi (8,290 sq km)

Highest point
Cerro Aconcagua, Argentina
22,834 ft (6,960 m)

Longest river
Amazon
4,000 mi (6,437 km)

POLITICAL

Population
378,000,000

Largest metropolitan area
São Paulo, Brazil:
Pop. 17,857,000

Largest country
Brazil
3,300,169 sq mi (8,547,403 sq km)

Most densely populated country
Ecuador
121 people per sq mi (47 per sq km)

Economy
Farming: cattle, coffee, fruit

Industry: mining, oil, manufacturing

Services

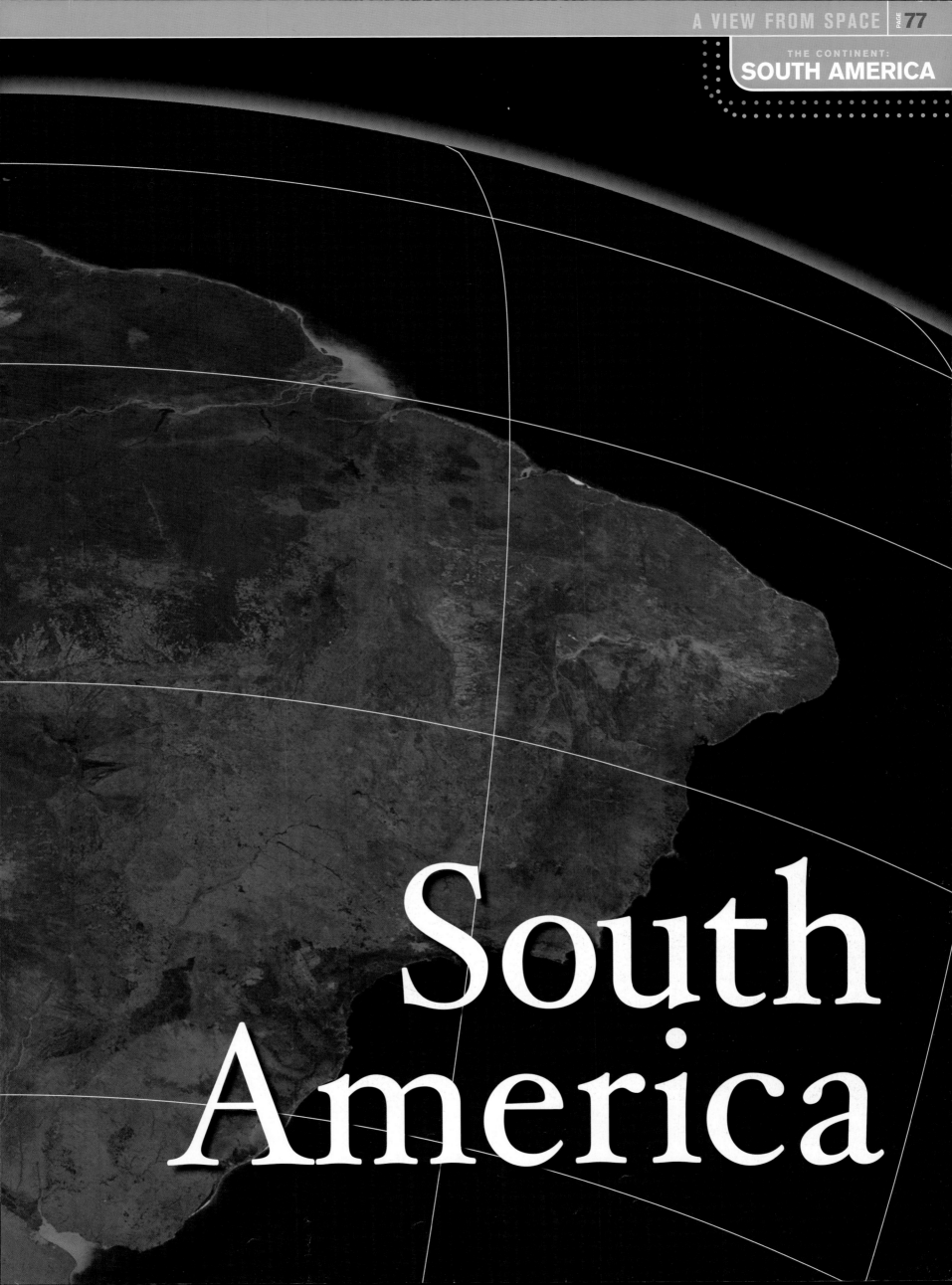

South America

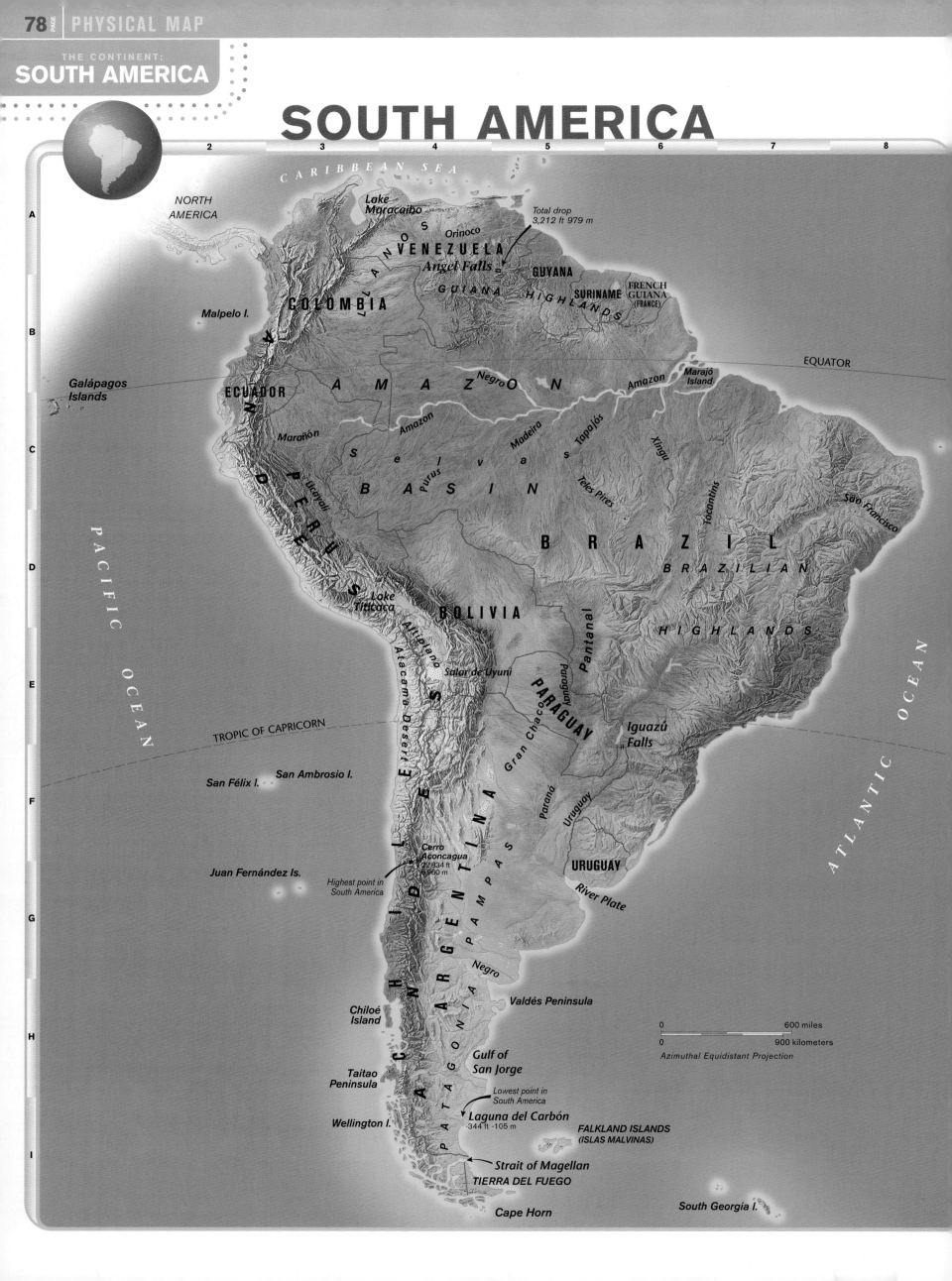

SOUTH AMERICA

2 3 4 5 6 7 8

A

B

C

D

E

F

G

H

I

CARIBBEAN SEA

NORTH
AMERICA

Lake
Maracaibo

Orinoco

L A N O S

Total drop
3,212 ft 979 m

VENEZUELA

Angel Falls

GUYANA

GUIANA HIGHLANDS

SURINAME

FRENCH
GUIANA
(FRANCE)

COLOMBIA

Malpelo I.

Galápagos
Islands

ECUADOR

A M A Z O N

Negro

Amazon

Marajó
Island

EQUATOR

Marañón

Amazon

Madeira

Tapajós

Xingu

São Francisco

S e l v a s

Purus

Teles Pires

Tocantins

B A S I N

Ucayali

PACIFIC

P E R U

Lake
Titicaca

BOLIVIA

B R A Z I L

BRAZILIAN

HIGHLANDS

Altiplano

Salar de Uyuni

Pantanal

Atacama Desert

PARAGUAY

Paraguay

Iguazú
Falls

OCEAN

TROPIC OF CAPRICORN

San Félix I.

San Ambrosio I.

Gran Chaco

Paraná

Uruguay

Juan Fernández Is.

Cerro
Aconcagua
22,834 ft
6,960 m

URUGUAY

River Plate

Highest point in
South America

A N D E S

A R G E N T I N A

PAMPAS

ATLANTIC OCEAN

Negro

Valdés Peninsula

Chiloé
Island

C H I L E

P A T A G O N I A

Gulf of
San Jorge

0   600 miles
0   900 kilometers

Azimuthal Equidistant Projection

Taitao
Peninsula

Lowest point in
South America

Laguna del Carbón
-344 ft -105 m

FALKLAND ISLANDS
(ISLAS MALVINAS)

Wellington I.

Strait of Magellan

TIERRA DEL FUEGO

Cape Horn

South Georgia I.

CARIBBEAN SEA

NORTH AMERICA

Santa Marta
Barranquilla
Cartagena
Maracaibo
Lake Maracaibo
Barquisimeto
Caracas
Valencia
Maracay
Ciudad Guayana
Cúcuta
Bucaramanga
San Cristóbal
Medellín
Manizales
Ibagué
Bogotá
COLOMBIA
Malpelo I.
(COLOMBIA)
Cali
Pasto
Esmeraldas
Quito
ECUADOR
Guayaquil
Cuenca
Iquitos
Piura
Chiclayo
Trujillo
Chimbote
Callao
Lima
Ayacucho
Cusco

VENEZUELA
Orinoco
ORINOCO
LLANOS
Angel Falls
GUIANA
GUYANA
Georgetown
Paramaribo
SURINAME
FRENCH GUIANA (FRANCE)
Cayenne
HIGHLANDS
Boundary claimed by Suriname
Boa Vista
Amapá
EQUATOR

Galápagos
Islands
(ECUADOR)

Negro
Amazon
AMAZON
Marajó Island
Belém
São Luís
Parnaíba
Manaus
Santarém
Marañón
Amazon (Solimões)
Selvas
Madeira
Tapajós
Marabá
Teresina
Fortaleza
BASIN
Purus
Xingu
Natal
João Pessoa
Campina Grande
Recife
Rio Branco
Porto Velho
Maceió
Aracaju
Teles pires
Tocantins
BRAZIL
BRAZILIAN
Feira de Santana
Machu Picchu
L. Titicaca
Trinidad
Salvador (Bahia)
Ilhéus
Arequipa
La Paz
BOLIVIA
Santa Cruz
Cochabamba
Brasília
Goiânia
HIGHLANDS
San Francisco
Arica
Oruro
Sucre
Altiplano
Salar de Uyuni
Uberlândia
Uberaba
Governador Valadares
Iquique
Tarija
Campo Grande
São José do Rio Preto
Ribeirão Preto
Belo Horizonte
PARAGUAY
Pantanal
Paraguay
ANDES
Londrina
Campinas
Nova Iguaçu
PACIFIC OCEAN
TROPIC OF CAPRICORN
Antofagasta
Salta
Gran Chaco
Asunción
Iguazú Falls
São Paulo
Santos
Rio de Janeiro
Curitiba
San Félix I.
San Ambrosio I.
(CHILE)
San Miguel de Tucumán
Resistencia
Corrientes
Paraná
Passo Fundo
Florianópolis
La Serena
Córdoba
Uruguaiana
Santa Maria
Porto Alegre
Cerro Aconcagua
22,834 ft
6,960 m
PAMPAS
Santa Fe
Uruguay
URUGUAY
Juan Fernández Is.
(CHILE)
Valparaíso
Santiago
Mendoza
Rosario
Buenos Aires
Montevideo
Talca
La Plata
River Plate
ATLANTIC OCEAN
Concepción
ARGENTINA
Mar del Plata
Temuco
Negro
Bahía Blanca
Puerto Montt
Viedma
Chiloé Island
PATAGONIA
Valdés Peninsula
Taitao Peninsula
Comodoro Rivadavia
Gulf of San Jorge
Wellington I.
Laguna del Carbón
-344 ft -105 m
Stanley
FALKLAND ISLANDS (ISLAS MALVINAS)
(UNITED KINGDOM)
Río Gallegos
Strait of Magellan
TIERRA DEL FUEGO
Punta Arenas
Ushuaia
Cape Horn
South Georgia I.
(U.K.)

0   600 miles
0   900 kilometers
Azimuthal Equidistant Projection

South America

A MIX OF OLD AND NEW

South America stretches from the warm waters of the Caribbean to the frigid ocean around Antarctica. Draining a third of the continent, the mighty Amazon carries more water than the world's next ten biggest rivers combined. Its basin contains the planet's largest rain forest. The Andes tower along the continent's western edge from Colombia to southern Chile. The Amerindian peoples who lived in the Andes were no match for the gold-seeking Spanish who arrived in 1532. They, along with the Portuguese, ruled most of the continent for almost 300 years. Centuries of ethnic blending have woven Amerindian, European, African, and Asian heritage into South America's rich cultural fabric.

⇧ SILENT STALKER. The jaguar is the largest member of the cat family native to the Americas. The largest populations of this at-risk species are found in the southern Amazon basin.

⇦ ROYAL CITY. Built by an Inca ruler between 1460 and 1470, Machu Picchu reveals the Inca's skill as stone masons. Massive blocks of granite were carved so carefully that all seams fit tightly without the use of mortar.

⇩ SOUTHERN METROPOLIS. A 1,300-foot (396-m)-high block of granite called Sugar Loaf dominates the harbor of Brazil's second largest city, Rio de Janeiro. Rio was Brazil's capital until 1960 and remains the country's most popular tourist destination.

⇦ NATURAL HERITAGE. Extending 2.5 miles (4 km) along the border between Brazil and Argentina, Iguazú Falls, which means "great water" in the local Guarani language, is clouded in mist as the water drops 269 feet (90 m) into the Iguazú River.

⇨ MOUNTAIN BUDDIES. An Aymara woman, with her llama, follows a traditional mountain lifestyle in the Andes of Peru.

more about
SOUTH AMERICA

⇧ STAPLE CROP. Corn, a food plant native to the Americas, is an important part of the diet of people throughout South America. Against a backdrop of Bolivia's Lake Titicaca, these men spread newly harvested corn to dry on a blanket. The dried corn will be stored for use throughout the year.

⇧ ICY COLD. Rising to an elevation of almost 11,000 feet (3,353 m), Fitzroy Massif in southern Argentina's Patagonia region presents major challenges to adventurous climbers who must contend with strong winds and bitter cold.

⇦ QUIET VIGIL. A young Pinare Indian sits beside a rushing stream in Venezuela, holding his traditional spear ready to catch a fish. Many groups of native people live in relative isolation from the modern world.

⇧ JUICY HARVEST. Grapes hang in heavy clusters ready for picking in a vineyard near Santiago, Chile. Second only to Italy, Chile produces almost one-quarter of the world's supply of fresh grapes. Grapes are Chile's leading fresh-fruit export.

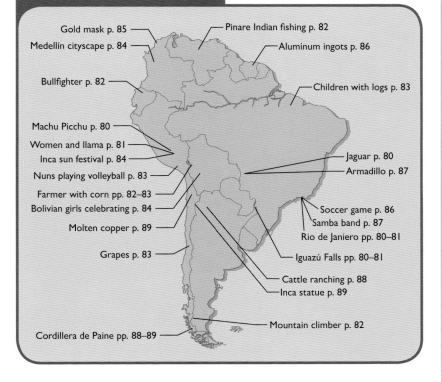

WHERE THE PICTURES ARE

Gold mask p. 85
Medellín cityscape p. 84
Pinare Indian fishing p. 82
Aluminum ingots p. 86
Bullfighter p. 82
Children with logs p. 83
Machu Picchu p. 80
Women and llama p. 81
Inca sun festival p. 84
Jaguar p. 80
Nuns playing volleyball p. 83
Armadillo p. 87
Farmer with corn pp. 82–83
Bolivian girls celebrating p. 84
Soccer game p. 86
Molten copper p. 89
Samba band p. 87
Rio de Janiero pp. 80–81
Grapes p. 83
Iguazú Falls pp. 80–81
Cattle ranching p. 88
Inca statue p. 89
Cordillera de Paine pp. 88–89
Mountain climber p. 82

⇧ ENVIRONMENTAL TRAGEDY. These giants of the rain forest dwarf two children in the Amazon village of Paragominas in Brazil. Harvesting such trees provides income for villagers but poses a serious long-term threat to the environment.

⇦ EL TORRO! Introduced to South America during the Spanish colonization, bullfighting is a popular sport and the focus of many festivals. Here, in Cayambe, Ecuador, a matador flashes his red cape before the bull.

⇩ BREAK TIME. Colonization of South America by Spain and Portugal in the 16th century brought a new religion—Roman Catholicism—to the region. Here, Catholic nuns in Arequipa, Peru, take a break from prayers to engage in a game of volleyball.

THE CONTINENT:
SOUTH AMERICA

THE BASICS

STATS

Largest country
Peru
496,224 sq mi (1,285,216 sq km)

Smallest country
Ecuador
109,483 sq mi (283,560 sq km)

Most populous country
Colombia
46,800,000

Least populous country
Bolivia
9,100,000

Predominant languages
Spanish, Amerindian languages and dialects, English

Predominant religion
Christianity (Roman Catholic)

Highest GDP per capita
Venezuela
$6,099

Lowest GDP per capita
Bolivia
$1,076

Highest life expectancy
Ecuador
74 years

Highest literacy rate
Colombia, Ecuador, Venezuela
93%

GEO WHIZ

On the llanos of Venezuela, capybaras, the world's largest rodents, are stalked and killed by anacondas, snakes weighing as much as 550 pounds (250 kg).

Some of the world's finest emeralds come from Colombia. Emeralds were sacred stones to the Inca, and some of the mines these ancient people worked are still a source of quality gemstones.

The world's only marine iguanas are among the unique animal species that live on the Galápagos, a volcanic chain of islands in the Pacific that belongs to Ecuador.

Bolivia's Madidi National Park is home to more plant and animal species than any other preserve in South America.

NORTHWESTERN SOUTH AMERICA

Like a huge letter "C," five countries crest the continent's northwest—Venezuela, Colombia, Ecuador, Peru, and Bolivia. Each has a seacoast except land-locked Bolivia. Dominated by the volcano-studded Andes range, the region contains huge rain forests in the upper Amazon and Orinoco River basins. Colombia and Venezuela share an extensive tropical grassland called Los Llanos. Though Spanish conquistador Pizarro defeated the Inca in the 16th century, Quechua, the Inca language, is still spoken by millions of Amerindians living in the altiplanos—high plateaus of the Andes. Rich oil resources are centered around Lake Maracaibo, in Venezuela. Many people in the region are poor, and drug wars have caused political instability, but recent democratic successes offer some hope for the future.

⇧ HAIL THE SUN. The ancient Inca celebrated the new year on June 24 in the festival of Inti Raymi. The tradition continues today in Cuzco, Peru, with the Festival of the Sun, when the celestial body is honored through music and dance.

⇩ FOLKLORE CENTER. Founded as a mining town, Oruro, Bolivia, is a UNESCO cultural heritage site. Each November a week-long festival celebrates traditional Andean culture with ancient dances, music, and rituals.

⇩ OLD MEETS NEW. Against a backdrop of skyscrapers, a modern urban train speeds past the old government palace in Medellín, Colombia. Known as a center of illegal drug trafficking, the city has worked hard to change its image, introducing economic and social changes that have improved safety.

← ANCIENT ARTISANS. Early cultures of Colombia left no great stone monuments, but they distinguished themselves with their fine gold work, which may have encouraged Europeans to search for El Dorado, the legendary City of Gold.

0   200 miles
0   300 kilometers
Azimuthal Equidistant Projection

CARIBBEAN SEA
Aruba (Neth.)
Bonaire (Neth.)
Curaçao (Neth.)
GRENADA

Santa Marta
Barranquilla
Cartagena
Gulf of Venezuela
gas
Maracaibo
L. Maracaibo
oil
Caracas
Cumaná
Puerto La Cruz
TRINIDAD & TOBAGO

Montería
gas
oil gas
oil
Mérida
Barquisimeto
Valencia

PANAMA
Cúcuta
San Cristóbal
+Pico Bolívar 16,427 ft 5,007 m
VENEZUELA
Ciudad Guayana
Ciudad Bolívar
oil

Bucaramanga

Medellín
Tunja
LLANOS

Pereira
Bogotá
COLOMBIA
Angel Falls Total drop 3,212 ft 979 m
Mt. Roraima + 9,094 ft 2,772 m
GUYANA

Cali
Ibagué
Neiva
San José del Guaviare
GUIANA HIGHLANDS

Popayán
Pasto
Florencia
Orinoco

EQUATOR

Cayambe
Quito
Portoviejo
ECUADOR
oil
Putumayo
AMAZON
Negro

Chimborazo 20,702 ft 6,310 m
Guayaquil
Cuenca
Machala
oil
Iquitos
Amazon (Solimões)

Talara
oil
Marañón
Ucayali
Amazon
BASIN

Piura
BRAZIL

Chiclayo
Cajamarca
Purus

Trujillo
Pucallpa
oil
Madeira

Chimbote
PERU
Nevado Huascarán 22,205 ft 6,768 m
Huánuco

Callao
Lima
Huancayo
Madre de Dios
Guaporé

Machu Picchu
Cusco
Ica
Apurímac
Mamoré

Lake Titicaca
Trinidad

Arequipa
La Paz (administrative capital)
BOLIVIA
Guaporé

ANDES
Altiplano
Cochabamba

Nevado Sajama 21,463 ft 6,542 m
Oruro
Santa Cruz

Sucre (constitutional capital)
Potosí
oil

Salar de Uyuni
Tarija
oil

CHILE
PARAGUAY
Pantanal

ARGENTINA

PACIFIC OCEAN

ATLANTIC OCEAN

Economy Symbols

- Cattle
- Fishing
- Bananas
- Corn
- Rice
- Sugarcane
- Potatoes
- Cacao
- Coffee
- Forest products
- Mining
- Oil
- Gas
- Manufacturing
- Tourism

INDIGENOUS PEOPLE

Bolivia	55%
Peru	45%
Ecuador	25%
Guyana	7%
Argentina	3%
Chile	3%
Suriname	2%
Brazil	0%
Colombia	0%
Paraguay	0%
Uruguay	0%
Venezuela	*

* Percentage unknown

Amerindians are concentrated largely in Andean countries. More than half of Bolivia's population is made up of these indigenous people.

NORTHEASTERN SOUTH AMERICA

THE BASICS

STATS

Largest country
Brazil
3,300,169 sq mi (8,547,403 sq km)

Smallest country
Suriname
63,037 sq mi (163,265 sq km)

Most populous country
Brazil
186,800,000

Least populous country
Suriname
500,000

Predominant languages
Portuguese, English, Dutch, Hindi

Predominant religions
Christianity (Roman Catholic, Protestant), Hindu, Islam

Highest GDP per capita
Brazil
$5,177

Lowest GDP per capita
Guyana
$1,095

Highest life expectancy
Brazil
71 years

Highest literacy rate
Guyana
99%

GEO WHIZ

Guyana has as many as 300 species of catfish, roughly a quarter of the total number living in South America. Locals hunt them and other fish for the international aquarium trade by probing hollow tree trunks submerged on river bottoms.

Paramaribo, Suriname's capital, is a melting pot of Dutch, Chinese, Hindu, East Indian, and Javanese cultures. Dutch is the only official language.

Brazil covers almost half of South America's land area. It is the world's largest Portuguese-speaking country and the largest Catholic country.

The Pantanal, the world's largest freshwater wetland, is almost ten times the size of the Florida Everglades. It is formed by the seasonal flooding of several rivers in southwestern Brazil.

⬆ GOAL! Maracana Stadium in Rio de Janeiro is packed with enthusiastic soccer fans. Brazil has a long history of producing world class soccer players and strong teams—winning the coveted World Cup five times.

Brazil dominates the region as well as the continent in size (it is the world's fifth largest country in area) and population (half of South America's 378 million people live here). Leading cities São Paulo and Rio de Janeiro are among the world's largest, and the country's vast agricultural lands make it a top global exporter of coffee, soybeans, beef, orange juice, and sugar. The vast Amazon rain forest, once a dense wilderness of unmatched biodiversity, is now threatened by farmers, loggers, and miners. To Brazil's north are lands colonized by the British, Dutch, and French— now sparsely settled Guyana, Suriname, and a French overseas department where the European Space Agency maintains its Spaceport, a launch site for explorations beyond Earth. Formerly known as the Guianas, these lands are populated by a mix of people with African, South Asian, and European heritage.

⬇ BAUXITE TO ALUMINUM. By exploiting rich deposits of bauxite, the ore from which aluminum is made, and inexpensive hydropower, the small country of Suriname produces aluminum ingots for export, such as these headed for global markets.

VAST WATERSHED

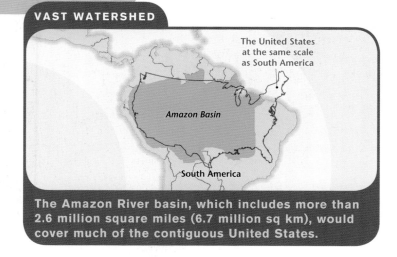

The United States at the same scale as South America

Amazon Basin

South America

The Amazon River basin, which includes more than 2.6 million square miles (6.7 million sq km), would cover much of the contiguous United States.

⇐ SIX-BANDED ARMADILLO, found throughout dry grassland areas of northeastern South America, lives on plants and
insects. Also known as the yellow armadillo, it is unlike others
of its species in that it remains active during the day.

Economy Symbols

- Cattle
- Fishing
- Bananas
- Citrus
- Corn
- Rice
- Sugarcane
- Cotton
- Coffee
- Tobacco
- Forest products
- Mining
- Manufacturing

0 — 400 miles
0 — 400 kilometers
Azimuthal Equidistant Projection

VENEZUELA

GUIANA HIGHLANDS

Georgetown

GUYANA

Paramaribo

SURINAME

Cayenne

FRENCH
GUIANA
(FRANCE)

COLOMBIA

Boa Vista

*Boundary claimed
by Suriname*

Macapá

EQUATOR

Pico da
Neblina
9,888 ft
3,014 m

rubber

rubber

Negro

A M A Z O N

Manaus

Amazon

Marajó
Island

Belém

São
Luís

Parnaíba

Santarém

Paragominas

Fortaleza

Putumayo

PERU

(Solimões)

Madeira

Tapajós

Marabá

Imperatriz

Teresina

S

Selvas

rubber

BASIN

Purus

rubber

Porto Velho

rubber

Xingu

Tocantins

Juazeiro

Natal

João Pessoa

Recife

Rio
Branco

Madre de
Dios

Teles Pires

Jurueña

B R A Z I L

Maceió

Aracaju

Feira de Santana

PERU

Guaporé

B R A Z I L I A N

São Francisco

Salvador (Bahia)

Mamoré

Cuiabá

Brasília

Vitória da Conquista

BOLIVIA

Lake
Titicaca

Pantanal

H I G H L A N D S

Goiânia

Uberlândia

Governador
Valadares

Campo
Grande

Ribeirão
Preto

Belo Horizonte

CHILE

São José do
Rio Preto

Juiz de Fora

Vitória

P A R A G U A Y

Paraguay

Londrina

São Paulo

São José dos Campos

Rio de Janeiro

TROPIC OF CAPRICORN

Paraná

Iguazú
Falls

Curitiba

Santos

Joinvile

ARGENTINA

Uruguay

Santa Maria

Porto Alegre

Patos
Lagoon

Pelotas

URUGUAY

ATLANTIC OCEAN

⇒ NATIONAL RHYTHM. Samba, often called Brazil's
national music, combines the music traditions of the
country's populations—Amerindian, Portuguese, and African.
Here a samba band practices on Rio de Janeiro's Ipanema Beach.

SOUTHERN SOUTH AMERICA

Four countries make up this region, which is sometimes called the Southern Cone because of its shape. Long north-south distances in Chile and Argentina result in varied environments. Chile's Atacama Desert in the north contrasts with much cooler, moister lands in the country's south where there are fjords and glaciers. Nine of ten Chileans live in Middle Chile, in and around booming Santiago. Similarly, most neighboring Argentinians live in the central Pampas region, where wheat and cattle flourish on the fertile plains. Farther south lie the arid, windswept plateaus of Patagonia. Landlocked Paraguay is small in comparison, less urbanized, and one of South America's poorest countries. Compact Uruguay is smaller still, but possesses a strong agricultural economy, including cattle and sheep-raising.

THE BASICS

STATS

Largest country
Argentina
1,073,518 sq mi (2,780,400 sq km)

Smallest country
Uruguay
68,037 sq mi (176,215 sq km)

Most populous country
Argentina
39,000,000

Least populous country
Uruguay
3,300,000

Predominant languages
Spanish, English, Italian, German, French

Predominant religion
Christianity (Roman Catholic, Protestant)

Highest GDP per capita
Chile
$8,570

Lowest GDP per capita
Paraguay
$1,460

Highest life expectancy
Chile
76 years

Highest literacy rate
Uruguay
98%

GEO WHIZ

Guanacos, a member of the camel family that is most numerous in the Patagonia region of Chile and Argentina, keeps enemies at bay by spitting at them.

The Itaipú Dam, which spans the Paraná River between Brazil and Paraguay, is currently the world's largest operating hydroelectric power plant.

Guaraní is the name of a people native to Paraguay, the country's basic unit of money, and one of its two official languages. Spanish is the other.

Argentinians eat 150 pounds (68 kg) of beef per person each year, making the country the world's largest per capita consumer of this meat.

Chile's Chuquicamata mine is among the largest open-pit copper mines.

⇨ COWBOYS OF THE PAMPAS.
Cattle are herded by gauchos, the Argentine term for cowboys. The country's extensive grass-covered plains support grain and cattle production on ranches called *estancias*.

⇨ FORBIDDING MOUNTAINS.
Rising to icy heights above Chile's narrow southern coast, the Cordillera de Paine lies about 1,500 miles (2,414 km) south of the capital, Santiago, in the Chilean part of Patagonia. The mountain is part of a national park that was made a world heritage site in 1978.

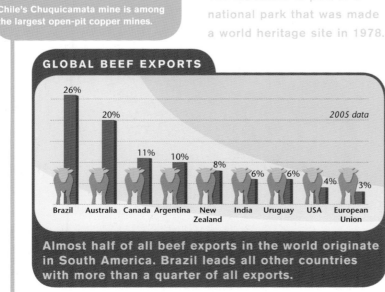

GLOBAL BEEF EXPORTS

2005 data

Brazil	26%	
Australia	20%	
Canada	11%	
Argentina	10%	
New Zealand	8%	
India	6%	
Uruguay	6%	
USA	4%	
European Union	3%	

Almost half of all beef exports in the world originate in South America. Brazil leads all other countries with more than a quarter of all exports.

⬅ INCA TREASURE. Near the frozen summit of Argentina's Cerro Llullaillaco, second highest active volcano in the world, archaeologists excavated Inca ruins and uncovered well-preserved mummies and 20 clothed statues, such as the one at left.

⬆ DESERT RICHES. Molten copper is poured into molds at a refinery near Chuquicamata, the world's largest copper deposit, located in northern Chile's Atacama Desert. Chile accounts for about 35 percent of the world's copper production.

PERU
BOLIVIA
BRAZIL

0   200 miles
0   300 kilometers
Azimuthal Equidistant Projection

Arica
Iquique
Puerto Esperanza
La Esmeralda
Concepción
Chuquicamata
oil
TROPIC OF CAPRICORN
Antofagasta
PARAGUAY
Salta
Asunción
Ciudad del Este
Iguazú Falls
San Miguel de Tucumán
Formosa
Villarrica
Paraná
Santiago del Estero
Resistencia
Corrientes
Posadas
Uruguay
La Serena
Santa Fe
Salto
Rivera
Patos Lagoon
San Juan
Córdoba
Paraná
Cerro Aconcagua 22,834 ft 6,960 m
Rosario
URUGUAY
Valparaíso
Mendoza
Buenos Aires
Santiago
oil   gas
ARGENTINA
Montevideo
Talca
San Justo
La Plata
River Plate
Concepción
Bahía Blanca
Mar del Plata
Temuco
Neuquén
oil   Colorado   Negro
gas
Puerto Montt
San Matías Gulf
Chiloé Island
Valdés Peninsula
Comodoro Rivadavia
oil
Gulf of San Jorge
gas
oil
Wellington I.
Laguna del Carbón -344 ft -105 m
FALKLAND ISLANDS (ISLAS MALVINAS) (U.K.)
Río Gallegos
oil   oil
gas   gas
Stanley
Strait of Magellan
Punta Arenas
gas
oil TIERRA DEL FUEGO
gas
Ushuaia
Cape Horn

PACIFIC OCEAN
ATLANTIC OCEAN
ANDES
Atacama Desert
Gran Chaco
PAMPAS
PATAGONIA

Economy Symbols

🐂 Cattle
🐑 Sheep
🐟 Fishing
🍓 Fruit
🌽 Corn
🌾 Rice
🌾 Other grains
Sugarcane
🌸 Cotton
🍷 Wine
Tobacco
🌲 Forest products
⛏ Mining
oil Oil
gas Gas
Manufacturing

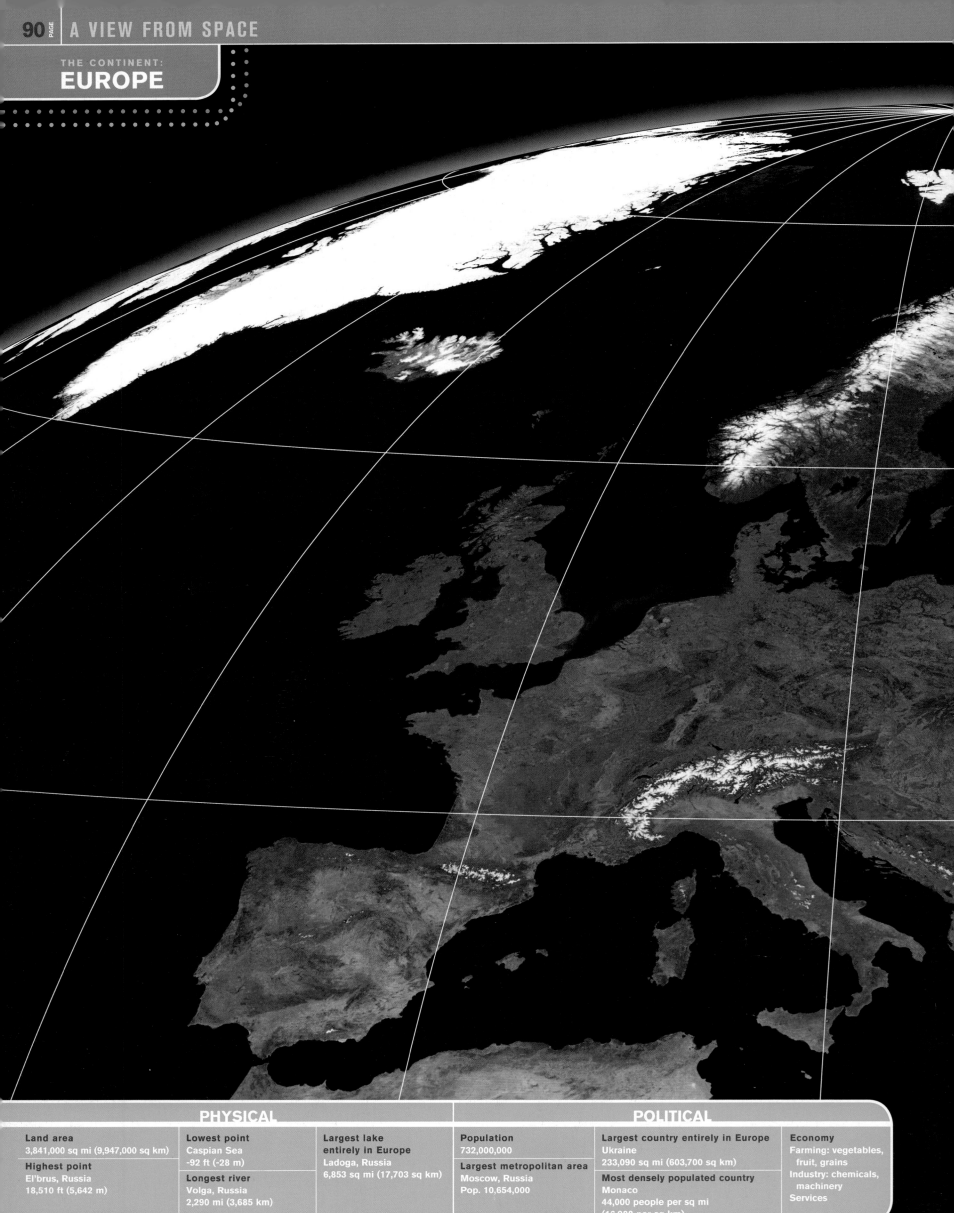

THE CONTINENT:
EUROPE

PHYSICAL

Land area
3,841,000 sq mi (9,947,000 sq km)

Highest point
El'brus, Russia
18,510 ft (5,642 m)

Lowest point
Caspian Sea
-92 ft (-28 m)

Longest river
Volga, Russia
2,290 mi (3,685 km)

**Largest lake
entirely in Europe**
Ladoga, Russia
6,853 sq mi (17,703 sq km)

POLITICAL

Population
732,000,000

Largest metropolitan area
Moscow, Russia
Pop. 10,654,000

Largest country entirely in Europe
Ukraine
233,090 sq mi (603,700 sq km)

Most densely populated country
Monaco
44,000 people per sq mi
(16,988 per sq km)

Economy
Farming: vegetables,
  fruit, grains
Industry: chemicals,
  machinery
Services

Europe

EUROPE

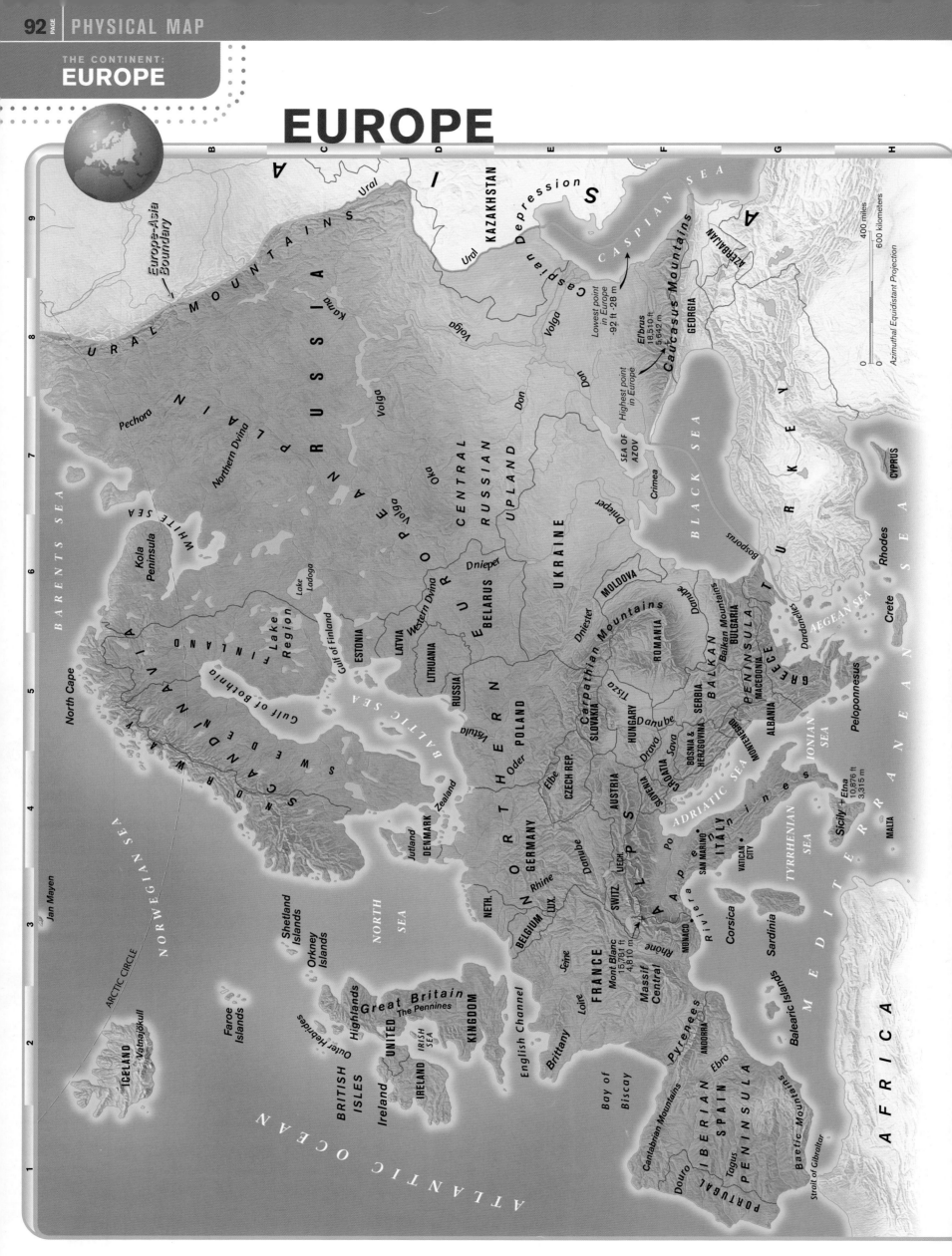

400 miles
600 kilometers
Azimuthal Equidistant Projection

KAZAKHSTAN

Ural Mountains

Europe-Asia Boundary

Caspian Depression

CASPIAN SEA

Caucasus Mountains

AZERBAIJAN

GEORGIA

Lowest point in Europe -92 ft -28 m

Elbrus 18,510 ft 5,642 m

Highest point in Europe

Ural

Kama

Pechora

Volga

Northern Dvina

RUSSIA

EAST EUROPEAN PLAIN

Volga

Oka

Don

Don

CENTRAL RUSSIAN UPLAND

SEA OF AZOV

Crimea

BLACK SEA

TURKEY

CYPRUS

BARENTS SEA

Kola Peninsula

WHITE SEA

Lake Ladoga

UKRAINE

Dnieper

Dnieper

Western Dvina

BELARUS

Rhodes

Crete

AEGEAN SEA

North Cape

SCANDINAVIA

Lake Region

FINLAND

Gulf of Finland

ESTONIA

LATVIA

LITHUANIA

RUSSIA

MOLDOVA

Dniester

Carpathian Mountains

Danube

ROMANIA

BULGARIA

Balkan Mountains

BALKAN PENINSULA

MACEDONIA

GREECE

Dardanelles

Bosporus

Peloponnesus

Gulf of Bothnia

SWEDEN

NORWAY

BALTIC SEA

Vistula

Oder

POLAND

Elbe

CZECH REP.

SLOVAKIA

HUNGARY

Tisza

Danube

Drava

Sava

CROATIA

SERBIA

BOSNIA & HERZEGOVINA

MONTENEGRO

ALBANIA

ADRIATIC SEA

IONIAN SEA

NORWEGIAN SEA

Jan Mayen

ARCTIC CIRCLE

ICELAND

Vatnajökull

Faroe Islands

Shetland Islands

Orkney Islands

Outer Hebrides

NORTH SEA

DENMARK

Jutland

Zealand

NETH.

GERMANY

BELGIUM

LUX.

Rhine

AUSTRIA

SLOVENIA

SWITZ.

LIECH.

ALPS

Po

Apennines

ITALY

SAN MARINO

VATICAN CITY

Corsica

Sardinia

TYRRHENIAN SEA

Sicily

Etna 10,876 ft 3,315 m

MALTA

MEDITERRANEAN SEA

BRITISH ISLES

Highlands

Great Britain

The Pennines

UNITED KINGDOM

Ireland

IRELAND

IRISH SEA

English Channel

Brittany

Seine

Loire

FRANCE

Mont Blanc 15,781 ft 4,810 m

Rhône

MONACO

Riviera

Massif Central

Bay of Biscay

Pyrenees

ANDORRA

Ebro

Cantabrian Mountains

IBERIAN PENINSULA

SPAIN

PORTUGAL

Douro

Tagus

Baetic Mountains

Strait of Gibraltar

Balearic Islands

ATLANTIC OCEAN

AFRICA

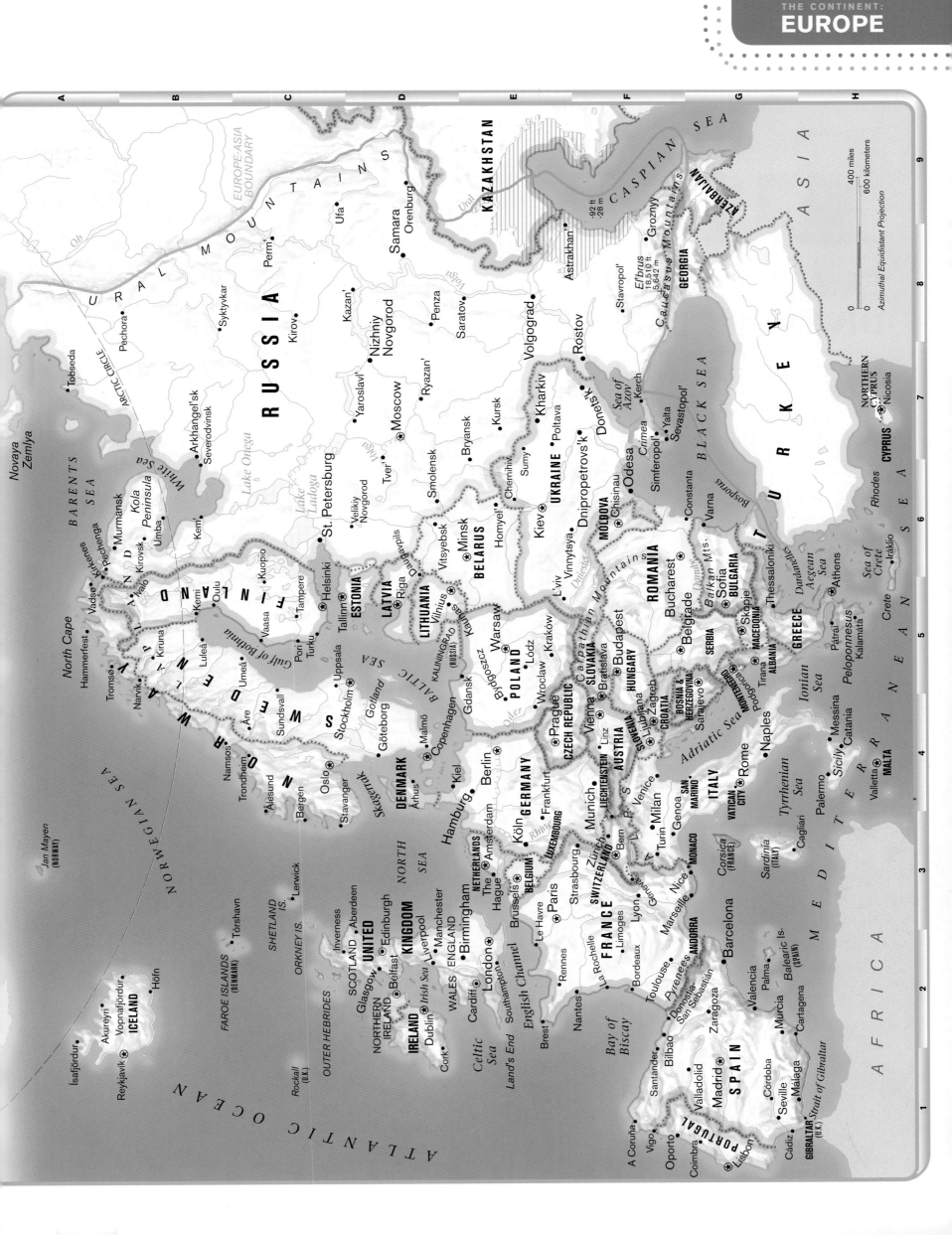

A B C D E F G H

KAZAKHSTAN

C A S P I A N   S E A

AZERBAIJAN

EUROPE-ASIA BOUNDARY

U R A L   M O U N T A I N S

Ob'

Tobseda

Pechora

Perm'

Ufa

Orenburg

Ural

Samara

-92 ft
-28 m

Astrakhan'

Grozny

El'brus
18,510 ft
5,642 m

GEORGIA

Caucasus Mountains

Syktyvkar

R U S S I A

Kirov

Kazan'

Nizhniy
Novgorod

Penza

Saratov

Volga

Volgograd

Stavropol'

ARCTIC CIRCLE

Pechenga

Arkhangel'sk

Severodvinsk

Lake Onega

Yaroslavl'

Moscow

Ryazan'

Rostov

Sea of
Azov

Kerch

T U R K E Y

*Novaya
Zemlya*

Tobseda

Kem'

Kirovsk

Umba

White Sea

*Lake
Ladoga*

St. Petersburg

Tver'

Smolensk

Bryansk

Kursk

Kharkiv

Donets'k

Crimea

Simferopol'

Sevastopol'

Yalta

B L A C K   S E A

Bosporus

NORTHERN
CYPRUS
Nicosia

B A R E N T S   S E A

Murmansk

Kola
Peninsula

Kandalaksha

Kuopio

Velikiy
Novgorod

Pskov

UKRAINE

L'viv

Vinnytsya

Dniester

Kiev

Dnipropetrovs'k

Sumy

Chernihiv

Poltava

Chisinau

MOLDOVA

Odesa

Constanta

Varna

Dardanelles

Aegean
Sea

CYPRUS

Rhodes

North Cape

Hammerfest

Vadsø

Kirkenes

Vardø

Ivalo

I C E L A N D

*Jan Mayen
(NORWAY)*

Tromsø

Narvik

Kiruna

Oulu

Tampere

Helsinki

Tallinn

ESTONIA

Riga

Daugavpils

Vitsyebsk

Minsk

Homyel'

BELARUS

LATVIA

LITHUANIA

Vilnius

Kaunas

KALININGRAD
(RUSSIA)

Warsaw

Balkan Mts.

ROMANIA

Bucharest

BULGARIA

Sofia

Skopje

Thessaloniki

MACEDONIA

GREECE

Athens

Pátrai

Peloponnesus

Kalamáta

*Ionian
Sea*

Crete

Iráklio

*Sea
of Crete*

N O R W E G I A N   S E A

Vaasa

Pori

Turku

Uppsala

Gulf of Bothnia

Are

Umeå

Luleå

Sundsvall

F I N L A N D

S W E D E N

B A L T I C   S E A

Gotland

Stockholm

Göteborg

Gdansk

Bydgoszcz

POLAND

Łódź

Kraków

Wrocław

Carpathian Mountains

Danube

SLOVAKIA

Bratislava

Budapest

HUNGARY

Belgrade

SERBIA

**BOSNIA &
HERZEGOVINA**

Sarajevo

Zagreb

CROATIA

SLOVENIA

Ljubljana

Tirana

ALBANIA

Podgorica

MONTENEGRO

Adriatic Sea

North Cape

Namsos

Trondheim

Ålesund

Bergen

Oslo

Stavanger

Skagerrak

Aarhus

DENMARK

Copenhagen

Malmö

Kiel

Berlin

Hamburg

GERMANY

Frankfurt

Köln

Prague

CZECH REPUBLIC

Vienna

Linz

AUSTRIA

Munich

LIECHTENSTEIN

Bern

SWITZERLAND

Zürich

Strasbourg

A L P S

Milan

Venice

Turin

Genoa

ITALY

Rome

**SAN
MARINO**

**VATICAN
CITY**

Naples

*Tyrrhenian
Sea*

Sicily

Messina

Catania

Palermo

Cagliari

Sardinia (ITALY)

Corsica (FRANCE)

MONACO

Nice

Marseille

Valletta

MALTA

M E D I T E R R A N E A N   S E A

Rhine

LUXEMBOURG

NETHERLANDS

The
Hague

Amsterdam

Brussels

BELGIUM

Lille

**FAROE ISLANDS
(DENMARK)**

Tórshavn

*SHETLAND
IS.*

Lerwick

ORKNEY IS.

Inverness

Aberdeen

SCOTLAND

Glasgow

Edinburgh

**UNITED
KINGDOM**

**NORTHERN
IRELAND**

Belfast

Dublin

IRELAND

Cork

Liverpool

Manchester

Birmingham

ENGLAND

WALES

Cardiff

London

Irish Sea

*Celtic
Sea*

*Rockall
(U.K.)*

OUTER HEBRIDES

N O R T H
S E A

Southampton

English Channel

Le Havre

Paris

Rennes

Brest

Nantes

La Rochelle

FRANCE

Limoges

Lyon

Bordeaux

Toulouse

Pyrenees

ANDORRA

Barcelona

SPAIN

Madrid

Valencia

Balearic Is. (SPAIN)

Palma

Murcia

Cartagena

Córdoba

Málaga

Seville

Granada

Cádiz

Strait of Gibraltar

GIBRALTAR (U.K.)

PORTUGAL

Lisbon

Coimbra

Oporto

Vigo

A Coruña

*Bay of
Biscay*

Santander

Bilbao

San Sebastián

Donostia

Zaragoza

Valladolid

A T L A N T I C   O C E A N

A F R I C A

A S I A

Ísafjörður

Akureyri

Reykjavík

Vopnafjörður

Höfn

400 miles
600 kilometers

Azimuthal Equidistant Projection

9
8
7
6
5
4
3
2
1

Europe
SMALL SPACES, DIVERSE PLACES

⇑ WIND POWER.
A traditional windmill stands silent in Spain, calling to mind scenes from the classic Spanish novel *Don Quixote*. Modern windmills are used to generate electricity and to pump water.

A cluster of islands and peninsulas jutting west from Asia, Europe is bordered by two oceans and more than a dozen seas, which are linked to inland areas by canals and navigable rivers such as the Rhine and Danube. The continent boasts a bounty of landscapes. Sweeping west from the Urals is the fertile Northern European Plain. Rugged uplands form part of Europe's western coast, while the Alps shield Mediterranean lands from frigid northern winds. Here, first Greek and then Roman civilizations laid Europe's cultural foundation. Its colonial powers built wealth from vast empires, while its inventors and thinkers revolutionized world industry, economy, and politics. Today, the 27-member European Union seeks to unite the continent's diversity.

⇩ CHEERY GREETINGS. Laughing children clown for the camera in Klaipeda, Lithuania. Klaipeda is the northernmost ice-free port on the eastern coast of the Baltic Sea.

⇐ ROCKY SENTINEL. Towering 14,693 feet (4,478 m) in elevation, the Matterhorn, on the border between Switzerland and Italy, is one of Europe's most famous mountains. Frequent avalanches on its steep slopes pose challenges for mountain climbers.

⇑ WATCHFUL GUARDIAN. A gargoyle stares out across the Paris skyline from a ledge of Notre Dame Cathedral. Gargoyles were first used in Gothic architecture as waterspouts but later were decorative additions meant to ward off evil spirits.

⇓ DAY'S END. The glow of sunset falls on buildings overlooking Strandvagen (Beach Street) in Stockholm, Sweden. This broad avenue has historic buildings, dating from the late 1800s, on one side and boat docks on the other.

more about
EUROPE

⇧ AGELESS TIME. The famous astronomical clock, built in 1410 in Prague, Czech Republic, has an astronomical dial on top of a calendar dial. Together they keep track of time as well as the movement of the sun, moon, and stars.

⇨ CLIFF DWELLERS. The town of Positano clings to the rocky hillside along Italy's Amalfi coast. In the mid-19th century, more than half the town's population emigrated, mainly to the United States. The economy today is based on tourism.

⇩ SEABIRDS OF THE NORTH. Colorful Atlantic puffins perch on a grass-covered cliff in Iceland, Europe's westernmost country. These unusual birds are skilled fishers but have difficulty becoming airborne and often crash upon landing.

⇧ CITY AT NIGHT. A winged victory statue atop the Metropolis Building, a classic example of early 20th-century architecture, appears to watch the evening traffic on the Gran Via in Madrid, Spain.

⇓ GLIMPSE OF THE PAST. Rome's Colosseum is a silent reminder of a once powerful empire that stretched from the British Isles to Persia (now Iran). The concrete, stone, and brick structure combined classic Greek and Roman architectural styles and could seat as many as 50,000 people.

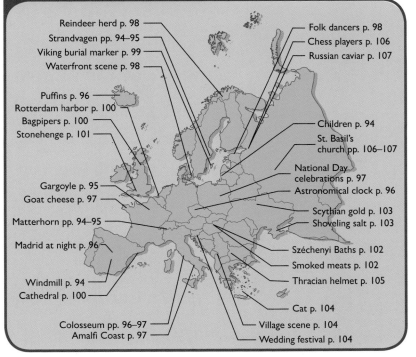

WHERE THE PICTURES ARE

Reindeer herd p. 98
Strandvagen pp. 94–95
Viking burial marker p. 99
Waterfront scene p. 98
Puffins p. 96
Rotterdam harbor p. 100
Bagpipers p. 100
Stonehenge p. 101
Gargoyle p. 95
Goat cheese p. 97
Matterhorn pp. 94–95
Madrid at night p. 96
Windmill p. 94
Cathedral p. 100
Colosseum pp. 96–97
Amalfi Coast p. 97

Folk dancers p. 98
Chess players p. 106
Russian caviar p. 107
Children p. 94
St. Basil's church pp. 106–107
National Day celebrations p. 97
Astronomical clock p. 96
Scythian gold p. 103
Shoveling salt p. 103
Széchenyi Baths p. 102
Smoked meats p. 102
Thracian helmet p. 105
Cat p. 104
Village scene p. 104
Wedding festival p. 104

⇐ LUNCHTIME! Varieties of creamy, fresh goat cheese are displayed in a market in the Brittany region of northern France.

⇓ NATIONAL PRIDE. Young women carry banners in a parade marking Poland's National Day. Celebrated each year on May 3, it is the anniversary of the 1997 proclamation of the Polish Constitution.

NORTHERN EUROPE

This entire region lies in latitudes similar to Canada's Hudson Bay, but the warm North Atlantic Drift current moderates temperatures in western parts of the region, from volcanically active Iceland to Denmark and Norway. The area's better farmlands lie in southern Sweden and the breezy lowlands of Denmark. Lightly populated but mostly urban, Northern Europe is home to slightly more than 30 million people. Sweden is the largest and most populous country. Forested, lake-dotted Finland shares a long border with Russia. Estonia, Latvia, and Lithuania—the so-called Baltic States—were republics of the Russian- dominated Soviet Union, which ceased to exist in 1991.

THE BASICS

STATS

Largest country
Sweden 173,732 sq mi (449,964 sq km)

Smallest country
Denmark 16,640 sq mi (43,098 sq km)

Most populous country
Sweden 9,100,000

Least populous country
Iceland 300,000

Predominant languages
Russian, Polish, Swedish, Finnish, Norwegian, Lithuanian, Latvian, Estonian, Icelandic

Predominant religion
Christianity (Lutheran, Roman Catholic, Orthodox)

Highest GDP per capita
Norway $71,674

Lowest GDP per capita
Latvia $8,349

Highest life expectancy
Iceland, Sweden 81 years

Highest literacy rate
Denmark, Estonia, Finland, Iceland, Latvia, Lithuania, Norway 100%

GEO WHIZ

Finland has more than 185,000 lakes. In fact, the southeastern part of the country is called the Lake Region.

The national symbol of Denmark is a statue of Hans Christian Andersen's Little Mermaid, in Copenhagen's harbor.

Vatnajokull, in Iceland, is the largest glacier in Europe.

According to Finnish folklore, Father and Mother Christmas live with their helpers on a mountain called Korvatunturi, in the country's Lapland region.

During Iceland's Thorrablot winter festival, locals celebrate by eating a Viking dish of rotten Greenland shark meat.

Legoland theme park, in Billund, Denmark, features miniature cities, models of famous landmarks such as the Taj Mahal, Statue of Liberty, Mount Rushmore, and more—all made from some 33 million Lego blocks.

⇨ COLORFUL TRADITION. Costumed folk dancers perform traditional dances at an open-air museum in Tallinn, Estonia.

⇧ NORDIC HERDERS. The Sami, indigenous people of northern Europe, herd their reindeer across the borders of Norway, Sweden, Finland, and Russia. Some use snowmobiles instead of horses.

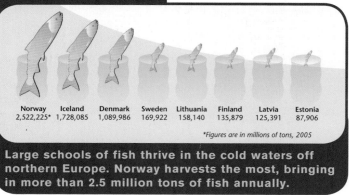

⇧ LINK TO THE PAST. Rainbow colored buildings line the canal in Nyhavn, Denmark. Dating back to the 12th century, it is part of Copenhagen's original harbor.

NORTHERN FISHERIES

Norway	Iceland	Denmark	Sweden	Lithuania	Finland	Latvia	Estonia
2,522,225*	1,728,085	1,089,986	169,922	158,140	135,879	125,391	87,906

*Figures are in millions of tons, 2005

Large schools of fish thrive in the cold waters off northern Europe. Norway harvests the most, bringing in more than 2.5 million tons of fish annually.

← MARKER FROM THE PAST. A stone memorial marks the burial site of Viking warriors in Sweden. Although their main activities were farming and trade, Vikings are better known for their ships and fierce raids on towns across Europe.

1 2 3 4 5 6 7 8

See map p. 93
ARCTIC CIRCLE
• Akureyri
ICELAND
Reykjavík
Vatnajökull
Kópavogur
Keflavík
0   200 miles
0   300 kilometers

SVALBARD (NORWAY)
See map p. 45
North East Land
Spitsbergen
• Longyearbyen
Edge Island
0   200 miles
0   300 kilometers

North Cape
BARENTS SEA

0   100 miles
0   150 kilometers
Azimuthal Equidistant Projection

• Hammerfest

reindeer

Economy Symbols

🐂 Cattle
🐖 Hogs
🐟 Fishing
🌾 Grain
🌱 Sugar beets
🌲 Forest products
⚒ Mining
🏭 Manufacturing

NORWEGIAN SEA

Tromsø •

LOFOTEN
VESTERÅLEN
Vestfjorden
• Bodø

ARCTIC CIRCLE

L A P L A N D

Kiruna •
Kebnekaise
6,926 ft
2,111 m

F I N L A N D

reindeer

• Rovaniemi

Kemi •
Luleå •
Skellefteå •

N O R R L A N D

Trondheim •
Trondheimsfjorden

Ångermanälven
Umeälven

Örnsköldsvik •
Östersund •
Umeå •

Oulu •
Oulu

R U S S I A

Ålesund •

Galdhøpiggen
8,100 ft
2,469 m

S W E D E N

Sundsvall •

Ljusnan

Vaasa •

Kuopio •
Joensuu •

Jyväskylä •
Mikkeli •

Lake Region

Gulf of Bothnia

Bergen •

Glåma

Falun •

Tampere •
Pori •

Lahti •
Lappeenranta •

Haugesund •
Drammen •
Oslo •

Klarälven

S v e a l a n d

Karlstad •
Örebro •

Uppsala •
Västerås •

Mälaren

Turku •
Helsinki •
Kotka •

ÅLAND IS.

Stavanger •
Skien •

Stockholm •

Hiiumaa

Gulf of Finland

Narva •

Vänern

Norrköping •

Tallinn •

Kristiansand •

Vättern

Linköping •

Saaremaa

Gulf of Riga

Pärnu •
Tartu •

ESTONIA

Lake Peipus

Skagerrak

Göteborg •
Borås •
Jönköping •

G ö t a l a n d

Visby •
Gotland

Riga •

Jelgava •
Daugavpils •

Western Dvina

Kattegat

Öland

Liepaja •

LATVIA

NORTH SEA

Århus •
JUTLAND
DENMARK
Esbjerg •
Odense •
Fyn

Copenhagen •
Helsingborg •

Zealand
Malmö •

Bornholm

Öland

B A L T I C   S E A

Siauliai •

Klaipeda •

LITHUANIA

KALININGRAD (RUSSIA)

Neman

Kaunas •
Vilnius •

BELARUS

GERMANY   POLAND

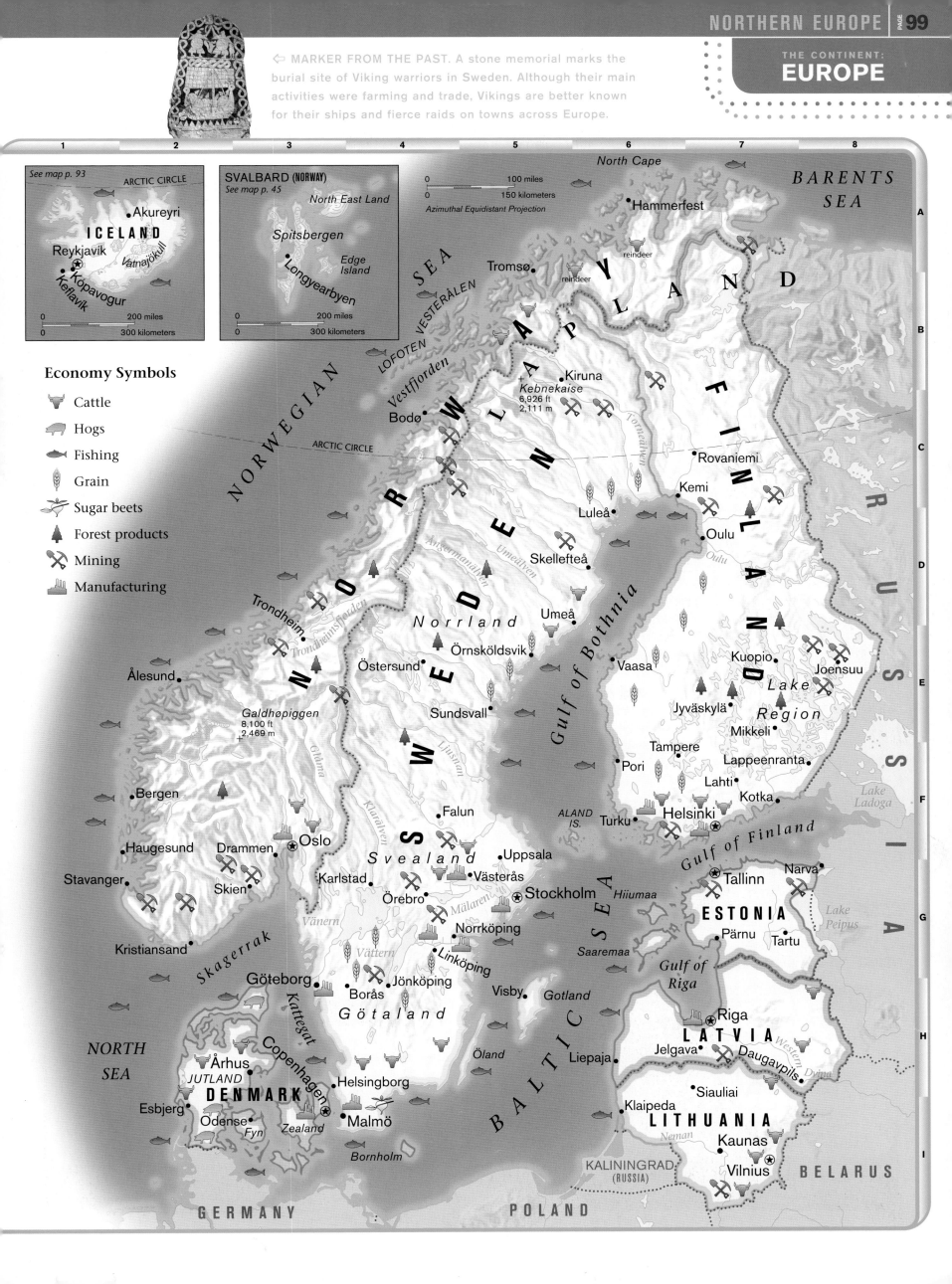

THE CONTINENT:
EUROPE

WESTERN EUROPE

Eighteen countries crowd this diverse region, which has enjoyed a central role in world affairs for centuries while suffering the results of devastating wars. The past half-century has seen bitter rivals become wiser allies, with today's European Union growing out of the need to rebuild economic and political stability after World War II. Fertile soil in the many river valleys, across the Northern European Plain, and on Mediterranean hillsides gives rise to abundant harvests of a wide variety of crops grown on rich farmland. France leads in agricultural production and area, while Germany is the most populous. These and other countries here face a population problem unlike most other regions: a decline in numbers.

THE BASICS

STATS

Largest country
France 210,026 sq mi (543,965 sq km)

Smallest country
Vatican City 0.2 sq mi (0.4 sq km)

Most populous country
Germany 82,400,000

Least populous country
Vatican City 798

Predominant languages
German, French, English, Italian, Spanish, Dutch, Portuguese

Predominant religion
Christianity (Roman Catholic, Protestant)

Highest GDP per capita
Liechtenstein $101,654

Lowest GDP per capita
Malta $13,802

Highest life expectancy
Andorra 84 years

Highest literacy rate
Andorra, Liechtenstein, Luxembourg, Vatican City
100%

GEO WHIZ

Fossil hunters discovered a new species of dinosaur in northern Spain in 2006. Measuring up to 120 feet (37 m) and weighing 48 tons (44 t), *Turiasaurus riodevemsis* is the largest dinosaur ever found in Europe.

The catacombs of Paris, which date from Roman times, contain the skeletons of some six million people, including some victims of the French Revolution.

Antwerp, Belgium, is the center of the world's diamond industry.

The ears on several rhinoceros images in France's Chauvet cave look so much like a certain fast-food chain's Golden Arches that researchers have nicknamed them McEars.

Portugal is the world's leading producer of cork.

Mount Etna, on Italy's island of Sicily, is known as the home of Zeus, ruler of all Greek gods. It is Europe's highest active volcano.

⇧ MONUMENT TO FAITH. The towering spires of La Sagrada Familia (The Holy Family) rise above Barcelona, Spain. This massive Roman Catholic church has been under construction for more than a century.

⇩ HIGHLAND TUNE. Bagpipers in formal dress parade through the streets of Edinburgh, Scotland. Bagpipes may have arrived with Roman invaders, but today they are most associated with the Scottish Highlands.

⇧ MODERN SPAN. Tall red arches support the Willem Bridge across the Maas River in Rotterdam, Netherlands. The Maas, which flows into the North Sea, is a major trade and transport artery, linking the Netherlands to the rest of Europe.

HOW BIG IS A COUNTRY?

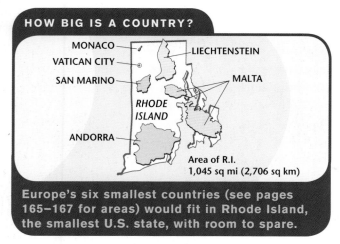

MONACO
VATICAN CITY
SAN MARINO
RHODE ISLAND
ANDORRA
LIECHTENSTEIN
MALTA

Area of R.I.
1,045 sq mi (2,706 sq km)

Europe's six smallest countries (see pages 165–167 for areas) would fit in Rhode Island, the smallest U.S. state, with room to spare.

⇐ CELTIC POWER. These rock pillars are part of Stonehenge, a puzzling arrangement of stones on the plains of southern England. Erected more than 5,000 years ago, Stonehenge is believed to be associated with sun worship.

Economy Symbols

Cattle	Vegetable oil
Sheep	Wine
Fishing	Forest products
Citrus	Mining
Other fruit	Coal
Corn	Oil
Other grains	Gas
Sugar beets	Manufacturing
Potatoes	Tourism

THE CONTINENT:
EUROPE

EASTERN EUROPE

1   2   3

THE BASICS

STATS

Largest country
Ukraine 233,090 sq mi (603,700 sq km)

Smallest country
Moldova 13,050 sq mi (33,800 sq km)

Most populous country
Ukraine 46,800,000

Least populous country
Moldova 4,000,000

Predominant languages
Ukrainian, Russian, Polish, Hungarian,
Czech, Belarussian, Slovak, Moldovan

Predominant religions
Christianity (Roman Catholic, Orthodox,
Protestant), Judaism, Islam

Highest GDP per capita
Czech Republic $13,654

Lowest GDP per capita
Moldova $927

Highest life expectancy
Czech Republic, Poland 75 years

Highest literacy rate
Czech Republic, Poland, Slovakia,
Belarus, Ukraine
100%

GEO WHIZ

The Wieliczka salt mine has been in
operation since the 13th century. Known
as the underground salt cathedral of
Poland, it features historical, religious,
and mythical figures, chambers, chapels,
and an exhibit about how salt is mined,
all carved in salt.

The Pinsk Marshes, one of Europe's
largest wetlands, covers thousands
of square miles in southern Belarus
and northwestern Ukraine. In 1970
the area was chosen as the site of
the Chornobyl' Nuclear Power Plant,
largely because few people lived there
and it had ready access to water. An
explosion closed the power plant in 1986,
and much of the area is still uninhabit-
able due to radioactive contaminants.

Budapest did not become a united city
until 1873. Until that time there were
two cities—Buda on the west bank
of the Danube and Pest on the east.
The first bridge between the cities
was built in the mid-1800s by Count
Istvan Széchenyi.

The so-called Velvet Revolution was
the non-violent uprising against the
communist government of
Czechoslovakia in 1989 that led to
the creation of two new countries: the
Czech Republic and Slovakia.

⇨ HEALING WATERS.
Budapest's Széchenyi Baths,
built in 1909–1913, are famous
for their medicinal thermal
waters, discovered in 1879.
A total of 15 baths, as well as
saunas and steam rooms, are
housed in buildings decorated
with sculptures and mosaics by
Hungary's leading artists.

⇧ TIME TO EAT. Smoked
sausages and bacon, ready
for purchase in the market,
are an important part of the
diet in the countries
of eastern Europe.

Eastern Europe stretches from the Baltic
Sea southeast to the Black Sea.
Before 1991, Ukraine, Belarus,
and Moldova were part of
the Soviet Union, with
the region's other
countries largely
under its control.
A small,
separated
segment of
Russia is
still nearby:
Kaliningrad. Much of the region has
a continental climate similar to that
of the U.S. Midwest. Nearly the size
of Texas, Ukraine is the region's largest country in both population and area.
Like Poland, it holds rich agricultural and
industrial resources. Warsaw is the region's
largest city, while the historic charms of
Prague and Budapest make them popular tourist stops. With the exceptions of Hungary and
Moldova, branches of Slavic language and ethnicity link
most people in these lands.

BALTIC SEA

Gdynia
Koszalin   Gdansk
Szczecin

Bydgoszcz   Vistula

Oder   Poznan

GERMANY   P O L A N

Kalisz

Legnica   Łódź

Liberec   Wrocław
                  Walbrzych

Prague   Opole

Pilsen   C Z E C H   Bytom

R E P U B L I C   Katowice

                  Ostrava   Kraków

Brno   C A R

Danube   S L O V A

                  oil

AUSTRIA   Bratislava

                  Gyor

                  Székesfehérvár   Tisza

SLOVENIA   Budapest   H U N G A

                  gas

                  Pécs   Szeged

CROATIA   Drava

                  SERBIA

                  Danube

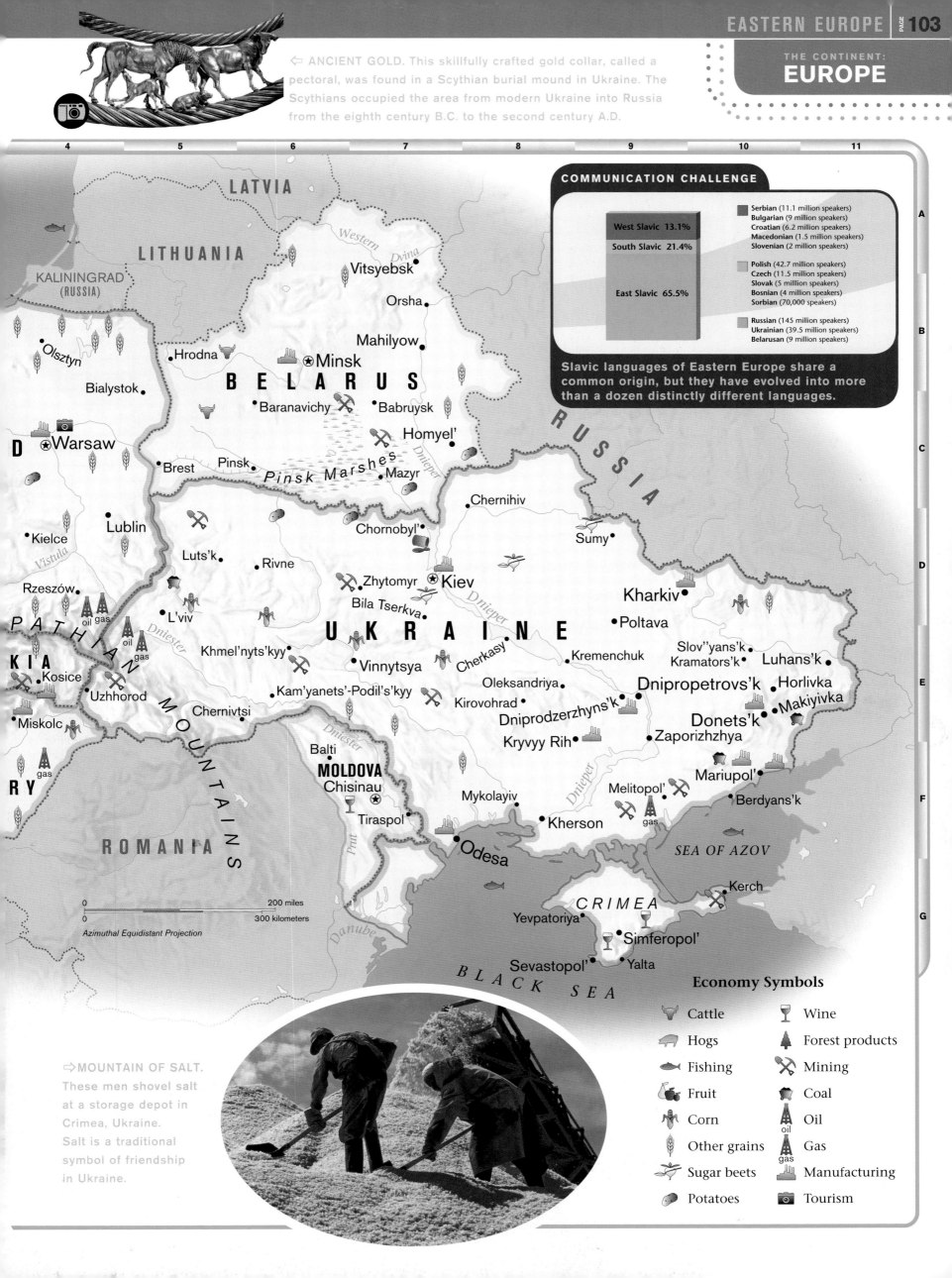

THE CONTINENT:
EUROPE

← ANCIENT GOLD. This skillfully crafted gold collar, called a pectoral, was found in a Scythian burial mound in Ukraine. The Scythians occupied the area from modern Ukraine into Russia from the eighth century B.C. to the second century A.D.

4   5   6   7   8   9   10   11

LATVIA

LITHUANIA

KALININGRAD (RUSSIA)

Western Dvina

Vitsyebsk

Orsha

Mahilyow

Olsztyn

Hrodna

★ Minsk

Bialystok

B E L A R U S

Baranavichy   Babruysk

Homyel'

Warsaw

Brest   Pinsk   *Pinsk Marshes*   Mazyr

Dnieper

Chernihiv

Lublin

Chornobyl'

Sumy

Kielce

Vistula

Luts'k   Rivne

Rzeszów

Zhytomyr   ★ Kiev

Kharkiv

Bila Tserkva

Poltava

oil gas

L'viv

U K R A I N E

oil

Dniester

Khmel'nyts'kyy

Cherkasy

Kremenchuk

Slov''yans'k

gas

Vinnytsya

Kramators'k   Luhans'k

KIA

Kosice

Kam'yanets'-Podil's'kyy

Oleksandriya

Dnipropetrovs'k   Horlivka

Uzhhorod

Kirovohrad

Dniprodzerzhyns'k   Makiyivka

Chernivtsi

Miskolc

Donets'k

Kryvyy Rih   Zaporizhzhya

gas

Balti

RY

Dniester

MOLDOVA

Melitopol'

Mariupol'

Chisinau

Mykolayiv

gas   Berdyans'k

Tiraspol

Kherson

R O M A N I A

Prut

Odesa

SEA OF AZOV

Kerch

200 miles

300 kilometers

Danube

C R I M E A

Azimuthal Equidistant Projection

Yevpatoriya

Simferopol'

Sevastopol'   Yalta

B L A C K   S E A

Economy Symbols

⇨ MOUNTAIN OF SALT. These men shovel salt at a storage depot in Crimea, Ukraine. Salt is a traditional symbol of friendship in Ukraine.

🐂 Cattle   🍷 Wine

🐖 Hogs   🌲 Forest products

🐟 Fishing   ⚒ Mining

🍎 Fruit   Coal

🌽 Corn   Oil (oil)

🌾 Other grains   Gas (gas)

🌱 Sugar beets   🏭 Manufacturing

🥔 Potatoes   📷 Tourism

COMMUNICATION CHALLENGE

West Slavic 13.1%	Serbian (11.1 million speakers)
	Bulgarian (9 million speakers)
South Slavic 21.4%	Croatian (6.2 million speakers)
	Macedonian (1.5 million speakers)
	Slovenian (2 million speakers)
	Polish (42.7 million speakers)
	Czech (11.5 million speakers)
	Slovak (5 million speakers)
East Slavic 65.5%	Bosnian (4 million speakers)
	Sorbian (70,000 speakers)
	Russian (145 million speakers)
	Ukrainian (39.5 million speakers)
	Belarusan (9 million speakers)

Slavic languages of Eastern Europe share a common origin, but they have evolved into more than a dozen distinctly different languages.

THE BASICS

STATS

Largest country
Romania 92,043 sq mi (238,391 sq km)

Smallest country
Cyprus 3,572 sq mi (9,251 sq km)

Most populous country
Romania 21,600,000

Least populous country
Cyprus 1,000,000

Predominant languages
Greek, Serbian, Croatian, Bulgarian, Albanian, Turkish, English

Predominant religions
Christianity (various Orthodox, Roman Catholic), Islam

Highest GDP per capita
Greece $21,925

Lowest GDP per capita
Bosnia and Herzegovina $2,568

Highest life expectancy
Greece 79 years

Highest literacy rate
Slovenia 100%

GEO WHIZ

Along the coast of Croatia there are huge fish farms where bluefin tuna are raised, making the country an important supplier of this highly edible, very popular fish.

The Dalmatian, a popular breed of dog, is named for its region of origin: Dalmatia, along the Adriatic coast of the Balkan peninsula.

Dracula tours abound in Romania, home of Vlad Dracula (also known as Vlad the Impaler), who ruled the region between the Danube and the Transylvanian Alps in the 15th century.

The famous Lipizzan horses of the Spanish Riding School in Vienna, Austria, trace their ancestry and their name back more than 400 years to a horse farm in Lipica, Slovenia.

Nicosia is the capital of both the independent Republic of Cyprus and the Rebublic of Northern Cyprus, which is under Turkish control.

BALKANS & CYPRUS

The Balkans—named for a Bulgarian mountain range—make up a rugged land with a rough history. Ethnic and religious conflict have long troubled the area. Since 1991, six new countries have emerged from the breakup of Yugoslavia (see inset on page 105). Kosovo may be next. The storied Danube River winds east across the Balkans, separating Bulgaria and Romania, the region's largest country in both area and population. Rimmed by four seas—the Black, Aegean, Ionian, and Adriatic—the Balkans, particularly Greece, have a long maritime history. With more than three million people, Greece's capital, Athens, is the largest city in the region. In 2004, Cyprus, which has been uneasily divided for three decades into Turkish and Greek sections, joined Greece as a member of the European Union.

⇧ TRADITIONAL LIFE. Villagers walk down a cobbled street in Gusinje, a rural town in northeastern Montenegro. A place of rugged mountains, Montenegro is one of the countries that emerged from the former Yugoslavia.

⇩ LAZY DAYS. A cat stretches out along a whitewashed wall on the Greek island of Thira. The blue dome in the background is part of a Greek Orthodox church.

⇧ JOYFUL SOUNDS. Young boys playing traditional instruments participate in a wedding festival in Crnomelj, Slovenia. Engaged couples, dancers, and musicians celebrate for four days. Then couples take their vows in a mass ceremony—an old Slovene wedding custom. Slovenia sponsors these festivals to preserve tradition in a fast changing world.

← ANCIENT WARRIORS. Soldiers and horsemen from Thrace, an ancient territory in present-day Bulgaria and Greece, wore masks as they rode into battle. Often serving as paid fighters in other armies, the Thracians were allies of Troy in Homer's *Iliad*.

SLOVAKIA

UKRAINE

HUNGARY

AUSTRIA

MOLDOVA

CARPATHIAN MTS.

• Satu Mare
• Baia Mare
• Botosani
Iasi •

• Oradea
Cluj-Napoca •
gas
• Târgu-Mures
oil

TRANSYLVANIA

ROMANIA

Maribor •
SLOVENIA
Ljubljana •
Sava
• Zagreb oil
CROATIA
Subotica •
Tisza
Danube
• Arad
• Timisoara
Sibiu •
• Brasov
Transylvanian Alps
oil
Galati •
Braila •

Gulf of Venice
• Rijeka
Drava
Osijek •
Novi Sad
• Resita
• Ploiesti
• Tulcea

D I N A R
• Banja Luka
Sava
oil
• Bucharest
Constanta •

Zadar •
BOSNIA AND
Zenica •
gas
SERBIA
Belgrade
Iron Gate Dam
oil
• Craiova
• Ruse

HERZEGOVINA
Sarajevo •
• Kragujevac
Danube
oil

Split •
• Mostar
• Pleven
• Varna

A D R I A T I C   S E A
D A L M A T I A
• Nis
BALKAN MOUNTAINS
oil

Dubrovnik •
MONTENEGRO
• Pec
KOSOVO
• Pristina
Sofia •
BULGARIA
• Sliven
• Burgas

ITALY
Podgorica •
Shkodër •
B A L K A N
• Stara Zagora

Tetovo •
Skopje •
RHODOPE MTS.
• Plovdiv

Tirana •
MACEDONIA
P E N I N S U L A

Durrës •
oil
• Bitola

Elbasan •
Kavála •
olive
Bosporus

ALBANIA
• Thessaloníki
oil
Sea of Marmara

Vlorë •
Olympus
9,570 ft
2,917 m

Economy Symbols

Limnos
TURKEY

🐂 Cattle
🍷 Wine
Dardanelles

🐑 Sheep
Tobacco
A E G E A N   S E A

🐟 Fishing
⛏ Mining
• Lárissa
Lesbos (Mitilíni)

Citrus
Coal
Chios

Other fruit
Oil oil
Corfu
I O N I A N   I S L A N D S

Corn
Gas gas
GREECE
Sámos

Other grains
Manufacturing
Ikaría

Sugar beets
📷 Tourism
I O N I A N   S E A
• Pátrai
• Athens
Náxos
DODECANESE

Vegetable oil
olive
Olympia
• Corinth
PELOPONNÉSUS
CYCLADES

• Sparta
Gulf of Messinia
Rhodes •
Rhodes

olive
Thíra (Santoríni)

M E D I T E R R A N E A N
SEA OF CRETE

olive
Iráklio •
Crete
olive

0   100 miles
0   100 kilometers
Azimuthal Equidistant Projection

B L A C K   S E A

Strait of Otranto

See map p.93 for position

NORTHERN CYPRUS
(recognized only by Turkey)

CYPRUS
Nicosia •

Same Scale as Main Map

REGION IN TURMOIL

AUSTRIA
HUNGARY
Former Yugoslavia Border (1991)
SLOVENIA
CROATIA
ROMANIA
BOSNIA AND HERZEGOVINA
SERBIA
Adriatic Sea
ITALY
BULGARIA
MONTENEGRO
ALBANIA
MACEDONIA
GREECE
TURKEY

Political and social change brought an end to the southern Slavic country of Yugoslavia. Six new countries emerged, but peace has been fragile.

THE CONTINENT:
EUROPE

EUROPEAN RUSSIA

THE BASICS

STATS*

Area	
6,592,850 sq mi (17,075,400 sq km)	
Population	
142,300,000	
Predominant languages	
Russian, minority languages	
Predominant religions	
Christianity (Russian Orthodox), Islam	
GDP per capita	
$6,861	
Life expectancy	
66 years	
Literacy rate	
100%	

*Note: These figures are for all of Russia. For Asian Russia, see pages 116–117.

GEO WHIZ

St. Petersburg's many canals and hundreds of bridges have earned it the nickname Venice of the North.

The fertile Northern European Plain, which stretches west from the Urals, is home to most of Russia's population and industry, while most of its mineral resources lie east of the Urals in the Asian portion of the country.

Two of the world's most famous ballet companies are in Russia: the Kirov in St. Petersburg and the Bolshoi in Moscow.

Arkhangel'sk, founded in 1584, is Russia's oldest Arctic port. The rich timber resources that surround it and make up the bulk of its exports have been nicknamed "green gold."

The official residence of the President of Russia is inside a walled fortress known as the Kremlin in downtown Moscow. The site on which the Kremlin stands has been continuously occupied since 2000 B.C.

During the Soviet era (1920–1991), the city Nizhniy Novgorod was named Gorky after author Maxim Gorky. "Gorky" is a Russian word meaning "bitter."

Soviet dictator Josef Stalin used the GUM department store, located on Moscow's Red Square, to display propaganda posters and the body of his wife, who committed suicide in 1932.

⇧ **CHECKMATE!** Bystanders watch intently as one player prepares to make his move in this chess game in a park in St. Petersburg. In Russia, chess is a national pastime, popular with people from all walks of life.

Home to four-fifths of Russia's 142 million people, European Russia contains most of the world's largest country's agriculture and industry. Here also is Moscow, its capital and Europe's largest city. Far to the north, Murmansk provides a year-round seaport—a gift of the warming currents of the North Atlantic Drift. This large, funnel-shaped portion of Russia, which spans 1,600 miles (2,575 km) from the icy Arctic to the imposing Caucasus Mountains, is home to the Volga, Europe's longest river, and Mount El'brus (18,510 ft/5,642 m), its highest peak. The Caucasus together with the mineral-rich Urals form a natural boundary between Europe and Asia. Although parts of Azerbaijan and Georgia in the south and Kazakhstan in the east span the continental boundary, only Russia is counted as part of Europe. To read about Asian Russia, see pages 116–117.

EUROPE'S GREAT RIVERS

Volga	3,685 km (2,290 mi)
Danube	2,888 km (1,795 mi)
Dnieper	2,290 km (1,423 mi)
Rhine	1,320 km (820 mi)
Elbe	1,091 km (678 mi)
Vistula	1,047 km (651 mi)
Tagus	1,038 km (645 mi)
Loire	1,012 km (629 mi)
Rhône	800 km (497 mi)
Po	652 km (405 mi)

Europe's rivers, many linked by canals, form a transportation network that connects its people and places to each other and the world beyond.

⇨ **CATHEDRAL ON THE SQUARE.** The onion-dome-topped towers of St. Basil's are a key landmark on Moscow's Red Square. Built between 1555 and 1561 to commemorate successful military campaigns by Ivan the Terrible, the building is rich in Christian symbolism.

◁ RUSSIAN DELICACY. Caviar, a distinctly Russian luxury food item, is the eggs (called roe) of sturgeon fish caught in the Caspian Sea. The eggs are aged in a salty brine before being packaged in cans (left) for shipment around the world.

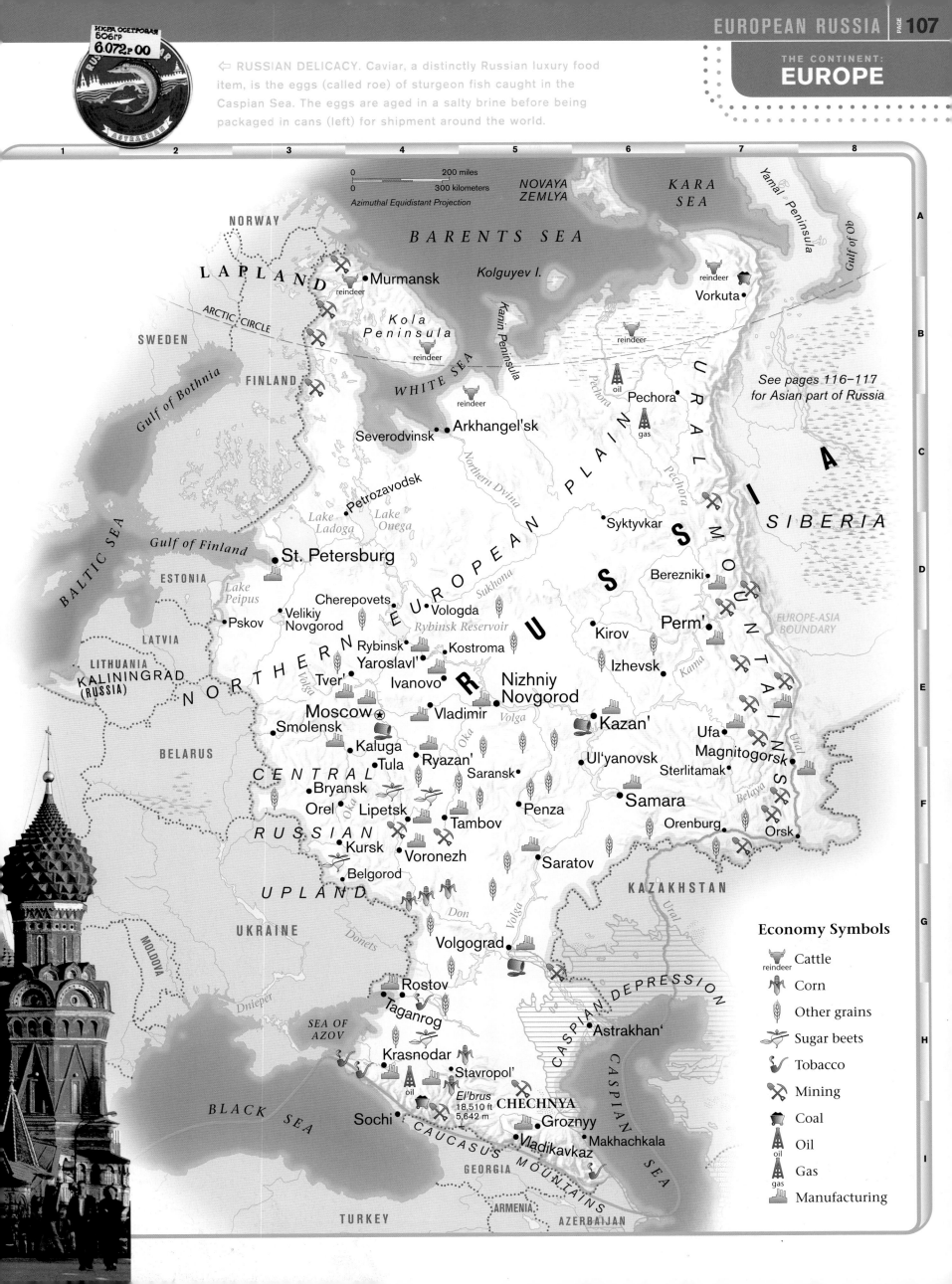

1 2 3 4 5 6 7 8

0 ——— 200 miles
0 ——— 300 kilometers
Azimuthal Equidistant Projection

NORWAY

BARENTS SEA

NOVAYA ZEMLYA

KARA SEA

Yamal Peninsula

Gulf of Ob

LAPLAND

Murmansk

Kolguyev I.

reindeer

Vorkuta

ARCTIC CIRCLE

SWEDEN

Kola Peninsula

reindeer

Kanin Peninsula

reindeer

oil

Pechora

Pechora

See pages 116–117
for Asian part of Russia

FINLAND

Gulf of Bothnia

WHITE SEA

reindeer

Arkhangel'sk

gas

U R A L

Northern Dvina

Severodvinsk

SIBERIA

M O U N T A I N S

Petrozavodsk

Syktyvkar

Lake Ladoga

Lake Onega

R U S S I A

Berezniki

EUROPE-ASIA BOUNDARY

Gulf of Finland

St. Petersburg

Sukhona

Perm'

ESTONIA

Lake Peipus

Cherepovets

Vologda

Rybinsk Reservoir

Kirov

Kama

Velikiy Novgorod

Izhevsk

Pskov

Rybinsk

Kostroma

LATVIA

Yaroslavl'

Volga

Nizhniy Novgorod

LITHUANIA

Tver'

Ivanovo

KALININGRAD (RUSSIA)

Moscow

Vladimir

Volga

Kazan'

Ufa

Smolensk

Oka

Magnitogorsk

Kaluga

Ul'yanovsk

Sterlitamak

BELARUS

Tula

Ryazan'

Belaya

C E N T R A L

Saransk

Samara

Bryansk

Penza

Orel

Lipetsk

Orenburg

Oka

Tambov

Orsk

R U S S I A N

Kursk

Voronezh

Saratov

Belgorod

Don

KAZAKHSTAN

U P L A N D

Volga

Ural

UKRAINE

Donets

KAZAKHSTAN

MOLDOVA

Dnieper

Volgograd

CASPIAN DEPRESSION

Rostov

Taganrog

SEA OF AZOV

Astrakhan'

Krasnodar

CASPIAN SEA

oil

Stavropol'

El'brus 18,510 ft 5,642 m

CHECHNYA

BLACK SEA

Sochi

Groznyy

Makhachkala

CAUCASUS MOUNTAINS

Vladikavkaz

GEORGIA

TURKEY

ARMENIA

AZERBAIJAN

Economy Symbols

Symbol	
reindeer	Cattle
	Corn
	Other grains
	Sugar beets
	Tobacco
	Mining
	Coal
oil	Oil
gas	Gas
	Manufacturing

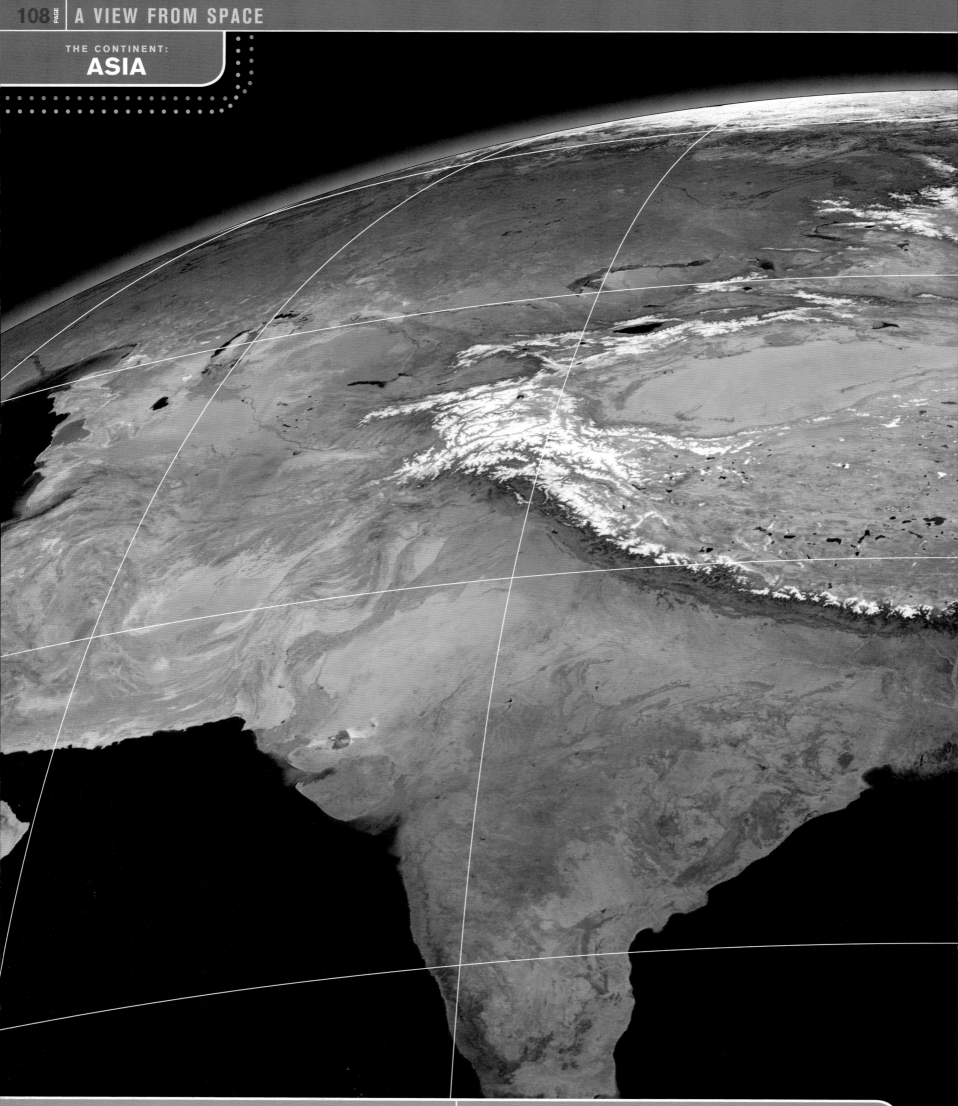

THE CONTINENT:
ASIA

PHYSICAL

Land area
17,208,000 sq mi
(44,570,000 sq km)

Highest point
Mount Everest, China-Nepal
29,035 ft (8,850 m)

Lowest point
Dead Sea, Israel-Jordan
-1,365 ft (-416 m)

Longest river
Yangtze (Chang), China
3,964 mi (6,380 km)

Largest lake entirely in Asia
Lake Baikal
12,200 sq mi (31,500 sq km)

POLITICAL

Population
3,968,000,000

Largest metropolitan area
Tokyo, Japan
Pop. 35,197,000

Largest country entirely in Asia
China 3,705,405 sq mi (9,596,960 sq km)

Most densely populated country
Singapore
18,652 people per sq mi (7,202 per sq km)

Economy
Farming: rice,
wheat
Industry: petroleum,
electronics
Services

Asia

ASIA

ATLANTIC OCEAN

ARCTIC OCEAN

PACIFIC OCEAN

BERING SEA

Bering Strait

Chukchi Peninsula

Kamchatka Peninsula

Commander Islands

Aleutian Islands

NORTH AMERICA

CHUKCHI SEA

Wrangel Island

EAST SIBERIAN SEA

New Siberian Islands

LAPTEV SEA

Taymyr Peninsula

North Land

KARA SEA

Gulf of Ob

ARCTIC CIRCLE

Kolyma Range

Chersky Range

Kolyma

Verkhoyansk Range

Aldan

Lena

SEA OF OKHOTSK

Sakhalin

Sikhote Alin Range

Amur

Yablonovy Range

Lake Baikal

Angara

Ural

Yenisey

SIBERIA

CENTRAL SIBERIAN PLATEAU

WEST SIBERIAN PLAIN

Ob

R U S S I A

BARENTS SEA

BALTIC SEA

RUSSIA

EUROPE

Europe-Asia Boundary

URAL MOUNTAINS

Volga

Ural

Aral Sea

THE STEPPES

KAZAKHSTAN

Lake Balkhash

Syr Darya

UZBEKISTAN

Amu Darya

TURKMENISTAN

Caspian Depression

Caspian Sea

BLACK SEA

Caucasus Mts.

GEORGIA

AZERBAIJAN

ARMENIA

Elburz Mountains

Zagros Mountains

IRAN

Tigris

Euphrates

Mesopotamia

Syrian Desert

SYRIA

Jordan

LEBANON

ISRAEL

Dead Sea
-1,365 ft
-416 m
World's lowest point

Sinai

Suez Canal

Mediterranean Sea

Aegean Sea

TURKEY

ANATOLIA

CYPRUS

RED SEA

SAUDI ARABIA

ARABIAN PENINSULA

Rub al Khali

YEMEN

Gulf of Aden

AFRICA

QATAR

BAHRAIN

KUWAIT

Persian Gulf

UNITED ARAB EMIRATES

OMAN

Gulf of Oman

ARABIAN SEA

MALDIVES

INDIAN OCEAN

EQUATOR

AFGHANISTAN

Hindu Kush

PAKISTAN

Indus

Great Indian Desert

Mt. Everest
29,035 ft
8,850 m
World's highest point

NEPAL

BHUTAN

BANGLADESH

Ganges

Brahmaputra

H I M A L A Y A

PLATEAU OF TIBET

KUNLUN MOUNTAINS

Qaidam Basin

TARIM BASIN

Taklimakan Desert

TIEN-SHAN

KYRGYZSTAN

TAJIKISTAN

ALTAY MOUNTAINS

MONGOLIA

Irtysh

Ob

GOBI

Greater Khingan Range

Manchurian Plain

Amur

North China Plain

Yellow

Yellow

C H I N A

Yangtze

Sichuan Basin

Gongga Shan
24,790 ft
7,556 m

Mekong

Salween

Mekong

Yangtze

I N D I A

DECCAN PLATEAU

Eastern Ghats

Western Ghats

BAY OF BENGAL

SRI LANKA

LACCADIVE SEA

Andaman Islands

Nicobar Islands

ANDAMAN SEA

MYANMAR (BURMA)

Irrawaddy

Salween

LAOS

THAILAND

CAMBODIA

VIETNAM

Gulf of Thailand

MALAY PENINSULA

MALAYSIA

SINGAPORE

Sumatra

Java

GREATER SUNDA ISLANDS

Borneo

BRUNEI

Hainan

SOUTH CHINA SEA

PHILIPPINES

PHILIPPINE ISLANDS

Luzon

Mindanao

SULU SEA

CELEBES SEA

Celebes

MOLUCCAS

I N D O N E S I A

Java Sea

LESSER SUNDA ISLANDS

Flores Sea

BANDA SEA

Timor

EAST TIMOR (TIMOR-LESTE)

TIMOR SEA

ARAFURA SEA

NEW GUINEA

AUSTRALIA

EAST CHINA SEA

YELLOW SEA

NORTH KOREA

SOUTH KOREA

SEA OF JAPAN (EAST SEA)

J A P A N

Hokkaido

Honshu

Shikoku

Kyushu

Ryukyu Islands

Taiwan

PHILIPPINE SEA

TROPIC OF CANCER

Nampo Shoto

Mariana Islands

CAROLINE ISLANDS

EQUATOR

Kuril Islands

0   1,000 miles

0   1,500 kilometers

Two-Point Equidistant Projection

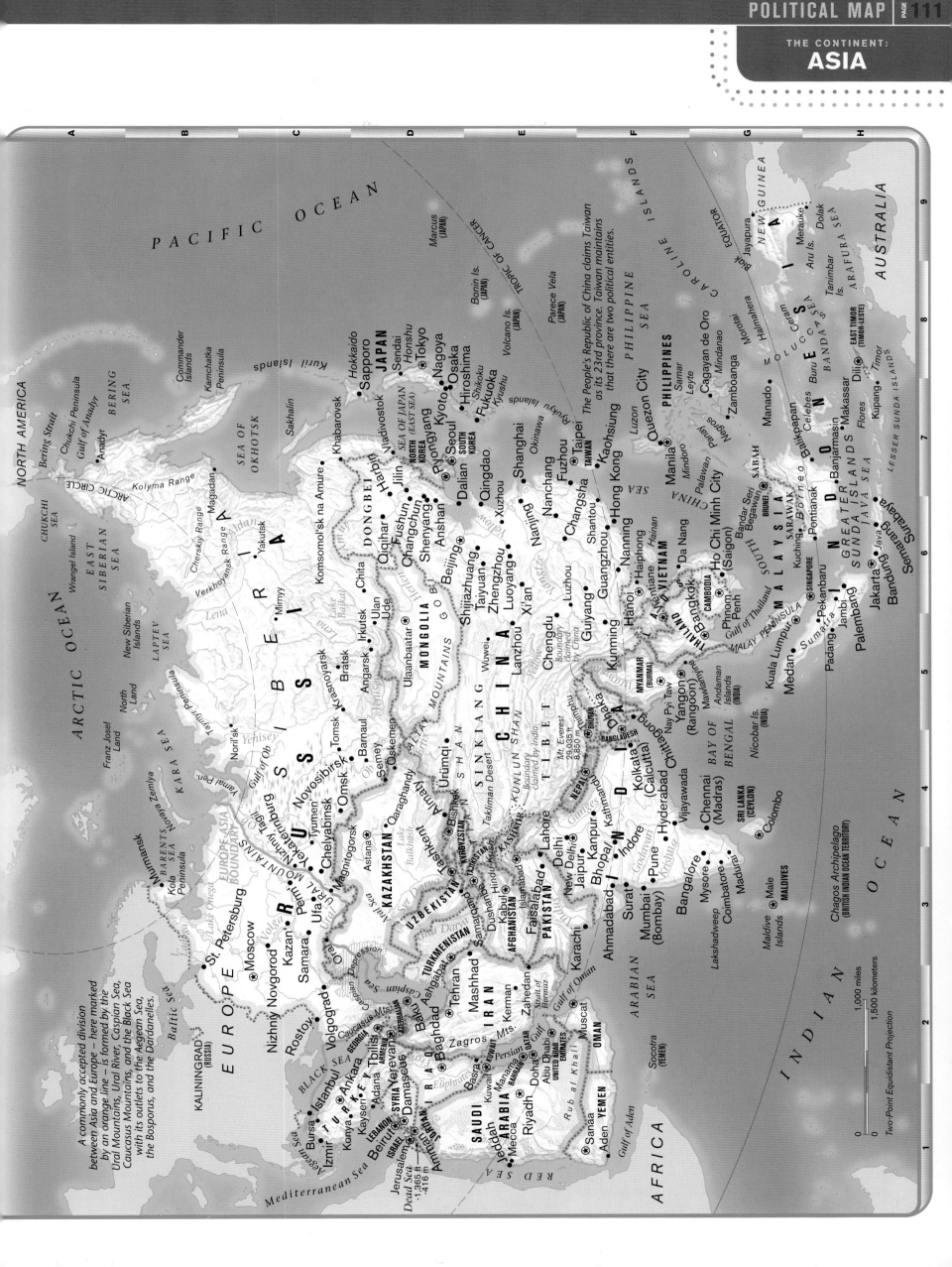

A B C D E F G H

9 8 7 6 5 4 3 2 1

PACIFIC OCEAN

NORTH AMERICA

ARCTIC OCEAN

NEW GUINEA

AUSTRALIA

The People's Republic of China claims Taiwan as its 23rd province. Taiwan maintains that there are two political entities.

A commonly accepted division between Asia and Europe – here marked by an orange line – is formed by the Ural Mountains, Ural River, Caspian Sea, Caucasus Mountains, and the Black Sea, with its outlets to the Aegean Sea, the Bosporus, and the Dardanelles.

Commander Islands
Kamchatka Peninsula
BERING SEA
Gulf of Anadyr
Anadyr
CHUKCHI SEA
Chukchi Peninsula
Bering Strait

Marcus (JAPAN)
Bonin Is. (JAPAN)
TROPIC OF CANCER
Parece Vela (JAPAN)
Volcano Is. (JAPAN)

Kuril Islands
SEA OF OKHOTSK
Sakhalin
Khabarovsk
Vladivostok
Komsomol'sk na Amure
Magadan
Kolyma Range
Chersky Range
Verkhoyansk Range
Yakutsk
Aldan
Cherskiy Range

Hokkaido
Sapporo
JAPAN
Sendai
Honshu
Tokyo
Nagoya
Osaka
Kyoto
Hiroshima
Shikoku
Fukuoka
Kyushu

SEA OF JAPAN (EAST SEA)
NORTH KOREA
Pyongyang
SOUTH KOREA
Seoul
Okinawa
Ryukyu Islands

PHILIPPINE SEA
CAROLINE ISLANDS

Biak
Merauke
EQUATOR
Jayapura
Dolak
Aru Is.
Tanimbar Is.
ARAFURA SEA

PHILIPPINES
Cagayan de Oro
Manila
Quezon City
Luzon
Mindoro
Samar
Leyte
Negros
Panay
Mindanao
Zamboanga
SOUTH CHINA SEA
Palawan

Manado
Morotai
Halmahera
MOLUCCAS
Buru
Ceram
BANDA SEA
Makassar
EAST TIMOR (TIMOR-LESTE)
Dili
Timor
Flores
Kupang
LESSER SUNDA ISLANDS

RUSSIA
SIBERIA
Mirnyy
Lena
Lake Baikal
Chita
Ulan Ude
Irkutsk
Angarsk
Bratsk
Krasnoyarsk
Noril'sk
Yenisey
Tomsk
Novosibirsk
Omsk
Ob
Barnaul
Semey
Oskemen

DONGBEI
Harbin
Qiqihar
Changchun
Jilin
Fushun
Shenyang
Anshan
Dalian
Qingdao
Yellow Sea

Beijing
Shijiazhuang
Taiyuan
Luoyang
Zhengzhou
Xuzhou
Nanjing
Shanghai
Hangzhou

MONGOLIA
Ulaanbaatar
GOBI
ALTAY MOUNTAINS
Ürümqi
SINKIANG
Taklimakan Desert
KUNLUN SHAN
TIBET
Lhasa

CHINA
Lanzhou
Xi'an
Chengdu
Wuwei
Guiyang
Kunming
Chongqing
Changsha
Nanchang
Fuzhou
Fuzhou
Guangzhou
Shantou
Hong Kong
Hainan
Nanning
Liuzhou
Yangtze

Nagoya
Wuhan

Boundary claimed by China
Boundary claimed by India

Mt. Everest 29,035 ft 8,850 m

NEPAL
Kathmandu
BHUTAN
Thimphu
BANGLADESH
Dhaka
Chittagong

MYANMAR (BURMA)
Nay Pyi Taw
Yangon (Rangoon)
Mawlamyine
IRRAWADDY

LAOS
Vientiane
Hanoi
Haiphong
VIETNAM
Da Nang
Ho Chi Minh City (Saigon)
THAILAND
Bangkok
Gulf of Thailand
CAMBODIA
Phnom Penh
MALAY PENINSULA

MALAYSIA
Kuala Lumpur
SINGAPORE
SARAWAK
SABAH
Bandar Seri Begawan
BRUNEI
Kuching
Pontianak
Banjarmasin
Balikpapan
BORNEO

INDONESIA
Medan
Pekanbaru
Padang
SUMATRA
Palembang
Jambi
Jakarta
Bandung
Semarang
Surabaya
JAVA
GREATER SUNDA ISLANDS
Celebes
JAVA SEA

KAZAKHSTAN
Astana
Qaraghandy
Almaty
Lake Balkhash
Aral Sea
Bishkek
KYRGYZSTAN
Tashkent
TAJIKISTAN
Dushanbe
UZBEKISTAN
Samarqand
TURKMENISTAN
Ashgabat
Amu Darya
Syr Darya

Yekaterinburg
Chelyabinsk
Magnitogorsk
Tyumen
Ufa
URAL MOUNTAINS
Perm
Kazan
Samara
Volga
EUROPE-ASIA BOUNDARY
Nizhniy Tagil

AFGHANISTAN
Kabul
HINDU KUSH
PAKISTAN
Islamabad
Faisalabad
Lahore
Karachi
KASHMIR
Gulf of Oman

INDIA
Delhi
New Delhi
Jaipur
Kanpur
Lucknow
Bhopal
Indore
Ahmadabad
Surat
Mumbai (Bombay)
Pune
Hyderabad
Bangalore
Mysore
Coimbatore
Chennai (Madras)
Vijayawada
Madurai
Krishna
Godavari
Ganges

SRI LANKA (CEYLON)
Colombo

MALDIVES
Male
Maldive Islands
Lakshadweep

Chagos Archipelago (BRITISH INDIAN OCEAN TERRITORY)

Andaman Islands (INDIA)
Nicobar Is. (INDIA)
BAY OF BENGAL

Kolkata (Calcutta)

ARABIAN SEA

INDIAN OCEAN

EUROPE
Moscow
St. Petersburg
Nizhniy Novgorod
Rostov
Volgograd
KALININGRAD (RUSSIA)
Baltic Sea
Lake Ladoga
Lake Onega
Murmansk
BARENTS SEA
Novaya Zemlya
Franz Josef Land
North Land
New Siberian Islands
Wrangel Island
KARA SEA
LAPTEV SEA
EAST SIBERIAN SEA
Kola Peninsula
Yamal Peninsula
Taymyr Peninsula
Gulf of Ob
ARCTIC CIRCLE

GEORGIA
Tbilisi
ARMENIA
Yerevan
AZERBAIJAN
Baku
Caucasus Mts.
BLACK SEA
Caspian Sea
Caspian Depression

IRAN
Tehran
Mashhad
Zagros Mts.
Kerman
Zahedan
Strait of Hormuz
Persian Gulf

IRAQ
Baghdad
Basra
Euphrates
Tigris

TURKEY
Istanbul
Ankara
Bursa
Izmir
Konya
Kayseri
Adana
Aegean Sea

SYRIA
Damascus
LEBANON
Beirut
ISRAEL
Jerusalem
JORDAN
Amman
Dead Sea -1,365 ft -416 m
Mediterranean Sea

SAUDI ARABIA
Riyadh
Mecca
Jeddah
Medina

KUWAIT
Kuwait
BAHRAIN
Manama
QATAR
Doha
UNITED ARAB EMIRATES
Abu Dhabi
OMAN
Muscat
YEMEN
Sanaa
Aden
Socotra (YEMEN)
Gulf of Aden
Rub' al Khali

RED SEA

AFRICA

1,000 miles
1,500 kilometers
0
Two-Point Equidistant Projection

Asia
WORLD CHAMPION

⇑ TASTY SNACK. This black and white giant panda, native to China, munches on a stalk of bamboo, the mainstay of its diet.

From Turkey to the eastern tip of Russia, Asia sprawls across nearly 180 degrees of longitude—almost half the globe! It boasts the highest (the Himalaya) and lowest (the Dead Sea) places on Earth's surface. Then there are Asia's people—almost four billion of them. That's more people than live on all the other continents put together. Asia has both the most farmers and the most million-plus cities. The world's first civilization arose in Sumer, in what is now southern Iraq. Rich cultures also emerged along rivers in present-day India and China, strongly influencing the world ever since.

⇩ NEW VS. OLD. An Afghan woman, completely covered by a traditional burka, sits among young girls dressed in Western clothes in Kabul.

⇦ LUNAR NEW YEAR.
Young men carry a
writhing paper dragon
on poles in this Chinese
New Year's parade in Singapore.

⇦ NEON AVENUE.
Bright lights and
neon signs highlight
bustling Nanjing Lu,
Shanghai's main
shopping street.
With a population of
more than 14 million,
Shanghai is China's
largest city.

⇨ WINGED HUNTER.
A Kazakh falconer sits
astride his pony as he
releases his golden eagle to
pursue prey on the dry Mongolian steppe.

more about
ASIA

⇧ EASTERN BELIEF. From its origins in the foothills of the Himalaya, Buddhism has spread across much of eastern Asia. Statues of the Buddha, such as this one in Bangkok, Thailand, appear frequently in the landscape.

⇩ UP AND DOWN. Traditional dress and a modern motorized walkway create sharp contrast in this mall in Doha, Qatar.

⇩ A FINAL TOUCH. Silk kimono and perfectly applied makeup are part of the tradition of a *maiko*, or apprentice geisha, in Kyoto, Japan.

⇩ STONE BARRIER. Construction on China's Great Wall began in 220 B.C. as a defense against invasion from the north and continued until the A.D. 1600s. Extending in sections for almost 4,000 miles (6,436 km), the wall attracts tourists from around the world.

WHERE THE PICTURES ARE

Kyrgyz goat herder p. 118
Ger and yak p. 119
Nenet woman and child p. 116
Samarkand market p. 119
Falconer p. 113
Diamond mine p. 117
Horse riders p. 118
Lenin's head p. 117
Girls talking p. 124
Brown bears p. 116
Stone head p. 123
Great Wall of China pp. 114–115
Galata Bridge p. 122
Woman in lab p. 120
Swimmers p. 123
Japanese snow monkeys p. 121
Petra p. 122
Tokyo city street pp. 120–121
Ring p. 125
Geisha p. 114
Horse and car pp. 124-125
Shanghai city lights p. 113
Terra cotta soldiers p. 121
Panda p. 112
Mall scene p. 114
Jeepney p. 129
Floating market p. 128
Drummer p. 124
Buddhist monk p. 128
Afghan girls p. 112
Golden Buddha p. 114
Rain forest p. 131
Taj Mahal p. 126
Boy with flag p. 130
Hindu god Shiva p. 127
Petronas Twin Towers p. 129
Orangutan p. 131
Elephant at work p. 128
Chinese New Year pp. 112-113
Terraced rice fields p. 115
Tigers p. 115
Ceremonial mask p. 131
Mountain climbers p. 126
Man and his cow p. 127
Jakarta at night p. 130

⇩ MOUNTAIN STAIRWAY. Terraces cut into a steep mountainside create fields for rice on the island of Bali, in Indonesia. Rice is the staple grain crop in much of eastern Asia. In the foreground, a man nimbly climbs a palm tree to harvest coconuts.

⇧ MOTHER KNOWS BEST. A Bengal tiger gently moves her cub to a safe hiding place before stalking her prey in India's Bandhavgarh National Park. Tigers are an endangered species.

THE CONTINENT:
ASIA

ASIAN RUSSIA

THE BASICS

STATS*

Area
6,592,850 sq mi (17,075,400 sq km)

Population
143,300,000

Predominant languages
Russian, minority languages

Predominant religions
Christianity (Russian Orthodox), Islam

GDP per capita
$6,861

Life expectancy
66 years

Literacy rate
100%

*These figures are for all of Russia. For European Russia, see pages 106–107.

GEO WHIZ

The name "Siberia" comes from the Turkic language and means "Sleeping Land."

Trophy hunting, oil and gas exploration, and gold mining have reduced the brown bear population on the Kamchatka Peninsula from 20,000 during the Soviet era, when the peninsula was restricted to military use, to about 12,500.

A region of northern coniferous forest called taiga stretches across northern Russia as far west as Norway. It covers an area that is more than 11 times the size of Texas.

It takes at least six days to travel 6,000 miles (9,656 km) on the Trans-Siberian Railroad from Moscow to the Pacific port of Vladivostok. The trip crosses eight time zones.

Russia produces more natural gas than the next six countries combined. More than a quarter of the world's proven reserves are in Russia, mainly in Siberia, the Urals, and the region around the Volga River.

Lake Baikal, nicknamed Siberia's "blue eye," is home to 1,500 unique species of plants and animals, including the nerpa, the world's only freshwater seal.

The Chukchi, the largest group of native people in Siberia, take their name from a word that means "rich in reindeer." They share their name with their homeland, a peninsula that borders the Arctic and Pacific Oceans.

⇧ NOMADIC HERDERS. A Nenet woman and her grandson prepare to follow the family reindeer herd into northern Siberia for spring and summer grazing.

Forming more than half of gigantic Russia, this region stretches from the Ural Mountains east to the Pacific, and from the Arctic Ocean south to mountains and deserts along borders with Central Asia and China. Siberia, as this region is commonly known, has limited croplands but bountiful forests (the taiga) and rich mineral resources such as natural gas, oil, and gold. The Trans-Siberian Railroad, built between 1891 and 1905, opened up the region for settlement—but not too much. Only about one-sixth of Russia's population—fewer than 25 million people—lives in sprawling Siberia.

⇨ FISHING FOR A MEAL. A brown bear and her cubs hunt for fish in a river below the snow-laced slopes of a volcano on Russia's Kamchatka Peninsula. Part of the Pacific Ring of Fire, this peninsula in far eastern Russia has 29 active volcanoes.

⇐ REVOLUTIONARY LEADER. Vladimir Ilyich Lenin, a founder of the Soviet Union, was honored with statues throughout the former Communist union and beyond. This one in Ulan Ude, in Siberia, is the largest still standing in Russia.

Economy Symbols

- Cattle
- Sheep
- Fishing
- Grain
- Forest products
- Mining
- Coal
- Oil
- Gas
- Manufacturing
- Pollution

CHUKCHI SEA

Wrangel Island

St. Lawrence Island (U.S.)

BERING SEA

EAST SIBERIAN SEA

ARCTIC OCEAN

Franz Josef Land

North Land (Severnaya Zemlya)

New Siberian Islands

BARENTS SEA

NOVAYA ZEMLYA

LAPTEV SEA

Commander Is.

KARA SEA

Taymyr Peninsula

Kolyma Range

KAMCHATKA PENINSULA

Central Range

Gulf of Ob

Yamal Peninsula

gas

Verkhoyansk Range

Lena

ARCTIC CIRCLE

Magadan

Petropavlovsk Kamchatskiy

SEA OF OKHOTSK

KURIL ISLANDS

MOUNTAINS

Noril'sk

CENTRAL

Yenisey

Ob

gas   gas   gas

SIBERIAN

Yakutsk

Dzhugdzhur Range

SAKHALIN

EUROPE-ASIA BOUNDARY

oil   gas

R U S S I A

WEST

Surgut

SIBERIAN

B E R E

PLATEAU

Lena

oil

Komsomol'sk na Amure

Yuzhno Sakhalinsk

Irtysh

PLAIN

Angara

Blagoveshchensk

Sikhote Alin Range

Tyumen'

Khabarovsk

Kurgan

Tomsk

Kemerovo

Krasnoyarsk

Ust' Ilimsk

Lake Baikal

Amur

SEA OF JAPAN (EAST SEA)

Hokkaido

Novosibirsk

Kansk

JAPAN

Omsk

Bratsk

Barnaul

Prokop'yevsk

Ob

Chita

CHINA

Ussuriysk

Novokuznetsk

Irkutsk

Ulan Ude

Yenisey

Rubtsovsk

KHSTAN

MONGOLIA

CHINA

NORTH KOREA

Vladivostok

PACIFIC OCEAN

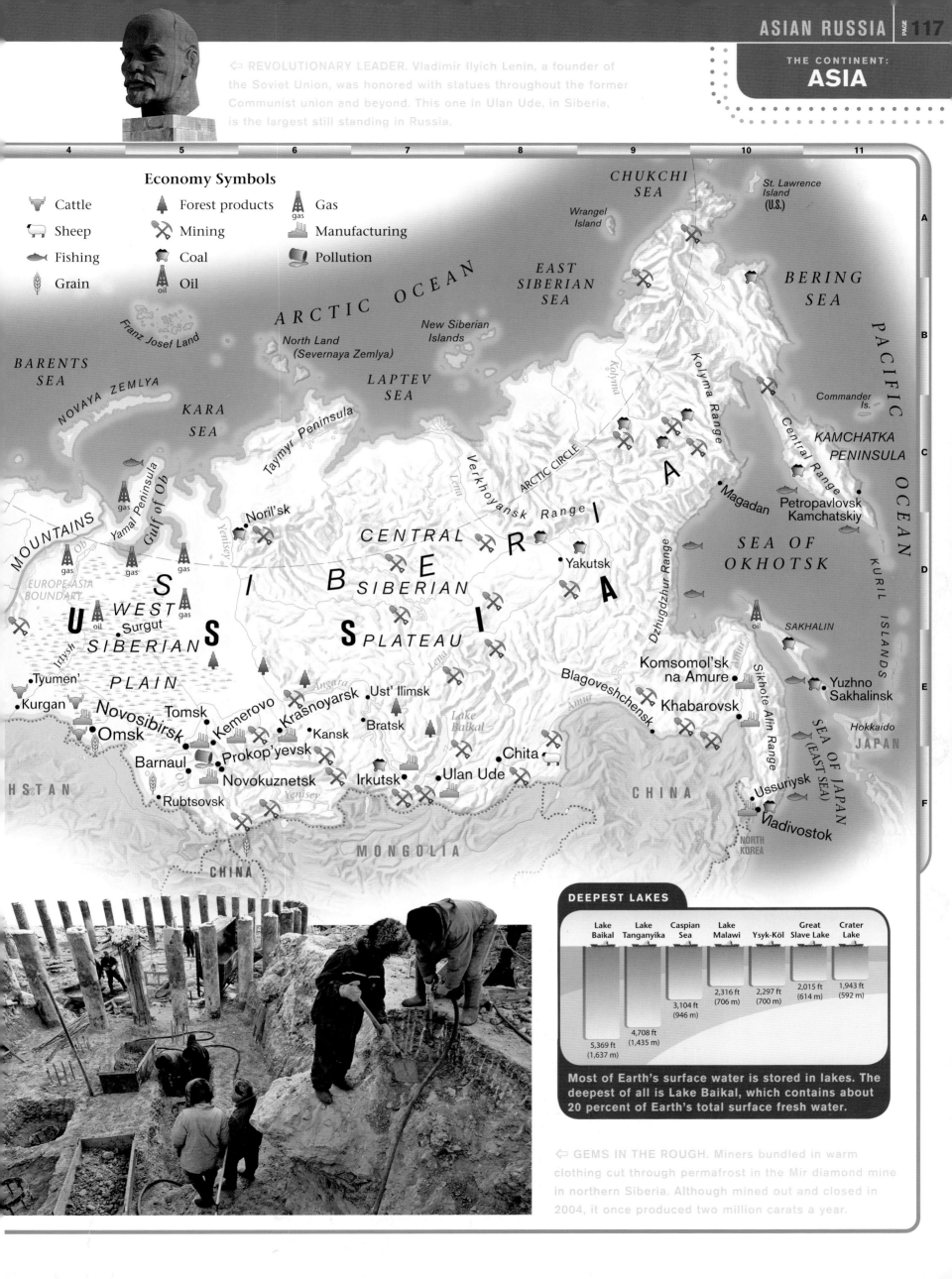

DEEPEST LAKES

Lake Baikal	Lake Tanganyika	Caspian Sea	Lake Malawi	Ysyk-Köl	Great Slave Lake	Crater Lake
5,369 ft (1,637 m)	4,708 ft (1,435 m)	3,104 ft (946 m)	2,316 ft (706 m)	2,297 ft (700 m)	2,015 ft (614 m)	1,943 ft (592 m)

Most of Earth's surface water is stored in lakes. The deepest of all is Lake Baikal, which contains about 20 percent of Earth's total surface fresh water.

⇐ GEMS IN THE ROUGH. Miners bundled in warm clothing cut through permafrost in the Mir diamond mine in northern Siberia. Although mined out and closed in 2004, it once produced two million carats a year.

THE BASICS

STATS

Largest country
Kazakhstan 1,049,155 sq mi (2,717,300 sq km)

Smallest country
Tajikistan 55,251 sq mi (143,100 sq km)

Most populous country
Uzbekistan 26,200,000

Least populous country
Mongolia 2,600,000

Predominant languages
Russian, Kazakh, Uzbek, Kyrgyz, Tajik, Mongol, Turkic

Predominant religions
Islam, Christianity (Orthodox), Buddhism

Highest GDP per capita
Kazakhstan $4,709

Lowest GDP per capita
Tajikistan $411

Highest life expectancy
Kyrgyzstan 68 years

Highest literacy rate
Kyrgyzstan, Tajikistan, Turkmenistan, Uzbekistan
99%

GEO WHIZ

The main instrument of the steppes in Kazakhstan is the dombra, a long-necked lute with two strings.

Uzbekistan is among the top ten gold-producing countries, and the world's largest open-pit gold mine is at Muruntau in the Qizilqum Desert some 250 miles (400 km) from Tashkent.

The world's only surviving breed of wild horse, the *takh*, or Prezewalski, was "discovered" in southwestern Mongolia in the 1880s by Count Prezewalski. The largest number—some 300—now live in zoos around the world, but a select few that have been reintroduced in the wild graze on the steppe in Mongolia's Hustai National Park.

Kazakhstan's Baikonur Cosmodrome, site of most space flights launched by the Soviet Union from the late 1950s to the 1980s, is the world's oldest space-launch facility. It is still managed by the Russian Federal Space Agency.

The Pamir and the Tian Shan are among the mountain ranges that cover more than 90 percent of Tajikistan.

⇨ SKILLED RIDERS. Young people ride their horses across the steppe in Darhad Valley, a region of nomadic herders in northern Mongolia. From the time of Genghis Khan's 13th-century armies, Mongolians have been known for their skill on horseback.

CENTRAL ASIA

Mongolia and five *stans*—"homelands"—make up Central Asia. Kazakhs, Turkmen, Uzbeks, Tajiks, and Kyrgyz outnumber others in their largely Muslim countries. Russians are still present in each, a result of decades of Soviet efforts to control these lands. Sparsely settled, largely Buddhist Mongolia consists of valley grasslands and dry basins beneath towering peaks. Kazakhstan's short-grass steppes give way to deserts, arid plateaus, and rugged mountains to the south. Irrigation provides water for wheat, cotton, and fruit crops. Though far from any ocean, this region possesses several inland seas, including the salty Caspian. Beneath its floor lie huge oil deposits, both tapped and undeveloped, which will add to the region's future importance.

⬆ BEST FRIENDS. A boy carries his goat in mountainous Kyrgyzstan where almost half the land is used for pasture and hay to support herds of goats and sheep.

⇐ HOME ON THE STEPPE. A ger, made of a wooden frame overlaid with felt, is the traditional Mongolian dwelling. The cowlike yak works as a pack animal and is a source of milk. Its waste is burned as fuel.

Economy Symbols

🐂 Cattle   🧶 Cotton   ⛏ Oil
🐑 Sheep   ⛏ Mining   ⛏ Gas
🍎 Fruit   ⬛ Coal   🏭 Manufacturing
🌾 Grain

0   500 miles
0   500 kilometers
Two-Point Equidistant Projection

MTS.

EUROPE-ASIA BOUNDARY

RUSSIA

Irtysch

Ertis

Petropavlovsk
Kökshetau
Pavlodar
Astana
S T E P P E S
Kasakh
Semey
Qaraghandy
Öskemen
K H S T A N
Uplands
BAYKONUR COSMODROME

Syr Darya
Lake Balkhash

Taldyqorghan

Shymkent
Taraz
Namangan
Bishkek
Almaty
Tashkent
KYRGYZSTAN
T A N
TIAN SHAN
Victory Peak
24,406 ft
7,439 m

gas
Samarqand
gas
TAJIKISTAN
Dushanbe
Pamirs
+ Communism Peak
24,590 ft 7,495 m

ANISTAN
PAKISTAN

Lake Baikal

DARHAD VALLEY

Yenisey

Selenga

Herlen

Choybalsan

Ertix

yaks
Hovd
yaks
Darhan
HUSTAI NAT. PARK
Ulaanbaatar
Mangolian Plateau

ALTAY MOUNTAINS
HANGAYN MOUNTAINS
M O N G O L I A
M O U N T A I N S

G O B I

Yellow

C H I N A

⇒ WHERE BARGAINING IS AN ART. Two men haggle over the price of cherries in a bazaar in Samarkand, Uzbekistan. Located on the fabled Silk Road, the country relies on agriculture, especially cotton production, to support its economy.

VANISHING SEA

KAZAKHSTAN

Extent of Aral Sea in 1965

Syr Darya

Aral Sea

Amu Darya

UZBEKISTAN

The Aral Sea has lost more than 60 percent of its area due to water from feeder rivers being used to irrigate millions of acres of cotton and rice.

THE CONTINENT:
ASIA

EAST ASIA

THE BASICS

STATS

Largest country
China 3,705,405 sq mi (9,596,960 sq km)

Smallest country
South Korea 38,321 sq mi (99,250 sq km)

Most populous country
China 1,318,900,000

Least populous country
North Korea 23,100,000

Predominant languages
Standard Chinese or Mandarin, Japanese, Korean, local dialects

Predominant religions
Daoism, Buddhism, Shintoism, Christianity, Confucianism

Highest GDP per capita
Japan $34,955

Lowest GDP per capita
North Korea $612

Highest life expectancy
Japan 82 years

Highest literacy rate
Japan, North Korea
99%

GEO WHIZ

The Seikan Tunnel, the world's longest railroad tunnel, links Japan's two largest islands: Honshu and Hokkaido.

Roughly 900 square miles (2,300 sq km) of farmland in northern China are blown away by the wind each year. Huge dust plumes travel hundreds of miles to Beijing and other cities. The clouds are often so thick that they hide the sun, slow traffic, and close airports.

Each year on October 9, people in South Korea celebrate their alphabet, which was created in 1446 to increase literacy.

Construction of the Three Gorges Dam across the Yangtze River created a reservoir that caused more than a million people to have to find new homes.

Kim Il-sung, who ruled North Korea from its founding in 1948 to his death in 1994, is referred to in the country's constitution as the Eternal President. Both his birthday and the anniversary of his death are public holidays.

Only about 18 percent of Japan's land is suitable for people to live on. Most of the people choose to live in cities along the narrow coastal plain.

China takes up most of this region, with the Koreas and Japan lining the Pacific edge. With more than 1.3 billion people, China's population is unrivalled in size. Rich river valleys have nourished Chinese civilization for more than four millennia. The Tibetan Plateau, dry basins, and the hulking Himalaya border China's western regions. Rugged uplands limit living space in Japan and the Koreas. Japan's economic success—especially in technology and manufacturing—has made it a global powerhouse. South Korea has followed similar economic paths, while North Korea's dictator prefers to isolate his country. A gradual move to capitalism has led communist China near the top of the global marketplace.

⇐ HIGH TECH. This young South Korean woman is working works in a laboratory that makes microcircuits in a semiconductor plant in Seoul.

1 2 3

RUSSIA

KAZAKHSTAN

ALTAY

oil

oil

KYRG.

TIAN SHAN ● Ürümqi
Turpan Depression
-505 ft
-154 m

TAJIKISTAN Tarim

● Kashi

SINKIANG

AFGHAN. oil TARIM BASIN
Taklimakan Desert Lop Nur

oil

PAKISTAN

K U N L U N ● Hotan ALTUN SHAN

oil

KASHMIR

Boundary claimed by India

S H A N

PLATEAU OF TIBET

Boundary claimed by China

TIBET

H I M A L A Y A

Mt. Everest
29,035 ft ● Lhasa
8,850 m Yarlung Zangbo
yaks yaks

NEPAL

INDIA BHUTAN

Ganges Brahmaputra

BANGLADESH

⇒ NIGHTLIGHTS. Tokyo's Shinjuku is both a shopping center and a theater district as well as the the city's busiest train station. It serves more than two million passengers daily.

AUTO GIANTS

9.0 million									
	5.4 million								
		4.3 million							
			3.4 million	3.1 million	3.1 million				
						2.1 million	2.0 million		
								1.6 million	1.4 million
Japan	Germany	USA	South Korea	France	China	Spain	Brazil	U.K.	Canada

2005 data

Once the leader in car production, the U.S. now ranks third. China's expanding production makes it a contender for top place in the future.

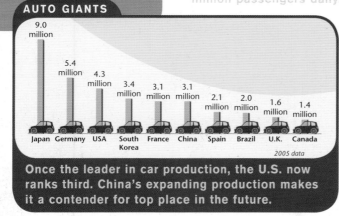

THE CONTINENT:
ASIA

STANDING GUARD. Lifelike terra cotta statues formed part of the "army" buried in 141 B.C. with Han Dynasty emperor Jing Di. The emperor believed the army, arranged in battle formation and facing enemy territory, would protect him after death.

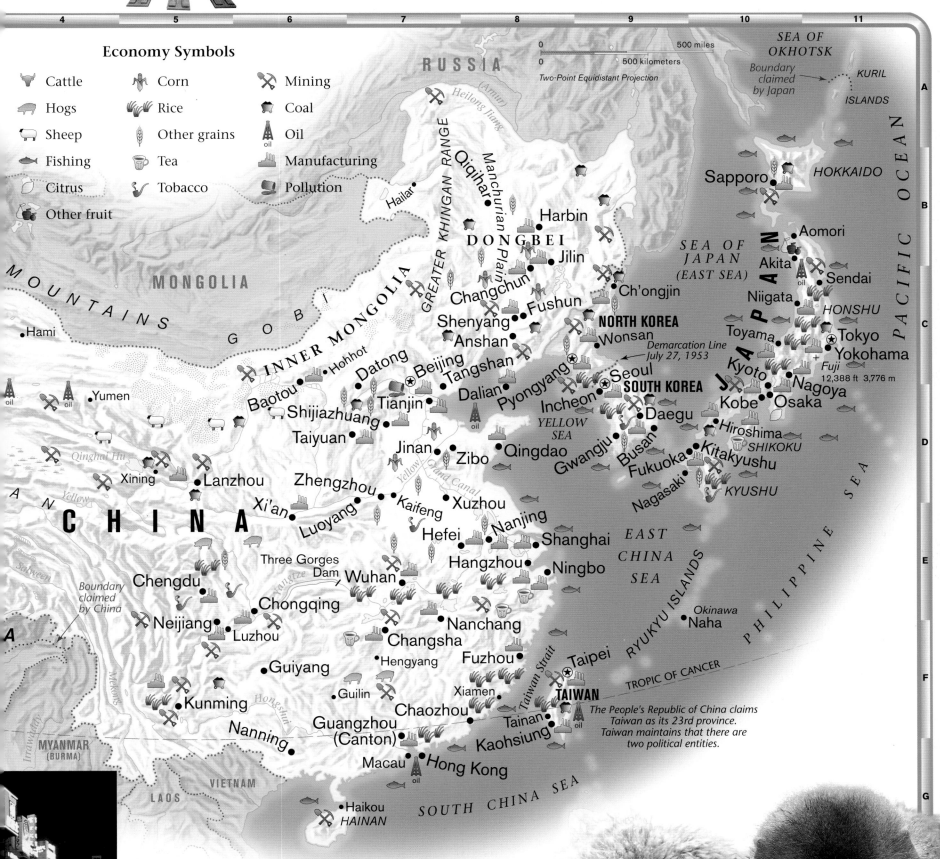

Economy Symbols

- Cattle
- Hogs
- Sheep
- Fishing
- Citrus
- Other fruit
- Corn
- Rice
- Other grains
- Tea
- Tobacco
- Mining
- Coal
- Oil
- Manufacturing
- Pollution

0 — 500 miles
0 — 500 kilometers
Two-Point Equidistant Projection

RUSSIA

SEA OF OKHOTSK

Boundary claimed by Japan

KURIL ISLANDS

Heilong Jiang (Amur)

Hailar

GREATER KHINGAN RANGE

Qiqihar

Manchurian Plain

Harbin

DONGBEI

Jilin

MONGOLIA

GOBI

INNER MONGOLIA

Changchun

Ch'ongjin

SEA OF JAPAN (EAST SEA)

HOKKAIDO

Sapporo

Aomori

Akita

Sendai

Niigata

HONSHU

JAPAN

Toyama

Tokyo

Yokohama

Fuji 12,388 ft 3,776 m

Hami

Shenyang

Fushun

Anshan

NORTH KOREA

Wonsan

Demarcation Line July 27, 1953

Hohhot

Datong

Beijing

Tangshan

Dalian

Pyongyang

Seoul

SOUTH KOREA

Kyoto

Nagoya

Kobe

Osaka

Baotou

Shijiazhuang

Tianjin

Incheon

Daegu

Hiroshima

SHIKOKU

Yumen

oil

oil

Taiyuan

Jinan

Zibo

Qingdao

Gwangju

Busan

Fukuoka

Kitakyushu

KYUSHU

Qinghai Hu

Xining

Lanzhou

Zhengzhou

Yellow

Grand Canal

Nagasaki

Yellow

Xi'an

Luoyang

Kaifeng

Xuzhou

Nanjing

YELLOW SEA

CHINA

Three Gorges Dam

Hefei

Shanghai

EAST CHINA SEA

Boundary claimed by China

Chengdu

Yangtze

Wuhan

Hangzhou

Ningbo

RYUKYU ISLANDS

PHILIPPINE SEA

Chongqing

Nanchang

Okinawa

Naha

Salween

Neijiang

Luzhou

Changsha

Fuzhou

Guiyang

Hengyang

Taipei

TROPIC OF CANCER

Kunming

Guilin

Chaozhou

Xiamen

TAIWAN

Tainan

Taiwan Strait

Nanning

Hongshui

Guangzhou (Canton)

Kaohsiung

The People's Republic of China claims Taiwan as its 23rd province. Taiwan maintains that there are two political entities.

Mekong

MYANMAR (BURMA)

Irrawaddy

Macau

Hong Kong

VIETNAM

LAOS

Haikou

HAINAN

SOUTH CHINA SEA

PACIFIC OCEAN

SILENT WATCHERS. Japanese macaques, or snow monkeys, cling to a rocky ledge on northern Honshu. Macaques live farther north than any other species of monkey. In winter they bathe in hot springs to stay warm. Japanese macaques are an endangered species.

EASTERN MEDITERRANEAN

THE BASICS

STATS

Largest country
Turkey 300,948 sq mi (779,452 sq km)

Smallest country
Lebanon 4,036 sq mi (10,452 sq km)

Most populous country
Turkey 73,700,000

Least populous country
Armenia 3,000,000

Predominant languages
Turkish, Arabic, Azeri, Hebrew, Armenian, Azerbaijani, Georgian, English, Kurdish

Predominant religions
Islam, Judaism, Christianity

Highest GDP per capita
Israel $19,878

Lowest GDP per capita
Armenia $1,234

Highest life expectancy
Israel 80 years

Highest literacy rate
Armenia, Azerbaijan, Georgia 99%

GEO WHIZ

A 1.75-million-year-old skull recently discovered in the Republic of Georgia is forcing scientists to rethink humankind's first great migration.

Nagorno-Karabakh is an Armenian Christian enclave surrounded by Muslim Azerbaijan that has been the focus of bitter conflict between Armenians and Azeris for decades.

Mount Ararat, near Turkey's border with Iran and Armenia, is believed by some to be the resting place for the ark that—according to the Bible—Noah built to survive the great flood.

To capture Tyre, capital of ancient Phoenicia and now a port in Lebanon, Alexander the Great destroyed the mainland portion of the city, then used the rubble to build a causeway to the island fortress.

Israelis capture runoff from seasonal rains to support crops in the Negev, a desert region that extends across more than half their country.

This region forms a bridge between Europe and Asia, from the Caucasus Mountains to the desert lands of Jordan. Turkey, framed by the Black, Aegean, and Mediterranean Seas, leads the region in population and area. The historic and life-giving Tigris and Euphrates Rivers begin in Turkey and flow southeast through arid Syria and Iraq. Israel, Lebanon, and Syria share the Mediterranean shore. While Islam claims the majority of followers across these lands, Jewish, Christian, and other faiths are present. Indeed, the holiest places to Christians and Jews occupy Israeli soil in Jerusalem, adjacent to the third-holiest site for Muslims, a situation that continues to cause tension and conflict.

⇧ ANCIENT MYSTERY. A camel walks before El-Khazneh in Petra, a World Heritage site in Jordan. Carved out of the mountainside more than 2,500 years ago, Petra was the capital of the Nabateans.

WEST BANK & GAZA STRIP
Captured by Israel in the 1967 Six Day War, areas of the West Bank and Gaza have limited Palestinian self rule under a 1993 peace agreement. The future for these areas and four million Palestinians is subject to Israeli-Palestinian negotiations.

BELOW SEA LEVEL

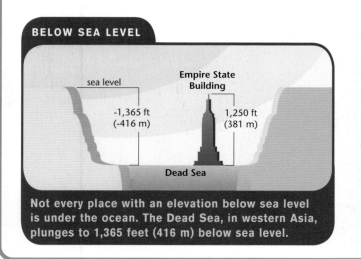

sea level

Empire State Building

-1,365 ft (-416 m)   1,250 ft (381 m)

Dead Sea

Not every place with an elevation below sea level is under the ocean. The Dead Sea, in western Asia, plunges to 1,365 feet (416 m) below sea level.

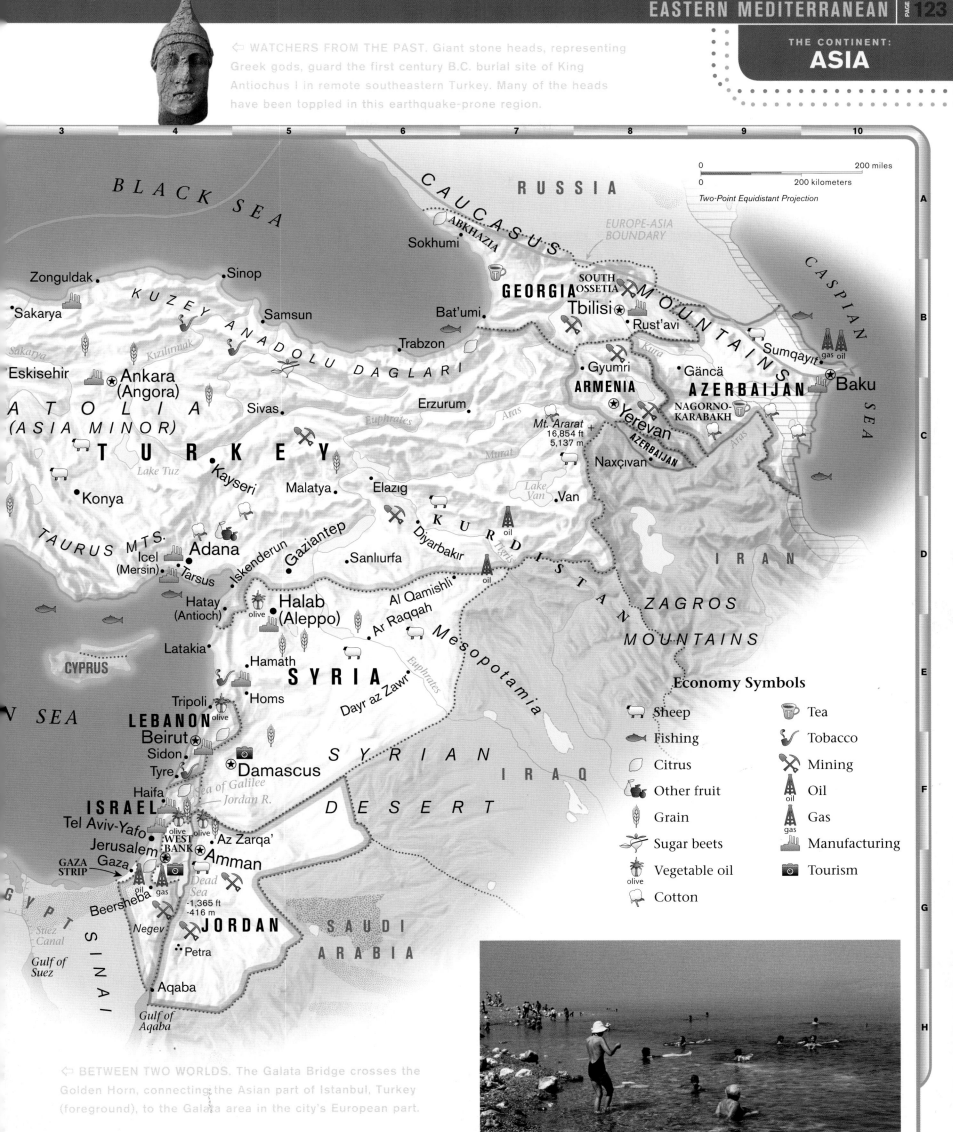

THE CONTINENT:
ASIA

⇐ WATCHERS FROM THE PAST. Giant stone heads, representing Greek gods, guard the first century B.C. burial site of King Antiochus I in remote southeastern Turkey. Many of the heads have been toppled in this earthquake-prone region.

0 ——— 200 miles
0 ——— 200 kilometers
Two-Point Equidistant Projection

3 4 5 6 7 8 9 10

B L A C K   S E A

C A U C A S U S

RUSSIA

A

ABKHAZIA

Sokhumi

EUROPE-ASIA
BOUNDARY

CASPIAN

Zonguldak
Sinop

GEORGIA
SOUTH
OSSETIA

Tbilisi

M
O
U
N
T
A
I
N
S

B

Sakarya
Samsun

Bat'umi

Rust'avi

Sumqayıt
gas oil

SEA

Eskişehir

K U Z E Y   A N A D O L U   D A G L A R I

Trabzon

Gyumri

Gäncä

Baku

Sakarya

Kızılırmak

Ankara
(Angora)

Erzurum

ARMENIA

AZERBAIJAN

NAGORNO-
KARABAKH

C

A T O L I A
(ASIA MINOR)

Sivas

Euphrates

Yerevan

Mt. Ararat
16,854 ft
5,137 m

AZERBAIJAN

T U R K E Y

Murat

Naxçıvan

I R A N

Lake Tuz

Kayseri

Malatya

Elazığ

Lake
Van

Van

Konya

K
U
R
D
I
S
T
A
N

Z A G R O S

D

T A U R U S   M T S.

Diyarbakır

oil

Adana

Gaziantep

Şanlıurfa

Tigris

M O U N T A I N S

İcel
(Mersin)

İskenderun

oil

Tarsus

Hatay
(Antioch)

Halab
(Aleppo)

Al Qamishli

olive

Ar Raqqah

M
e
s
o
p
o
t
a
m
i
a

E

CYPRUS

Latakia

Hamath

Euphrates

S Y R I A

Dayr az Zawr

Economy Symbols

Tripoli

olive

Homs

🐑 Sheep   🍵 Tea

N   S E A

LEBANON

Beirut

S Y R I A N

🐟 Fishing   🪈 Tobacco

F

Sidon

Damascus

🍋 Citrus   ⛏ Mining

Tyre

Haifa

Sea of Galilee

D E S E R T

🍎 Other fruit   🛢 Oil
oil

Tel Aviv-Yafo

Jordan R.

🌾 Grain   gas Gas

ISRAEL

olive

olive

Jerusalem

WEST
BANK

Az Zarqa'

🌱 Sugar beets   🏭 Manufacturing

G

GAZA
STRIP

Gaza

Amman

🌿 Vegetable oil 📷 Tourism
olive

oil

gas

*Dead
Sea*

-1,365 ft
-416 m

🍂 Cotton

Beersheba

E G Y P T

*Suez
Canal*

Negev

JORDAN

S A U D I

*Gulf of
Suez*

S I N A I

Petra

A R A B I A

H

*Gulf of
Aqaba*

Aqaba

⇐ BETWEEN TWO WORLDS. The Galata Bridge crosses the Golden Horn, connecting the Asian part of Istanbul, Turkey (foreground), to the Galata area in the city's European part.

⇒ SALTY EXTREME. The land between Israel and Jordan plunges down to the surface of the Dead Sea, which lies at 1,365 feet (416 m) below sea level. The water of the sea is almost six times saltier than the ocean.

THE CONTINENT:
ASIA

SOUTHWEST ASIA

This region, made up largely of deserts and mountains, includes the countries of the Arabian Peninsula and those that border the Persian Gulf. Islam is the dominant religion in each, and the two holiest places for Muslims—Mecca and Medina—are here. Arabic is the principal language everywhere but Iran, where most people speak Farsi. While water has been the most important natural resource here for millennia, global attention has focused in recent decades on the region's oil wealth. With the majority of the world's reserves found here, oil has brought outside influences and military conflict. Long a cradle of civilization, Southwest Asia continues to hold the world's gaze.

THE BASICS

STATS

Largest country
Saudi Arabia 756,985 sq mi (1,960,582 sq km)

Smallest country
Bahrain 277 sq mi (717 sq km)

Most populous country
Iran 70,300,000

Least populous country
Bahrain 700,000

Predominant languages
Arabic, Farsi (modern-day Persian)

Predominant religion
Islam

Highest GDP per capita
Qatar $56,512

Lowest GDP per capita
Yemen $649

Highest life expectancy
Kuwait 78 years

Highest literacy rate
Bahrain, Qatar 89%

GEO WHIZ

Rub' al Khali (Empty Quarter), the world's largest sand desert, covers 225,000 square miles (583,000 sq km), an area larger than France.

More than 4,000 years ago, the Sumerians built the first cities in the world on the plain between the Tigris and Euphrates Rivers in what is now Iraq.

The ancient Romans called Yemen "Arabia Felix," meaning "Happy Arabia."

Five times a day, every day, Muslims all over the world face the city of Mecca, in Saudi Arabia, to pray. Mecca is the birthplace of the prophet Muhammad, the founder of Islam.

Iran drilled the first oil wells in the region in 1908.

Causeways connect Bahrain Island—the largest of the 35 islands that make up the country of Bahrain—to two others and to the mainland of Saudi Arabia.

⇧ GIRL TALK. Young Iranian girls get together at a film festival in Tehran. The scarves they are wearing are part of the Islamic dress code *hijab*, which says that women and girls must cover their heads and dress modestly.

⇧ HE'S GOT THE BEAT. This Omani drummer plays at a dance in the Arabian Sea port of Qurayyat. Though modernizing in many ways, Oman works hard to preserve its traditional culture.

⇨ DIFFERENT WORLDS. A contrast between horse and horsepower, this roadside meeting in Qatar also displays both traditional Arab and Western clothing styles. This Persian Gulf country preserves a rich history of Arabian horse breeding and continues to produce champions.

REGIONAL OIL RESERVES

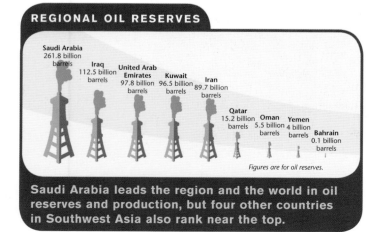

Saudi Arabia 261.8 billion barrels
Iraq 112.5 billion barrels
United Arab Emirates 97.8 billion barrels
Kuwait 96.5 billion barrels
Iran 89.7 billion barrels
Qatar 15.2 billion barrels
Oman 5.5 billion barrels
Yemen 4 billion barrels
Bahrain 0.1 billion barrels

Figures are for oil reserves.

Saudi Arabia leads the region and the world in oil reserves and production, but four other countries in Southwest Asia also rank near the top.

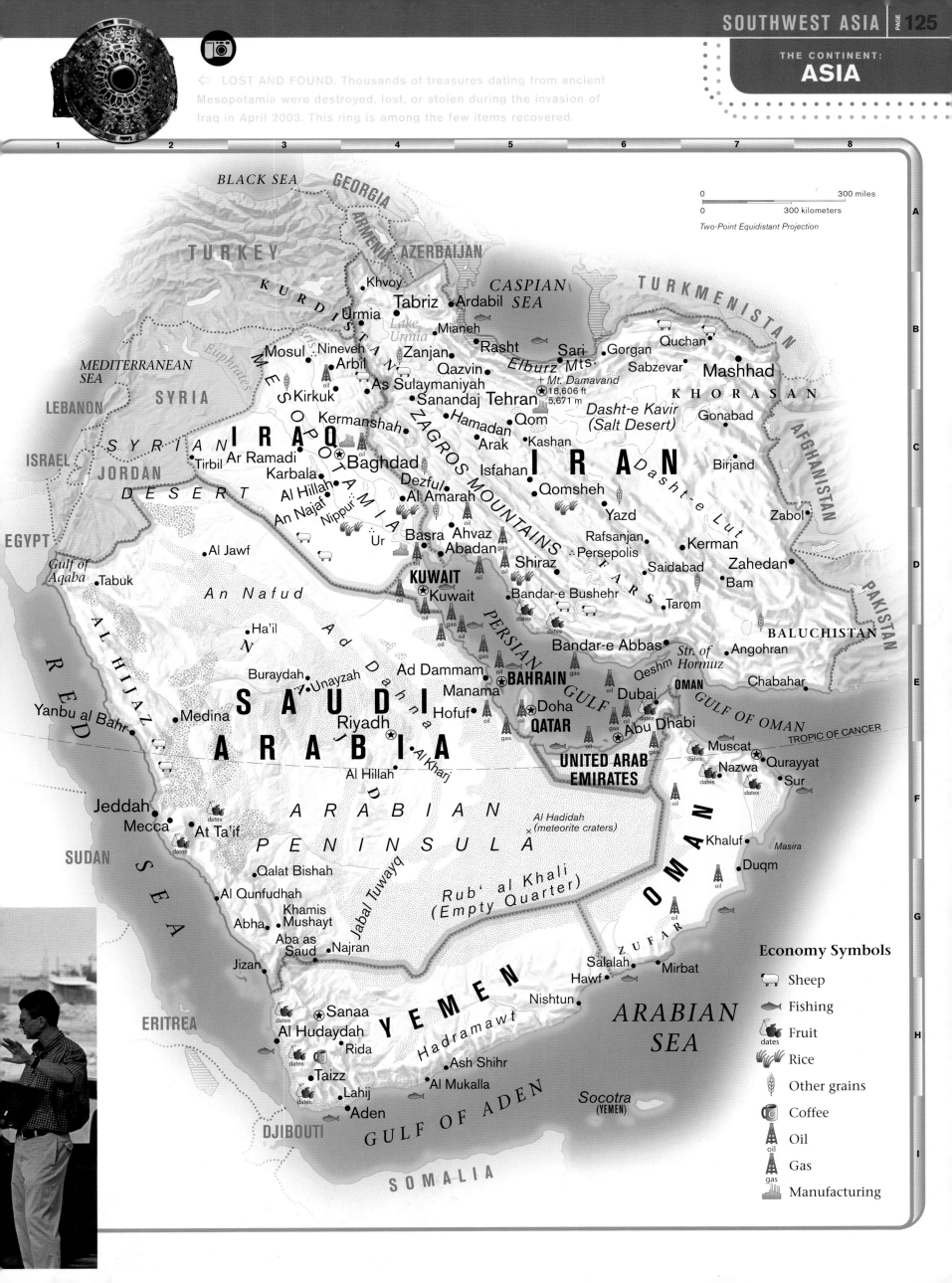

← LOST AND FOUND. Thousands of treasures dating from ancient Mesopotamia were destroyed, lost, or stolen during the invasion of Iraq in April 2003. This ring is among the few items recovered.

0   300 miles
0   300 kilometers
Two-Point Equidistant Projection

BLACK SEA
GEORGIA
ARMENIA
AZERBAIJAN
TURKEY
CASPIAN SEA
TURKMENISTAN
Khvoy
Tabriz • Ardabil
Urmia
Lake Urmia
Mianeh
Sari • Gorgan
Quchan
KURDISTAN
Mosul • Nineveh
Zanjan • Rasht
Sabzevar
Mashhad
MEDITERRANEAN SEA
Arbil
Qazvin
Elburz Mts.
KHORASAN
LEBANON
Kirkuk
As Sulaymaniyah
Sanandaj
Tehran
+ Mt. Damavand
18,606 ft
5,671 m
Dasht-e Kavir
(Salt Desert)
Gonabad
SYRIA
Kermanshah
Hamadan
Qom
IRAN
ISRAEL
Tirbil
Ar Ramadi
IRAQ
Arak
Kashan
Birjand
JORDAN
Karbala
Baghdad
MESOPOTAMIA
Dezful
Isfahan
Dasht-e Lut
DESERT
Al Hillah
Al Amarah
ZAGROS MOUNTAINS
Qomsheh
Yazd
Zabol
An Najaf
Nippur
Ur
Basra
Ahvaz
Abadan
Shiraz
Rafsanjan
Persepolis
Kerman
Zahedan
EGYPT
Al Jawf
KUWAIT
Kuwait
Bandar-e Bushehr
Saidabad
Bam
Gulf of Aqaba
Tabuk
An Nafud
FARS
Tarom
PAKISTAN
Ha'il
Bandar-e Abbas
Str. of Hormuz
Angohran
BALUCHISTAN
AL HIJAZ
AD DAHNA
Buraydah
Unayzah
Ad Dammam
BAHRAIN
PERSIAN GULF
Qeshm
Chabahar
Yanbu al Bahr
Medina
SAUDI ARABIA
Riyadh
Manama
Hofuf
Doha
QATAR
Dubai
Abu Dhabi
OMAN
GULF OF OMAN
TROPIC OF CANCER
Muscat
Nazwa
Qurayyat
Sur
RED SEA
Al Hillah
Al Kharj
UNITED ARAB EMIRATES
Jeddah
Mecca
At Ta'if
ARABIAN PENINSULA
Al Hadidah
× (meteorite craters)
OMAN
Khaluf
Masira
SUDAN
Qalat Bishah
Jabal Tuwayq
Duqm
Al Qunfudhah
Khamis Mushayt
Abha
Rub' al Khali
(Empty Quarter)
ZUFAR
Aba as Saud
Najran
Salalah
Mirbat
Jizan
Nishtun
Hawf
ARABIAN SEA
ERITREA
Sanaa
YEMEN
Hadramawt
Al Hudaydah
Rida
Ash Shihr
Taizz
Lahij
Al Mukalla
Socotra
(YEMEN)
DJIBOUTI
Aden
GULF OF ADEN
SOMALIA

Economy Symbols

🐑 Sheep
🐟 Fishing
🍇 Fruit
  dates
🌾 Rice
Other grains
☕ Coffee
⛏ Oil
  oil
Gas
  gas
🏭 Manufacturing

THE CONTINENT: ASIA

THE BASICS

STATS

Largest country
India 1,269,221 sq mi (3,287,270 sq km)

Smallest country
Maldives 115 sq mi (298 sq km)

Most populous country
India 1,121,800,000

Least populous country
Maldives 300,000

Predominant languages
Hindi, English, Punjabi, Bangla, Dari, Burmese, Pashtu, Urdu, Sinhala, Nepali, Dzongha

Predominant religions
Hindu, Islam, Buddhism

Highest GDP per capita
Maldives $2,757

Lowest GDP per capita
Myanmar $230

Highest life expectancy
Sri Lanka 73 years

Highest literacy rate
Maldives 97%

GEO WHIZ

India's rail system transports four billion passengers each year across nearly 38,000 miles (61,155 km) of track.

Bhutan, a Himalayan country known as Land of the Thunder Dragon, is the world's only Buddhist kingdom.

Nepal has the only national flag that is not a rectangle or a square. Its shape evokes the high Himalayan peaks that dominate its landscape (see page 168).

Mountains of the Hindu Kush in northeastern Afghanistan have been a source of rubies, silver, and other mineral wealth for thousands of years. The lapis lazuli that adorns the golden funeral mask of Egypt's King Tutankhamun was mined in this region.

Beaches along the southern and western coasts of Sri Lanka are nesting sites for five species of endangered sea turtle. The December 2004 tsunami wiped out several hatcheries, but the devastation has not kept the turtles from returning to their traditional nesting areas.

SOUTH ASIA

This region is home to the world's highest peaks, and three of the world's storied rivers—the Indus, Ganges, and Brahmaputra—support the hundreds of millions of

⬆ TAJ MAHAL. In 1631 in Agra, India, the Mughal emperor Shah Jehan began construction of this magnificent marble memorial to his deceased wife.

people who live here. India is at the center, with greater area than the other countries combined and three times their population. Born in India, Hinduism and Buddhism were spread to other places by traders, teachers, and priests. Muslims form the majority in Afghanistan, Pakistan, and Bangladesh, while there are large numbers of Buddhists in Bhutan, Nepal, Sri Lanka, and Myanmar.

Poverty and prosperity live side by side across the region, with streams of migrants flowing from rural areas to mushrooming cities.

⇨ TOP OF THE WORLD. Climbers make their way through Nepal's treacherous Khumbu Icefall on their approach to Mount Everest.

TOP OF THE WORLD

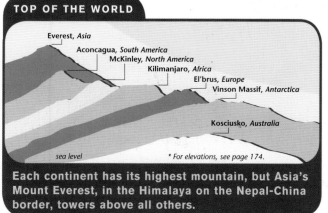

Everest, *Asia*
Aconcagua, *South America*
McKinley, *North America*
Kilimanjaro, *Africa*
El'brus, *Europe*
Vinson Massif, *Antarctica*
Kosciusko, *Australia*

sea level   * For elevations, see page 174.

Each continent has its highest mountain, but Asia's Mount Everest, in the Himalaya on the Nepal-China border, towers above all others.

← EASTERN BELIEF. The god Shiva is part of the Hindu trinity, which also includes the gods Brahma and Vishnu. With more than 900 million followers, Hinduism is the world's third largest religion, after Christianity and Islam.

Economy Symbols

Cattle	Rice	Forest products
Sheep	Other grains	Mining
Fishing	Sugarcane	Coal
Fruit	Cotton	Manufacturing
Tea		Tourism

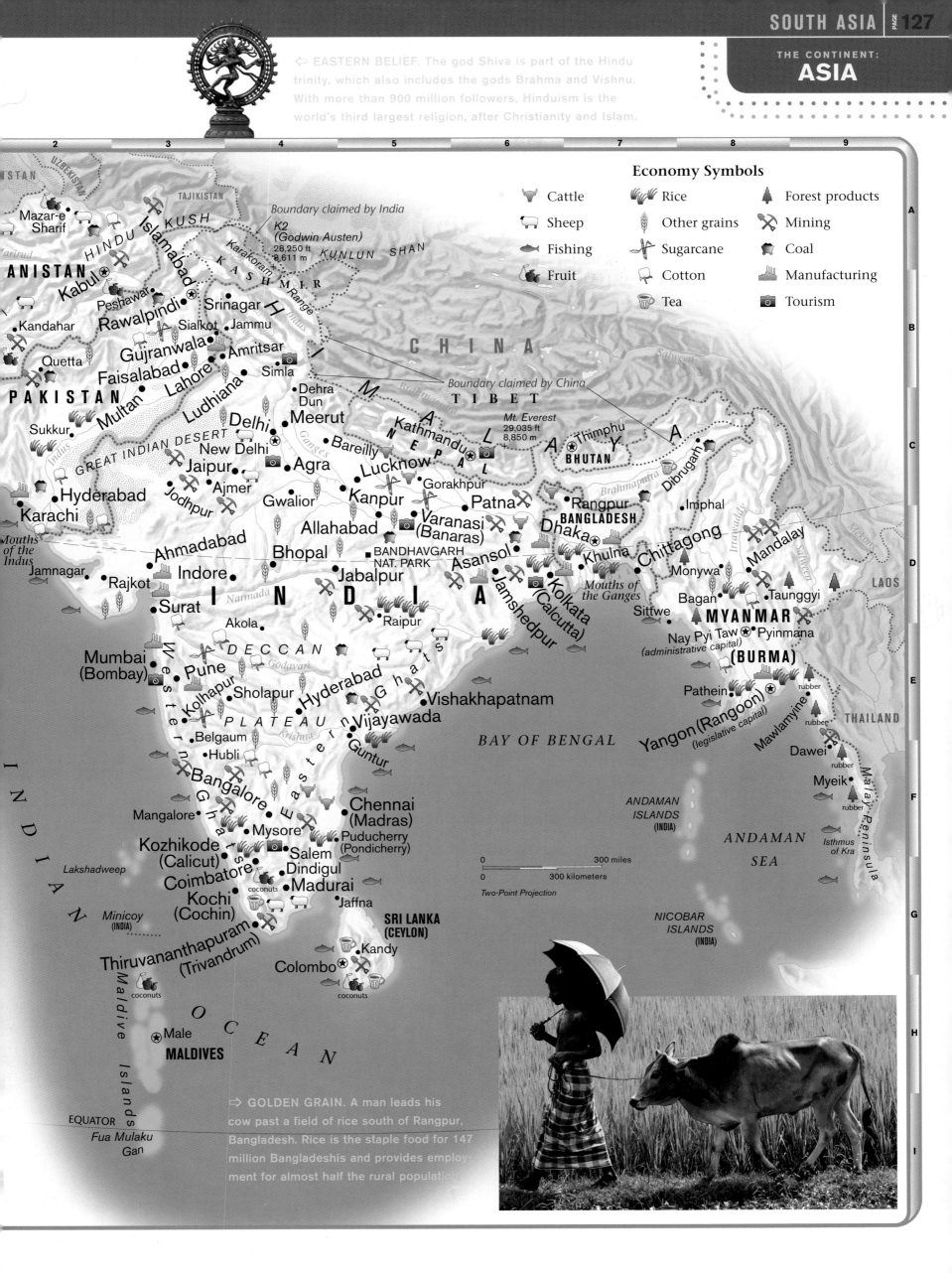

TAJIKISTAN

UZBEKISTAN

Mazar-e Sharif

Kabul

HINDU KUSH

ANISTAN

Peshawar

Islamabad

KASHMIR

Karakoram Range

K2 (Godwin Austen) 28,250 ft 8,611 m

Boundary claimed by India

KUNLUN SHAN

C H I N A

Salween

Kandahar

Rawalpindi

Sialkot

Jammu

Srinagar

Quetta

Gujranwala

Amritsar

Simla

H I M A L A Y A

TIBET

Boundary claimed by China

Mt. Everest 29,035 ft 8,850 m

Thimphu

BHUTAN

Dibrugarh

Faisalabad

Lahore

Ludhiana

Dehra Dun

PAKISTAN

Multan

Sukkur

GREAT INDIAN DESERT

Delhi

Meerut

New Delhi

Kathmandu

N E P A L

Brahmaputra

Rangpur

BANGLADESH

Imphal

Indus

Jaipur

Agra

Bareilly

Lucknow

Gorakhpur

Patna

Dhaka

Jodhpur

Ajmer

Gwalior

Kanpur

Hyderabad

Karachi

Ahmadabad

Varanasi (Banaras)

Allahabad

Asansol

Khulna

Chittagong

Mandalay

Monywa

Mouths of the Indus

Jamnagar

Rajkot

Bhopal

Narmada

BANDHAVGARH NAT. PARK

Jabalpur

I N D I A

Jamshedpur

Kolkata (Calcutta)

Mouths of the Ganges

Sittwe

Bagan

Taunggyi

LAOS

Surat

Indore

Akola

Raipur

Mumbai (Bombay)

Pune

DECCAN

Godavari

Nay Pyi Taw

Pyinmana

MYANMAR

(administrative capital)

(BURMA)

Kolhapur

Sholapur

Hyderabad

Eastern Ghats

Vishakhapatnam

Pathein

rubber

Belgaum

PLATEAU

Krishna

Vijayawada

Guntur

Yangon (Rangoon)

(legislative capital)

Mawlamyine

THAILAND

rubber

Hubli

Bangalore

Western Ghats

Chennai (Madras)

BAY OF BENGAL

Dawei

rubber

Mangalore

Mysore

Puducherry (Pondicherry)

Kozhikode (Calicut)

Salem

Dindigul

Madurai

ANDAMAN ISLANDS (INDIA)

ANDAMAN SEA

Myeik

rubber

Malay Peninsula

Isthmus of Kra

Coimbatore

Lakshadweep

Kochi (Cochin)

coconuts

Jaffna

SRI LANKA (CEYLON)

Thiruvananthapuram (Trivandrum)

Minicoy (INDIA)

I N D I A N

0 300 miles

0 300 kilometers

Two-Point Projection

NICOBAR ISLANDS (INDIA)

Kandy

Colombo

coconuts

O C E A N

Maldive Islands

Male

MALDIVES

EQUATOR

Fua Mulaku Gan

→ GOLDEN GRAIN. A man leads his cow past a field of rice south of Rangpur, Bangladesh. Rice is the staple food for 147 million Bangladeshis and provides employment for almost half the rural population.

THE CONTINENT:
ASIA

SOUTHEAST ASIA

The countries of Southeast Asia have long been influenced by neighboring giants India and China. The result is a dazzling mix of cultures, rich histories, terrible conflicts, and future promise. Cambodia's spectacular 12th-century Angkor temple complex provides a glimpse of former greatness. Colonial rule brought division and change, while struggles for independence took a heavy toll, as in Vietnam. Mainland countries are largely Buddhist, while peninsular Malaysia is mostly Muslim, and Christians dominate the Philippines. All but Laos have ocean access, with fisheries providing jobs and food for millions. Rivers like the Chao Phraya and the mighty Mekong provide transport and water-rich croplands dominated by rice growing. Tiny Singapore has gained global importance with its bustling port operations and high-tech focus.

THE BASICS

STATS

Largest country
Thailand 198,115 sq mi (513,115 sq km)

Smallest country
Singapore 255 sq mi (660 sq km)

Most populous country
Philippines 86,300,000

Least populous country
Brunei 400,000

Predominant languages
Filipino (based on Tagalog), English, Vietnamese, Thai, Khmer, Lao, French, Malay, Bahasa Melayu, Mandarin

Predominant religions
Christianity, Buddhism, Islam

Highest GDP per capita
Brunei $30,415

Lowest GDP per capita
Cambodia $459

Highest life expectancy
Singapore 79 years

Highest literacy rate
Brunei 94%

GEO WHIZ

Cambodia's Mekong Fish Conservation Project pays fishermen more than the market price to release any giant fish they catch. Catfish as long as 10 feet (3 m) weigh up to 600 pounds (270 kg).

The Philippines has one of the highest rates of deforestation in the world. Based on the current rate of removal, studies estimate that the country's virgin forests are in danger of disappearing as soon as 2010.

The Cathedral of Notre Dame in Ho Chi Minh City, capital of predominantly Buddhist Vietnam, was built in the late 1800s during French colonial times, when the city was named Saigon.

The Plain of Jars, in northern Laos, takes its name from hundreds of huge stone urns spread across the ground. Archaeologists believe the jars were made by Bronze Age people who used them to hold the cremated remains of their dead.

"Thailand" means "Land of the Free." It is the only country in Southeast Asia that has never been ruled by a colonial power.

Singapore is a melting pot of cultures. Its name comes from the Sanskrit *Singha Pura* (Lion City), its national anthem is sung in Malay, and English is the lingua franca.

⬆ SMILING BUDDHA. A Buddhist monk admires a sculpture on a temple wall near Siem Reap, Cambodia. Built between A.D. 800 and 1200 by the Khmer, the Angkor complex includes Buddhist and Hindu temples.

⬆ WILLING WORKER. Smaller and more easily tamed than the African variety, Asian elephants have been a part of the workforce for centuries. They are found from India to Indonesia.

⇨ FLOATING MARKET. This market scene in Laos is typical of much of Southeast Asia. People in small boats move about selling or trading goods and produce.

⇐ FLASHY RIDE. Colorful Philippine taxis, called jeepneys, are a common sight on the streets of Manila. Originally rebuilt WWII jeeps, these wildly decorated vehicles offer inexpensive, but crowded, transportation.

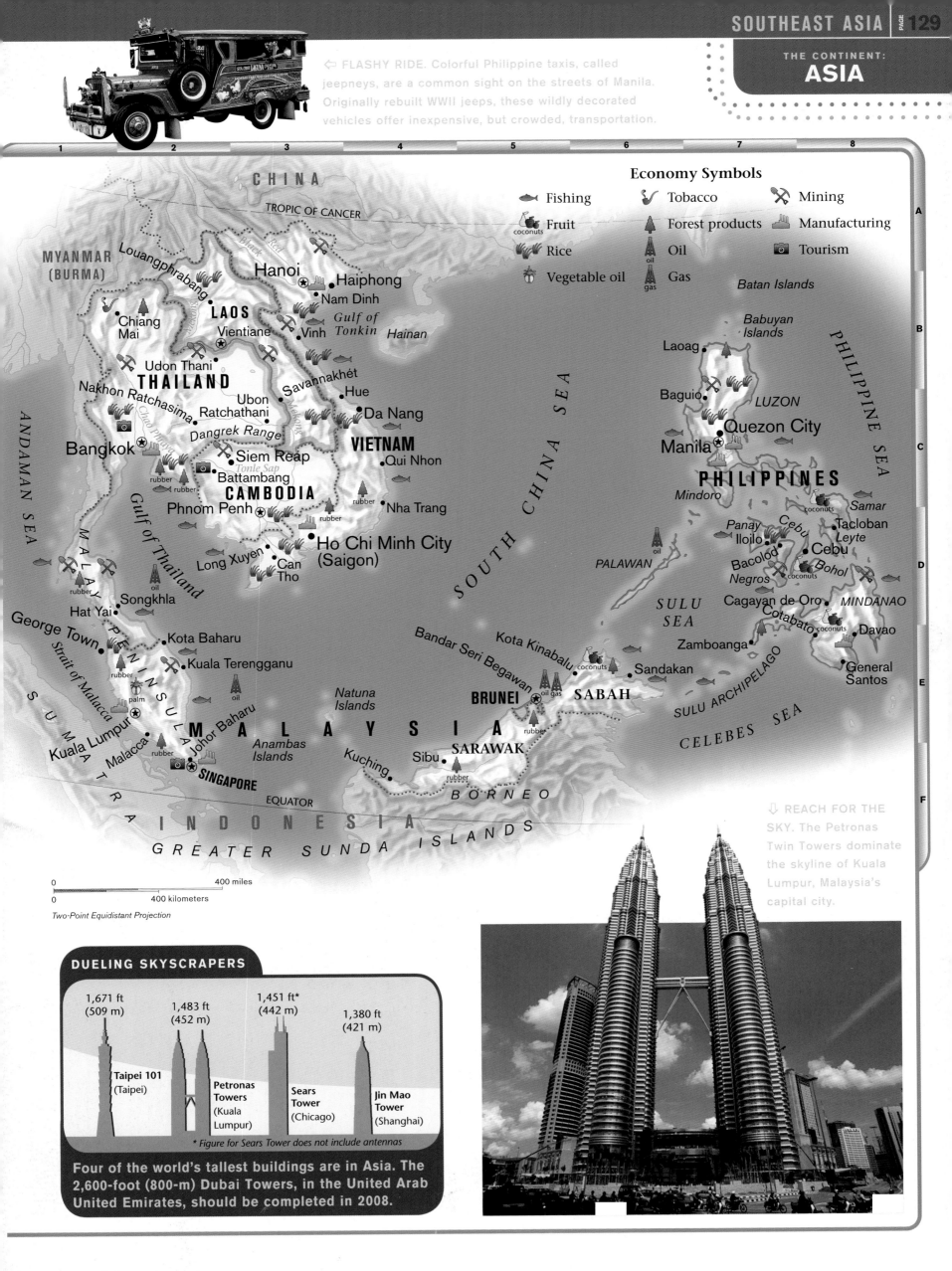

Economy Symbols

- Fishing
- Tobacco
- Mining
- Fruit (coconuts)
- Forest products
- Manufacturing
- Rice
- Oil
- Tourism
- Vegetable oil
- Gas

CHINA

TROPIC OF CANCER

MYANMAR (BURMA)

Louangphrabang
Chiang Mai
Hanoi
Haiphong
Nam Dinh
LAOS
Vientiane
Vinh
Gulf of Tonkin
Hainan
Batan Islands
Black
Red
Babuyan Islands
Laoag
Baguio
LUZON
Udon Thani
THAILAND
Nakhon Ratchasima
Savannakhét
Hue
Quezon City
Ubon Ratchathani
Chao Phraya
Da Nang
Manila
Dangrek Range
Siem Reap
VIETNAM
Mekong
Bangkok
Tonle Sap
Qui Nhon
PHILIPPINES
rubber
Battambang
Mindoro
Samar
CAMBODIA
Panay
Cebu
Tacloban
rubber
Phnom Penh
Nha Trang
Iloilo
Leyte
rubber
Bacolod
Cebu
Long Xuyen
Ho Chi Minh City (Saigon)
Negros
Bohol
ANDAMAN SEA
Can Tho
PALAWAN
Cagayan de Oro
MINDANAO
oil
SULU SEA
Hat Yai
Songkhla
oil
SOUTH CHINA SEA
Cotabato
Davao
George Town
rubber
Zamboanga
coconuts
Kota Baharu
Kota Kinabalu
General Santos
MALAY PENINSULA
Kuala Terengganu
Bandar Seri Begawan
SULU ARCHIPELAGO
STRAIT OF MALACCA
rubber
oil
Sandakan
Kuala Lumpur
palm
Natuna Islands
SABAH
CELEBES SEA
SUMATRA
Malacca
rubber
Johor Baharu
MALAYSIA
oil gas
BRUNEI
rubber
SINGAPORE
Anambas Islands
Kuching
Sibu
SARAWAK
EQUATOR
INDONESIA
rubber
BORNEO
GREATER SUNDA ISLANDS

PHILIPPINE SEA

Gulf of Thailand

0 ——— 400 miles
0 ——— 400 kilometers
Two-Point Equidistant Projection

⇓ REACH FOR THE SKY. The Petronas Twin Towers dominate the skyline of Kuala Lumpur, Malaysia's capital city.

DUELING SKYSCRAPERS

- 1,671 ft (509 m) — **Taipei 101** (Taipei)
- 1,483 ft (452 m) — **Petronas Towers** (Kuala Lumpur)
- 1,451 ft* (442 m) — **Sears Tower** (Chicago)
- 1,380 ft (421 m) — **Jin Mao Tower** (Shanghai)

Figure for Sears Tower does not include antennas

Four of the world's tallest buildings are in Asia. The 2,600-foot (800-m) Dubai Towers, in the United Arab United Emirates, should be completed in 2008.

THE CONTINENT:
ASIA

THE BASICS

STATS

Largest country
Indonesia 742,308 sq mi (1,922,570 sq km)

Smallest country
East Timor 5,640 sq mi (14,609 sq km)

Most populous country
Indonesia 225,500,000

Least populous country
East Timor 1,000,000

Predominant languages
Indonesian, English, Dutch, Javanese, Tetum, Portuguese

Predominant religions
Islam, Christianity

Highest GDP per capita
Indonesia $1,581

Lowest GDP per capita
East Timor $347

Highest life expectancy
Indonesia 68 years

Highest literacy rate
Indonesia
88%

GEO WHIZ

Two species of sharks that use their fins to "walk" on coral reefs were discovered off the northwestern coast of Indonesia's Papua province in 2006. Scientists believe they might be similar to the first vertebrates that moved from sea to land.

In an effort to reduce crowding on Java, the government adopted a program of relocating landless people to more remote islands, a policy that has created tensions and that helped lead to East Timor's independence in 2002.

With a length of 10 feet (3 m) and weighing more than 300 pounds (135 kg), the Komodo dragon is Earth's heaviest lizard. This meat eater lives only on Indonesia's Lesser Sunda Islands where it eats all types of prey—sometimes people!

When seen from the air, Timor Island resembles a crocodile. According to local legend, a crocodile turned itself into the island as a way of saying thank you to a boy who saved its life.

In December 2004 an earthquake off the coast of Sumatra, measuring 9.1 on the Richter scale, triggered a massive tsunami that killed hundreds of thousands of people and left millions homeless in countries around the Indian Ocean, from Indonesia to Africa's east coast.

⇨ CITY ON THE MOVE. Skyscrapers and a busy freeway are just one face of Jakarta, Indonesia. In this city of more than 10 million people—national capital and center of trade and industry—the modern and traditional, the rich and poor, live side by side. Just like Indonesia as a whole, the city has a very diverse population.

EAST TIMOR & INDONESIA

Stretching more than 2,200 miles (3,520 km) from Sumatra to New Guinea, Indonesia is the world's largest island nation and the fourth most populous country. Most of its 226 million people live on the volcanically active island of Java. Indonesia shares rainforested Borneo with Malaysia and Brunei. Most Indonesians are of Malay ethnicity, though there are large numbers of Melanesians, Chinese, and East Indians. Arab traders brought Islam to the islands in the 13th century, and today six of seven Indonesians are Muslim. East Timor gained independence from Indonesia in 2002. It and the Philippines are Asia's only predominantly Catholic countries.

⇧ NEWLY INDEPENDENT. A young boy smiles broadly as he waves East Timor's flag in Dili, the capital city. The country's official name is Timor-Leste.

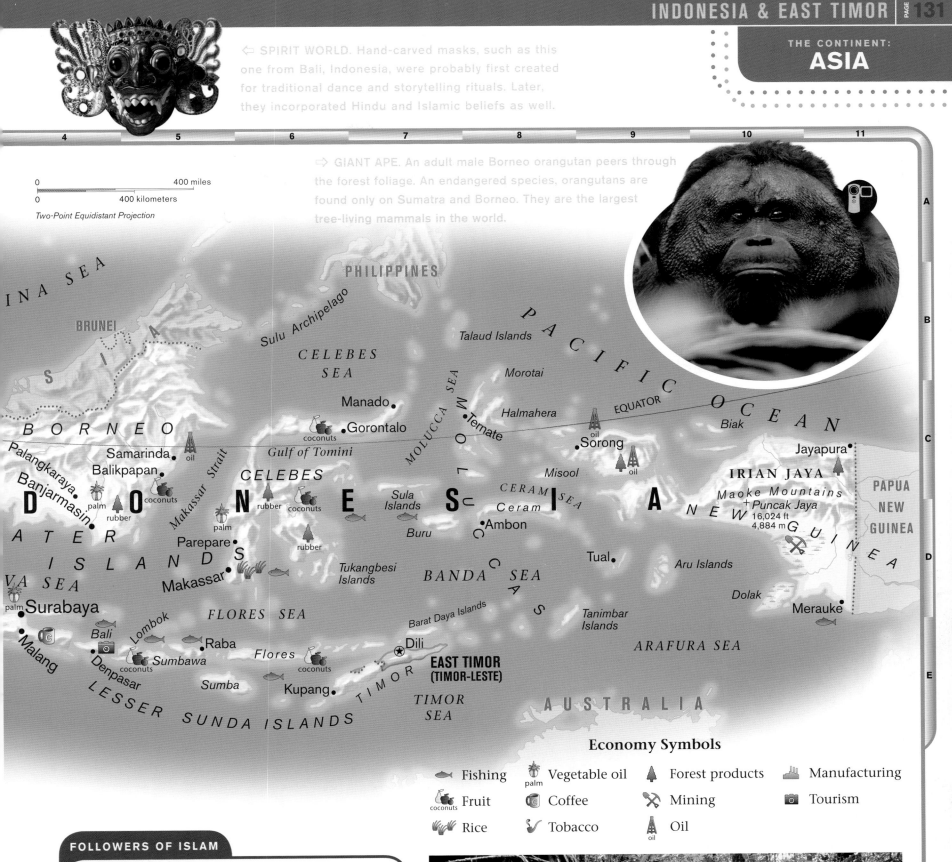

⟵ SPIRIT WORLD. Hand-carved masks, such as this one from Bali, Indonesia, were probably first created for traditional dance and storytelling rituals. Later, they incorporated Hindu and Islamic beliefs as well.

⟹ GIANT APE. An adult male Borneo orangutan peers through the forest foliage. An endangered species, orangutans are found only on Sumatra and Borneo. They are the largest tree-living mammals in the world.

0 — 400 miles
0 — 400 kilometers
Two-Point Equidistant Projection

PHILIPPINES

INA SEA
BRUNEI
SIA
BORNEO
Palangkaraya
Samarinda · oil
Balikpapan
Banjarmasin · palm · rubber
DONESIA
Sula Islands
CELEBES SEA
Manado
Gorontalo · coconuts
CELEBES
Makassar Strait
rubber
palm
coconuts
Parepare · palm
Makassar
ATER ISLANDS
VA SEA
palm Surabaya
Malang
Bali · 📷
Denpasar · coconuts
Lombok
Sumbawa
Raba
Sumba
FLORES SEA
Flores · coconuts
Kupang
LESSER SUNDA ISLANDS
TIMOR

Talaud Islands
CELEBES SEA
Morotai
Halmahera
Ternate
Sorong · oil
EQUATOR
MOLUCCA SEA
Misool
CERAM SEA
Ceram
Ambon
Buru
rubber
Tukangbesi Islands
BANDA SEA
MOLUCCAS
Barat Daya Islands
Tanimbar Islands
Dili
EAST TIMOR (TIMOR-LESTE)
TIMOR SEA
ARAFURA SEA

PACIFIC OCEAN
Biak
Jayapura
IRIAN JAYA
Maoke Mountains
+ Puncak Jaya
16,024 ft
4,884 m
NEW GUINEA
PAPUA NEW GUINEA
Tual
Aru Islands
Dolak
Merauke

AUSTRALIA

Economy Symbols

Symbol		Symbol		Symbol		Symbol	
🐟	Fishing	palm	Vegetable oil	🌲	Forest products	🏭	Manufacturing
coconuts	Fruit	☕	Coffee	⛏	Mining	📷	Tourism
🌾	Rice	🚬	Tobacco	oil	Oil		

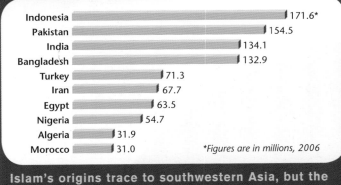

FOLLOWERS OF ISLAM

Country	Millions
Indonesia	171.6*
Pakistan	154.5
India	134.1
Bangladesh	132.9
Turkey	71.3
Iran	67.7
Egypt	63.5
Nigeria	54.7
Algeria	31.9
Morocco	31.0

*Figures are in millions, 2006

Islam's origins trace to southwestern Asia, but the religion has spread around the world. The country with the largest Muslim population is Indonesia.

⟹ GENETIC STOREHOUSE. About 75 percent of Indonesia's Kalimantan Province in eastern Borneo remains covered in rain forest that is home to 221 different types of mammals and 450 different species of birds. The forest and its inhabitants are at risk due to widespread logging and mining.

THE CONTINENT:
AFRICA

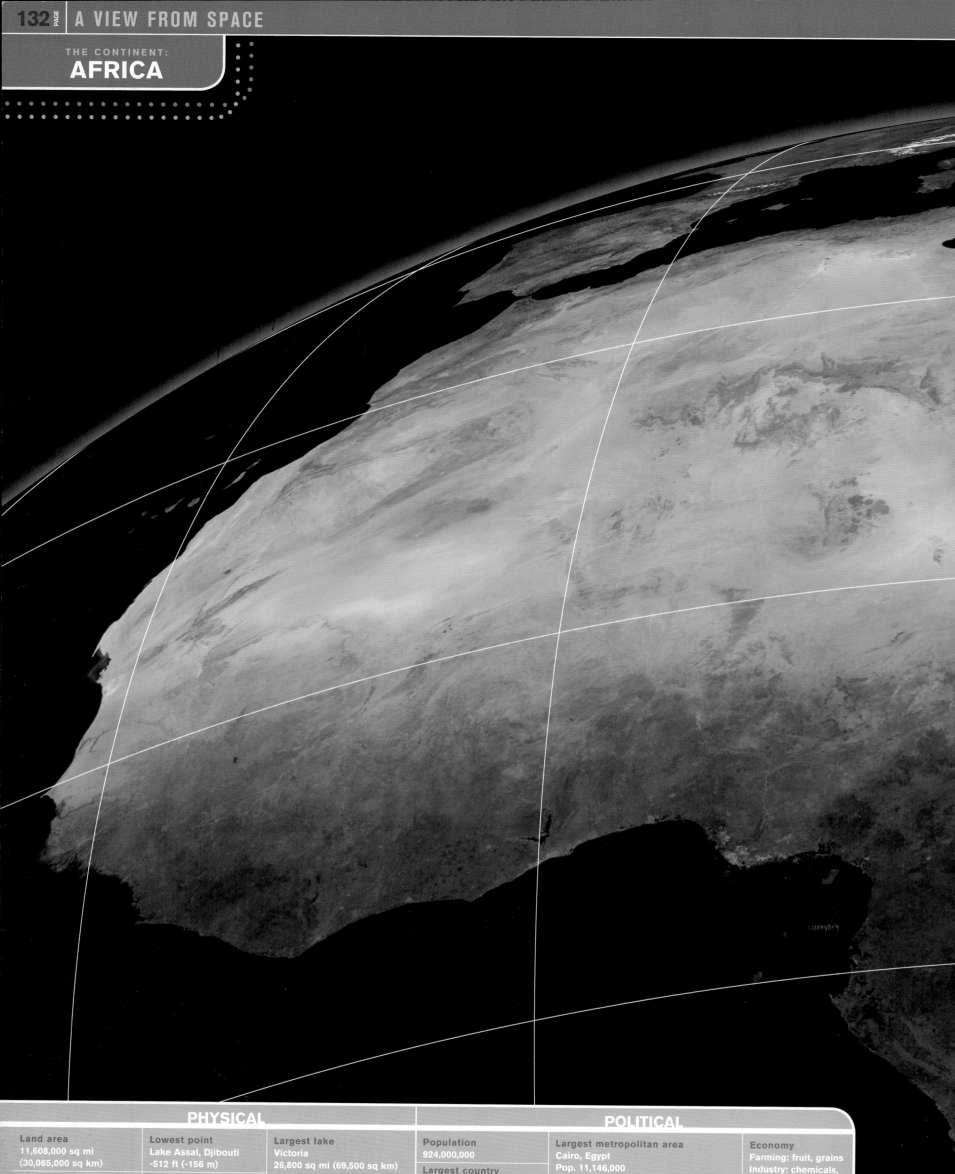

Kilimanjaro, Tanzania

PHYSICAL			POLITICAL		
Land area 11,608,000 sq mi (30,065,000 sq km)	**Lowest point** Lake Assal, Djibouti -512 ft (-156 m)	**Largest lake** Victoria 26,800 sq mi (69,500 sq km)	**Population** 924,000,000	**Largest metropolitan area** Cairo, Egypt Pop. 11,146,000	**Economy** **Farming:** fruit, grains **Industry:** chemicals, mining, cement **Services**
Highest point Kilimanjaro, Tanzania 19,340 ft (5,895 m)	**Longest river** Nile 4,241 mi (6,825 km)		**Largest country** Sudan 967,500 sq mi (2,505,813 sq km)	**Most densely populated country** Mauritius 1,592 people per sq mi (615 per sq km)	

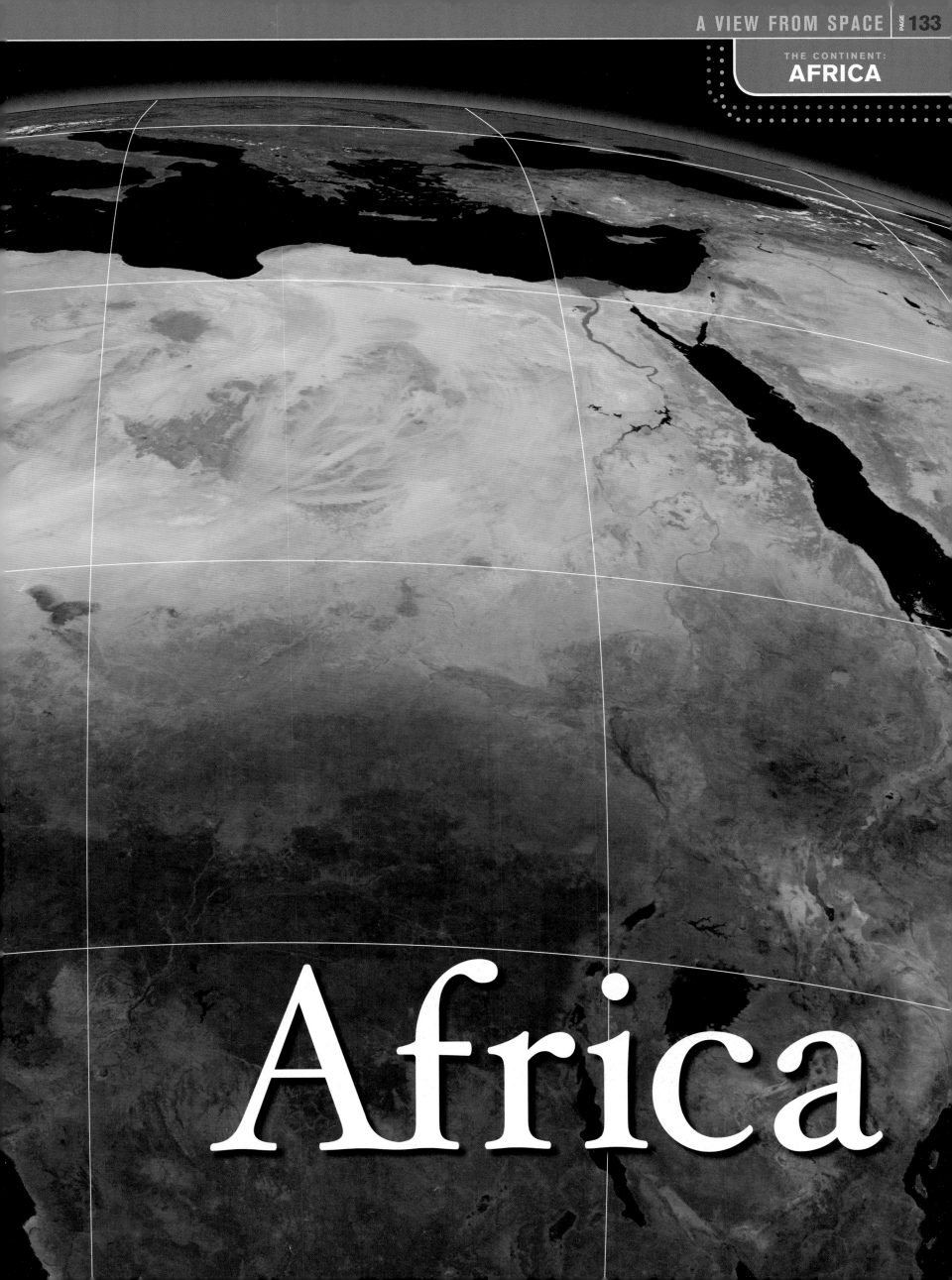

Africa

AFRICA

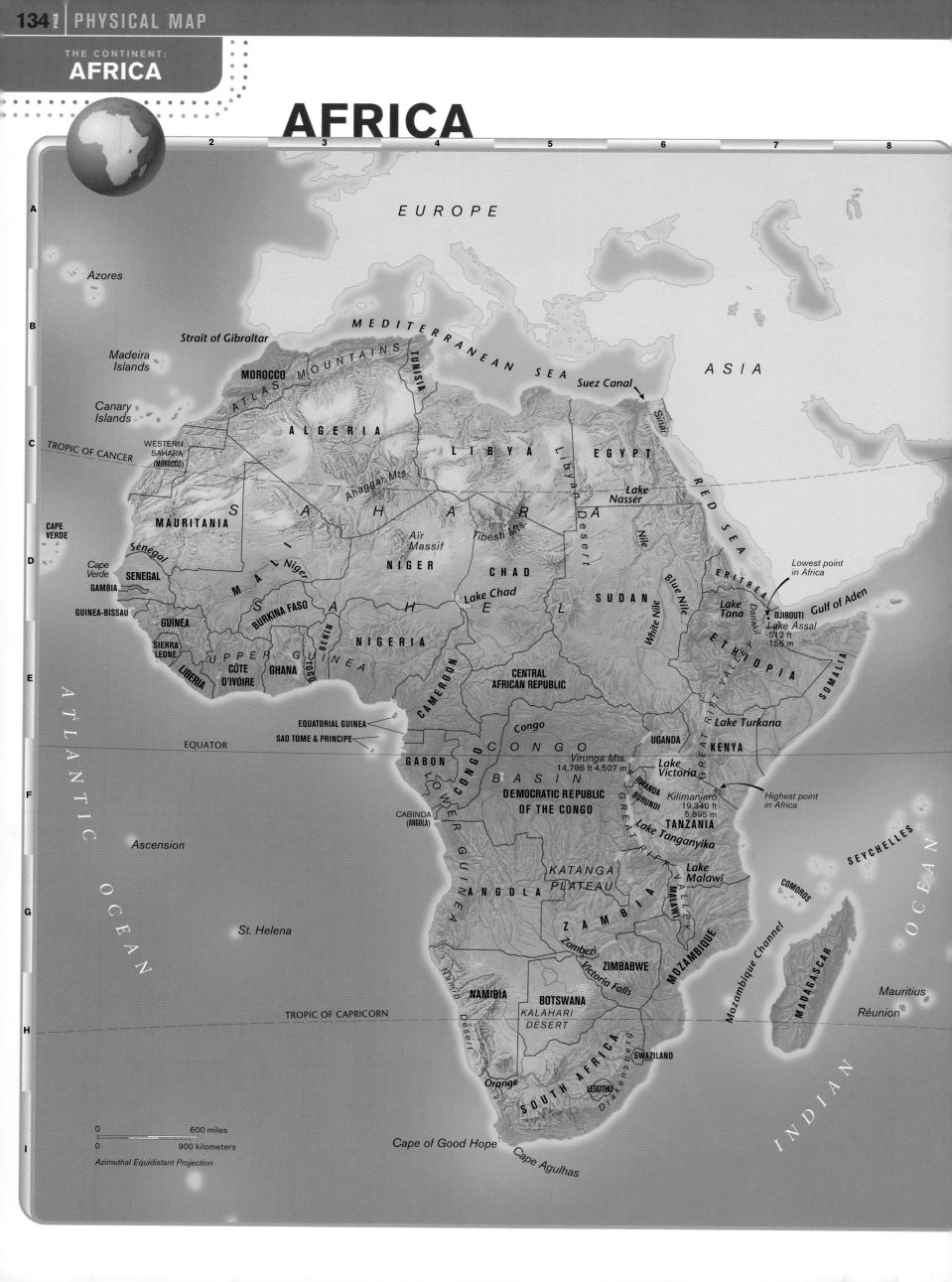

EUROPE

ASIA

MEDITERRANEAN SEA

Azores

Strait of Gibraltar

Madeira
Islands

MOROCCO

ATLAS MOUNTAINS

TUNISIA

Suez Canal

Sinai

Canary
Islands

ALGERIA

LIBYA

EGYPT

TROPIC OF CANCER

WESTERN
SAHARA
(MOROCCO)

Ahaggar Mts.

Lake
Nasser

RED SEA

CAPE
VERDE

MAURITANIA

S   A   H   A   R   A

Aïr
Massif

Tibesti Mts.

Libyan Desert

Nile

Lowest point
in Africa

ERITREA

Gulf of Aden

Cape
Verde

Sénégal

MALI

Niger

NIGER

CHAD

SUDAN

Blue Nile

Lake
Tana

Danakil

DJIBOUTI
Lake Assal
-512 ft
-156 m

SENEGAL

GAMBIA

S   A   H   E   L

White Nile

ETHIOPIA

SOMALIA

GUINEA-BISSAU

BURKINA FASO

GUINEA

BENIN

NIGERIA

SIERRA
LEONE

UPPER   GUINEA

CÔTE
D'IVOIRE

GHANA

TOGO

CENTRAL
AFRICAN REPUBLIC

LIBERIA

CAMEROON

EQUATORIAL GUINEA

Congo

UGANDA

Lake Turkana

KENYA

SAO TOME & PRINCIPE

EQUATOR

GABON

C O N G O

CONGO

Virunga Mts.
14,786 ft 4,507 m

Lake
Victoria

ATLANTIC OCEAN

B A S I N

DEMOCRATIC REPUBLIC
OF THE CONGO

RWANDA

BURUNDI

Kilimanjaro
19,340 ft
5,895 m

Highest point
in Africa

CABINDA
(ANGOLA)

LOWER   GUINEA

GREAT RIFT VALLEY

TANZANIA

Lake Tanganyika

SEYCHELLES

Ascension

KATANGA
PLATEAU

Lake
Malawi

COMOROS

St. Helena

GREAT RIFT VALLEY (MALAWI)

ANGOLA

ZAMBIA

Mozambique Channel

MADAGASCAR

Mauritius

Zambezi

ZIMBABWE

MOZAMBIQUE

Réunion

Namib Desert

NAMIBIA

BOTSWANA

KALAHARI
DESERT

Victoria Falls

TROPIC OF CAPRICORN

SOUTH AFRICA

SWAZILAND

Drakensberg

INDIAN OCEAN

Orange

LESOTHO

0   600 miles
0   900 kilometers

Azimuthal Equidistant Projection

Cape of Good Hope

Cape Agulhas

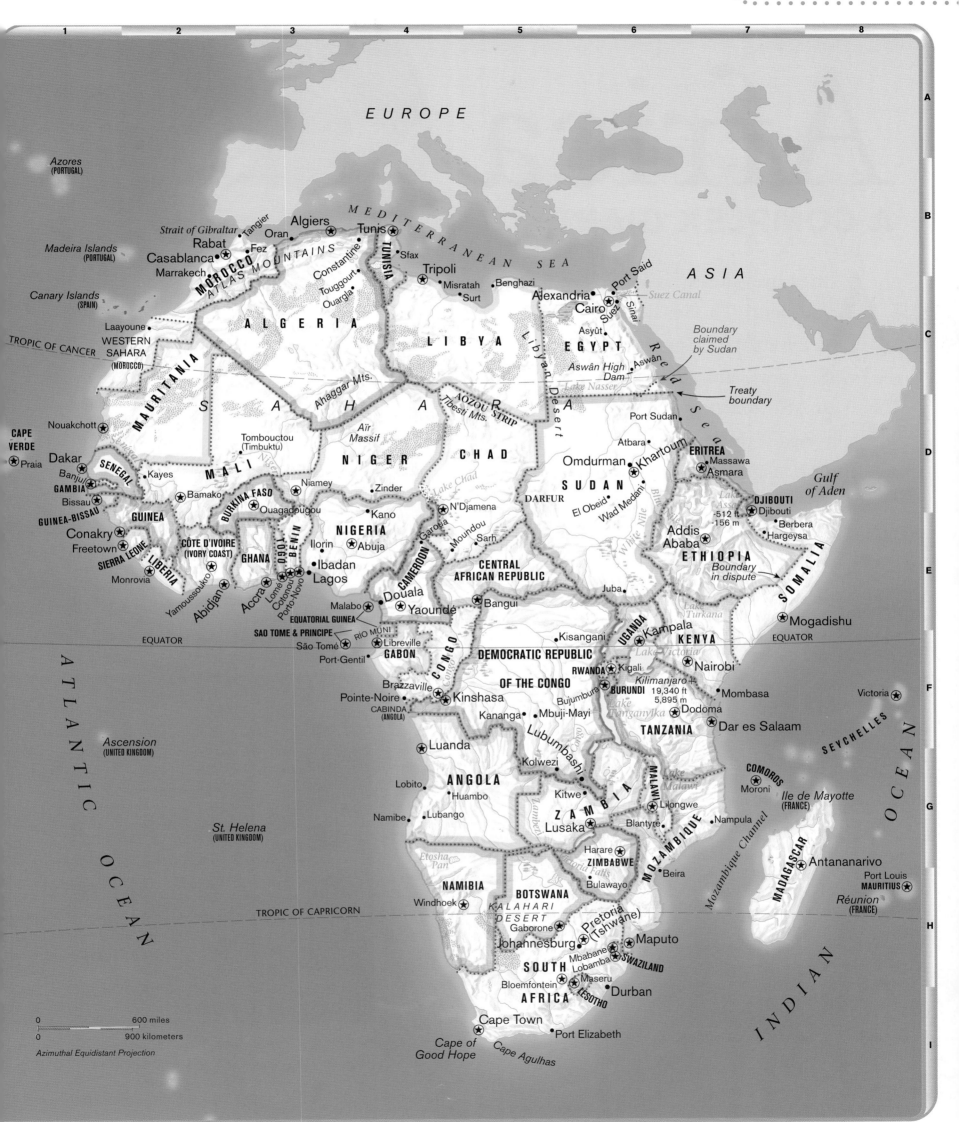

EUROPE

ASIA

MEDITERRANEAN SEA

Azores
(PORTUGAL)

Madeira Islands
(PORTUGAL)

Strait of Gibraltar
Tangier
Oran
Algiers
Tunis
Rabat
Fez
TUNISIA
Sfax
Tripoli
Casablanca
Misratah
Benghazi
Port Said
Marrakech
Constantine
Surt
Alexandria
Suez Canal
Touggourt
Cairo
Suez
Sinai
Ouargla
MOROCCO
ATLAS MOUNTAINS
Asyût

Canary Islands
(SPAIN)

ALGERIA
LIBYA
EGYPT
Boundary
claimed
by Sudan

Laayoune
TROPIC OF CANCER
WESTERN
SAHARA
(MOROCCO)
Aswân High
Dam
Aswân
Lake Nasser
Treaty
boundary

MAURITANIA
S A H A R A
Ahaggar Mts.
AOZOU
STRIP
Tibesti Mts.
Libyan Desert
Port Sudan

CAPE
VERDE
Nouakchott
Aïr
Massif
Tombouctou
(Timbuktu)
CHAD
Atbara
ERITREA
Massawa
Asmara
Dakar
Praia
Kayes
MALI
NIGER
Zinder
Lake Chad
Omdurman
Khartoum
SUDAN
DARFUR
El Obeid
Wad Medani
Gulf
of Aden
DJIBOUTI
Djibouti
Banjul
GAMBIA
Bamako
Niamey
Kano
N'Djamena
-512 ft
-156 m
Bissau
BURKINA FASO
Ouagadougou
NIGERIA
Garoua
Berbera
GUINEA-BISSAU
GUINEA
Moundou
Sarh
Addis
Ababa
Hargeysa
Conakry
CÔTE D'IVOIRE
(IVORY COAST)
GHANA
Ilorin
Abuja
CAMEROON
CENTRAL
AFRICAN REPUBLIC
ETHIOPIA
Boundary
in dispute
Freetown
BENIN
TOGO
Ibadan
Lagos
Juba
SOMALIA
SIERRA LEONE
LIBERIA
Lomé
Cotonou
Porto Novo
Douala
Yaoundé
Bangui
Lake
Turkana
Monrovia
Yamoussoukro
Accra
Malabo
UGANDA
Kampala
Mogadishu
Abidjan
EQUATORIAL GUINEA
SAO TOME & PRINCIPE
RIO MUNI
Libreville
Kisangani
Lake Victoria
Nairobi
KENYA
EQUATOR
São Tomé
GABON
CONGO
DEMOCRATIC REPUBLIC
OF THE CONGO
RWANDA
Kigali
Kilimanjaro
19,340 ft
5,895 m
Mombasa
Victoria
Port-Gentil
Brazzaville
BURUNDI
Bujumbura
Nairobi
SEYCHELLES
Pointe-Noire
Kinshasa
Kananga
Mbuji-Mayi
Dodoma
Dar es Salaam
CABINDA
(ANGOLA)
Lake
Tanganyika
TANZANIA
Luanda
Lubumbashi
COMOROS
Moroni
Ile de Mayotte
(FRANCE)
Ascension
(UNITED KINGDOM)
ANGOLA
Kolwezi
Lake
Malawi
Lobito
Huambo
Kitwe
MALAWI
Nampula
Namibe
Lubango
ZAMBIA
Lilongwe
St. Helena
(UNITED KINGDOM)
Lusaka
Blantyre
Harare
MOZAMBIQUE
Beira
Etosha
Pan
ZIMBABWE
Bulawayo
MADAGASCAR
Antananarivo
Port Louis
MAURITIUS
NAMIBIA
BOTSWANA
Mozambique Channel
Réunion
(FRANCE)
TROPIC OF CAPRICORN
Windhoek
KALAHARI
DESERT
Gaborone
Pretoria
(Tshwane)
Maputo
Johannesburg
Mbabane
Lobamba
SWAZILAND
SOUTH
Maseru
Durban
Bloemfontein
LESOTHO
AFRICA
Cape Town
Cape of
Good Hope
Port Elizabeth
Cape Agulhas

ATLANTIC OCEAN

INDIAN OCEAN

Red Sea
White Nile
Blue Nile
Congo
Zambezi
Niger
Senegal
Lake
Ass

0   600 miles
0   900 kilometers

Azimuthal Equidistant Projection

THE CONTINENT:
AFRICA

Africa
A COMPLEX GIANT

Africa spans nearly as far west to east as it does north to south. The Sahara—the world's largest desert—covers Africa's northern third, while to the south lie bands of grassland, tropical rain forest, and more desert. The East African Rift system marks where shifting plates are splitting off the continent's edge. Africa has a wealth of cultures, speaking some 1,600 languages—more than on any other continent. Though still largely rural, Africans increasingly migrate to booming cities like Cairo, Lagos, and Johannesburg. While rich in natural resources, from oil and coal to gemstones and precious metals, Africa is the poorest continent, long plagued by outside interference, corruption, and disease.

⇧ **FASHION STATEMENT.** Maasai women in Kenya adorn themselves with distinctive, colorful bead jewelry.

⇩ **CHARGE!** Sensing danger, an African elephant charges. The world's largest land mammal, African elephants are at risk due to poaching and loss of habitat.

⇧ **SEA OF COLOR.** Women balance trays of dates on their heads in a Saqqara market in Egypt. By tradition, only unmarried women dress in bright colors.

⇩ AFRICAN SAVANNA. Zebras graze on the tall grasses of the Serengeti Plain, in East Africa. Each year more than 200,000 zebras migrate through Serengeti, following the seasonal rains.

⇩ CRYSTAL WATERS. A snorkeler swims in the clear blue waters off the Seychelles, one of Africa's island countries. Made up of 116 granite and coral islands, it lies about 1,000 miles (1,600 km) east of Kenya.

⇨ FREE RIDE. A woman in Kumasi, Ghana, with her infant wrapped snugly on her back in a colorful cloth, goes about her daily chores.

more about
AFRICA

⇩ **DESERT WORSHIPPERS.** Muslim faithful gather before the Great Mosque in Mopti, Mali. An earthen structure typical of Muslim architecture in Africa's Sahel, the mosque was built between 1936 and 1943.

⇨ **WINDOW ON THE PAST.** Traditional Egyptian sailing vessels called feluccas skim along the Nile River below the ruins at Qubbat al Hawa. Tombs from ancient Egypt's sixth dynasty are carved into the hillside.

⇩ **MODERN SKYLINE.** Established in 1899 as a railway supply depot, Nairobi, Kenya, is now one of Africa's most modern cities. In Maasai, the name means "place of cold water."

⇐ TALL LOAD. A woman carries a stack of brightly dyed cotton cloth, called wax prints, through a market in Lomé, Togo.

WHERE THE PICTURES ARE

Muslims praying p. 138
Folk dancers p. 140
Mother and child p. 137
Woman with stack of fabric p. 139
Bronze head from Benin p. 141
Freight boats p. 140
Peanuts for export pp. 140–141
Gold miners p. 139
Chokwe mask p. 145
Gorilla p. 145
Elephant p. 136
Women carrying wood p. 144
Cape Town skyline p. 147

Migrant workers p. 144
Treasure from Tut's tomb p. 143
Camels and pyramids p. 142
Marketplace pp. 136–137
Feluccas on the Nile pp. 138–139
Shipping terminal p. 143
Coffee beans p. 142
Maasai women p. 136
Nairobi skyline p. 138
Fody bird p. 139
Snorkeler p. 137
Zebras pp. 136–137
Classroom scene p. 142
Ring-tailed lemur p. 146
Early man skull p. 147
Victoria Falls p. 146

⇓ DIGGING FOR GOLD. Miners dig a pit mine near the edge of the rain forest in Gabon. While searching for traces of gold, they expose the fragile soil to erosion. Oil and mineral extraction is an important part of Gabon's economy.

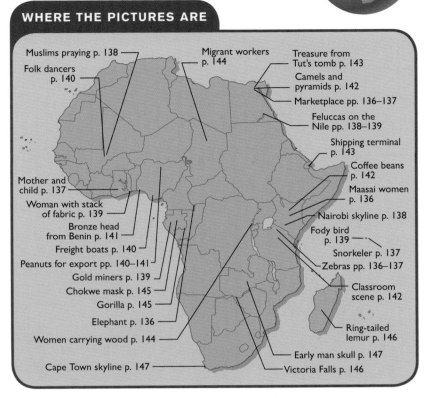

⇧ TROPICAL JEWEL. A ruby red fody bird perches on a forest branch on Mahe Island in the Seychelles. Native to neighboring Madagascar, the fody eats seeds and insects.

THE CONTINENT:
AFRICA

NORTHWEST AFRICA

This region stretches from the Gulf of Guinea north to the Atlas Mountains, which rise between Mediterranean waters and Sahara  sands. Early kingdoms thrived in Mali, Ghana, and Benin, but European invasions disrupted the social order and took out vast wealth, leaving a colonial legacy of disorder and conflict. Palm oil, rubber, and cacao are produced in tropical areas. Drier lands grow peanuts and cotton, and olives are raised along the Mediterranean Sea.

⇧ RIVER TRANSPORT. Traditional river boats are an important link in the movement of cargo and people along the Niger River.

Energy fuels the economies of several countries: Nigeria, Libya, and Algeria produce great quantities of oil and natural gas. The region's 20 countries are largely poor, with fast-growing populations totaling more than 350 million people.

THE BASICS

STATS

Largest country
Algeria 919,595 sq mi (2,381,741 sq km)

Smallest country
Cape Verde 1,558 sq mi (4,036 sq km)

Most populous country
Nigeria 134,500,000

Least populous country
Cape Verde 500,000

Predominant languages
Arabic, French, English, various indigenous languages and dialects

Predominant religions
Islam, Christianity, indigenous beliefs

Highest GDP per capita
Libya $8,300

Lowest GDP per capita
Guinea-Bissau $192

Highest life expectancy
Libya 76 years

Highest literacy rate
Libya
83%

GEO WHIZ

Nigeria is Africa's largest producer and exporter of oil. Port Harcourt, in the Niger River delta, is the center of the country's oil industry.

Ibn Battuta, who was born in Tangier, Morocco, in 1304, set off on a pilgrimage to Mecca that turned into a 29-year, 75,000-mile (120,675-km) journey that took him from the Middle East to India, China, the East Indies, and back home.

For more than 300 years, the Slave House on Senegal's Gorée Island served as a holding pen for slaves before they were sent to the Americas and elsewhere. Today it is a museum and a memorial to those slaves.

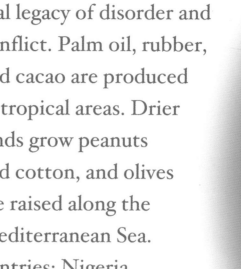

CAPE VERDE

✶ Praia

ATLANTIC

⇦ COLORFUL COSTUMES. Folk dancers perform in a festival in Djenné, Mali. Built as a center for trade between the desert to the north and the rain forest to the south, Djenné is the oldest known city in Sub-Saharan Africa.

⇨ WAITING FOR SHIPMENT. Sacks of peanuts create an artificial mountain in Kano, Nigeria, where they wait for transport to Lagos and then export to world markets. The Kano region produces about half of Nigeria's peanut crop.

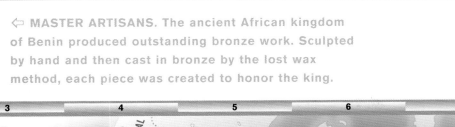

← **MASTER ARTISANS.** The ancient African kingdom of Benin produced outstanding bronze work. Sculpted by hand and then cast in bronze by the lost wax method, each piece was created to honor the king.

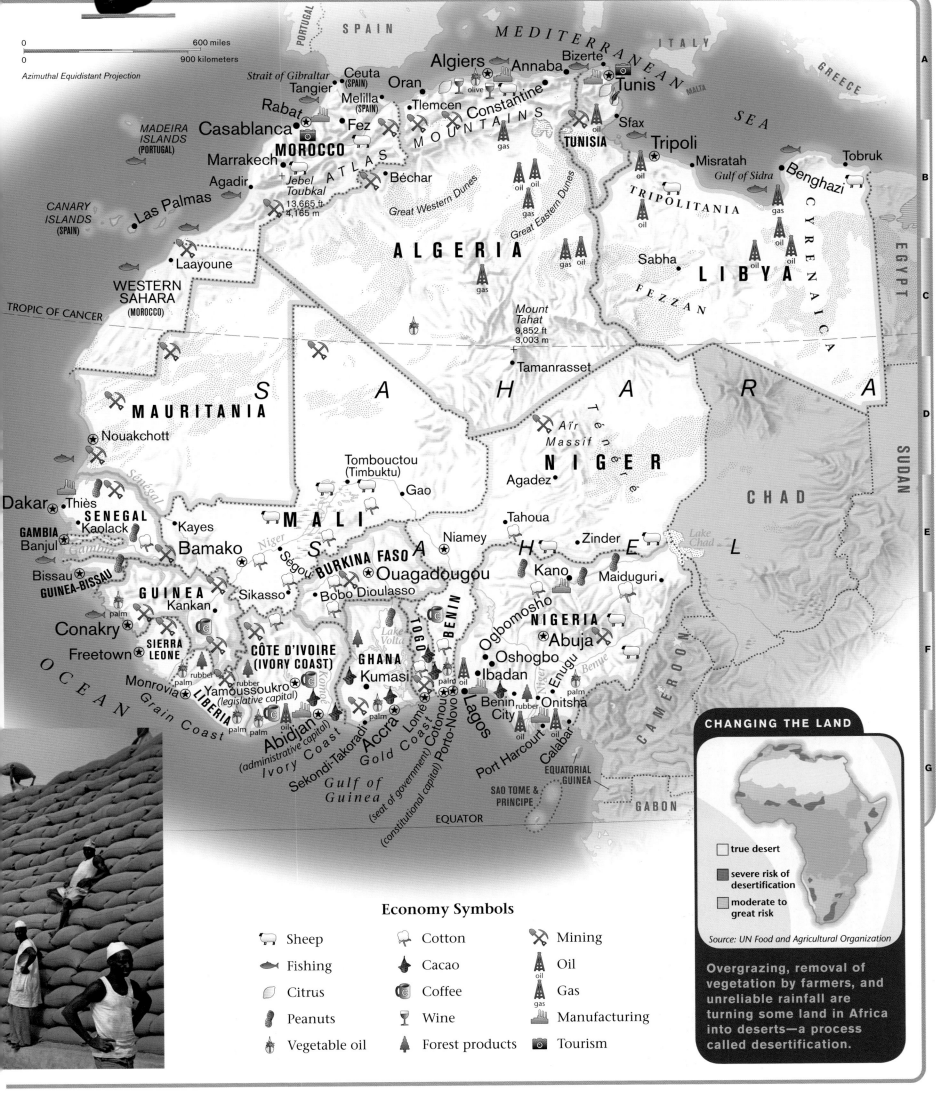

0 600 miles
0 900 kilometers
Azimuthal Equidistant Projection

SPAIN
MEDITERRANEAN
ITALY
GREECE
PORTUGAL

Strait of Gibraltar
Tangier
Ceuta (SPAIN)
Melilla (SPAIN)
Algiers
Annaba
Bizerte
Tunis
MALTA
SEA

Oran
Tlemcen
Constantine
Sfax
Tripoli
Misratah
Tobruk

Rabat
Fez
MOUNTAINS
TUNISIA
Gulf of Sidra
Benghazi

Casablanca
MOROCCO
oil
gas
oil

MADEIRA ISLANDS (PORTUGAL)

Marrakech
Béchar
Great Western Dunes
oil oil
gas
oil
TRIPOLITANIA
oil
oil oil
gas

Agadir
+ Jebel Toubkal 13,665 ft 4,165 m
ATLAS
Great Eastern Dunes
gas oil
oil oil
CYRENAICA

CANARY ISLANDS (SPAIN)
Las Palmas

Laayoune
ALGERIA
Sabha
LIBYA

WESTERN SAHARA (MOROCCO)
gas
FEZZAN

TROPIC OF CANCER
Mount Tahat 9,852 ft 3,003 m

EGYPT

Tamanrasset
S   A   H   A   R   A

MAURITANIA
Aïr Massif
NIGER
SUDAN

Nouakchott
Tombouctou (Timbuktu)
Gao
Agadez
Ténéré
CHAD

Dakar Thiès
Sénégal
Kayes
MALI
Tahoua
Lake Chad

SENEGAL
Kaolack
Niger
Niamey
Zinder

GAMBIA
Banjul
Bamako
Segou
BURKINA FASO
S   A   H   E   L

Gambia
Bissau
GUINEA-BISSAU
Sikasso
Ouagadougou
Bobo Dioulasso
Kano
Maiduguri

GUINEA
Kankan
BENIN
NIGERIA
Ogbomosho

Conakry
palm
rubber
palm
CÔTE D'IVOIRE (IVORY COAST)
GHANA
Kumasi
TOGO
Lake Volta
Abuja

Freetown
SIERRA LEONE
Yamoussoukro (legislative capital)
palm
oil
Oshogbo
Ibadan
Enugu

OCEAN
Monrovia
Grain Coast
LIBERIA
rubber
palm
Abidjan (administrative capital)
Ivory Coast
Komoé
Kumasi
Accra
Gold Coast
Sekondi-Takoradi
Lomé
Cotonou
Porto-Novo (constitutional capital)
oil
Lagos
Benin City
rubber
palm
Onitsha
Benue
Port Harcourt
Calabar

Gulf of Guinea
EQUATOR
SAO TOME & PRINCIPE
EQUATORIAL GUINEA
GABON
CAMEROON

CHANGING THE LAND

☐ true desert
■ severe risk of desertification
☐ moderate to great risk

Source: UN Food and Agricultural Organization

Overgrazing, removal of vegetation by farmers, and unreliable rainfall are turning some land in Africa into deserts—a process called desertification.

Economy Symbols

🐑 Sheep	Cotton	⛏ Mining
🐟 Fishing	Cacao	🛢 Oil
Citrus	© Coffee	Gas
Peanuts	🍷 Wine	🏭 Manufacturing
Vegetable oil	🌲 Forest products	📷 Tourism

THE CONTINENT:
AFRICA

THE BASICS

STATS

Largest country
Sudan 967,500 sq mi (2,505,813 sq km)

Smallest country
Djibouti 8,958 sq mi (23,200 sq km)

Most populous country
Sudan 41,200,000

Least populous country
Djibouti 800,000

Predominant languages
French, English, Arabic, Swahili, various
indigenous languages and dialects

Predominant religions
Christianity, Islam, various indigenous
beliefs

Highest GDP per capita
Egypt $1,432

Lowest GDP per capita
Burundi $125

Highest life expectancy
Egypt 70 years

Highest literacy rate
Kenya
85%

GEO WHIZ

Lakes Malawi, Tanganyika, and Albert
are part of a chain of lakes that mark
where the Somali Plate (see page 19)
is breaking away from Africa. Millions
of years from now, much of the region
from Djibouti to Mozambique could be
one big island.

As part of a coming-of-age ritual,
each Maasai boy must kill a lion.
Read the true-life story of Joseph
Lemasolai Lekuton in *Facing
the Lion*, published by National
Geographic Children's Books.

Lake Nasser, formed by the Aswan High
Dam, is the world's third largest reservoir. Built to provide water for farms
along the Nile in years of drought, it
also produces more than 10 billion
kilowatt hours of electricity every year.

In 2006 the 3.3-million-year-old
fossilized remains of a child were
found in the Danakil area of
northern Ethiopia. The find was
not far from where the 2.3-million-
year-old remains of Lucy, an adult
female of the same primitive human
species, were found in 1974.

NORTHEAST AFRICA

The world's longest river—the Nile—winds through much of this region. Along its banks rose one of Earth's greatest civilizations: Ancient Egypt. Today, more than nine of ten Egyptians live within a few miles of its life-giving water, and Cairo, the region's largest urban area, lies near its delta. Volcanic peaks such as Kilimanjaro—Africa's highest mountain—tower above fertile farmlands in Tanzania and Kenya. Tree-dotted grasslands, called savannas, are home to vast herds of wildlife that attract tourists from across the globe. For more than 50 years, religious and ethnic conflicts have fueled warfare throughout much of the region, especially in Sudan, where millions suffer in refugee camps in Darfur.

⇑ EAGER LEARNERS. Tanzania, a poor country with a literacy rate of only 78 percent, lags in education. Students in this crowded village school compete for the teacher's attention.

⇐ FROM FIELD TO CUP. A worker on a coffee estate in Kenya holds freshly harvested coffee berries, which will soon be on their way to the world market. Coffee production was introduced to Kenya in 1900. Today, it employs 250,000 workers.

⇓ SYMBOLS OF ANCIENT EGYPT. Camels plod through the desert as the sun sets behind the ancient pyramids of Giza. Built 4,500 years ago, the pyramids were monumental tombs of the pharaohs.

PROTECTING THE ENVIRONMENT

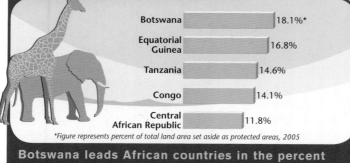

Country	Percent
Botswana	18.1%*
Equatorial Guinea	16.8%
Tanzania	14.6%
Congo	14.1%
Central African Republic	11.8%

*Figure represents percent of total land area set aside as protected areas, 2005

Botswana leads African countries in the percent of land set aside as special parks and reserves to protect the habitats of animals.

⇐ SPIRIT OF THE PAST. A gold hawk pendant adorned with semiprecious stones and colored glass may represent the god Horus, one of the oldest Egyptian gods. This treasure was found in the tomb of King Tut.

⇓ INTERNATIONAL PORT. Shipping containers look like colorful ribbons at a port terminal in Djibouti. The recently modernized and expanded port facility, with its deep natural harbor, is the mainstay of this small East African country's economy.

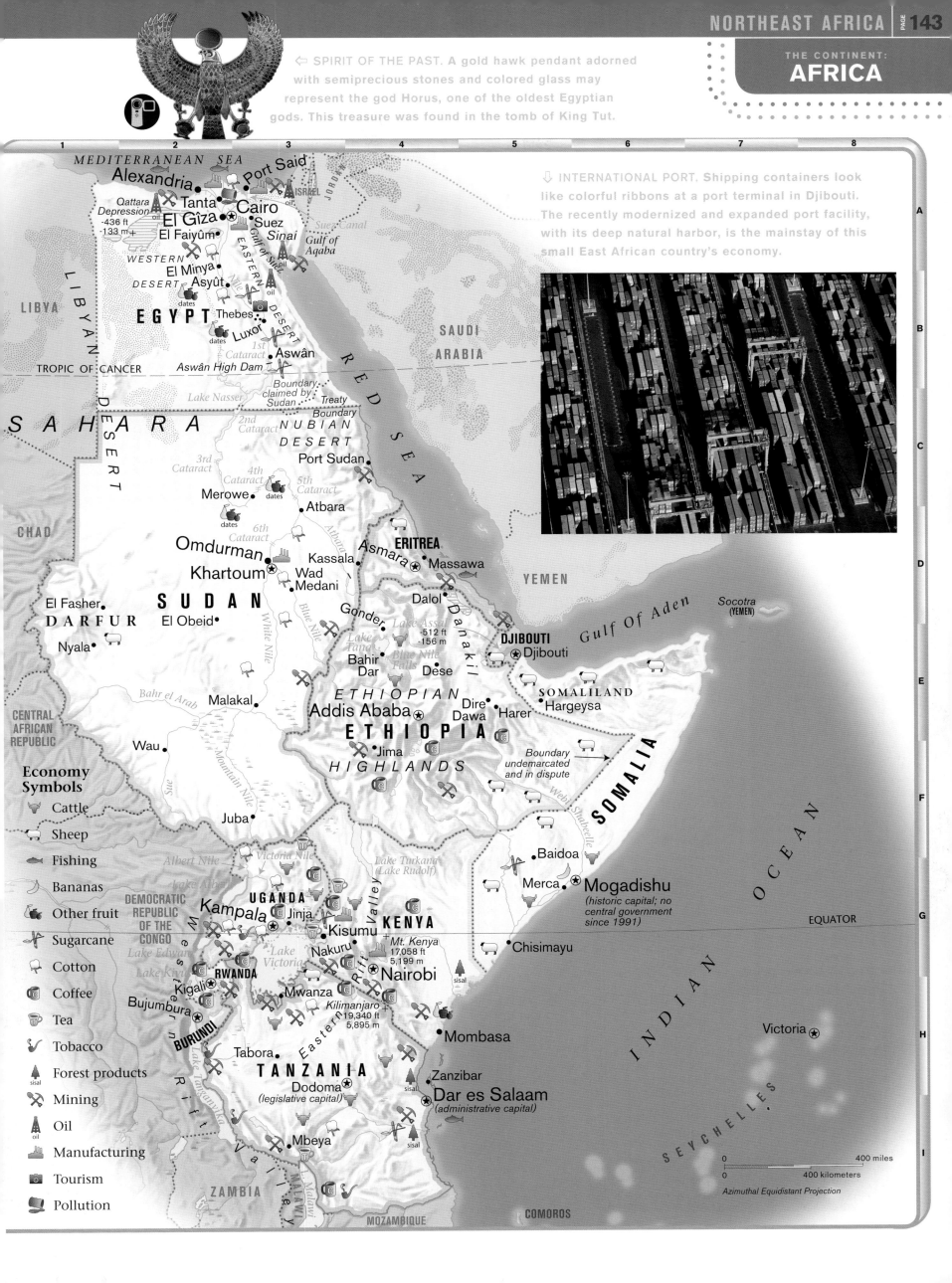

MEDITERRANEAN SEA

Alexandria
Port Said
Tanta
Cairo
ISRAEL
Qattara
Depression
-436 ft
-133 m
El Gîza
Suez
El Faiyûm
Sinai
Gulf of Aqaba
Gulf of Suez
WESTERN
El Minya
DESERT
Asyût

LIBYA

EGYPT
dates
Thebes
Luxor
dates
1st Cataract
Aswân
Aswân High Dam

TROPIC OF CANCER

SAHARA DESERT

LIBYAN DESERT

Lake Nasser
Boundary claimed by Sudan
Treaty Boundary
2nd Cataract
NUBIAN DESERT
3rd Cataract
4th Cataract
5th Cataract

RED SEA

SAUDI ARABIA

Port Sudan
Merowe
dates
Atbara
dates
6th Cataract

CHAD

Omdurman
Khartoum
Kassala
Wad Medani

SUDAN

El Fasher
DARFUR
El Obeid
Nyala

White Nile
Blue Nile

Asmara
ERITREA
Massawa
Dalol
Danakil

YEMEN

Socotra (YEMEN)

Gulf Of Aden

Gonder
Lake Tana
Bahir Dar
Blue Nile Falls
Dese
Lake Assal
-512 ft
-156 m
DJIBOUTI
Djibouti

CENTRAL AFRICAN REPUBLIC

Bahr el Arab
Malakal
Mountain Nile

ETHIOPIAN
Addis Ababa
Dire Dawa
Harer
SOMALILAND
Hargeysa

ETHIOPIA
Wau
Jima
HIGHLANDS

Boundary undemarcated and in dispute

SOMALIA

Sue

Juba

Economy Symbols

🐂 Cattle
🐑 Sheep
🐟 Fishing
🍌 Bananas
🍇 Other fruit
🌾 Sugarcane
🌱 Cotton
☕ Coffee
🍵 Tea
🚬 Tobacco
🌲 Forest products
⚒ Mining
🛢 Oil
🏭 Manufacturing
📷 Tourism
💨 Pollution

Albert Nile
Victoria Nile
Lake Turkana (Lake Rudolf)

Baidoa
Merca
Mogadishu
(historic capital; no central government since 1991)

Western Rift Valley

DEMOCRATIC REPUBLIC OF THE CONGO

UGANDA
Kampala
Jinja
Lake Edward
Lake Kivu
Kisumu
Nakuru
KENYA
Mt. Kenya
17,058 ft
5,199 m
Nairobi

EQUATOR

Chisimayu

RWANDA
Kigali
Lake Victoria
Mwanza
Bujumbura
BURUNDI
Kilimanjaro
19,340 ft
5,895 m
sisal
Mombasa

Lake Tanganyika
Tabora
TANZANIA
Dodoma
(legislative capital)
Zanzibar
sisal
Dar es Salaam
(administrative capital)

INDIAN OCEAN

Victoria

Eastern Rift Valley

Mbeya
sisal

SEYCHELLES

ZAMBIA

Lake Malawi
MALAWI

0   400 miles
0   400 kilometers
Azimuthal Equidistant Projection

MOZAMBIQUE
COMOROS

Webi Shabeelle

THE CONTINENT:
AFRICA

CENTRAL AFRICA

THE BASICS

STATS

Largest country
Democratic Republic of the Congo
905,365 sq mi (2,344,885 sq km)

Smallest country
São Tomé and Principe
386 sq mi (1,001 sq km)

Most populous country
Democratic Republic of the Congo
62,700,000

Least populous country
São Tomé and Principe 200,000

Predominant languages
Various indigenous languages and
dialects, French, English, Spanish

Predominant religions
Christianity, various indigenous
beliefs, Islam

Highest GDP per capita
Equatorial Guinea $7,817

Lowest GDP per capita
Democratic Republic of the Congo $115

Highest life expectancy
São Tomé and Principe 63 years

Highest literacy rate
Equatorial Guinea
86%

GEO WHIZ

Income from oil production gives
Equatorial Guinea the highest GDP
per capita in the region, but wealth is
unevenly distributed. Most people still
practice subsistence farming and enjoy
few benefits from oil revenues.

Biologist and conservationist J. Michael
Fay hiked 2,000 miles (3,200 km)
through dense tropical forest to
survey the land and wildlife of
the Congo River basin.

The Mbuti Pygmies, hunter-gatherers
of the Ituri forest in the Democratic
Republic of the Congo, hunt cat-size
antelope. They yodel as they beat the
bush to drive the animals into their
nets, a practice that is more than a
thousand years old.

Measuring a foot (32 cm) long and
weighing seven pounds (3 kg), the
goliath frog has a hind foot
bigger than a man's palm. The
world's largest frog lives only in
the rain forests of Cameroon and
Equatorial Guinea.

French is the official language of most of this region. The Congo, the region's longest river and chief commercial highway, flows through rain forests that, despite efforts to save them, are being cut for timber and palm oil plantations. Oil fields dot the coasts of Gabon and Cameroon, while diamonds and reserves of metals such as copper and chromium are mined for export in the Central African Republic and the Democratic Republic of the Congo. Coffee is grown in highland regions, and Chadians raise livestock as well as cotton and other crops. Extended drought and diversion of water for agriculture have reduced Lake Chad to one-twentieth of its former size.

⇧ CATCHING A RIDE. A big flatbed truck, diesel engine churning, carries people and freight across the dusty brown Sahara. Men from poverty-stricken Chad travel to Libya, along with their belongings, for short-term work, then return home.

⇨ WOMEN'S WORK. Villagers throughout Africa depend on wood as their main source of fuel to cook and heat their homes. This helps cause widespread deforestation. These women carry wood out of Virunga National Park in the Democratic Republic of the Congo.

VANISHING FORESTS

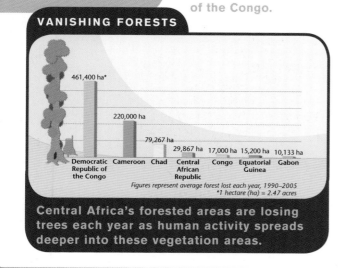

461,400 ha*

220,000 ha

79,267 ha

29,867 ha   17,000 ha   15,200 ha   10,133 ha

Democratic   Cameroon Chad   Central   Congo Equatorial Gabon
Republic of   African   Guinea
the Congo   Republic

Figures represent average forest lost each year, 1990–2005
*1 hectare (ha) = 2.47 acres

Central Africa's forested areas are losing
trees each year as human activity spreads
deeper into these vegetation areas.

⇦ CELEBRATING A KING. The Chokwe people of Central Africa used masks such as this to celebrate the inauguration of a new king. Considered sacred, the mask could only be worn by the current chief of a group.

⇩ WESTERN LOWLAND GORILLAS. This gorilla in Gabon faces threats from disease, poaching, and habitat loss. Gabon is protecting lowland gorillas in its national parks.

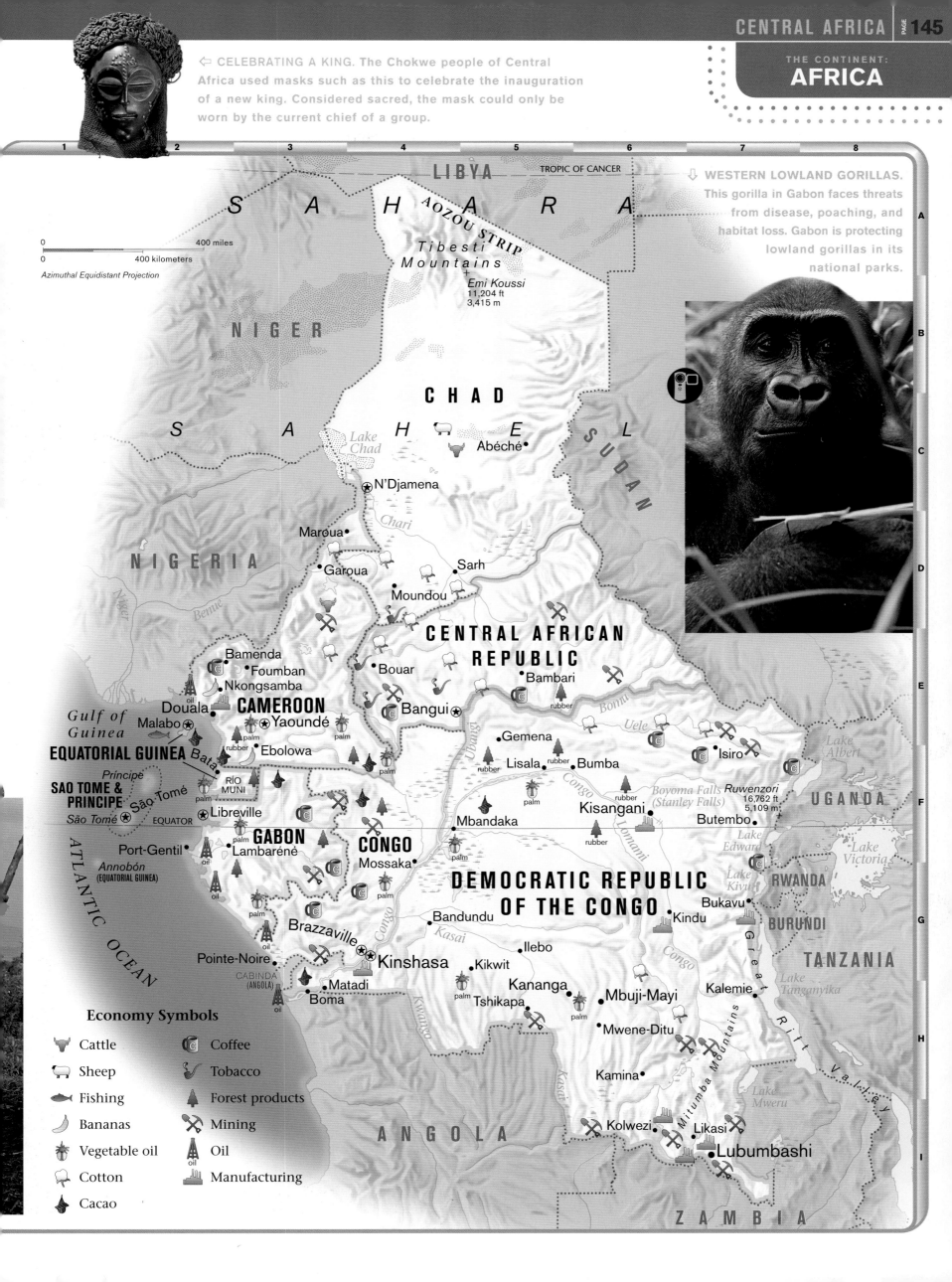

LIBYA

TROPIC OF CANCER

S A H A R A

Aozou Strip

Tibesti Mountains

+ *Emi Koussi* 11,204 ft 3,415 m

NIGER

0 ——— 400 miles
0 ——— 400 kilometers
Azimuthal Equidistant Projection

C H A D

S A H E L

SUDAN

Lake Chad

Abéché •

N'Djamena ★

Chari

NIGERIA

Maroua •

Garoua •

Sarh •

Moundou •

Benue

Niger

CENTRAL AFRICAN REPUBLIC

Bamenda •

Foumban •

Bouar •

Bambari •

Nkongsamba •

oil

Douala •

CAMEROON

Yaoundé ★

Bangui ★

rubber

Gemena •

Bomu

Uele

Gulf of Guinea

Malabo ★

palm

palm

EQUATORIAL GUINEA

Bata •

rubber

Ebolowa •

Lisala •

Bumba •

rubber

Isiro •

Lake Albert

Príncipe

SAO TOME & PRINCIPE

RÍO MUNI

São Tomé

palm

Congo

rubber

Boyoma Falls (Stanley Falls)

Ruwenzori 16,762 ft 5,109 m

UGANDA

São Tomé ★

EQUATOR

Libreville ★

Ubangi

palm

Kisangani •

Mbandaka •

Butembo •

GABON

palm

rubber

Lake Edward

Port-Gentil •

oil

Lambaréné •

CONGO

Lomami

RWANDA

Annobón (EQUATORIAL GUINEA)

oil

Mossaka •

palm

DEMOCRATIC REPUBLIC OF THE CONGO

Lake Kivu

Bukavu •

BURUNDI

ATLANTIC OCEAN

palm

Brazzaville ★

Bandundu •

Congo

Kasai

Kindu •

Great Rift Valley

TANZANIA

Pointe-Noire •

Kinshasa ★

Kikwit •

Ilebo •

Kananga •

Kalemie •

Lake Tanganyika

CABINDA (ANGOLA)

Matadi •

palm

Tshikapa •

palm

Mbuji-Mayi •

Boma •

oil

Mwene-Ditu •

Kamina •

Mitumba Mountains

Lake Mweru

ANGOLA

Kolwezi •

Likasi •

Lubumbashi •

Z A M B I A

Economy Symbols

🐂 Cattle
🐑 Sheep
🐟 Fishing
🍌 Bananas
⚘ Vegetable oil
Cotton
Cacao

☕ Coffee
Tobacco
🌲 Forest products
⚒ Mining
oil Oil
🏭 Manufacturing

THE CONTINENT:
AFRICA

THE BASICS

STATS

Largest country
Angola 481,354 sq mi (1,246,700 sq km)

Smallest country
Seychelles 176 sq mi (455 sq km)

Most populous country
South Africa 47,300,000

Least populous country
Seychelles 1,000

Predominant languages
English, French, various indigenous languages and dialects

Predominant religions
Christianity, Islam, various indigenous beliefs

Highest GDP per capita
Seychelles $8,246

Lowest GDP per capita
Malawi $164

Highest life expectancy
Mauritius 72 years

Highest literacy rate
Seychelles 92%

GEO WHIZ

South Africa's Kruger National Park, largest in Africa, covers more area than the entire country of Israel. Within its boundary are 14 different ecological zones that provide habitat to a great variety of plants, birds, and other animals, including the "big five": lions, elephants, leopards, rhinos, and buffaloes.

Great Zimbabwe National Monument has the largest ancient stone ruins south of the Sahara. This massive fortress city was the center of an empire that flourished from the 11th to the 15th century.

The Makgadikgadi salt pans in the eastern Kalahari of Botswana are what is left of an immense lake. Each spring, rains flood the area and attract herds of migrating zebras and wildebeests.

Namibia is famed for sand dunes that are reportedly the highest in the world. The largest, Big Daddy, towers 1,200 feet (366 m) above the the surrounding land. Along Namibia's northwestern coast, treacherous crosscurrents have caused countless shipwrecks, earning it the nickname Skeleton Coast.

SOUTHERN AFRICA

Ringed by uplands, the region's central basin holds the seasonally lush Okavango Delta and scorch-

⇧ NATURAL WONDER. Victoria Falls, third largest waterfall in the world, is 5,500 feet (1,676 m) wide and 355 feet (108 m) high.

ing Kalahari Desert. The mighty Zambezi thunders over Victoria Falls on its way to the Indian Ocean, where Madagascar is home to plants and animals found nowhere else in the world. Bantu and San are among the indigenous people who saw their hold on the land give way to Portuguese, Dutch, and British traders and colonists. The region offers a range of mineral resources and a variety of climates and soils that in some places yield bumper crops of grains, grapes, and citrus. Rich deposits of coal, gold, and diamonds have helped make South Africa the continent's economic powerhouse.

⇦ STARING EYES. This ring-tailed lemur sits on a forest tree branch. The ring-tail, found only in Madagascar, spends time both on the ground and in the trees. It eats fruits, leaves, insects, small birds, and even lizards.

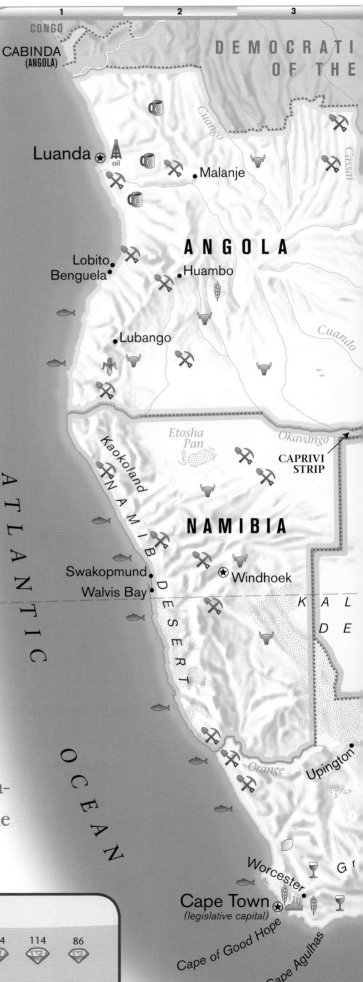

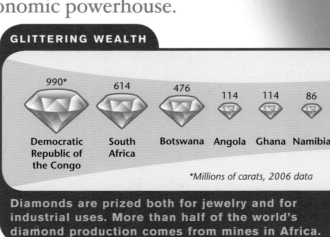

GLITTERING WEALTH

990*	614	476	114	114	86
Democratic Republic of the Congo	South Africa	Botswana	Angola	Ghana	Namibia

*Millions of carats, 2006 data

Diamonds are prized both for jewelry and for industrial uses. More than half of the world's diamond production comes from mines in Africa.

⇐ EARLY MAN. Dating back perhaps 70,000 years, this skull of "Broken Hill Man," found in Zimbabwe, is thought to represent a transitional type between *Homo erectus* and *Homo sapiens.*

Economy Symbols

Cattle	Coffee	Coal
Fishing	Tea	Oil
Citrus	Wine	Manufacturing
Corn	Tobacco	
Other grains	Mining	

0 _____ 200 miles
0 _____ 300 kilometers
Azimuthal Equidistant Projection

DEMOCRATIC REPUBLIC OF THE CONGO

TANZANIA

Lake Tanganyika

Lake Malawi

Rovuma

SEYCHELLES

Moroni ⊛

COMOROS

Pemba

Îles Glorieuses (FRANCE)

Cap d'Ambre

Antsiranana

Mayotte (FRANCE)

Maromokotro
9,436 ft
2,876 m

Zambezi

Mufulira
Chingola
Kitwe Ndola
Kabwe
ZAMBIA
Mongo
Lusaka ⊛

Lilongwe ⊛

MALAWI

Tete

Blantyre

MOZAMBIQUE

Moçambique

Nampula

Mahajanga

MADAGASCAR

Antsirabe

Antananarivo ⊛

Toamasina

Juan De Nova (FRANCE)

Victoria Falls
Livingstone

Lake Kariba

Harare ⊛

ZIMBABWE

Bulawayo

Great Zimbabwe

Quelimane

Beira

Mozambique Channel

Fianarantsoa

Okavango Delta

Makgadikgadi Pans

BOTSWANA

Serowe

Bassas Da India (FRANCE)

Île Europa (FRANCE)

Toliara

TROPIC OF CAPRICORN

Limpopo

Inhambane

Xai-Xai

Maputo

Mbabane *(administrative capital)*
SWAZILAND
Lobamba *(legislative and royal capital)*

Cap Ste. Marie

For Mauritius and Réunion, see maps on pages 134–135.

KALAHARI DESERT

Gaborone ⊛
Kanye

Polokwane (Pietersburg)

Pretoria (Tshwane) *(administrative capital)*

Johannesburg

Klerksdorp

SOUTH

Welkom
Kimberley
Bloemfontein ⊛ *(judicial capital)*

AFRICA

Kroonstad

Maseru ⊛
LESOTHO

Pietermaritzburg

Durban

INDIAN OCEAN

Vaal
Orange

Drakensberg

Great Karroo
Queenstown
Oudtshoorn Grahamstown
Port Elizabeth
East London

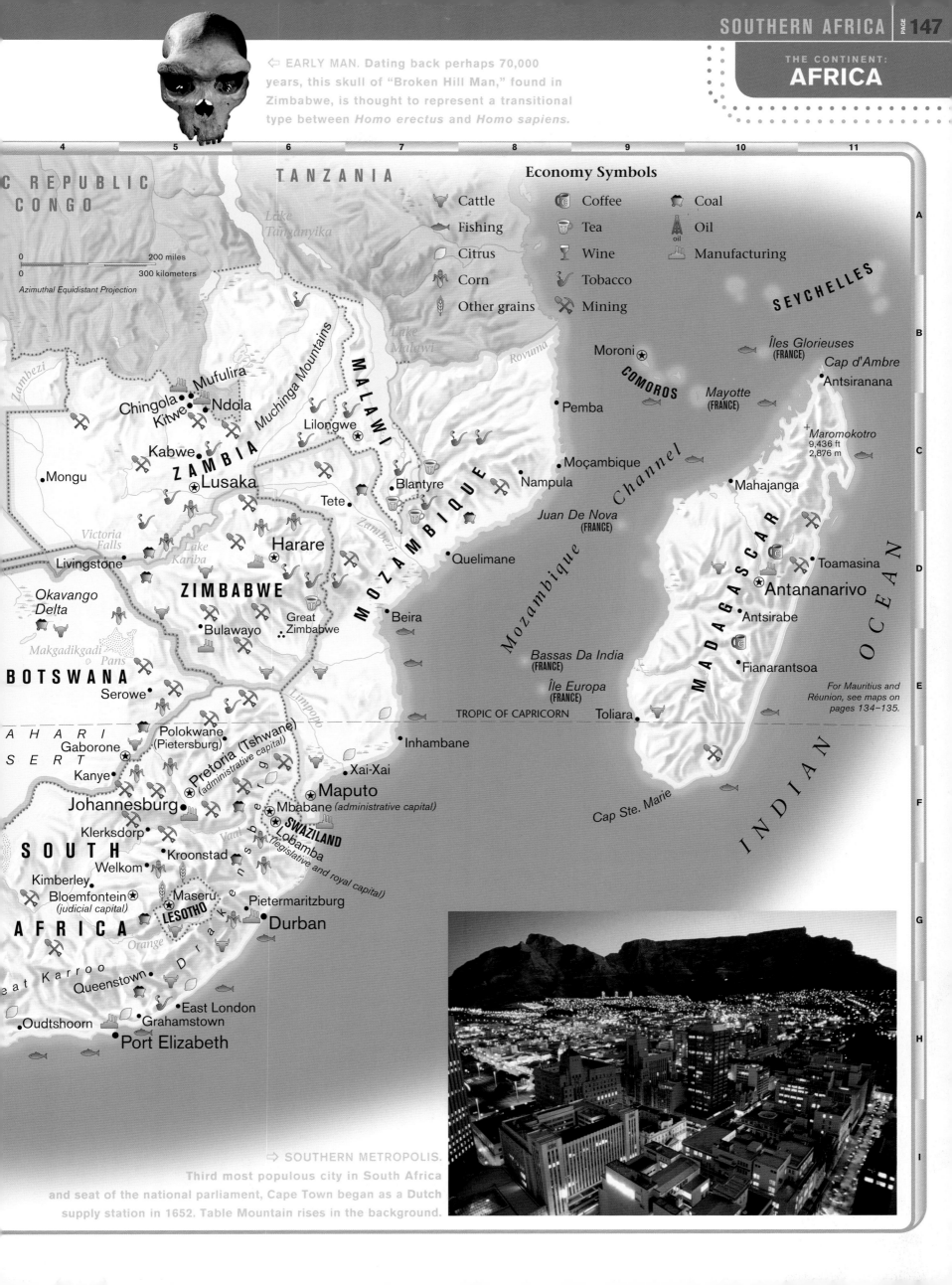

⇒ SOUTHERN METROPOLIS. Third most populous city in South Africa and seat of the national parliament, Cape Town began as a Dutch supply station in 1652. Table Mountain rises in the background.

THE REGION:

AUSTRALIA,
NEW ZEALAND, & OCEANIA

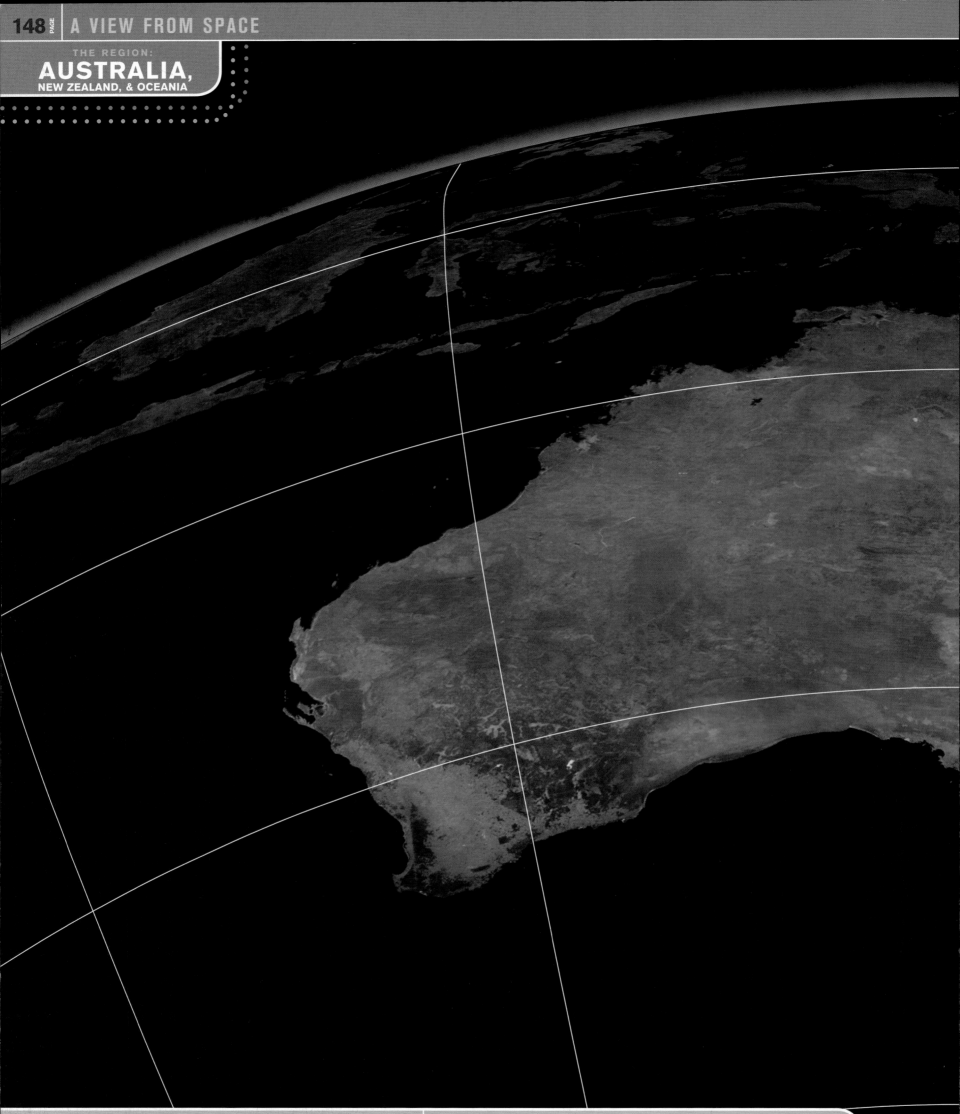

PHYSICAL			POLITICAL		
Area and population totals are for the independent counties in the region only.	Highest point **Mount Wilhelm, Papua New Guinea** **14,793 ft (4,509 m)**	Longest river **Murray-Darling, Australia** **2,310 mi (3,718 km)**	Population **32,840,000**	Largest country **Australia** **2,969,906 sq mi (7,692,024 sq km)**	Economy **Farming: livestock, wheat, fruit**
Land area **3,278,000 sq mi** **(8,490,000 sq km)**	Lowest point **Lake Eyre, Australia** **-52 ft (-16 m)**	Largest lake **Lake Eyre, Australia** **3,430 sq mi (8,884 sq km)**	Largest metropolitan area **Sydney, Australia** **Pop. 4,274,000**	Most densely populated country **Nauru** **1,529 people per sq mi (590 per sq km)**	Industry: mining, wool, oil Services

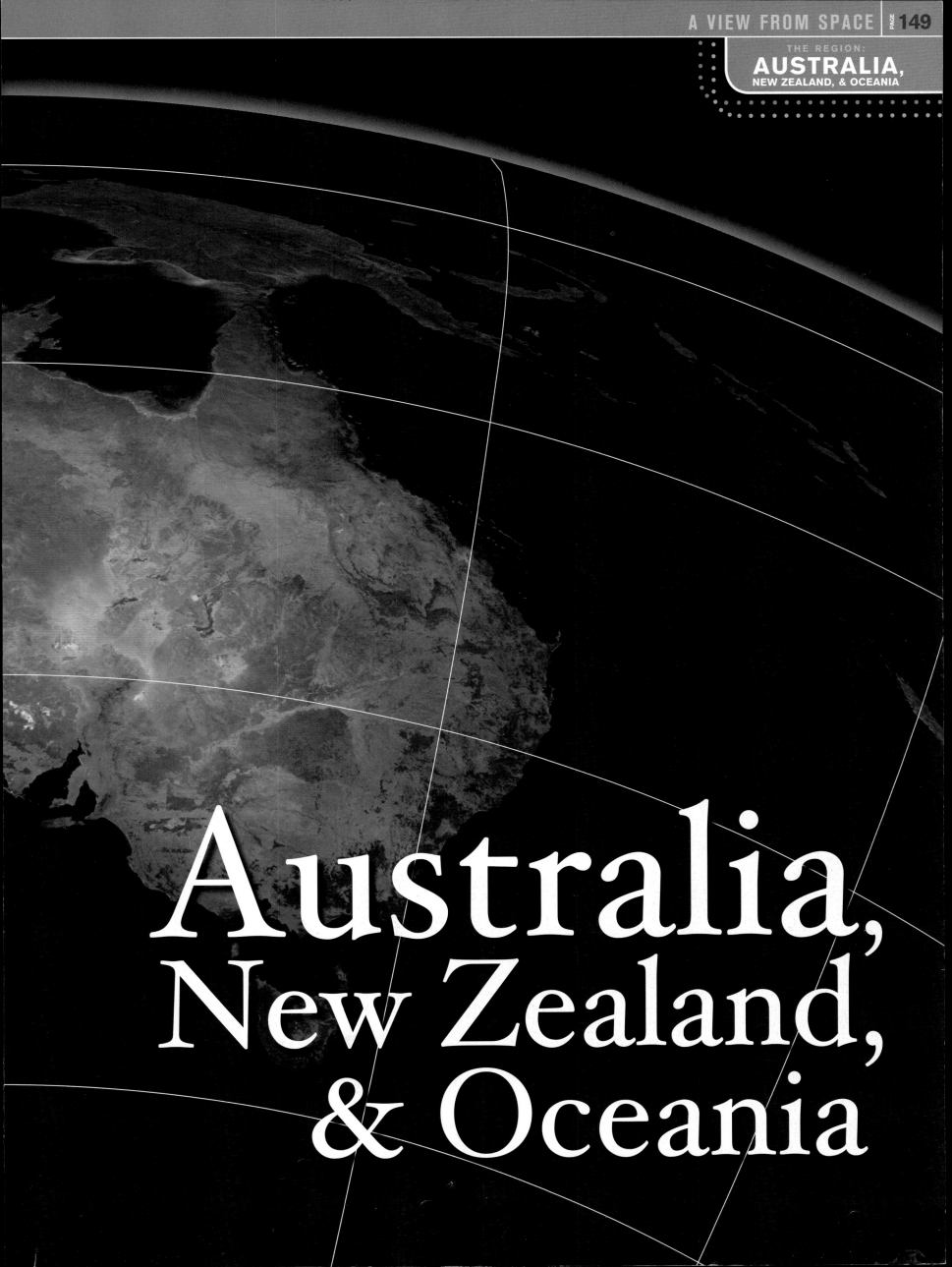

Australia, New Zealand, & Oceania

AUSTRALIA
NEW ZEALAND, & OCEANIA

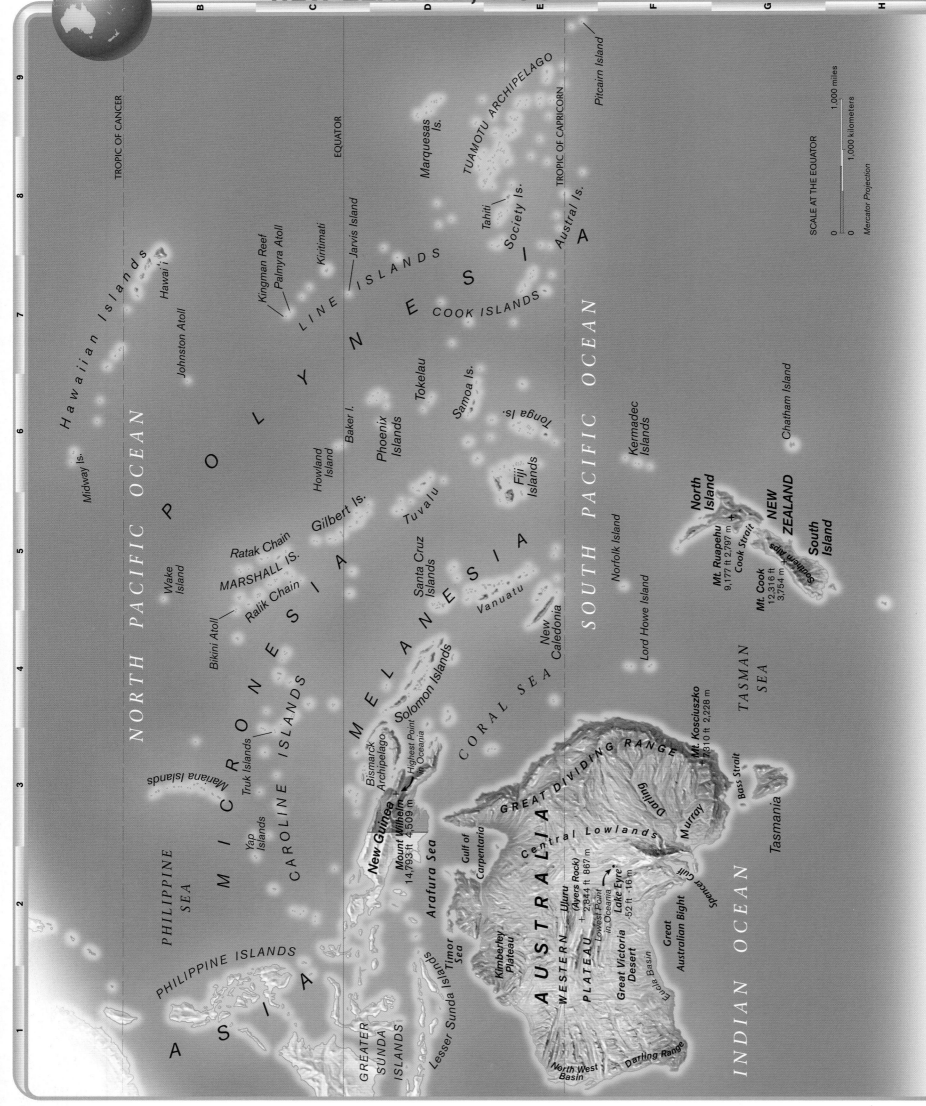

SCALE AT THE EQUATOR

1,000 miles

1,000 kilometers

Mercator Projection

TROPIC OF CANCER

EQUATOR

TROPIC OF CAPRICORN

Pitcairn Island

TUAMOTU ARCHIPELAGO

Marquesas Is.

Tahiti

Society Is.

Austral Is.

COOK ISLANDS

LINE ISLANDS

Kingman Reef
Palmyra Atoll
Kiritimati

Jarvis Island

Hawaiian Islands

Hawai'i

Johnston Atoll

Midway Is.

NORTH PACIFIC OCEAN

P O L Y N E S I A

Chatham Island

Baker I.
Howland Island
Phoenix Islands

Tokelau

Samoa Is.

Tonga Is.

Fiji Islands

Tuvalu

Gilbert Is.

Ratak Chain
MARSHALL IS.
Ralik Chain

Wake Island

Bikini Atoll

Yap Islands
Truk Islands

Mariana Islands

MICRONESIA

CAROLINE ISLANDS

M E L A N E S I A

Santa Cruz Islands

Vanuatu

New Caledonia

Kermadec Islands

Norfolk Island

Lord Howe Island

North Island

NEW ZEALAND

South Island

Mt. Ruapehu
9,177 ft 2,797 m

Cook Strait

Mt. Cook
12,316 ft
3,754 m

Southern Alps

SOUTH PACIFIC OCEAN

TASMAN SEA

Bass Strait

Tasmania

PHILIPPINE SEA

PHILIPPINE ISLANDS

GREATER SUNDA ISLANDS

Lesser Sunda Islands

Timor Sea

A S I A

New Guinea

Mount Wilhelm
14,793 ft 4,509 m

Bismarck Archipelago

Highest Point in Oceania

Solomon Islands

Arafura Sea

Gulf of Carpentaria

CORAL SEA

A U S T R A L I A

WESTERN PLATEAU

Kimberley Plateau

Great Victoria Desert

Uluru
(Ayers Rock)
+ 2,844 ft 867 m

Lake Eyre
-52 ft -16 m
Lowest Point in Oceania

Central Lowlands

GREAT DIVIDING RANGE

Darling

Murray

Mt. Kosciuszko
+ 7,310 ft 2,228 m

Eyola Basin

Spencer Gulf

Great Australian Bight

Darling Range

North West Basin

INDIAN OCEAN

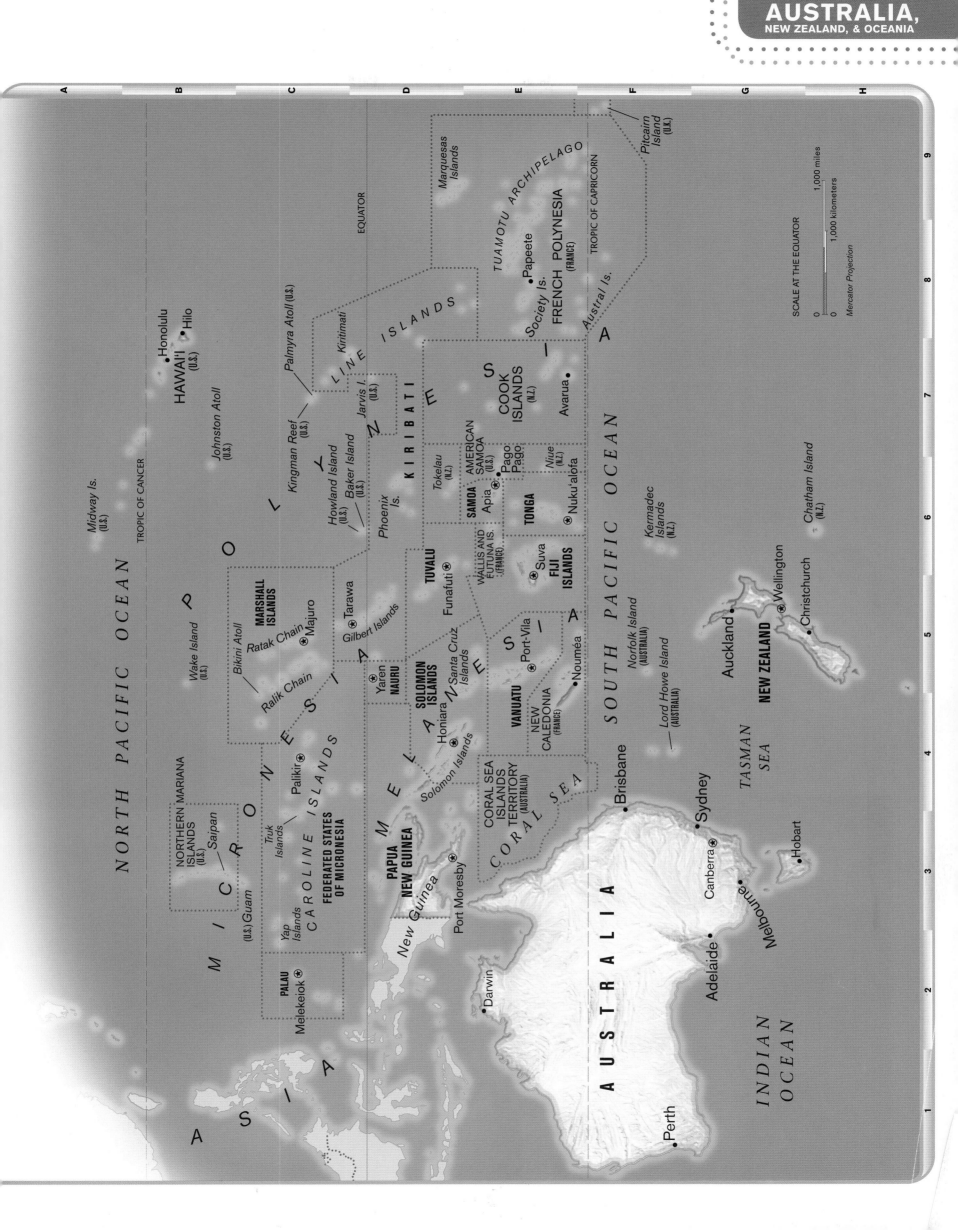

A B C D E F G H

NORTH PACIFIC OCEAN

EQUATOR

TROPIC OF CANCER

Midway Is. (U.S.)

Honolulu
Hilo
HAWAI'I (U.S.)

Johnston Atoll (U.S.)

Palmyra Atoll (U.S.)

Kingman Reef (U.S.)

LINE ISLANDS

Kiritimati

Jarvis I. (U.S.)

Howland Island (U.S.)
Baker Island (U.S.)

Phoenix Is.

KIRIBATI

Tokelau (N.Z.)

AMERICAN SAMOA (U.S.)
Pago Pago

SAMOA
Apia

Niue (N.Z.)

Nuku'alofa

TONGA

Marquesas Islands

TUAMOTU ARCHIPELAGO

TROPIC OF CAPRICORN

Society Is.
Papeete
FRENCH POLYNESIA (FRANCE)

Austral Is.

COOK ISLANDS (N.Z.)
Avarua

POLYNESIA

Pitcairn Island (U.K.)

SCALE AT THE EQUATOR
1,000 miles
1,000 kilometers
Mercator Projection

NORTH PACIFIC OCEAN

Wake Island (U.S.)

MARSHALL ISLANDS

Bikini Atoll
Ratak Chain
Majuro

Ralik Chain

Tarawa
Gilbert Islands

TUVALU
Funafuti

WALLIS AND FUTUNA IS. (FRANCE)

Suva
FIJI ISLANDS

MICRONESIA

NORTHERN MARIANA ISLANDS (U.S.)
Saipan

Truk Islands

Palikir
CAROLINE ISLANDS

FEDERATED STATES OF MICRONESIA

(U.S.) Guam

Yap Islands

Yaren NAURU

SOLOMON ISLANDS
Honiara

Santa Cruz Islands

MELANESIA

Port-Vila
VANUATU

NEW CALEDONIA (FRANCE)
Nouméa

SOUTH PACIFIC OCEAN

Norfolk Island (AUSTRALIA)

Lord Howe Island (AUSTRALIA)

Kermadec Islands (N.Z.)

Chatham Island (N.Z.)

Wellington
NEW ZEALAND
Auckland
Christchurch

TASMAN SEA

ASIA

PALAU
Melekeiok

PAPUA NEW GUINEA
New Guinea
Port Moresby

Solomon Islands

CORAL SEA ISLANDS TERRITORY (AUSTRALIA)

CORAL SEA

AUSTRALIA

Darwin

Brisbane
Sydney
Canberra
Melbourne
Adelaide
Hobart

Perth

INDIAN OCEAN

1 2 3 4 5 6 7 8 9

Australia,
New Zealand, & Oceania
WORLDS APART

This vast region includes Australia—the world's smallest continent—New Zealand, and a fleet of mostly tiny island worlds scattered across the Pacific Ocean. Apart from Australia, New Zealand, and Papua New Guinea, Oceania's other 11 independent countries cover about 25,000 square miles (65,000 sq km), an area only slightly larger than half of New Zealand's North Island. Twenty-one other island groups are dependencies of the United States, France, Australia, New Zealand, or the United Kingdom. Long isolation has allowed the growth of diverse marine communities such as Australia's Great Barrier Reef and the evolution of platypuses, kangaroos, and other land animals that live nowhere else on the planet.

⇧ AUSTRALIAN TEDDY BEAR. Koalas, which are not bears at all, are native to the eucalyptus forests of eastern Australia.

⇐ ANCIENT VOYAGERS. The Maoris are believed to have sailed to New Zealand from islands, far to the northeast. Maori warriors traditionally adorned themselves with elaborate tattoos to frighten enemies.

⇓ PLACE OF LEGENDS. Sacred to native Aborigines, Uluru, also known as Ayers Rock, glows a deep red in the rays of the setting sun. Uluru is the tip of a massive sandstone block—part of an ancient seabed exposed by erosion.

⇐ TROPICAL HABITAT. Brilliantly colored fish swim among branching corals in the warm waters of the Vatuira Channel in the Fiji Islands. The waters around Fiji have some of the richest and most diverse fish populations in the world.

⇒ NATIVE COWBOYS. Competition is fierce during a rodeo in Hope Vale, an Aboriginal community on Australia's Cape York Peninsula. Hope Vale is home to several Aboriginal clan groups.

more about AUSTRALIA, NEW ZEALAND & OCEANIA

⇧ BIG JUMPER. The red kangaroo, largest living marsupial—an animal that carries its young in a pouch—is at home on the dry inland plains of Australia. It can cover 30 feet (9 m) in a single hop.

⇦ HOT SPOT. This geothermal pool at Waiotapu, on New Zealand's North Island, is evidence of ongoing volcanic activity. Minerals dissolved in superheated water give the pool its vivid colors.

⇦ FESTIVAL DRESS. Women of Tanna Island, in Vanuatu, wear face paint and ceremonial clothes in preparation for a festival. Traditional festivals often involve an elaborate exchange of gifts, such as pigs, mats, and baskets, between villages to gain social status.

⇓ A WATER WORLD. Located just 7 degrees north of the Equator in the western Pacific Ocean, the islands of the Republic of Palau were a United Nations Trust Territory until 1994, when they gained independence.

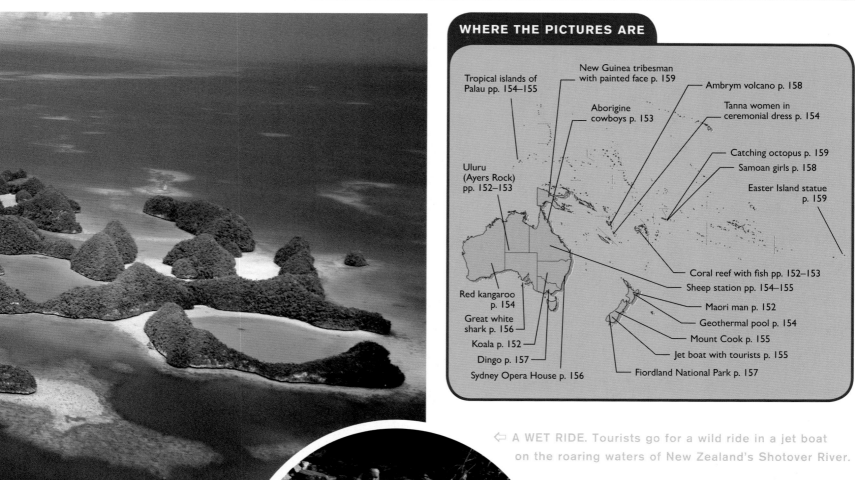

WHERE THE PICTURES ARE

Tropical islands of Palau pp. 154–155

New Guinea tribesman with painted face p. 159

Ambrym volcano p. 158

Aborigine cowboys p. 153

Tanna women in ceremonial dress p. 154

Uluru (Ayers Rock) pp. 152–153

Catching octopus p. 159

Samoan girls p. 158

Easter Island statue p. 159

Red kangaroo p. 154

Great white shark p. 156

Koala p. 152

Dingo p. 157

Sydney Opera House p. 156

Coral reef with fish pp. 152–153

Sheep station pp. 154–155

Maori man p. 152

Geothermal pool p. 154

Mount Cook p. 155

Jet boat with tourists p. 155

Fiordland National Park p. 157

⇐ A WET RIDE. Tourists go for a wild ride in a jet boat on the roaring waters of New Zealand's Shotover River.

⇓ SNOWY PEAK. New Zealand's Mount Cook rises above the clouds. Legend says the peak is a frozen Maori warrior.

⇓ A SEA OF SHEEP. Sheep outnumber people in Australia and New Zealand. Wool production is an important part of the economy of these two countries.

THE BASICS

STATS

Largest country
Australia 2,969,906 sq mi
(7,692,024 sq km)

Smallest country
New Zealand 104,454 sq mi
(270,534 sq km)

Most populous country
Australia 20,600,000

Least populous country
New Zealand 4,100,000

Predominant languages
English, Maori

Predominant religion
Christianity

Highest GDP per capita
Australia $36,016

Lowest GDP per capita
New Zealand $25,566

Highest life expectancy
Australia 80 years

Highest literacy rate
Australia
100%

GEO WHIZ

Australian Aborigines use a small tree trunk hollowed out by termites to make a musical instrument called a didgeridoo.

One fourth of New Zealand's population lives in Auckland, on North Island, making it the largest city in Polynesia.

Lake Eyre is Australia's largest lake, but it is very shallow—not quite 20 feet (6 m) when full. Most of the rivers that flow into it dry up before they reach the lake. During the last 150 years, it has filled to capacity only three times.

Australia's location south of the Equator earned it the nickname Land Down Under.

The ceilings of grottoes in New Zealand's Waitomo Caves look like starry night skies thanks to the light given off by thousands of glowworms.

The Tasmanian devil is a meat-eating marsupial that lives only in Tasmania. Its high-pitched screeches can be heard at night when the animal is most active. This protected species is the symbol of the Tasmanian National Parks and Wildlife Service.

AUSTRALIA & NEW ZEALAND

Most people in Australia live along the coast, far from the country's dry interior, known as the Outback. The most populous cities and the best croplands are in the southeast. This "Land Down Under" is increasingly linked by trade to Asian countries and to 4 million "neighbors" in New Zealand. Twelve hundred miles (1,930 km) across the Tasman Sea, New Zealand is cooler, wetter, and more mountainous than Australia. It is geologically active and has ecosystems ranging from subtropical forests on North Island to snowy peaks on South Island. Both countries enjoy high standards of living and strong agricultural and mining outputs, including wool, wines, gold, coal, and iron ore.

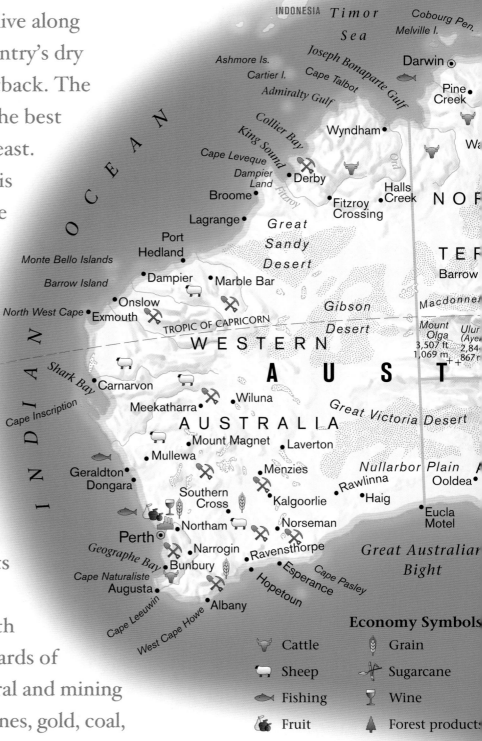

Economy Symbols

- Cattle
- Sheep
- Fishing
- Fruit
- Grain
- Sugarcane
- Wine
- Forest products

⇐ KILLER OF THE DEEP. Great white sharks inhabit the warm waters off the coast of southern Australia. These warm-blooded marine predators can grow up to 20 feet (6 m) in length.

⇒ SAILS AT SUNSET. Reminiscent of a ship in full sail, the Sydney Opera House, in Sydney Harbor, has become a symbol of Australia that is recognized around the world.

⇐ DOG OF THE OUTBACK. The dingo is a wild dog found throughout Australia except for Tasmania. Unlike most domestic dogs, the dingo does not bark, although it howls. Aborigines sometimes use dingos as hunting companions or guard dogs.

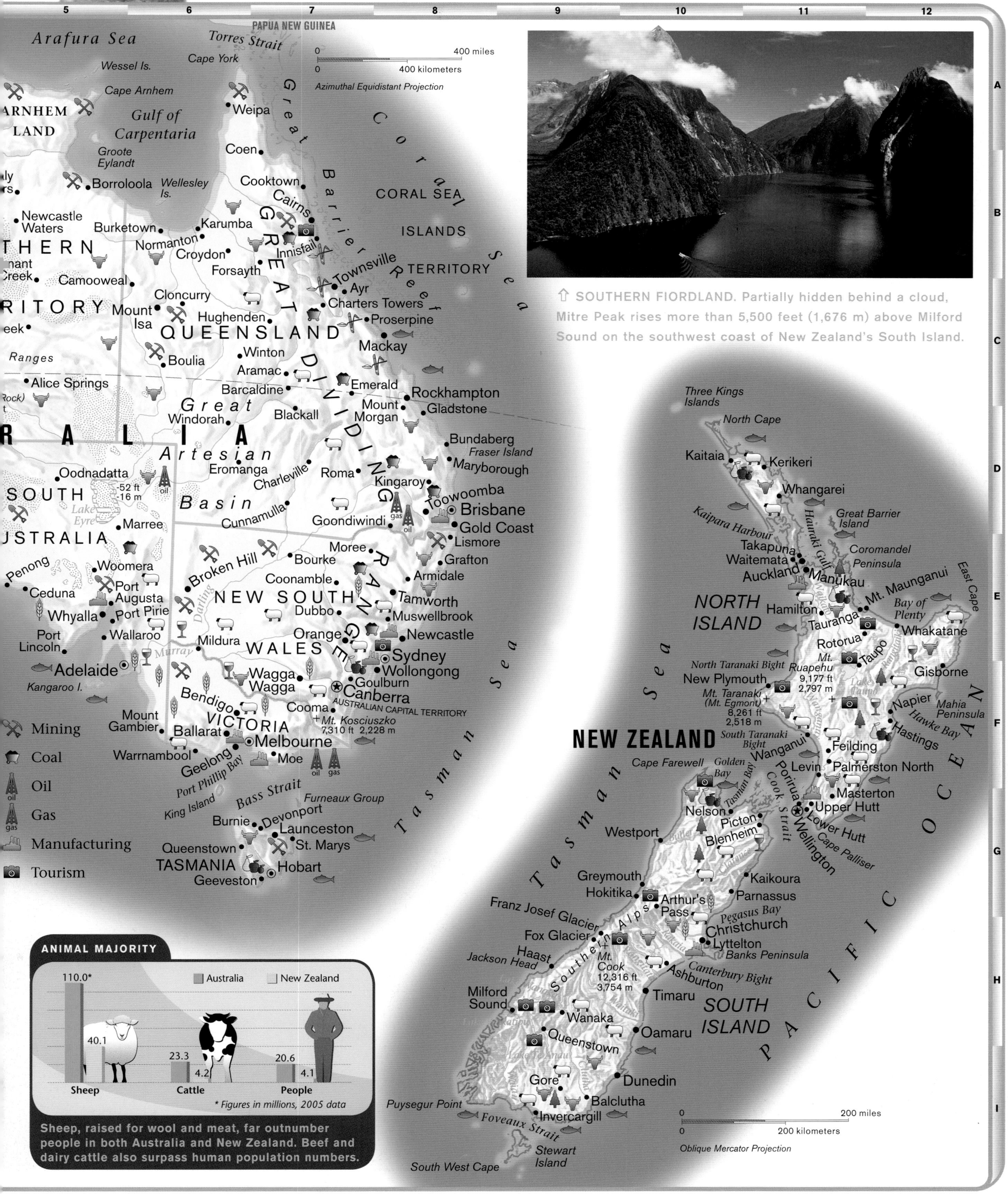

⇑ SOUTHERN FIORDLAND. Partially hidden behind a cloud, Mitre Peak rises more than 5,500 feet (1,676 m) above Milford Sound on the southwest coast of New Zealand's South Island.

Map labels — Australia

Arafura Sea
Torres Strait
PAPUA NEW GUINEA
Wessel Is.
Cape York
Cape Arnhem
ARNHEM LAND
Gulf of Carpentaria
Groote Eylandt
Weipa
Coen
Wellesley Is.
Borroloola
Cooktown
Cairns
Coral Sea
CORAL SEA ISLANDS
Newcastle Waters
Burketown
Karumba
Normanton
Croydon
Innisfail
Townsville
TERRITORY
Forsayth
Ayr
GREAT BARRIER REEF
Camooweal
Cloncurry
Hughenden
Charters Towers
Proserpine
Mount Isa
QUEENSLAND
Boulia
Winton
Mackay
Ranges
Aramac
Emerald
Rockhampton
Alice Springs
Barcaldine
Mount Morgan
Gladstone
Great
Blackall
Windorah
Artesian
Eromanga
Charleville
Roma
Kingaroy
Bundaberg
Fraser Island
Maryborough
Oodnadatta
-52 ft -16 m
oil
Basin
Cunnamulla
Toowoomba
Brisbane
SOUTH
Lake Eyre
Goondiwindi
Gold Coast
Marree
Moree
Lismore
AUSTRALIA
Bourke
Grafton
Penong
Broken Hill
Coonamble
Armidale
Woomera
Ceduna
Coonable
NEW SOUTH
Tamworth
Whyalla
Port Augusta
Dubbo
Muswellbrook
Port Pirie
Orange
Newcastle
Port Lincoln
Wallaroo
Mildura
WALES
Sydney
Adelaide
Wagga Wagga
Wollongong
Kangaroo I.
Bendigo
Goulburn
Canberra
AUSTRALIAN CAPITAL TERRITORY
Cooma
Mount Gambier
VICTORIA
Mt. Kosciuszko 7,310 ft 2,228 m
Ballarat
Melbourne
Warrnambool
Geelong
Moe
Port Phillip Bay
oil gas
King Island
Bass Strait
Furneaux Group
Burnie
Devonport
Tasman Sea
Queenstown
Launceston
St. Marys
TASMANIA
Hobart
Geeveston

Map labels — New Zealand

Three Kings Islands
North Cape
Kaitaia
Kerikeri
Whangarei
Great Barrier Island
Kaipara Harbour
Takapuna
Coromandel Peninsula
Waitemata
Auckland
Manukau
Hauraki Gulf
East Cape
NORTH ISLAND
Hamilton
Tauranga
Mt. Maunganui
Bay of Plenty
Rotorua
Whakatane
North Taranaki Bight
Mt. Ruapehu 9,177 ft 2,797 m
Taupo
New Plymouth
Mt. Taranaki (Mt. Egmont) 8,261 ft 2,518 m
Gisborne
Napier
Mahia Peninsula
NEW ZEALAND
South Taranaki Bight
Hastings
Wanganui
Feilding
Hawke Bay
Cape Farewell
Golden Bay
Levin
Palmerston North
Porirua
Nelson
Wanganui
Masterton
Westport
Picton
Upper Hutt
Blenheim
Lower Hutt
Cook Strait
Wellington
Cape Palliser
Greymouth
Kaikoura
Hokitika
Parnassus
Franz Josef Glacier
Arthur's Pass
Pegasus Bay
Fox Glacier
Southern Alps
Christchurch
Haast
Lyttelton
Jackson Head
Mt. Cook 12,316 ft 3,754 m
Banks Peninsula
Ashburton
Milford Sound
Canterbury Bight
Wanaka
Timaru
SOUTH ISLAND
Queenstown
Oamaru
PACIFIC OCEAN
Gore
Dunedin
Puysegur Point
Balclutha
Foveaux Strait
Invercargill
Stewart Island
South West Cape

Legend
⛏ Mining
🪨 Coal
🛢 Oil
Gas
🏭 Manufacturing
📷 Tourism

ANIMAL MAJORITY

	Australia	New Zealand
Sheep	110.0*	40.1
Cattle	23.3	4.2
People	20.6	4.1

*Figures in millions, 2005 data

Sheep, raised for wool and meat, far outnumber people in both Australia and New Zealand. Beef and dairy cattle also surpass human population numbers.

Scale / projection notes
400 miles
400 kilometers
Azimuthal Equidistant Projection

200 miles
200 kilometers
Oblique Mercator Projection

THE BASICS

STATS

Largest country
Papua New Guinea
178,703 sq mi (462,840 sq km)

Smallest country
Nauru 8 sq mi (21 sq km)

Most populous country
Papua New Guinea 6,000,000

Least populous country
Tuvalu 10,000

Predominant languages
English, various indigenous
languages and dialects

Predominant religion
Christianity, various indigenous
beliefs

Highest GDP per capita
Palau $6,717

Lowest GDP per capita
Solomon Islands $585

Highest life expectancy
Samoa 73 years

Highest literacy rate
Samoa
100%

GEO WHIZ

Tuvalu's highest point is roughly 16 feet
(5 m) above sea level. Predictions that
rising sea levels due to global warming could drown the island within the
next 50 years have caused some of its
people to emigrate to New Zealand and
other countries with higher elevations.

 For centuries in Fiji, tribal officials would
bring out their best utensils for
special people—not to serve them,
but to eat them. Cannibalism in
the islands ended in the late 1800s,
when Christianity was adopted.

Only 36 of Tonga's 170 islands are
inhabited. It was in Tongan waters that
the infamous mutiny aboard the British
ship HMAV *Bounty* took place in 1789.

The interior highland region of Papua
New Guinea is so mountainous and
forested that it wasn't explored
by outsiders until the 1930s.
Europeans were surprised to find
people living there whose cultures
hadn't changed since the Stone Age.

Kennedy Island, in the Solomon
Islands, is named for U.S. President
John F. Kennedy. During World War II
he and some of his crew swam to this
island—known as Plum Pudding at the
time—after their PT boat was rammed
by a Japanese destroyer.

⇨ LIVING EARTH.
Ambrym volcano, in Vanuatu,
is one of the most active
volcanoes in Oceania. First
observed by Captain Cook in
1774, Ambrym continues to
erupt regularly, adding to the
island's black sand beaches.

OCEANIA

Although in its broadest sense Oceania includes
Australia and New Zealand, more commonly it
refers to some 25,000 islands that make up
three large cultural
regions in the
Pacific Ocean.
Melanesia,
which extends
from Papua
New Guinea
to Fiji, is clos-
est to Australia.
Micronesia lies
mostly north of
the Equator and
includes Palau and the Federated States of
Micronesia. New Zealand, Hawai'i, and Rapa
Nui (Easter Island) mark the western, northern,
and eastern limits of Polynesia, with Tahiti, Samoa,
and Tonga near its heart. Oceania's people often
face problems of limited living space and fresh water.
Plantation agriculture, fishing, tourism, or mining form
the economic base for most of the islands in this region.

⇧ SUNDAY SERVICES. These
Samoan girls are dressed for
church. The London Missionary
Society brought Christianity to
Samoa in the mid-1800s. The
eastern islands became a U.S.
territory in 1900.

SCALE AT THE EQUATOR
0   1,000 miles
0   1,000 kilometers
Mercator Projection

JAPAN

Bonin Islands
(JAPAN)

Volcano Islands
(JAPAN)

Minami Tori
Shima (Marcus)
(JAPAN)

PHILIPPINE
SEA

NORTHERN MARIANA
ISLANDS
(U.S.)

○ Saipan

M I C R O N

N O R

Guam
(U.S.)

Eneweta
Ato

Yap
Islands

PHILIPPINES

CAROLINE   ISLANDS

coconuts

Senyavin Is.

PALAU
Melekeiok

Palikir

Pohnpe

FEDERATED STATES
OF MICRONESIA

coconuts

Kapingamarangi
Atoll

Admiralty Is.

M E L A

Mount
Wilhelm
14,793 ft
4,509 m

Bismarck
Archipelago

New Ireland

New Britain

Bougainville

Solomon

NEW GUINEA

INDONESIA

coconuts

PAPUA NEW GUINEA

FI

ARAFURA SEA

Torres Strait

Port Moresby

Solomon Sea

coconuts

Honiara

Guadalcanal

C O R A L

CORAL SEA
ISLANDS
TERRITORY
(AUSTRALIA)

AUSTRALIA

S E A

← UNSOLVED MYSTERY. Carved from volcanic rock, the giant stone heads of Rapa Nui, also known as Easter Island, remain a mystery. Although culturally Polynesian, the island belongs to Chile, 2,400 miles (3,862 km) to the east (see page 44).

↓ LONG ARMS. Octopuses live on coral reefs in the warm tropical waters of the South Pacific Ocean. They use the suckers on their tentacles to move around and to catch crustaceans and small fish.

4   5   6   7   8   9   10   11

A
B
C
D
E
F

Midway Islands (U.S.)

H A W A I ' I (UNITED STATES)

TROPIC OF CANCER

Honolulu   O'ahu
            Hawai'i

Wake Island (U.S.)

NORTH PACIFIC OCEAN

Johnston Atoll (U.S.)

P O L Y

Bikini Atoll

MARSHALL ISLANDS

coconuts

Ratak Chain

Ralik Chain

Majuro

Kingman Reef (U.S.)
Palmyra Atoll (U.S.)

Kiritimati (Christmas I.)
coconuts

Gilbert Islands

Tarawa

Yaren
NAURU

coconuts

K I R I B A T I

Howland Island (U.S.)
Baker Island (U.S.)

L I N E   I S L A N D S

EQUATOR

Jarvis Island (U.S.)

Malden Island

Starbuck Island

Vostok Island

Caroline I.

Flint Island

MARQUESAS ISLANDS (FRANCE)

Phoenix Islands
coconuts

TUVALU
Funafuti
coconuts

TOKELAU (NEW ZEALAND)

SOLOMON ISLANDS

Santa Cruz Is.
coconuts

Rotuma

Wallis & Futuna (FRANCE)

SAMOA
Apia

AMERICAN SAMOA (U.S.)
Pago Pago

Samoa Islands

C o o k   I s l a n d s (NEW ZEALAND)

P O L Y N E S I A

Society Islands

coconuts
Tahiti
Papeete

TUAMOTU ARCHIPELAGO

FRENCH POLYNESIA (FRANCE)

Austral Islands
coconuts

VANUATU
Port-Vila
Éfaté
coconuts

Vanua Levu

FIJI ISLANDS
Viti Levu   Suva
coconuts

Mt. Panié + 5,341 ft 1,628 m

Nouméa
New Caledonia (FRANCE)

TONGA
Nuku'alofa

TROPIC OF CAPRICORN

SOUTH   PACIFIC   OCEAN

Henderson Island (U.K.)
Ducie Island (U.K.)

Pitcairn Island (U.K.)

Sala-y-Gómez (CHILE)

Rapa Nui (Easter Island) (CHILE)

For Easter Island, see page 44.

Norfolk Island
Phillip Island (AUSTRALIA)

Kermadec Islands (NEW ZEALAND)

NEW ZEALAND

Economy Symbols

Fishing		Cacao	
Bananas		Coffee	
Other fruit		Forest products	
coconuts			
Sugarcane		Mining	
		Tourism	

← MELANESIAN CUSTOM. In the Huli culture of Papua New Guinea's Eastern Highlands, men adorn themselves with colorful paints, feathers, and grasses in preparation for a festival.

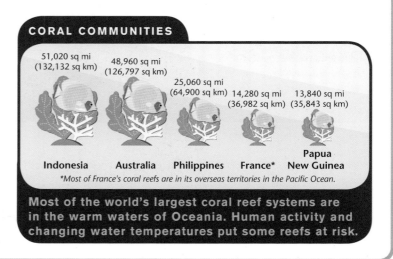

CORAL COMMUNITIES

51,020 sq mi (132,132 sq km)	48,960 sq mi (126,797 sq km)	25,060 sq mi (64,900 sq km)	14,280 sq mi (36,982 sq km)	13,840 sq mi (35,843 sq km)
Indonesia	Australia	Philippines	France*	Papua New Guinea

Most of France's coral reefs are in its overseas territories in the Pacific Ocean.

Most of the world's largest coral reef systems are in the warm waters of Oceania. Human activity and changing water temperatures put some reefs at risk.

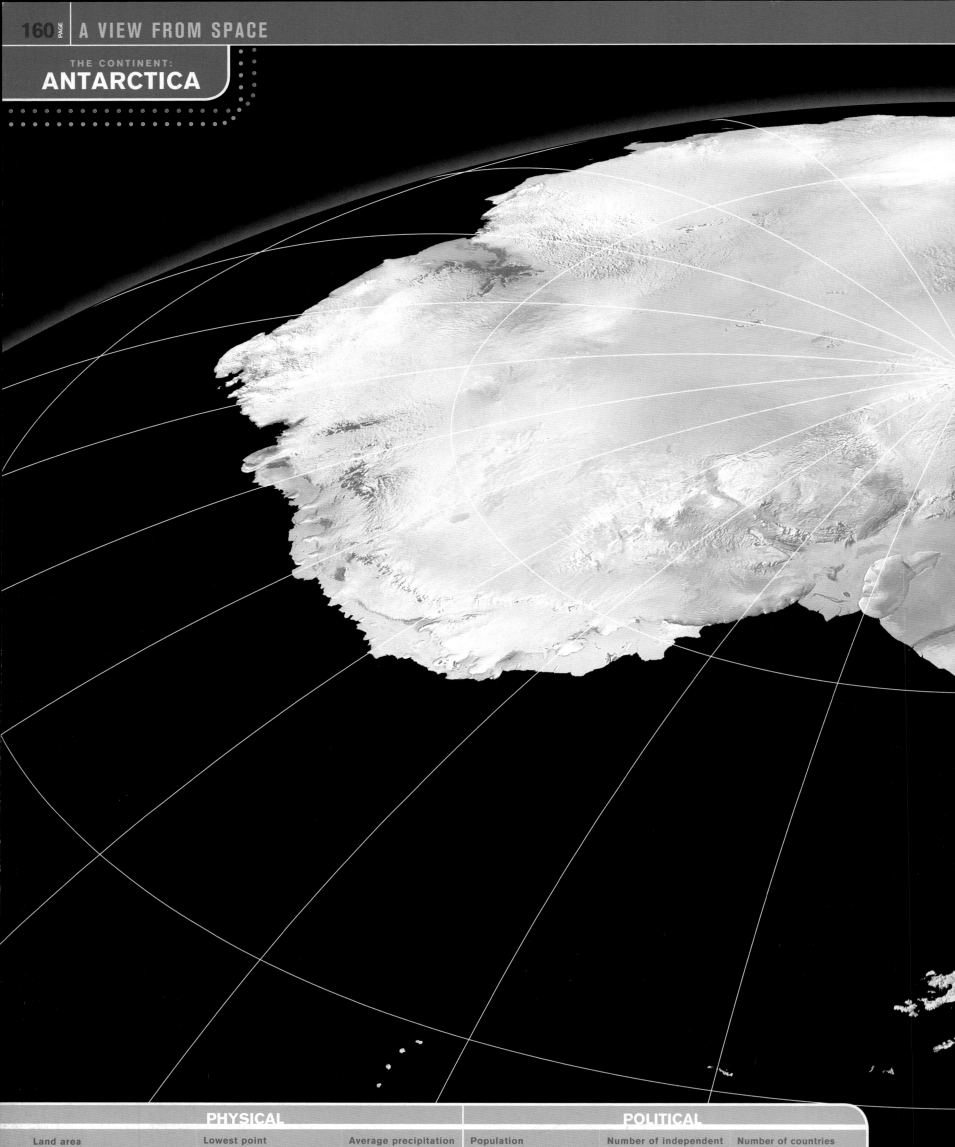

THE CONTINENT:
ANTARCTICA

PHYSICAL

Land area
5,100,000 sq mi (13,209,000 sq km)

Highest point
Vinson Massif
16,067 ft (4,897 m)

Lowest point
Bentley Subglacial Trench
-8,383 ft (-2,555 m)

Coldest place
Plateau Station
Annual average temperature
−70°F (-56.7°C)

**Average precipitation
on the polar plateau**
Less than 2 in (5 cm)
per year

POLITICAL

Population
There are no indigenous
inhabitants, but there
are both permanent and
summer-only staffed
research stations.

**Number of independent
countries**
0

**Number of countries
claiming land**
7

**Number of countries
operating year-round
research stations**
19

**Number of year-round
research stations**
45

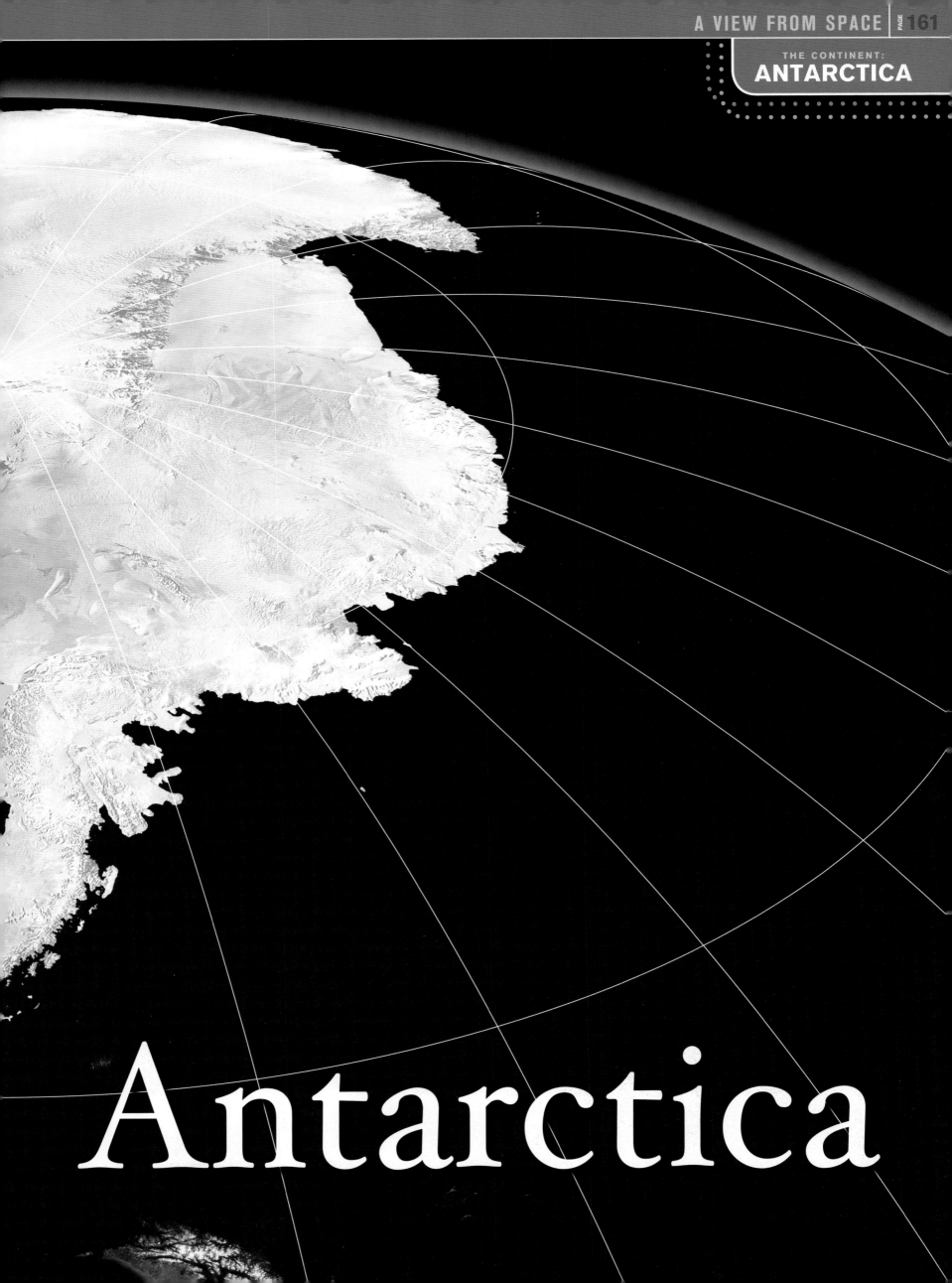

Antarctica

ANTARCTICA

THE BASICS

Antarctica is the only continent that has no sovereign boundaries and no economy or permanent population. Seven countries claim portions of the landmass (see map below), but according to the Antarctic Treaty, which preserves the continent for peaceful use and scientific study, no country rules the continent.

GEO WHIZ

In winter, sea ice averaging six feet (2 m) deep more than doubles the size of the continent as it forms a belt ranging from 300 miles (483 km) to more than 1,000 miles (1,620 km) wide.

The Antarctic Convergence, an area where the waters of the Pacific, Atlantic, and Indian Oceans meet the cold Antarctic Circumpolar Current, is one of Earth's richest marine ecosystems.

The largest iceberg ever spotted in Antarctic waters measured 208 miles (335 km) long by 60 miles (97 km) wide, making it slightly larger than Belgium.

Krill, a tiny shrimplike creature that thrives in the waters around the continent Antarctica, is important in the Antarctic food chain. Whales, seals, and penguins are among the creatures that depend on it for survival.

A small insect known as the wingless midge is Antarctica's largest land animal.

Five species of penguins live on the continent and nearby islands. The Emperor penguin is the only one that breeds during the winter.

Fierce, bitter cold winds batter the coast at speeds of as much as 180 miles per hour (300 kmph).

Mount Erebus is the world's southernmost volcano. Polar explorer James Clark Ross named it after one of his ships.

The Antarctic Treaty was signed in 1959 by 12 countries. To date, 46 countries have signed the document, agreeing to cooperate in scientific research and forbidding military action, nuclear tests, and the dumping of radioactive waste on the continent and in its waters.

⇧ SOUTHERN HEIGHTS. Standing on the rocky summit of Mount Bearskin, named for a member of the team that established the 1956–57 IGY (International Geophysical Year) South Pole Station, a climber looks out across a vast snow field.

Antarctica is the coldest, windiest, and even the driest continent. Though its immense ice cap holds 70 percent of the world's fresh water, its interior averages less than 2 inches (5 cm) of precipitation per year. Hidden beneath the ice is a continent of valleys, mountains, and lakes, but less than 2 percent of the land breaks through the ice cover. Reaching toward South America is the Antarctic Peninsula, the most visited of Antarctic regions. Though it is remote and mostly inhospitable, issues of human impact abound: fishing in rich but fragile waters that are sometimes called the Southern Ocean, future mining rights, and concern about the impact of global warming on the ice sheet.

1

South Orkney Is.

South Shetland Islands

Joinville I.

Larsen Ice Shelf

Antarctic

Alexander I.

Bellingshausen Sea

Thurston I.

PACIFIC

(Map)

30°S

0°

30°W   ATLANTIC OCEAN   AFRICA   30°E

SOUTH AMERICA

Falkland Is. (U.K.)

60°W   60°S   60°E

ARGENTINA

0   2,000 mi

0   2,000 km

Azimuthal Equidistant Projection

CHILE

ANTARCTIC CIRCLE

NORWAY

CHILE

AUSTRALIA

90°W   UNCLAIMED   90°E

INDIAN OCEAN

120°W   120°E

NEW ZEALAND

PACIFIC OCEAN

FRANCE

AUSTRALIA

150°W   150°E

NEW ZEALAND

180°

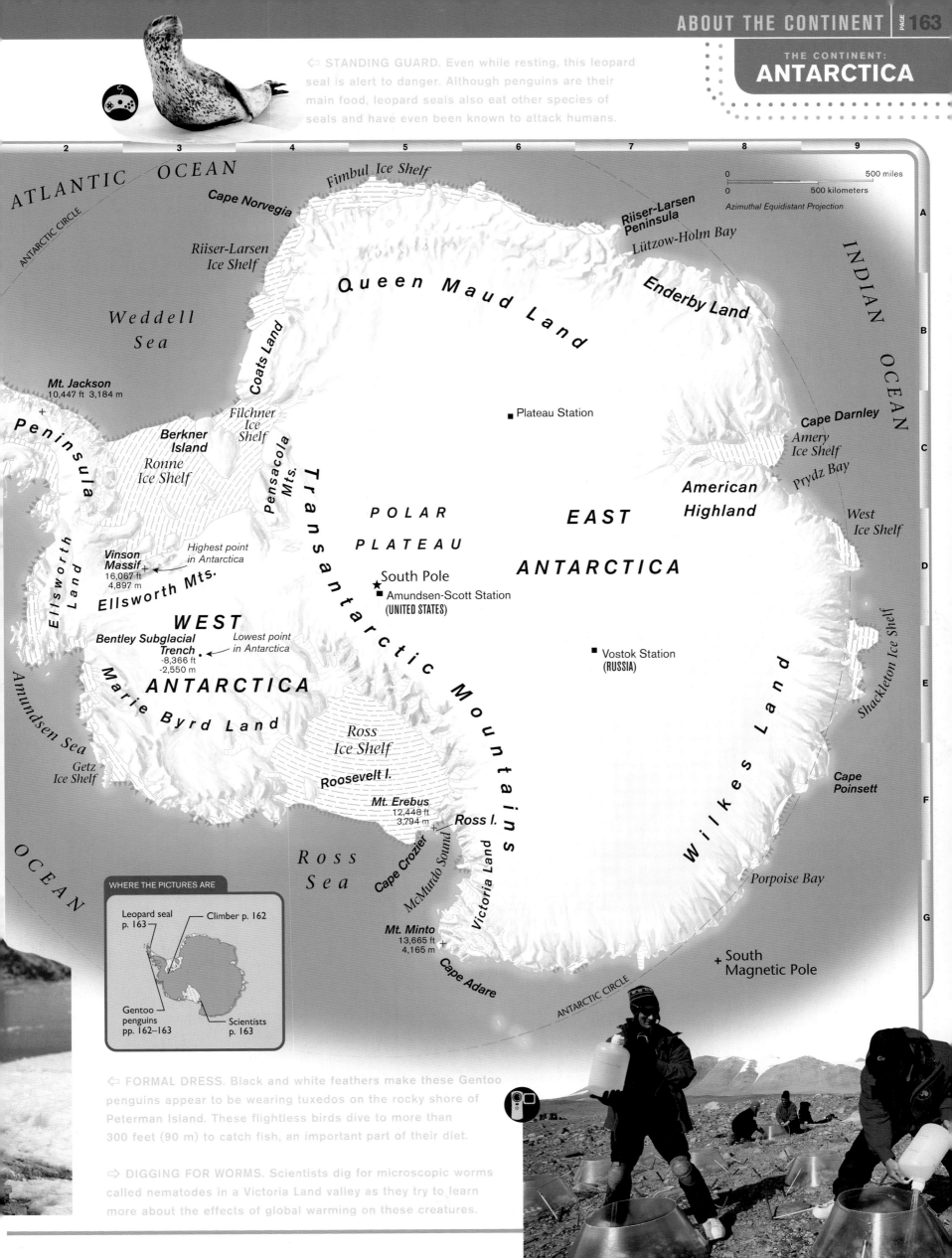

⇐ STANDING GUARD. Even while resting, this leopard seal is alert to danger. Although penguins are their main food, leopard seals also eat other species of seals and have even been known to attack humans.

ATLANTIC OCEAN

ANTARCTIC CIRCLE

Cape Norvegia

Fimbul Ice Shelf

Riiser-Larsen Peninsula

Lützow-Holm Bay

0   500 miles
0   500 kilometers
Azimuthal Equidistant Projection

INDIAN OCEAN

Riiser-Larsen Ice Shelf

Queen Maud Land

Enderby Land

Weddell Sea

Coats Land

Cape Darnley
Amery Ice Shelf
Prydz Bay

Mt. Jackson
10,447 ft 3,184 m

Filchner Ice Shelf

Berkner Island

Ronne Ice Shelf

Pensacola Mts.

Plateau Station

American Highland

West Ice Shelf

Peninsula

POLAR PLATEAU

EAST ANTARCTICA

Transantarctic Mountains

Ellsworth Land

Vinson Massif
16,067 ft
4,897 m

Highest point in Antarctica

South Pole
Amundsen-Scott Station
(UNITED STATES)

Ellsworth Mts.

WEST ANTARCTICA

Bentley Subglacial Trench
-8,366 ft
-2,550 m

Lowest point in Antarctica

Vostok Station
(RUSSIA)

Marie Byrd Land

Shackleton Ice Shelf

Amundsen Sea

Getz Ice Shelf

Ross Ice Shelf

Roosevelt I.

Wilkes Land

Mt. Erebus
12,448 ft
3,794 m

Ross I.

Cape Poinsett

OCEAN

Ross Sea

Cape Crozier

McMurdo Sound

Victoria Land

Porpoise Bay

WHERE THE PICTURES ARE

Leopard seal p. 163

Climber p. 162

Gentoo penguins pp. 162–163

Scientists p. 163

Mt. Minto
13,665 ft
4,165 m

Cape Adare

South Magnetic Pole

ANTARCTIC CIRCLE

⇐ FORMAL DRESS. Black and white feathers make these Gentoo penguins appear to be wearing tuxedos on the rocky shore of Peterman Island. These flightless birds dive to more than 300 feet (90 m) to catch fish, an important part of their diet.

⇒ DIGGING FOR WORMS. Scientists dig for microscopic worms called nematodes in a Victoria Land valley as they try to learn more about the effects of global warming on these creatures.

FLAGS & STATS

These flags and fact boxes represent the world's 193 independent countries—those with national governments that are recognized as having the highest legal authority over the land and people within their boundaries. The flags shown are national flags recognized by the United Nations. Area figures include land plus surface areas for inland bodies of water. Population figures are for mid-2006 as provided by the Population Reference Bureau of the United States. The languages listed are either the ones most commonly spoken within a country or official languages of a country.

NORTH AMERICA

Antigua and Barbuda
Area: 171 sq mi
(442 sq km)
Population: 100,000
Capital: St. John's
Languages: English (official),
local dialects

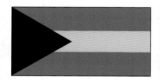

Bahamas
Area: 5,382 sq mi
(13,939 sq km)
Population: 300,000
Capital: Nassau
Languages: English (official),
Creole

Barbados
Area: 166 sq mi
(430 sq km)
Population: 300,000
Capital: Bridgetown
Language: English

Belize
Area: 8,867 sq mi
(22,965 sq km)
Population: 300,000
Capital: Belmopan
Languages: English (official),
Spanish, Maya, Garifuna
(Carib), Creole

Canada
Area: 3,855,101 sq mi
(9,984,670 sq km)
Population: 32,600,000
Capital: Ottawa
Languages: English, French
(both official)

Costa Rica
Area: 19,730 sq mi
(51,100 sq km)
Population: 4,300,000
Capital: San José
Languages: Spanish
(official), English

Cuba
Area: 42,803 sq mi
(110,860 sq km)
Population: 11,300,000
Capital: Havana
Language: Spanish

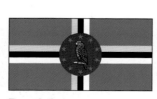

Dominica
Area: 290 sq mi
(751 sq km)
Population: 100,000
Capital: Roseau
Languages: English (official),
French patois

Dominican Republic
Area: 18,704 sq mi
(48,442 sq km)
Population: 9,000,000
Capital: Santo Domingo
Language: Spanish

El Salvador
Area: 8,124 sq mi
(21,041 sq km)
Population: 7,000,000
Capital: San Salvador
Languages: Spanish, Nahua

Grenada
Area: 133 sq mi
(344 sq km)
Population: 100,000
Capital: St. George's
Languages: English (official),
French patois

Guatemala
Area: 42,042 sq mi
(108,889 sq km)
Population: 13,000,000
Capital: Guatemala City
Languages: Spanish,
23 Amerindian languages

Haiti
Area: 10,714 sq mi
(27,750 sq km)
Population: 8,500,000
Capital: Port-au-Prince
Languages: French,
Creole (both official)

Honduras
Area: 43,433 sq mi
(112,492 sq km)
Population: 7,400,000
Capital: Tegucigalpa
Languages: Spanish,
Amerindian dialects

Jamaica
Area: 4,244 sq mi
(10,991 sq km)
Population: 2,700,000
Capital: Kingston
Languages: English,
patois English

México
Area: 758,449 sq mi
(1,964,375 sq km)
Population: 108,300,000
Capital: México City
Languages: Spanish, Maya,
Nahuatl, other indigenous
languages

Nicaragua
Area: 50,193 sq mi
(130,000 sq km)
Population: 5,600,000
Capital: Managua
Languages: Spanish
(official), English,
indigenous languages

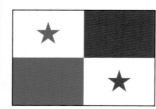

Panama
Area: 29,157 sq mi
(75,517 sq km)
Population: 3,300,000
Capital: Panama City
Languages: Spanish
(official), English

St. Kitts and Nevis
Area: 104 sq mi
(269 sq km)
Population: 50,000
Capital: Basseterre
Language: English

St. Lucia
Area: 238 sq mi
(616 sq km)
Population: 200,000
Capital: Castries
Languages: English (official),
French patois

St. Vincent and the Grenadines
Area: 150 sq mi
(389 sq km)
Population: 100,000
Capital: Kingstown
Languages: English, French
patois

Trinidad and Tobago
Area: 1,980 sq mi
(5,128 sq km)
Population: 1,300,000
Capital: Port-of-Spain
Languages: English (official),
Hindi, French, Spanish,
Chinese

United States
Area: 3,794,083 sq mi
(9,826,630 sq km)
Population: 300,000,000
Capital: Washington, D.C.
Languages: English, Spanish

SOUTH AMERICA

Argentina
Area: 1,073,518 sq mi
(2,780,400 sq km)
Population: 39,000,000
Capital: Buenos Aires
Languages: Spanish (official),
English, Italian, German, French

Bolivia
Area: 424,164 sq mi
(1,098,581 sq km)
Population: 9,100,000
Capitals: La Paz, Sucre
Languages: Spanish,
Quechua, Aymara (all official)

Brazil
Area: 3,300,169 sq mi
(8,547,403 sq km)
Population: 186,800,000
Capital: Brasília
Language: Portuguese (official)

Chile
Area: 291,930 sq mi
(756,096 sq km)
Population: 16,400,000
Capital: Santiago
Language: Spanish

Colombia
Area: 440,831 sq mi
(1,141,748 sq km)
Population: 46,800,000
Capital: Bogotá
Language: Spanish

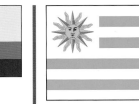

Ecuador
Area: 109,483 sq mi
(283,560 sq km)
Population: 13,300,000
Capital: Quito
Languages: Spanish (official),
Quechua, other Amerindian
languages

Guyana
Area: 83,000 sq mi
(214,969 sq km)
Population: 700,000
Capital: Georgetown
Languages: English,
Amerindian dialects, Creole,
Hindi, Urdu

Paraguay
Area: 157,048 sq mi
(406,752 sq km)
Population: 6,300,000
Capital: Asunción
Languages: Spanish, Guaraní
(both official)

Peru
Area: 496,224 sq mi
(1,285,216 sq km)
Population: 28,400,000
Capital: Lima
Languages: Spanish, Quechua
(both official), Aymara, minor
Amazonian languages

Suriname
Area: 63,037 sq mi
(163,265 sq km)
Population: 500,000
Capital: Paramaribo
Languages: Dutch (official),
English, Sranang Tongo (Taki-
Taki), Hindustani, Javanese

Uruguay
Area: 68,037 sq mi
(176,215 sq km)
Population: 3,300,000
Capital: Montevideo
Languages: Spanish, Portunol,
Brazilero

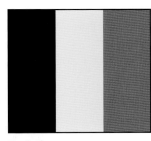

Venezuela
Area: 352,144 sq mi
(912,050 sq km)
Population: 27,000,000
Capital: Caracas
Languages: Spanish
(official), many indigenous
languages

EUROPE

Albania
Area: 11,100 sq mi
(28,748 sq km)
Population: 3,200,000
Capital: Tirana
Languages: Albanian
(official), Greek, Vlach,
Romani, Slavic dialects

Andorra
Area: 181 sq mi
(468 sq km)
Population: 100,000
Capital: Andorra la Vella
Languages: Catalan
(official), French, Castilian,
Portuguese

Austria
Area: 32,378 sq mi
(83,858 sq km)
Population: 8,300,000
Capital: Vienna
Languages: German (official),
Slovene, Croatian, Hungarian

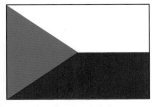

Belarus
Area: 80,153 sq mi
(207,595 sq km)
Population: 9,700,000
Capital: Minsk
Languages: Belarusian,
Russian

Belgium
Area: 11,787 sq mi
(30,528 sq km)
Population: 10,500,000
Capital: Brussels
Languages: Flemish (Dutch),
French, German (all official)

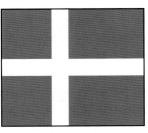

**Bosnia and
Herzegovina**
Area: 19,741 sq mi
(51,129 sq km)
Population: 3,900,000
Capital: Sarajevo
Languages: Croatian, Serbian,
Bosnian

Bulgaria
Area: 42,855 sq mi
(110,994 sq km)
Population: 7,700,000
Capital: Sofia
Languages: Bulgarian, Turkish

Croatia
Area: 21,831 sq mi
(56,542 sq km)
Population: 4,400,000
Capital: Zagreb
Language: Croatian

Cyprus
Area: 3,572 sq mi
(9,251 sq km)
Population: 1,000,000
Capital: Nicosia
Languages: Greek, Turkish,
English

Czech Republic
Area: 30,450 sq mi
(78,866 sq km)
Population: 10,300,000
Capital: Prague
Language: Czech

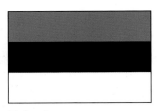

Denmark
Area: 16,640 sq mi
(43,098 sq km)
Population: 5,400,000
Capital: Copenhagen
Languages: Danish, Faroese,
Greenlandic, German

Estonia
Area: 17,462 sq mi
(45,227 sq km)
Population: 1,300,000
Capital: Tallinn
Languages: Estonian (official),
Russian

FLAGS & STATS

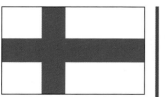

Finland
Area: 130,558 sq mi
(338,145 sq km)
Population: 5,300,000
Capital: Helsinki
Languages: Finnish, Swedish
(both official)

France
Area: 210,026 sq mi
(543,965 sq km)
Population: 61,200,000
Capital: Paris
Language: French

Germany
Area: 137,847 sq mi
(357,022 sq km)
Population: 82,400,000
Capital: Berlin
Language: German

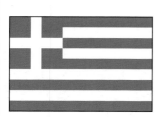

Greece
Area: 50,949 sq mi
(131,957 sq km)
Population: 11,100,000
Capital: Athens
Language: Greek

Hungary
Area: 35,919 sq mi
(93,030 sq km)
Population: 10,100,000
Capital: Budapest
Language: Hungarian

Iceland
Area: 39,769 sq mi
(103,000 sq km)
Population: 300,000
Capital: Reykjavik
Languages: Icelandic, English,
Nordic languages

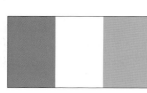

Ireland
Area: 27,133 sq mi
(70,273 sq km)
Population: 4,200,000
Capital: Dublin
Languages: Irish (Gaelic),
English

Italy
Area: 116,345 sq mi
(301,333 sq km)
Population: 59,000,000
Capital: Rome
Languages: Italian (official),
German, French, Slovene

Latvia
Area: 24,938 sq mi
(64,589 sq km)
Population: 2,300,000
Capital: Riga
Languages: Latvian (official),
Russian

Liechtenstein
Area: 62 sq mi
(160 sq km)
Population: 40,000
Capital: Vaduz
Language: German (official)

Lithuania
Area: 25,212 sq mi
(65,300 sq km)
Population: 3,400,000
Capital: Vilnius
Languages: Lithuanian
(official), Polish, Russian

Luxembourg
Area: 998 sq mi
(2,586 sq km)
Population: 500,000
Capital: Luxembourg
Languages: Luxembourgish
(official), German, French

Macedonia
Area: 9,928 sq mi
(25,713 sq km)
Population: 2,000,000
Capital: Skopje
Languages: Macedonian,
Albanian

Malta
Area: 122 sq mi
(316 sq km)
Population: 400,000
Capital: Valletta
Languages: Maltese, English
(both official)

Moldova
Area: 13,050 sq mi
(33,800 sq km)
Population: 4,000,000
Capital: Chişinău
Languages: Moldovan
(official), Russian, Gagauz

Monaco
Area: 1 sq mi
(2 sq km)
Population: 30,000
Capital: Monaco
Languages: French (official),
English, Italian, Monegasque

Montenegro
Area: 5,416 sq mi
(14,026 sq km)
Population: 600,000
Capital: Podgorica
Languages: Serbian (official),
Bosnian, Albanian, Croatian

Netherlands
Area: 16,034 sq mi
(41,528 sq km)
Population: 16,400,000
Capital: Amsterdam
Languages: Dutch, Frisian
(both official)

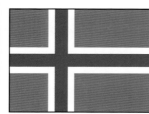

Norway
Area: 125,004 sq mi
(323,758 sq km)
Population: 4,700,000
Capital: Oslo
Language: Norwegian (official)

Poland
Area: 120,728 sq mi
(312,685 sq km)
Population: 38,100,000
Capital: Warsaw
Language: Polish

Portugal
Area: 35,655 sq mi
(92,345 sq km)
Population: 10,600,000
Capital: Lisbon
Languages: Portuguese,
Mirandese (both official)

Romania
Area: 92,043 sq mi
(238,391 sq km)
Population: 21,600,000
Capital: Bucharest
Languages: Romanian (official),
Hungarian, German

Russia
Area: 6,592,850 sq mi
(17,075,400 sq km)
Population: 142,300,000
Capital: Moscow
Languages: Russian, many
minority languages

San Marino
Area: 24 sq mi
(61 sq km)
Population: 30,000
Capital: San Marino
Language: Italian

Serbia
Area: 34,119 sq mi
(88,361 sq km)
Population: 9,500,000
Capital: Belgrade
Languages: Serbian (official),
Romanian, Hungarian, Slovak,
Croatian

Slovakia
Area: 18,932 sq mi
(49,035 km)
Population: 5,400,000
Capital: Bratislava
Languages: Slovak (official),
Hungarian

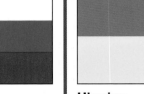

Slovenia
Area: 7,827 sq mi
(20,273 sq km)
Population: 2,000,000
Capital: Ljubljana
Languages: Slovene

Spain
Area: 195,363 sq mi
(505,988 sq km)
Population: 45,500,000
Capital: Madrid
Languages: Castilian Spanish
(official), Catalan, Galician,
Basque

Sweden
Area: 173,732 sq mi
(449,964 sq km)
Population: 9,100,000
Capital: Stockholm
Language: Swedish

Switzerland
Area: 15,940 sq mi
(41,284 sq km)
Population: 7,500,000
Capital: Bern
Languages: German,
French, Italian (all official),
Romansch

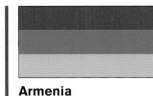

Ukraine
Area: 233,090 sq mi
(603,700 sq km)
Population: 46,800,000
Capital: Kiev
Languages: Ukrainian (official),
Russian

United Kingdom
Area: 93,788 sq mi
(242,910 sq km)
Population: 60,500,000
Capital: London
Languages: English, Welsh,
Scottish form of Gaelic

Vatican City
Area: 0.2 sq mi
(0.4 sq km)
Population: 798
Languages: Italian, Latin,
French

ASIA

Afghanistan
Area: 251,773 sq mi
(652,090 sq km)
Population: 31,100,000
Capital: Kabul
Languages: Afghan Persian
(Dari), Pashtu (both official),
Turkic languages

Armenia
Area: 11,484 sq mi
(29,743 sq km)
Population: 3,000,000
Capital: Yerevan
Language: Armenian

Azerbaijan
Area: 33,436 sq mi
(86,600 sq km)
Population: 8,500,000
Capital: Baku
Language: Azerbaijani (Azeri)

Bahrain
Area: 277 sq mi
(717 sq km)
Population: 700,000
Capital: Manama
Languages: Arabic, English,
Farsi, Urdu

Bangladesh
Area: 56,977 sq mi
(147,570 sq km)
Population: 146,600,000
Capital: Dhaka
Languages: Bangla (Bengali)
(official), English

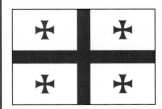

Bhutan
Area: 17,954 sq mi
(46,500 sq km)
Population: 900,000
Capital: Thimphu
Languages: Dzongkha
(official), Tibetan dialects,
Nepali dialects

Brunei
Area: 2,226 sq mi
(5,765 sq km)
Population: 400,000
Capital: Bandar Seri Begawan
Languages: Malay (official),
English, Chinese

Cambodia
Area: 69,898 sq mi
(181,035 sq km)
Population: 14,100,000
Capital: Phnom Penh
Language: Khmer (official)

China
Area: 3,705,405 sq mi
(9,596,960 sq km)
Population: 1,311,400,000
Capital: Beijing
Languages: Standard Chinese
(Mandarin), Yue, Wu, Minbei,
other dialects and minority
languages

East Timor
(Timor-Leste)
Area: 5,640 sq mi
(14,609 sq km)
Population: 100,000
Capital: Dili
Languages: Tetum, Portuguese
(official), Indonesian, English

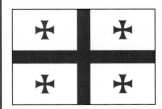

Georgia
Area: 26,911 sq mi
(69,700 sq km)
Population: 4,400,000
Capital: T'bilisi
Languages: Georgian (official),
Russian, Armenian, Azeri

India
Area: 1,269,221 sq mi
(3,287,270 sq km)
Population: 1,121,800,000
Capital: New Delhi
Languages: Hindi, English
(both official), 21 other official
languages

Indonesia
Area: 742,308 sq mi
(1,922,570 sq km)
Population: 225,500,000
Capital: Jakarta
Languages: Bahasa Indonesian
(official), English, Dutch, Javanese

Iran
Area: 636,296 sq mi
(1,648,000 sq km)
Population: 70,300,000
Capital: Tehran
Languages: Farsi (modern-day
Persian), Turkic, Kurdish

Iraq
Area: 168,754 sq mi
(437,072 sq km)
Population: 29,600,000
Capital: Baghdad
Languages: Arabic, Kurdish,
Assyrian, Armenian

Israel
Area: 8,550 sq mi
(22,145 sq km)
Population: 7,200,000
Capital: Jerusalem
Languages: Hebrew (official),
Arabic, English

FLAGS & STATS

Japan
Area: 145,902 sq mi
(377,887 sq km)
Population: 127,800,000
Capital: Tokyo
Language: Japanese

Kuwait
Area: 6,880 sq mi
(17,818 sq km)
Population: 2,700,000
Capital: Kuwait
Languages: Arabic (official),
English

Maldives
Area: 115 sq mi
(298 sq km)
Population: 300,000
Capital: Male
Languages: Maldivian Dhivehi,
English

Pakistan
Area: 307,374 sq mi
(796,095 sq km)
Population: 165,800,000
Capital: Islamabad
Languages: Urdu, English
(both official), Punjabi, Sindhi,
Siraiki, Pashtu

Sri Lanka
Area: 25,299 sq mi
(65,525 sq km)
Population: 19,900,000
Capital: Colombo
Languages: Sinhala
(official), Tamil, English

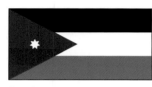

Jordan
Area: 34,495 sq mi
(89,342 sq km)
Population: 5,600,000
Capital: Amman
Languages: Arabic (official),
English

Kyrgyzstan
Area: 77,182 sq mi
(199,900 sq km)
Population: 5,200,000
Capital: Bishkek
Languages: Kyrgyz, Russian
(both official)

Mongolia
Area: 603,909 sq mi
(1,564,116 sq km)
Population: 2,600,000
Capital: Ulaanbaatar
Languages: Khalkha Mongol,
Turkic, Russian

Philippines
Area: 115,831 sq mi
(300,000 sq km)
Population: 86,300,000
Capital: Manila
Languages: Filipino (based on
Tagalog), English (both official),
8 major dialects

Syria
Area: 71,498 sq mi
(185,180 sq km)
Population: 19,500,000
Capital: Damascus
Languages: Arabic (official),
Kurdish, Armenian, Aramaic,
Circassian

Kazakhstan
Area: 1,049,155 sq mi
(2,717,300 sq km)
Population: 15,300,000
Capital: Astana
Languages: Kazakh (Qazaq),
Russian (official)

Laos
Area: 91,429 sq mi
(236,800 sq km)
Population: 6,100,000
Languages: Lao (official),
French, English, various ethnic
languages

Myanmar (Burma)
Area: 261,218 sq mi
(676,552 sq km)
Population: 51,000,000
Capitals: Nay Pyi Taw,
Yangon (Rangoon)
Languages: Burmese, minority
ethnic languages

Qatar
Area: 4,448 sq mi
(11,521 sq km)
Population: 800,000
Capital: Doha
Languages: Arabic (official),
English

Tajikistan
Area: 55,251 sq mi
(143,100 sq km)
Population: 7,000,000
Capital: Dushanbe
Languages: Tajik (official),
Russian

Korea, North
Area: 46,540 sq mi
(120,538 sq km)
Population: 23,100,000
Capital: Pyongyang
Language: Korean

Lebanon
Area: 4,036 sq mi
(10,452 sq km)
Population: 3,900,000
Capital: Beirut
Languages: Arabic (official),
French, English, Armenian

Nepal
Area: 56,827 sq mi
(147,181 sq km)
Population: 26,000,000
Capital: Kathmandu
Languages: Nepali, Maithali,
Bhojpuri, Tharu, Tamang,
English

Saudi Arabia
Area: 756,985 sq mi
(1,960,582 sq km)
Population: 24,100,000
Capital: Riyadh
Language: Arabic

Thailand
Area: 198,115 sq mi
(513,115 sq km)
Population: 65,200,000
Capital: Bangkok (Krung Thep)
Languages: Thai, English,
ethnic and regional dialects

Korea, South
Area: 38,321 sq mi
(99,250 sq km)
Population: 48,500,000
Capital: Seoul
Languages: Korean,
English widely taught

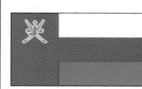

Malaysia
Area: 127,355 sq mi
(329,847 sq km)
Population: 26,900,000
Capital: Kuala Lumpur
Languages: Bahasa Melayu
(official), English, Chinese
dialects, Tamil, Telugu,
indigenous languages

Oman
Area: 119,500 sq mi
(309,500 sq km)
Population: 2,600,000
Capital: Muscat
Languages: Arabic (official),
English, Baluchi, Urdu, Indian
dialects

Singapore
Area: 255 sq mi
(660 sq km)
Population: 4,500,000
Capital: Singapore
Languages: Mandarin, English,
Malay, Hokkien

Turkey
Area: 300,948 sq mi
(779,452 sq km)
Population: 73,700,000
Capital: Ankara
Languages: Turkish (official),
Kurdish, Arabic, Armenian,
Greek

Turkmenistan
Area: 188,300 sq mi
(488,100 sq km)
Population: 5,300,000
Capital: Ashgabat
Languages: Turkmen, Russian,
Uzbek

United Arab Emirates
Area: 30,000 sq mi
(77,700 sq km)
Population: 4,900,000
Capital: Abu Dhabi
Languages: Arabic (official),
Persian, English, Hindi, Urdu

Uzbekistan
Area: 172,742 sq mi
(447,400 sq km)
Population: 26,200,000
Capital: Tashkent
Languages: Uzbek, Russian

Vietnam
Area: 127,844 sq mi
(331,114 sq km)
Population: 84,200,000
Capital: Hanoi
Languages: Vietnamese
(official), English, French,
Chinese, Khmer

Yemen
Area: 207,286 sq mi
(536,869 sq km)
Population: 21,600,000
Capital: Sanaa
Language: Arabic

AFRICA

Algeria
Area: 919,595 sq mi
(2,381,741 sq km)
Population: 33,500,000
Capital: Algiers
Languages: Arabic (official),
French, Berber dialects

Angola
Area: 481,354 sq mi
(1,246,700 sq km)
Population: 15,800,000
Capital: Luanda
Languages: Portuguese
(official), Bantu, other African
languages

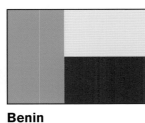

Benin
Area: 43,484 sq mi
(112,622 sq km)
Population: 8,700,000
Capitals: Porto-Novo, Cotonou
Languages: French (official),
Fon, Yoruba, tribal languages

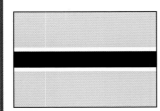

Botswana
Area: 224,607 sq mi
(581,730 sq km)
Population: 1,800,000
Capital: Gaborone
Languages: English (official),
Setswana, Kalanga, Sekgalgadi

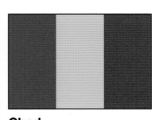

Burkina Faso
Area: 105,869 sq mi
(274,200 sq km)
Population: 13,600,000
Capital: Ouagadougou
Languages: French (official),
indigenous languages

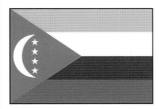

Burundi
Area: 10,747 sq mi
(27,834 sq km)
Population: 7,800,000
Capital: Bujumbura
Languages: Kirundi, French
(both official), Swahili

Cameroon
Area: 183,569 sq mi
(475,442 sq km)
Population: 17,300,000
Capital: Yaoundé
Languages: French, English
(both official), 24 major African
language groups

Cape Verde
Area: 1,558 sq mi
(4,036 sq km)
Population: 500,000
Capital: Praia
Languages: Portuguese,
Crioulo

Central African
Republic
Area: 240,535 sq mi
(622,984 sq km)
Population: 4,300,000
Capital: Bangui
Languages: French (official),
Sangho, tribal languages

Chad
Area: 495,755 sq mi
(1,284,000 sq km)
Population: 10,000,000
Capital: N'Djamena
Languages: French, Arabic
(both official), Sara, more
than 120 other languages
and dialects

Comoros
Area: 719 sq mi
(1,862 sq km)
Population: 700,000
Capital: Moroni
Languages: Arabic, French
(both official), Shikomoro

Congo
Area: 132,047 sq mi
(342,000 sq km)
Population: 3,700,000
Capital: Brazzaville
Languages: French (official),
Lingala, Monokutuba,
many local languages
and dialects

Congo,
Democratic
Republic of the
Area: 905,365 sq mi
(2,344,885 sq km)
Population: 62,700,000
Capital: Kinshasa
Languages: French (official),
Lingala, Kingwana, Kikongo,
Tshiluba

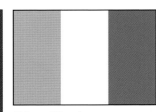

Côte d'Ivoire
Area: 124,503 sq mi
(322,462 sq km)
Population: 19,700,000
Capitals: Abidjan, Yamoussoukro
Languages: French (official),
Dioula, 60 native dialects

Djibouti
Area: 8,958 sq mi
(23,200 sq km)
Population: 800,000
Capital: Djibouti
Languages: French, Arabic
(both official), Somali, Afar

Egypt
Area: 386,874 sq mi
(1,002,000 sq km)
Population: 75,400,000
Capital: Cairo
Languages: Arabic (official),
English, French

Equatorial Guinea
Area: 10,831 sq mi
(28,051 sq km)
Population: 500,000
Capital: Malabo
Languages: Spanish, French
(both official), pidgin English,
Fang, Bubi, Ibo

Eritrea
Area: 46,774 sq mi
(121,144 sq km)
Population: 4,600,000
Capital: Asmara
Languages: Afar, Arabic,
Tigre, Kunama, Tigrinya, other
Cushitic languages

FLAGS & STATS

Ethiopia
Area: 437,600 sq mi
(1,133,380 sq km)
Population: 74,800,000
Capital: Addis Ababa
Languages: Amharic, Tigrinya,
Oromigna, Guaragigna, Somali

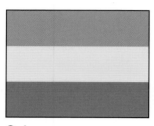

Gabon
Area: 103,347 sq mi
(267,667 sq km)
Population: 1,400,000
Capital: Libreville
Languages: French (official),
Fang, Myene, Nzebi,
Bapounou/Eschira

Gambia
Area: 4,361 sq mi
(11,295 sq km)
Population: 1,500,000
Capital: Banjul
Languages: English (official),
Mandinka, Wolof, Fula

Ghana
Area: 92,100 sq mi
(238,537 sq km)
Population: 22,600,000
Capital: Accra
Languages: English (official),
Akan, Moshi-Dagomba, Ewe, Ga

Guinea
Area: 94,926 sq mi
(245,857 sq km)
Population: 9,800,000
Capital: Conakry
Languages: French (official),
indigenous languages

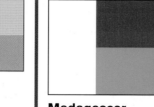

Guinea-Bissau
Area: 13,948 sq mi
(36,125 sq km)
Population: 1,400,000
Capital: Bissau
Languages: Portuguese
(official), Crioulo, indigenous
languages

Kenya
Area: 224,081 sq mi
(580,367 sq km)
Population: 34,700,000
Capital: Nairobi
Languages: English, Kiswahili
(both official), indigenous
languages

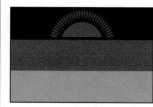

Lesotho
Area: 11,720 sq mi
(30,355 sq km)
Population: 1,800,000
Capital: Maseru
Languages: Sesotho, English
(official), Zulu, Xhosa

Liberia
Area: 43,000 sq mi
(111,370 sq km)
Population: 3,400,000
Capital: Monrovia
Languages: English (official),
20 ethnic group languages

Libya
Area: 679,362 sq mi
(1,759,540 sq km)
Population: 5,900,000
Capital: Tripoli
Languages: Arabic, Italian,
English

Madagascar
Area: 226,658 sq mi
(587,041 sq km)
Population: 17,800,000
Capital: Antananarivo
Languages: French, Malagasy
(both official)

Malawi
Area: 45,747 sq mi
(118,484 sq km)
Population: 12,800,000
Capital: Lilongwe
Languages: Chichewa (official),
Chinyanja, Chiyao, Chitumbuka

Mali
Area: 478,841 sq mi
(1,240,192 sq km)
Population: 13,900,000
Capital: Bamako
Languages: French, Bambara
(both official), numerous
African languages

Mauritania
Area: 397,955 sq mi
(1,030,700 sq km)
Population: 3,200,000
Capital: Nouakchott
Languages: Arabic (official), Pulaar,
Soninke, French, Hassaniya, Wolof

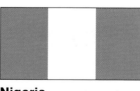

Mauritius
Area: 788 sq mi
(2,040 sq km)
Population: 1,300,000
Capital: Port Louis
Languages: Creole, Bhojpuri,
French (official)

Morocco
Area: 274,461 sq mi
(710,850 sq km)
Population: 31,700,000
Capital: Rabat
Languages: Arabic (official),
Berber dialects, French

Mozambique
Area: 308,642 sq mi
(799,380 sq km)
Population: 19,900,000
Capital: Maputo
Languages: Emakhuwa,
Xichangana, Portuguese (official),
Elomwe, Cisena, Echuwabo

Namibia
Area: 318,261 sq mi
(824,292 sq km)
Population: 2,100,000
Capital: Windhoek
Languages: English (official),
Afrikaans, German, indigenous
languages

Niger
Area: 489,191 sq mi
(1,267,000 sq km)
Population: 14,400,000
Capital: Niamey
Languages: French (official),
Hausa, Djerma

Nigeria
Area: 356,669 sq mi
(923,768 sq km)
Population: 134,500,000
Capital: Abuja
Languages: English (official),
Hausa, Yoruba, Igbo (Ibo), Fulani

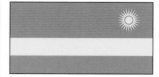

Rwanda
Area: 10,169 sq mi
(26,338 sq km)
Population: 9,100,000
Capital: Kigali
Languages: Kinyarwanda,
French, English (all official),
Kiswahili

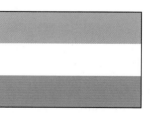

São Tomé and
Principe
Area: 386 sq mi
(1,001 sq km)
Population: 200,000
Capital: São Tomé
Language: Portuguese
(official)

Senegal
Area: 75,955 sq mi
(196,722 sq km)
Population: 11,900,000
Capital: Dakar
Languages: French (official),
Wolof, Pulaar, Jola, Mandinka

Seychelles
Area: 176 sq mi
(455 sq km)
Population: 100,000
Capital: Victoria
Languages: English (official),
Creole

Sierra Leone
Area: 27,699 sq mi
(71,740 sq km)
Population: 5,700,000
Capital: Freetown
Languages: English (official),
Mende, Temne, Krio

Somalia
Area: 246,201 sq mi
(637,657 sq km)
Population: 8,900,000
Capital: Mogadishu
Languages: Somali (official),
Arabic, Italian, English

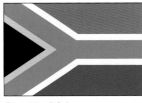

South Africa
Area: 470,693 sq mi
(1,219,090 sq km)
Population: 47,300,000
Capitals: Pretoria (Tshwane),
Cape Town, Bloemfontein
Languages: IsiZulu, IsiXhosa,
Afrikaans, Sepedi, English,
Setswana

Sudan
Area: 967,500 sq mi
(2,505,813 sq km)
Population: 41,200,000
Capital: Khartoum
Languages: Arabic (official),
Nubian, Ta Bedawie, many
local dialects

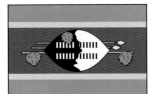

Swaziland
Area: 6,704 sq mi
(17,363 sq km)
Population: 1,100,000
Capitals: Mbabane, Lobamba
Languages: English, siSwati
(both official)

Tanzania
Area: 364,900 sq mi
(945,087 sq km)
Population: 37,900,000
Capitals: Dar es Salaam, Dodoma
Languages: Swahili, English
(both official), Arabic, many local
languages

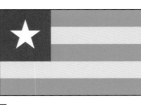

Togo
Area: 21,925 sq mi
(56,785 sq km)
Population: 6,300,000
Capital: Lomé
Languages: French (official),
Ewe, Mina, Kabye, Dagomba

Tunisia
Area: 63,170 sq mi
(163,610 sq km)
Population: 10,100,000
Capital: Tunis
Languages: Arabic (official),
French

Uganda
Area: 93,104 sq mi
(241,139 sq km)
Population: 27,700,000
Capital: Kampala
Languages: English (official),
Ganda or Luganda, many local
languages

Zambia
Area: 290,586 sq mi
(752,614 sq km)
Population: 11,900,000
Capital: Lusaka
Languages: English (official),
75 indigenous languages

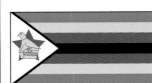

Zimbabwe
Area: 150,872 sq mi
(390,757 sq km)
Population: 13,100,000
Capital: Harare
Languages: English (official),
Shona, Sindebele

AUSTRALIA, NEW ZEALAND, & OCEANIA

Australia
Area: 2,969,906 sq mi
(7,692,024 sq km)
Population: 20,600,000
Capital: Canberra
Language: English

Fiji Islands
Area: 7,095 sq mi
(18,376 sq km)
Population: 800,000
Capital: Suva
Languages: English (official),
Fijian, Hindustani

Kiribati
Area: 313 sq mi
(811 sq km)
Population: 100,000
Capital: Tarawa
Languages: English (official),
I-Kiribati

Marshall Islands
Area: 70 sq mi
(181 sq km)
Population: 100,000
Capital: Majuro
Languages: Marshallese
(official), English

Micronesia
Population: 271 sq mi
(702 sq km)
Population: 100,000
Capital: Palikir
Languages: English (official),
Trukese, Pohnpeian, Yapese,
Kosrean

Nauru
Area: 8 sq mi
(21 sq km)
Population: 10,000
Capital: Yaren
Languages: Nauruan
(official), English

New Zealand
Area: 104,454 sq mi
(270,534 sq km)
Population: 4,100,000
Capital: Wellington
Languages: English, Maori
(both official)

Palau
Area: 189 sq mi
(489 sq km)
Population: 20,000
Capital: Melekeok
Languages: Palauan, Filipino,
English, Chinese

Papua New Guinea
Area: 178,703 sq mi
(462,840 sq km)
Population: 6,000,000
Capital: Port Moresby
Languages: Melanesian pidgin,
715 indigenous languages

Samoa
Area: 1,093 sq mi
(2,831 sq km)
Population: 200,000
Capital: Apia
Languages: Samoan
(Polynesian), English

Solomon Islands
Area: 10,954 sq mi
(28,370 sq km)
Population: 500,000
Capital: Honiara
Languages: Melanesian pidgin,
120 indigenous languages

Tonga
Area: 289 sq mi
(748 sq km)
Population: 100,000
Capital: Nuku'alofa
Languages: Tongan, English

Tuvalu
Area: 10 sq mi
(26 sq km)
Population: 10,000
Capital: Funafuti
Languages: Tuvaluan, English,
Samoan, Kiribati

Vanuatu
Area: 4,707 sq mi
(12,190 sq km)
Population: 200,000
Capital: Port-Vila
Languages: over 100 local
languages, pidgin (Bislama or
Bichelama)

GLOSSARY

acid rain precipitation containing acid droplets resulting from the mixture of moisture in the air with carbon dioxide, nitrogen oxide, sulfur dioxide, and hydrocarbons released by factories and motor vehicles

archipelago a group or chain of islands

bathymetry measurement of depth at various places in the ocean or other body of water

bay a body of water, usually smaller than a gulf, that is partially surrounded by land

biomass the total volume of organic material in a certain area or ecosystem that can be used as a renewable energy source

border the area on either side of a boundary

boundary most commonly, a line that has been established by people to mark the limit of one political unit, such as a country or state, and the beginning of another; geographical features such as mountains sometimes act as boundaries

breakwater a structure, such as a wall, that protects a harbor or beach from pounding waves

caloric supply a measure of the amount of food available to a particular person, household, or community

canal a human-made waterway that is used by ships or to carry water for irrigation

canyon a deep, narrow valley that has steep sides

cape a point of land that extends into an ocean, a lake, or a river

carat a unit of weight for precious stones equal to 200 milligrams

cataract a steplike series of waterfalls or rapids such as occur on the Nile River

cliff a very steep rock face, usually along a coast but also on the side of a mountain

continent one of the seven main landmasses on Earth's surface

country a territory whose government is the highest legal authority over the land and people within its boundaries

delta lowland formed by silt, sand, and gravel deposited by a river at its mouth

desert a hot or cold region that receives 10 inches (25 cm) or less of rain or other kinds of precipitation a year

desertification the spread of desertlike conditions in semiarid regions resulting from climatic changes and increasing human pressures, such as overgrazing, removal of natural vegetation, and cultivation of land

dialect a regional variation of a language

divide an elevated area drained by different river systems flowing in different directions

elevation distance above sea level, usually measured in feet or meters

escarpment a cliff that separates two nearly flat land areas that lie at different elevations

fault a break in Earth's crust along which movement up, down, or sideways occurs

fork in a river, the place where two streams come together

geographic pole 90°N, 90°S latitude; location of the ends of Earth's axis

geomagnetic pole point where the axis of Earth's magnetic field intersects Earth's surface; compass needles align with Earth's magnetic field so that one end points to the magnetic north pole, the other to the magnetic south pole

glacier a large, slow-moving mass of ice

global warming a theory explaining that the recent increase in Earth's average global temperature is due to a buildup of greenhouse gases, such as carbon dioxide and methane, in excess of natural levels due mainly to human activities

greenhouse gases atmospheric gases, such as carbon dioxide and methane, in excess of natural levels due mainly to human activities

gross domestic product (GDP) the total market value of goods and services produced by a country's economy in a year

gulf a portion of the ocean that cuts into the land; usually larger than a bay

harbor a body of water, sheltered by natural or artificial barriers, that is deep enough for ships

hemisphere literally half a sphere; Earth has four hemispheres: Northern, Southern, Eastern, and Western

highlands an elevated area or the more mountainous region of a country

hybrid car a car that is powered by gasoline and electricity

hydrothermal vent a crack in the ocean floor that releases mineral-rich, superheated water

inlet a narrow opening in the land that is filled with water flowing from an ocean, a lake, or a river

island a landmass, smaller than a continent, that is completely surrounded by water

isthmus a narrow strip of land that connects two larger landmasses and has water on two sides

lagoon a shallow body of water that is open to the sea but also protected from it by a reef or sandbar

lake a body of water that is surrounded by land; large lakes are sometimes called seas

landform a physical feature that is shaped by tectonic activity and weathering and erosion; the four major kinds on earth are plains, mountains, plateaus, and hills

landmass a large area of Earth's crust that lies above sea level, such as a continent

large-scale map a map, such as a street map, that shows a small area in great detail

Latin America cultural region generally considered to include Mexico, Central America, South America, and the West Indies; Portuguese and Spanish are the prinicipal languages

latitude distance north and south of the Equator, which is 0° latitude

leeward the side away from or sheltered from the wind

lingua franca a language not native to the local population but that is used as a common or commercial language

longitude distance east and west of the prime meridian, which is 0° longitude

magma molten rock in Earth's mantle

mesa an eroded plateau, broader than it is high, that is found in arid or semiarid regions

metropolitan area a city and its surrounding suburbs or communities

Middle East term commonly used for the countries of Southwest Asia but can also include northern Africa from Morocco to Somalia

molten liquefied by heat; melted

mountain a landform, higher than a hill, that rises at least 1,000 feet (300 m) above the surrounding land and is wider at its base than at its top, or peak; a series of mountains is called a range

nation people who share a common culture; often used as another word for "country," although people within a country may be of many cultures

ocean the large body of saltwater that surrounds the continents and covers more than two-thirds of Earth's surface

peninsula a piece of land that is almost completely surrounded by water

permafrost a permanently frozen sub-surface soil in frigid regions

plain a large area of relatively flat land that is often covered with grasses

plateau a relatively flat area, larger than a mesa, that rises above the surrounding landscape

poaching the illegal killing or taking of animals from their natural habitats

point a narrow piece of land smaller than a cape that extends into a body of water

population density in a country, the number of people living on each square mile or square kilometer of land (calculated by dividing population by land area)

Prairie Provinces popular name for the Canadian provinces of Manitoba, Saskatchewan, and Alberta

prime meridian an imaginary line that runs through Greenwich, England, and is accepted as the line of 0° longitude

projection the process of representing the round Earth on a flat surface, such as a map

rain shadow the dry region on the leeward side of a mountain range

reef an offshore ridge made of coral, rocks, or sand

renewable resources resources that are replenished naturally, but the supply of which can be endangered by overuse and pollution

Sahel a semiarid grassland in Africa along the Sahara's southern border

savanna a tropical grassland with scattered trees

scale on a map, a means of explaining the relationship between distances on the map and actual distances on Earth's surface

sea the ocean or a partially enclosed body of saltwater that is connected to the ocean; completely enclosed bodies of saltwater, such as the Dead Sea, are really lakes

slot canyon a very narrow, deep canyon formed by water and wind erosion

small-scale map a map, such as a country map, that shows a large area without much detail

sound a long, broad inlet of the ocean that lies parallel to the coast and often separates an island and the mainland

Soviet Union shortened name for the Union of Soviet Socialist Republics (U.S.S.R.), a former Communist republic (1920–1991) in eastern Europe and northern and central Asia that was made up of 15 republics of which Russia was the largest

spit a long, narrow strip of land, often of sand or silt, extending into a body of water from the land

staple a chief ingredient of a people's diet

steppe a Slavic word referring to relatively flat, mostly treeless temperate grasslands that stretch across much of central Europe and central Asia

strait a narrow passage of water that connects two larger bodies of water

territory land that is under the jurisdiction of a country but that is not a state or a province

tributary a stream that flows into a larger river

tropics region lying within 23 1/2° north and south of the Equator that experiences warm temperatures year-round

topography the relief features that are evident on a planet's surface

upwelling process by which nutrient-rich water rises from ocean depths to the surface

valley a long depression, usually created by a river, that is bordered by higher land

virgin forest a forest made up of trees that have never been cut down by humans

volcano an opening in Earth's crust through which molten rock erupts

windward the unsheltered side toward which the wind blows

GEO FACTS & FIGURES

PLANET EARTH

Mass: 6,583,348,000,000,000,000,000 tons
(5,974,000,000,000,000,000,000 metric tons)
Distance around the Equator: 24,901 mi
(40,073 km)
Area: 196,938,000 sq mi (510,066,000 sq km)
Land area: 57,393,000 sq mi (148,647,000 sq km)
Water area: 139,545,000 sq mi
(361,419,000 sq km)

The Continents

Asia: 17,208,000 sq mi (44,570,000 sq km)
Africa: 11,608,000 sq mi (30,065,000 sq km)
North America: 9,449,000 sq mi
(24,474,000 sq km)
South America: 6,880,000 sq mi
(17,819,000 sq km)
Antarctica: 5,100,000 sq mi (13,209,000 sq km)
Europe: 3,841,000 sq mi (9,947,000 sq km)
Australia: 2,968,000 sq mi (7,687,000 sq km)

Highest Mountain on Each Continent

Everest, Asia: 29,035 ft (8,850 m)
Aconcagua, South America: 22,834 ft (6,960 m)
McKinley (Denali), North America:
20,320 ft (6,194 m)
Kilimanjaro, Africa: 19,340 ft (5,895 m)
El'brus, Europe: 18,510 ft (5,642 m)
Vinson Massif, Antarctica: 16,067 ft (4,897 m)
Kosciuszko, Australia: 7,310 ft (2,228 m)

Lowest Point on Each Continent

Bentley Subglacial Trench, Antarctica: −8,383 ft
(−2,555 m)
Dead Sea, Asia: −1,365 ft (−416 m)
Lake Assal, Africa: −512 ft (−156 m)
Death Valley, North America: −282 ft (−86 m)
Laguna del Carbón, South America: −344 ft
(−105 m)
Caspian Sea, Europe: −92 ft (−28 m)
Lake Eyre, Australia: −52 ft (−16 m)

Longest Rivers

Nile, Africa: 4,241 mi (6,825 km)
Amazon, South America: 4,000 mi (6,437 km)
Yangtze (Chang), Asia: 3,964 mi (6,380 km)
Mississippi-Missouri, North America: 3,710 mi
(5,971 km)
Yenisey-Angara, Asia: 3,440 mi (5,536 km)
Yellow (Huang), Asia: 3,395 mi (5,464 km)
Ob-Irtysh, Asia: 3,362 mi (5,410 km)
Congo (Zaire), Africa: 2,715 mi (4,370 km)
Amur, Asia: 2,744 mi (4,416 km)
Lena, Asia: 2,734 mi (4,400 km)

Largest Islands

Greenland: 836,000 sq mi (2,166,000 sq km)
New Guinea: 306,000 sq mi (792,500 sq km)
Borneo: 280,100 sq mi (725,500 sq km)
Madagascar: 226,600 sq mi (587,000 sq km)
Baffin: 196,000 sq mi (507,500 sq km)
Sumatra: 165,000 sq mi (427,300 sq km)
Honshu: 87,800 sq mi (227,400 sq km)
Great Britain: 84,200 sq mi (218,100 sq km)
Victoria: 83,900 sq mi (217,300 sq km)
Ellesmere: 75,800 sq mi (196,200 sq km)

Largest Lakes (by area)

Caspian Sea, Europe-Asia: 143,200 sq mi
(371,000 sq km)
Superior, North America: 31,700 sq mi
(82,100 sq km)
Victoria, Africa: 26,800 sq mi (69,500 sq km)
Huron, North America: 23,000 sq mi
(59,600 sq km)
Michigan, North America: 22,300 sq mi
(57,800 sq km)
Tanganyika, Africa: 12,600 sq mi (32,600 sq km)
Baikal, Asia: 12,200 sq mi (31,500 sq km)
Great Bear, North America: 12,100 sq mi
(31,300 sq km)
Malawi, Africa: 11,200 sq mi (28,900 sq km)
Great Slave Lake, Canada: 11,000 sq mi
(28,600 sq km)

Oceans

Pacific: 65,436,200 sq mi (169,479,000 sq km)
Atlantic: 35,338,500 sq mi (91,526,400 sq km)
Indian: 28,839,800 sq mi (74,694,800 sq km)
Arctic: 5,390,000 sq mi (13,960,100 sq km)

Largest Seas (by area)

Coral: 1,615,260 sq mi (4,183,510 sq km)
South China: 1,388,570 sq mi (3,596,390 sq km)
Caribbean: 1,094,330 sq mi (2,834,290 sq km)
Bering: 972,810 sq mi (2,519,580 sq km)
Mediterranean: 953,320 sq mi (2,469,100 sq km)
Sea of Okhotsk: 627,490 sq mi (1,625,190 sq km)
Gulf of Mexico: 591,430 sq mi (1,531,810 sq km)
Norwegian: 550,300 sq mi (1,425,280 sq km)
Greenland: 447,050 sq mi (1,157,850 sq km)
Sea of Japan: 389,290 sq mi (1,008,260 sq km)

Geographic Extremes

Highest Mountain

Everest, China/Nepal:
29,035 ft (8,850 m)

Deepest Point in the Ocean

Challenger Deep, Mariana Trench, Pacific:
-35,827 ft (-10,920 m)

Hottest Place

Dalol, Danakil Depression, Ethiopia:
annual average temperature 93° F (34° C)

Coldest Place

Plateau Station, Antarctica:
annual average temperature -70° F (-56.7° C)

Wettest Place

Mawsynram, Assam, India: annual average rainfall
467 in (1,187 cm)

Driest Place

Arica, Atacama Desert, Chile: barely measurable
rainfall

Largest Hot Desert

Sahara, Africa: 3,475,000 sq mi (9,000,000 sq km)

Largest Cold Desert

Antarctica: 5,100,000 sq mi (13,209,000 sq km)

People

Most People by Continent

Asia: 3,968,000,000

Least People by Continent

Antarctica: 2,000 (transient)
Australia: 20,600,000

Most Densely Populated Country

Monaco: 44,000 people per sq mi/16,988 per sq km

Least Densely Populated Country

Mongolia: 4 people per sq mi/1.5 per sq km

Biggest Metropolitan Areas

Tokyo, Japan: 35,200,000
México City, México: 19,400,000
New York, United States: 18,700,000
São Paulo, Brazil: 18,300,000
Mumbai (Bombay), India: 18,200,000
Delhi, India: 15,000,000
Shanghai, China: 14,500,000
Kolkata (Calcutta), India: 14,300,000
Jakarta, Indonesia: 13,200,000
Buenos Aires, Argentina: 12,600,000

Countries with the Highest Life Expectancy

Andorra: 84 years
Japan: 82 years
Iceland: 81 years
San Marino: 81 years
Spain: 81 years
Sweden: 81 years
Switzerland: 81 years

Countries with the Lowest Life Expectancy

Botswana: 34 years
Swaziland: 34 years
Lesotho: 36 years
Zambia: 37 years
Zimbabwe: 37 years
Angola: 41 years
Sierra Leone: 41 years

Countries with the Highest Annual Income per Person

Luxembourg: $65,630
Norway: $59,590
Switzerland: $54,930
Denmark: $47,390
Iceland: $46,320

Countries with the Lowest Annual Income per Person

Burundi: $100
Democratic Rep. of the Congo: $120
Liberia: $130
Malawi: $160
Ethiopia: $160

OUTSIDE WEB SITES

The following Web sites will provide you with additional valuable information about various topics discussed in this atlas. You can find direct links to each by going to the atlas URL (www.nationalgeographic.com/kids-world-atlas) and clicking on "Other Stuff."

Antarctic wildlife:
http://www.antarcticconnection.com/antarctic/wildlife/index.shtml

Biomes:
http://www.blueplanetbiomes.org

Currency converter:
http://www.xe.com/ucc

Earth's climates:
http://www.worldclimate.com

Earth's geologic history:
Earthquakes: http://earthquake.usgs.gov/
Tsunamis: http://www.noaa.gov/tsunamis.html
Volcanoes: http://www.geo.mtu.edu/volcanoes/

Extreme facts about the world:
http://www.extremescience.com

Flags of the world:
http://www.fotw.us/flags/index.html

Languages of the world:
http://www.ipl.org/div/kidspace/hello/
http://www.nvtc.gov/lotw/index.html

Mapping sites:
http://earth.google.com/
http://www.skylineglobe.com/

National anthems:
http://www.nationalanthems.info

Political world (lots of statistics):
https://www.cia.gov/cia/publications/factbook/index.html

Religions of the world:
http://www.adherents.com/Religions_By_Adherents.html

Solar system:
http://learn.arc.nasa.gov/planets/main/overview.html

Time differences between places:
http://www.worldtimeserver.com

Time zone map:
http://aa.usno.navy.mil/faq/docs/world_tzones.html

Tracking Quakes (p. 33 lo left):
http://www.iris.edu/seismon/

Weather around the world right now:
http://www.weather.com

World heritage sites:
(important historic places around the world):
http://whc.unesco.org/en/list

INDEX

Map references are in bold-face (**50**) type. Letters and numbers following in lightface (D12) locate the place-names using the map grid. (Refer to page 7 for more details.)

PLACE-NAMES

Anadyr — Bitola

Ciudad del Este — England

English Channel — Guinea, Gulf of

Guinea-Bissau — Kansas

Lord Howe Island — Moroni

Osijek — Rangitata

Severn — The Hague

Wau — Cape Verde Plain

Cargados Carajos Bank — Lau Ridge

Lesser Sunda Islands — Somerset Island

South Australian Basin — Zhokhova

Illustrations Credits

Abbreviations for terms appearing below: lo = lower; NGS = National Geographic Society.

All continent opening spreads (60–61, 76–77, 90–91, 108–109, 132–133, 148–149, 160–161) Blue Marble: Next Generation was produced by Reto Stöckli, NASA Earth Observatory (NASA Goddard Space Flight Center) http://earthobservatory.nasa.gov/Newsroom/BlueMarble/. The satellite imagery was captured for the month of May.

All graphic illustrations by Stuart Armstrong unless otherwise noted.

All locator globes created by Theophilus Britt Griswold and NGS.

Front cover globe, Premium Stock/Corbis; front cover photos, (left to right), Ron Kimball Stock, Jose Fuste Raga/Corbis, Sexh, Brand X; back cover photos (top to bottom), Richard Nowitz/NGS, Roy Toft/NGS, Roy Toft/NGS, Arthur ThÉvenart/Corbis.

Front of the Book

1, Premium Stock/Corbis; 2 up, Premium Stock/Corbis; 2 lo (left to right), Roy Toft/NGS, Tom Murphy/NGS, Cary Wolinsky/NGS, Richard Nowitz/NGS; 3 (left to right), far left, Ron Kimball Stock, Jose Fuste Raga/Corbis, Sexh, Brand X; 4 left, Raymond Gehman/NGS; 4 up right, Todd Gipstein/NGS; 4 lo right, Cary Wolinsky/NGS; 5 left, Richard Nowitz/NGS; 5 center up, Frans Lanting/NGS; 5 center lo, Justin Guariglia/NGS; 5 up right, Gordon Wiltsie/NGS.

Understanding Maps

10 (all), 3D Globe visualizations provided by SkylineGlobe (www.skylineglobe.com); 12 lo left (art) Shusei Nagaoka; 12 lo right, Mark Thiessen/NGS; 12 lo left (art), Lockheed Martin; 14–15 (art), Shusei Nagaoka.

Planet Earth

16 lo (art), Shusei Nagaoka; 16–17 (art), David Aguillar; 17 lo (art), Robert Hynes; 18 up right (art), Tibor G. Tóth/NGS; 18 lo (all art), Christopher R. Scotese/PALEOMAP Project, University of Texas, Arlington; 19 lo (all art), NGS.

Physical World

22 far left, Maria Stenzel/NGS; 22 left, Bill Hatcher/NGS; 22 right, Carsten Peter/NGS; 22 far right, Carsten Peter/NGS; 22–23 (ART), Shusei Nagaoka; 23 far left, Gordon Wiltsie/NGS; 23 left, James P. Blair/NGS; 23 right, Thomas J. Abercrombie/NGS; 23 far right, Anne Keiser/NGS; 27 up right, Kevin Rivoli/Associated Press; 27, up left, O. Brown, R. Evans, and M. Carle, University of Miami Rosenstiel School of Marine and Atmospheric Science, Miami, Florida; 27 lo right (both), Weiss and Overpeck, The University of Arizona; 26–27 (art), NGS. 28 far left, Raymond Gehman/NGS; 28 left, George F. Mobley/NGS; 28 right, Paul Nicklen/NGS; 28 far right, Raymond Gehman/NGS; 29 far left, Annie Griffiths Belt/NGS; 29 left, Beverly Joubert/NGS; 29 right, Michael Melford/NGS; 29 far right, Maria Stenzel/NGS; 30 left a, George Grall/NGS; 30 left b, Nicole Duplaix/NGS; 30 left c, Michael Nichols/NGS; 30 left d, William Albert Allard/NGS; 30 left e, Michael Nichols/NGS; 30 left f, Paul Sutherland/NGS; 30 right, James P. Blair/NGS; 31 left, William Thompson/NGS; 31 center, Steve McCurry/NGS; 31 right, Peter Essick/NGS; 32 up, NSSL/NOAA Photo Librry; 32 lo, Getty Images; 33 up, Dave Harlow/USGS; 33 lo left, The Seismic Monitor is an online product of the IRIS Consortium and displays earthquake locations from the U.S. Geological Survey; 33 lo right, Mario Tama/Getty Images.

The Oceans

35 lo left, Scripps Institute of Oceanography; 35 up right, NOAA; 35 lo right, NASA; 36 up, Wolcott Henry/NGS; 36 lo, Karen Kasmauski/NGS; 38 up, Tom Murphy/NGS; 38 lo left, Emory Kristof/NGS; 38 lo right, John Eastcott and Yva Momatiuk/NGS; 40, Hans Fricke/NGS; 42 up, Norbet Rosing/NGS; 42 lo, Paul Nicklen/NGS.

Political World

47, Justin Guariglia/NGS; 48, Maria Stenzel/NGS; 49 left, Justin Guariglia/NGS; 49 right, Phillipe Lissac/Godong/Corbis; 50 left, Martin Gray/NGS; 50 center, Randy Olson/NGS; 50 right, Amit Dave/Reuters/Corbis; 51 left, Reza/NGS; 51 right, Richard Nowitz/NGS; 52, Justin Guariglia/NGS; 53 left, George F. Mobley/NGS; 53 right, Phil Schermeister/NGS; 54, Jodi Cobb/NGS; 55 lo (art), NGS 57 left, James P. Blair/NGS; 57 up right, Stephen St. John/NGS; 57 center right, Joel Sartore/NGS; 57 lo right, Michael Nichols/NGS; 58 lo (art), NGS; 59 far left, Walter Rawlings/Robert Harding World Imagery/Corbis; 59 left, Richard Nowitz/NGS; 59 right, Sarah Leen/NGS; 59 far right, Priit Vesilind/NGS.

North America

64 up, Raymond Gehman/NGS; 64 lo, Tomas Tomaszewski/NGS; 64–65 up, Michael Melford/NGS; 64–55 lo, Rex Stucky/NGS; 65 lo, Jeff Vanuga/Corbis; 66 up left, Ira Block/NGS; 66 up right, NGS; 66 lo left, George F. Mobley/NGS; 66 lo right, Martin Gray/NGS; 67 up, David Doubilet/NGS; 67 lo left, Mark Cosslett/NGS; 67 lo right, Glen Allison/Stone/Getty Images; 68 center, William Albert Allard/NGS; 68 lo left, Michael S. Yamashita/NGS; 68 lo right, Richard Nowitz/NGS; 69 up, Tim Laman/NGS; 69 right, William Albert Allard/NGS; 70 up, NASA; 70 lo left, Todd Gipstein/NGS; 70 lo right, Norbet Rosing/NGS; 71 up, Brooks Walker/NGS; 72 up, Kenneth Garrett/NGS; 72 lo, Kenneth Garrett/NGS; 73up left, MacDuff Everton/NGS; 73 up right, Steve Winter/NGS; 73 lo, Roy Toft/NGS; 74 up, Pablo Corral Vega/Corbis; 74 lo left, Steve Raymer/NGS; 74-75 lo, Bill Curtsinger/NGS; 75 up, Michael Melford/NGS; 75 lo right, Jose Fuste Raga/Corbis.

(Continued on page 192)

Published by the National Geographic Society

John M. Fahey, Jr.
President and Chief Executive Officer

Gilbert M. Grosvenor
Chairman of the Board

Nina D. Hoffman
Executive Vice President; President, Book Publishing Group

Prepared by the Book Division

Nancy Laties Feresten,
Vice President, Editor in Chief, Children's Books

Bea Jackson, Director of Design and Illustrations, Children's Books

Amy Shields, Executive Editor, Series, Children's Books

Carl Mehler, Director of Maps

Staff for this book

Suzanne Patrick Fonda, Project Editor

Bea Jackson, Art Director and Book Design

Lori Epstein, Illustrations Editor

David M. Seager, Nancy Sabato, Designers

Ruthie Thompson, Production Design

Al Morrow, Production Design Assistant

Susan Kehnemui Donnelly, Researcher

Thomas L. Gray, Nicholas P. Rosenbach, Map Editors
Matt Chwastyk, Sven M. Dolling, Steven D. Gardner,
Michael McNey, Gregory Ugiansky, Mapping Specialists, and
XNR Productions, Map Research and Production

Tibor G. Tóth, Map Relief

Martha B. Sharma, Consultant

Mark H. Bockenhauer, Martha B. Sharma, Writers

Dan Sherman, Web Page Design

Alex Novak, Web Page Editor

Stuart Armstrong, Graphics Illustrator

Stacy Gold, Nadia Hughes, Illustrations Research Editors

Rebecca Baines, Editorial Assistant

Jean Cantu, Illustrations Specialist

Debbie Guthrie Haer, Copy Editor

Lindsey Marie Shields, Research Assistant

Lewis R. Bassford, Production Project Manager

Jennifer A. Thornton, Managing Editor

Gary Colbert, Production Director

Manufacturing and Quality Management

Christopher A. Liedel, Chief Financial Officer

Phillip L. Schlosser, Vice President

John T. Dunn, Technical Director

Chris Brown, Director

Maryclare Tracy, Manager

Nicole Elliott, Manager

Founded in 1888, the National Geographic Society is one of the largest nonprofit scientific and educational organizations in the world. It reaches more than 285 million people worldwide each month through its official journal, NATIONAL GEOGRAPHIC, and its four other magazines; the National Geographic Channel; television documentaries; radio programs; films; books; videos and DVDs; maps; and interactive media. National Geographic has funded more than 8,000 scientific research projects and supports an education program combating geographic illiteracy.

For more information, please call 1-800-NGS LINE (647-5463) or write to the following address:

NATIONAL GEOGRAPHIC SOCIETY
1145 17th Street N.W., Washington, D.C. 20036-4688 U.S.A.

Visit us online at www.nationalgeographic.com/books

For information about special discounts for bulk purchases, please contact National Geographic Books Special Sales: ngspecsales@ngs.org

For rights or permissions inquiries, please contact National Geographic Books Subsidiary Rights: ngbookrights@ngs.org

(Continued from page 191)

South America

80 up, Tim Laman/NGS; 80 lo left, Pablo Corral Vega/NGS; 80-81 up, Stephanie Maze/NGS; 81 lo left, Anne Keiser/NGS; 81 lo right, Todd Gipstein/NGS; 82 up left, Jimmy Chin/NGS; 82 up right, Kenneth Garrett/NGS; 82 lo left, Pablo Corral Vega/NGS; 82 lo right, Ed George/NGS; 83 up, Richard Nowitz/NGS; 83 lo left, Joel Sartore/NGS; 83 lo right, Melissa Farlow/NGS; 84 up, William Albert Allard/NGS; 84 lo left, Pablo Corral Vega/NGS; 84 lo right, Meredith Davenport/NGS; 85 up, O. Louis Mazzatenta/NGS; 86 up, Priit Vesilind/NGS; 86 lo left, MacDuff Everton/NGS; 86-87 lo, James L. Amos/NGS; 87 up, Joel Sartore/NGS; 88 up, O. Louis Mazzatenta/NGS; 88–89 lo, Skip Brown/NGS; 89 up, Maria Stenzel/NGS; 89 center, Joel Sartore/NGS.

Europe

94 up, Richard Nowitz/NGS; 94 lo left, Priit Vesilind/NGS; 94–95 up, Melissa Farlow/NGS; 94–95 lo, Richard Nowitz/NGS; 95 up right, Richard Nowitz/NGS; 96 up left, Taylor S. Kennedy/NGS; 96 lo left, Steve McCurry/NGS; 96 lo right, Sisse Brimberg/NGS; 96–97 up, Richard Nowitz/NGS; 97 lo left, Richard Nowitz/NGS; 97 center, Nicole Duplaix/NGS; 97 lo right, James P. Blair/NGS; 98 up, Sisse Brimberg & Cotton Coulson, Keepress/NGS; 98 lo left, Karen Kasmauski/NGS; 98 lo right, Priit Vesilind/NGS; 99 up, The Art Archive/Corbis; 100 up, Cees Van Leeuwen; Cordaiy Photo Library Ltd./Corbis; 100 lo left, Jim Richardson/NGS; 100 lo right, Richard Nowitz/NGS; 101 up, Richard Nowitz/NGS; 102 up, Catherine Karnow/NGS; 102 lo, Catherine Karnow/NGS; 103 up left, Sisse Brimberg/NGS; 103 right, Sisse Brimberg/NGS; 104 up, James P. Blair/NGS; 104 lo left, James P. Blair/NGS; 104 lo right, Todd Gipstein/NGS; 105 up, James L. Stanfield/NGS; 106 up, Steve Raymer/NGS; 106 lo, Steve Raymer/NGS 107 up, Richard Nowitz/NGS.

Asia

112 up, Taylor S. Kennedy/NGS; 112 lo left, Steve McCurry/NGS; 112–113 up, Steve Raymer/NGS; 112–113 lo, Justin Guariglia/NGS; 113 lo right, David Edwards/NGS; 114 up left, Fred de Noyelle/Godong/Corbis; 114 lo left, Jodi Cobb/NGS; 114 lo right, Justin Guariglia/NGS; 114–115 up, Todd Gipstein/NGS; 115 lo left, Michael Nichols/NGS; 115 lo right, Justin Guariglia/NGS; 116 up, Maria Stenzel/NGS; 116 lo, Steve Winter/NGS; 117 up, Steve Raymer/NGS; 117 lo, Cary Wolinsky/NGS; 118 up, Medford Taylor/NGS; 118 lo, Gordon Wiltsie/NGS; 119 up, David Edwards/NGS; 119 lo, Dean Conger/NGS; 120 up, H. Kim/NGS; 120–121 lo, Justin Guariglia/NGS; 121 up, O. Louis Mazzatenta/NGS; 121 lo, Roy Toft/NGS; 122 up, James L. Stanfield/NGS; 122 lo, Alex Webb/NGS; 123 up, Martin Gray/NGS; 123 lo, Priit Vesilind/NGS; 124 up left, Morteza Nikoubazl/Reuters/Corbis; 124 up right, Arthur Thèvenart/Corbis; 124 lo, Robb Kendrick/NGS; 125 up, Bill Lyons/NGS; 126 up, Ed George/NGS; 126 lo, Bobby Model/NGS; 127 up, Jason Horowitz/zefa/Corbis; 127 lo, James P. Blair/NGS; 128 up left, Paul Chesley/NGS; 128 up right, MacDuff Everton/NGS; 128 lo, Paul Chesley/NGS; 129 up, Jack Fields/Corbis; 129 lo, Steve Raymer/NGS; 130 up, Reuters/Corbis; 130 lo, Richard Nowitz/NGS; 131 up left, Paul Chesley/NGS; 131 up right, Tim Laman/NGS; 131 lo, Tim Laman/NGS.

Africa

136 up, George F. Mobley/NGS; 136 lo left, Michael Nichols/NGS 136-137 up, Skip Brown/NGS; 136-137 lo, Kenneth Garrett/NGS; 137 lo left, Bill Curtsinger/NGS; 137 lo right, Cary Wolinsky/NGS; 138 up, Georg Gerster/NGS; 138 lo left, Digital Vision/Getty Images; 138 lo right, Kenneth Garrett/NGS; 139 up, Cary Wolinsky/NGS; 139 lo left, Bill Curtsinger/NGS; 139 lo right, Michael Nichols/NGS 140 up, W. Robert Moore/NGS; 140 lo left, Sarah Leen/NGS; 140–141 lo, NGS; 141 up, James L. Stanfield/NGS; 142 up, Randy Olson/NGS; 142 lo left, Michael Lewis/NGS; 142 lo right, Richard Nowitz/NGS; 143 up left, Kenneth Garrett/NGS; 143 up right, Bobby Haas/NGS; 144 up, George Steinmetz/NGS; 144 lo, Michael Nichols/NGS; 145 up, Werner Forman/Corbis; 145 up right, Michael Nichols/NGS; 146 up, George F. Mobley/NGS; 146 lo, Tim Laman/NGS; 147 up, Kenneth Garrett/NGS; 147 lo, Bob Krist/Corbis.

Australia, New Zealand, and Oceania

152 up, Nicole Duplaix/NGS; 152 lo left, Frans Lanting/NGS; 152–153 up, Art Wolfe/NGS; 152–153 lo, Tim Laman/NGS; 153 lo right, Nicole Duplaix/NGS; 154 up left, Medford Taylor/NGS; 154 lo left, Carsten Peter/NGS; 154 center, Frans Lanting/NGS 154–155 up, Tim Laman/NGS; 154–155 lo, Winfield Parks/NGS; 155 center, Paul Chesley/NGS; 155 lo right, Mark Cosslett/NGS; 156 lo left, Bill Curtsinger/NGS; 156 lo right, Sam Abell/NGS; 157 up left, Jason Edwards/NGS; 157 up right, Paul Chesley/NGS; 158 up, Randy Olson/NGS; 158 lo, Carsten Peter/NGS; 159 up left, Martin Gray/NGS; 159 up right, Randy Olson/NGS; 159 lo, Jodi Cobb/NGS.

Antarctica

162 up, Gordon Wiltsie/NGS; 162 lo, Gordon Wiltsie/NGS; 163 up, Paul Nicklen/NGS; 163 lo, Maria Stenzel/NGS.

Library of Congress Cataloging-in-Publication Data available upon request.

ISBN-13: 978-1-4263-0088-2 (hardcover)

Printed in Italy